A PERFECT STORM OF INJUSTICE

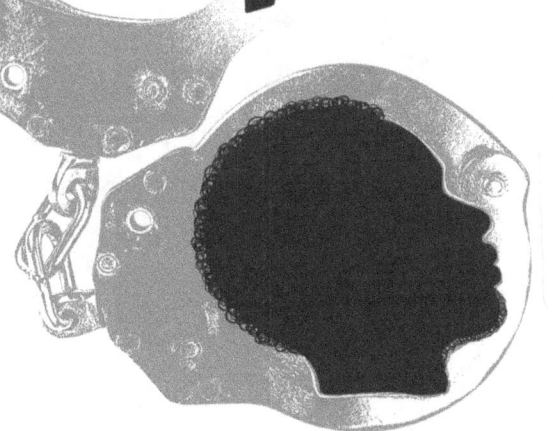

A NOVEL

I0608091

Can't Put it Down
BOOKS

JACK SAARELA

WHAT THEY ARE SAYING ABOUT
A PERFECT STORM OF INJUSTICE

Good writing starts with what you know, continues with thorough research, and then expands with that imaginative entry into the world of "what if?"

Jack Saarela knows death row and the Florida prison system. He draws on his years as a campus minister at the University of Florida in the 1980s and 1990s, a ministry that connected him to death row at nearby Florida State Prison. He has been inside that prison, walked the corridors of death row cells, and listened to the stories of the men who lived with the reality that the governor could sign their death warrant on any given day.

Saarela has taken this experience and created the story of Charles Wilkerson, an African American man married to a white woman, and their three-year-old son, Travis. When Dana is murdered in her bedroom one morning just after Charles has gone to work, Charles falls into the nightmare scenario of what is all too typical of Florida's criminal justice system, and winds up on death row.

The difficulty of writing fiction about capital punishment in Florida is that reality itself is so bizarre. If Sheriff Buck Davidson in Saarela's *A Perfect Storm of Injustice* seems excessively unscrupulous, consider the real-life Sheriff Willis Virgil McCall, elected for seven consecutive terms in Lake County, Florida, who actually shot two of the four defendants known as the "Groveland Four" while driving them from Florida State Prison back to Groveland for a rehearing. Racial disparity in Florida is multifaceted like a fine diamond, specifically targeting African Americans accused of killing whites.

Most stories of the fights for justice for the wrongly incarcerated are told from the perspective of the lawyers who pursue their cases. Saarela takes us into the life of the defendant who spends two and a half decades in prison.

Saarela gives us a journey through the injustice of the American legal system, which is all too common, especially for people of color. It's a gripping read with intriguing legal information and a fascinating window into what it is like to be the person living this terror.

Larry Reimer, Pastor Emeritus, The United Church of Gainesville

A Perfect Storm of Injustice
A Novel
Copyright 2021 by Jack Saarela

ISBN: 978-1-7365979-1-0
Printed in the United States of America

This is a work of fiction. Names, characters, places and incidents are either a product of the author's imagination or are used fictitiously. Any resemblance to actual events, or persons or locales, living or dead, is purely coincidental.

The **exceptions** are **the Innocence Project** and its co-founder **Barry Scheck.** The Innocence Project is an actual 501(c)(3) nonprofit legal organization based at the Cardozo School of Law at Yeshiva University in New York that is committed to exonerating individuals who it claims have been wrongly convicted. Though the Innocence Project and Mr. Scheck assisted in the exoneration of several inmates on whom the fictional case of Charles Wilkerson is based, their participation in the fictional case in this novel are products of the author's imagination.

Published by
Can't Put It Down Books
An imprint of
Open Door Publications
Willow Spring, NC

Cover Design by Eric Labacz, labaczdesign.com

*This story of the descent into the purgatory
of wrongful conviction
and
redemption from it
is dedicated to
Susan Cary, public defender and advocate for death row inmates,
and the Innocence Project,
both wellsprings of compassion.*

EXCERPT FROM *THE PHILADELPHIA INQUIRER* BY SAMANTHA MELAMED

JANUARY 22, 2020

On Tuesday morning, January 21, after 28 years in prison for a triple murder he did not commit, Theophalis "Bilaal" Wilson heard the words he had been waiting for.

"Theophalis Wilson, you are free to go," Common Pleas Court Judge Tracy Brandeis-Roman said as extended family and friends who packed the courtroom wailed, hugged and wept.

"It is time for Mr. Wilson to be allowed to go home with an apology," unit chief Patricia Cummings said in court, her voice trembling. "No words can express what we put these people through; what we put Mr. Wilson through; what we put his family through."

Brandeis-Roman ordered him released immediately, finding violations of his right to due process and effective counsel, as well as to the withholding of exculpatory evidence in his case.

"This is a great day," Wilson said after his release. "Now we have to go back and get the other guys. There's a lot of innocent people in jail."

Wilson, now 48, was a teenager when he was accused of participating in the slaying of three men in North Philadelphia.

"Wilson's trial was infected by serious prosecutorial misconduct, Brady violations, a critical witness who supplied false testimony, and ineffective assistance of counsel," the Philadelphia District Attorney Larry Krasner's Office wrote in a filing that called the case "a perfect storm of injustice."

CHAPTER 1

FEBRUARY 17,1987,RAIFORD,FL

THE DOOR SLAMMED SHUT with emphasis.

Not with the clunk of wood against wood as when a bedroom door is closed.

Rather, with the long, hard scraping of cold steel sliding against hardened metal tracks on the floor and ceiling followed by a cold, bone-rattling boom that sent a sharp metallic echo reverberating down the long corridor.

The portal to the world Charles Wilkerson was being forced to leave behind grew smaller as the barrier of thick, pastel green steel bars clanged into place.

It was late in the day when two taciturn guards dressed in their standard Florida Department of Corrections (FDOC) sand-colored, short-sleeve shirt and milk chocolate-colored slacks ushered Charles into the corridor beyond the door. Each guard held Charles by his elbow as though he were an elderly invalid who could easily trip and fall onto the shiny tile floor. Charles kept his eyes riveted on the end of the corridor. He could smell the sour odor of the guards' sweat.

As the trio progressed down the corridor, Charles was aware that other inmates were scrutinizing him from behind the bars on their cell doors. One or two greeted him with "Welcome to your last home, buddy," but he knew from the preparation he had received from his defense team not to look them in the eye.

No, not in prison, especially not on death row.

They had to stop again when they reached another locked steel door. "Open two!" one of the guards yelled out. As they waited, Charles could see a third guard at a control panel behind a glass window press a button. "Door number two open," the guard announced from behind the glass door.

Once more Charles heard the scraping noise of the door sliding closed, followed by the clang of the door against the steel of its waiting dock. The process was replicated a third time when they reached yet another locked door.

Charles would never forget that haunting sound of multiple doors closing behind him one after another. The sound put an exclamation mark after the prosecution's statement to the jury that Charles was no longer fit to walk freely.

With the accumulated wisdom of fifteen years as a prison guard, one of them said in a neutral tone, "Don't look so freaked out, buddy. You'll get used to the sound."

The two guards delivered him to a tiny cell the width of which measured about the height of a six-foot man. The cell's length was not much more, perhaps, than if the imaginary man were to stretch his arms above his head as far as they could extend. Charles' eyes widened in disbelief as he surveyed the tiny space and wondered about claustrophobia.

Having fulfilled their mission and delivered their human cargo, the two guards left Charles in the cell, locked the barred door with a key hanging from the belt of one of them, and departed wordlessly.

Charles was alone in the cell. He would remain alone there often for up to twenty-three hours of every day to hear over and over again, night and day, the echo of closing sliding steel doors reverberating against the hard plaster walls of the hallway. Starting on that first day, Charles knew he would see the world he was being forced to give up beyond the walls of the Florida State Prison (FSP) only through the figurative keyhole of a door that he could not unlock.

His fear of death aside, his most urgent struggle was to prove the innocence he had claimed from the beginning, that he was innocent of the horrendous, indescribable crime for which Palm Beach County was single-mindedly intent on charging, trying, and punishing him.

Bear in mind that of the approximately 380 prisoners on Florida's death row at the beginning of their sentence, rightly or wrongly, a high percentage swear up and down that they are innocent of the crime for which they were sentenced. For many of those, however, the pretense of innocence is just that and evaporates in due time into the hot, sweaty air of the FSP.

But, with a naïve faith in the American system of justice inculcated in him during his childhood and youth, a faith that, it turned out in his case, was largely undeserved, Charles Wilkerson continued to maintain his belief that surely, the court's error would be discovered and rectified. He was confident and determined that someday the barred steel doors would slide wide open and permit him to walk freely out of FSP and places like it forever.

CHAPTER 2

JUNE 1970

SIXTEEN-YEAR-OLD CHARLES WILKERSON sat erect in the back seat of the '67 Ford Galaxy, gazing out of the window in wonderment.

"Man, look at all those palm trees! It's like we've driven to another country," he uttered uncharacteristically of a teenager after two full days with his middle-aged parents.

A smile came over the face of his father, Richard, as he signaled that they were about to exit I-95. He glanced over knowingly to his wife, Eileen, beside him in the front bench seat.

"I read more than three dozen different species of palms line the streets of Boynton Beach."

"We're not in Buffalo anymore, Toto," Charles responded. "Where's the beach? I don't see the ocean."

"Well, Charles dear, judging from the map the realtor gave us, our new house won't be far from the beach or the ocean," Eileen assured him as she turned her head back toward her son. "We'll go see it soon enough."

"Once we've made some reasonable progress unloading the car and letting Mother decide where she wants the movers to set the furniture when they arrive," Richard appended.

"Work before play," she added.

Charles didn't find those words at all unusual. All his life he had heard his parents' mantra "work before play," or some variation of it. "Complete your homework before you can watch the television.... Finish all your chores and then you can go out and play with your friends, son.... Help your mother clear the dinner table and wash the dishes, and then you'll be free to play with your toys until bedtime."

Their home had a predictable routine; his parents' stable and accustomed roles differed from what Charles found in many of those of his friends back in Buffalo, whether they were white or black. When his friends came over to visit and hang out, they marveled at the showroom neatness and orderliness of the rooms at the Wilkerson home, even the small garage attached to the house. It was so plainly unlike their own home and garage. When the others weren't listening, his black friends asked Charles, "Is this how all white kids grow up?" His white friends asked much the same about black homes.

His friends felt free to ask him because Charles had black skin and was categorized as "African-American" by the school board, but he hardly ever sounded like the other black students in class. He sounded "white" like Theodore and Wally in *Leave It to Beaver*. This was a source of reassurance and relief to the parents of his white buddies. They could rest, assured that Charles had been taught how to play fairly with other children, to speak politely to his friends' parents, to not wander off by himself into rooms whose doors were closed, and to keep his hands off the knickknacks around their living and dining rooms, leaving them where he found them. The parents of his black friends were surprised the first time either Richard or Eileen stopped by their home to bring Charles back home for dinner. They had not expected his parents to be white.

It was an unusual family structure, even in 1970. It was even more strange in the mid-1950s when, after years of trying to conceive their own child, Richard and Eileen made an appointment at Child and Family Services (CFS) to begin the application and education process for becoming adoptive parents. They didn't go to the adoption agency with the intention of choosing a black child. It's just that when they received "the call" on the telephone from CFS and were introduced to the eighteen-month-old Charles, they were immediately enamored with the bright-eyed, quietly active, intelligent-looking child whose birth mother had named him Charles. Richard and Eileen looked at each other and passed the little ball of cuteness to each other's arms, and their commitment to become Charles' adoptive parents was cemented.

In his preschool and elementary school years, Charles stood out among his classmates. In the fourth grade, his teachers named him as the school's "Student of the Year" for his academic excellence and model behavior. The principal lauded him at the school assembly in the cafetorium for his affability and exemplary ability to be on good terms with his peers—both white and black.

His homeroom teacher, Miss Sample, sent him a card of appreciation and congratulations, expressing her good wishes for the fifth grade and beyond. "With your praiseworthy behavior, agreeable nature, active curiosity about life, and obvious intelligence, you will have the whole world at your fingertips, Charles. I predict good things for your future. You will go far in life. It has been a distinct pleasure to have you in my class.

CHAPTER 3

MAY 5, 1972

CHARLES AND A SMALL GROUP OF SENIORS sat at the concrete picnic table by the flagpole in front of their school. They gathered to eat their sandwich lunches in good weather, as it was on this day in early May. Other students were accustomed to seeing this group of white students and a single black one together. The white students wouldn't dare to grab the table before this particular group because there was a black student there, and the black students wouldn't think of presuming they were invited to sit there just because there was one black student in the group—particularly this black student.

"It's a perfect day to go eat outside today," Roddy Carmichael remarked while they were still inside the cafeteria. "June will be here before we know it, and it'll be too hot."

"June can't come soon enough," said Ray Barnett. "I remind you of graduation, guys."

"Yeah, but finals before that," Gene Schneider pointed out.

"Don't ruin our good mood, Gene," Charles warned. "It's too nice a day to ruin it with thoughts of final exams."

"What are you going to do after graduation, Charles? Any idea?" Roddy asked. "You gonna join us at the 'U'?"

"Probably not," Ray interjected. "Charles is more Duke or Vandy material." His comment was neither critical nor envious. It was just what everyone expected of Charles—that he would attend one of the elite Southern schools, sometimes called the "Southern Ivy League."

"You think so?" Gene inquired, not really surprised by Ray's assessment, just making conversation.

"Let's ask the man himself."

"That where you're headed, Charles?"

"Actually, I'm undecided. I'll miss you guys if you all go to Miami. But I'm not a real football guy. I wonder if I'd fit in down there."

Roddy chimed in. "Everybody's at the Orange Bowl on Saturday afternoons. If that's not your scene, friend, you can always spend the afternoon at South Pointe Pier in Miami Beach. You might meet a hot girl there."

"My parents are encouraging me to stay close to home at FAU," Charles informed them.

The conversation came to a sudden halt.

It seemed that the closer he was to graduation, the more keenly people took an interest in where Charles was headed. His guidance counselor and teachers, for instance, couldn't hold back their recommendations, but as well-intentioned as they might have been, Charles wasn't really interested in their advice.

"Yes, Charles. FAU is worth taking a look at, of course, since it's so close to home," Mr. Peters, his guidance counselor, told him. "But it's an awfully new school and unproven. You've got the smarts to think about Duke. We don't have any Ivy League schools here in the south. That's what you're capable of, you know. Duke is the nearest thing to an Ivy school."

Charles' parents didn't hide their shock at the tuition and living costs at Duke, the opportunity for good financial aid notwithstanding. His homeroom teacher, Mr. Roberts, his only black teacher and an alumnus of the University of Florida in Gainesville, some six hours north of Boynton by car, strongly encouraged Charles to go there and take advantage of the improving diversity of its student body and the wide range of academic offerings.

"But I'm not really familiar with your goals in choosing a college," the teacher added. "What are they?"

Charles shifted uncomfortably in his chair in Mr. Roberts' office.

"That makes two of us, Mr. Roberts. The goal? Oh, I don't know. To get out as soon as possible and start earning a living, I suppose. A college is a college as far as I'm concerned, whether it's Duke or Princeton or FAU. In any case, it's a hoop to jump through to earn a decent livelihood and not have to depend on my parents all the time."

"But they're supportive of your continuing your education and going on to college, aren't they?"

"Oh yes, sir. Very supportive. They were a little shocked at the costs at Duke, but they've never put pressure on me to keep the college costs as low as possible. Honestly, Mr. Roberts, that pressure is from inside *me*."

"That's completely understandable, Charles. I was in your position once. It cost my family a lot to send this black kid from Homestead to college in Gainesville. But I think that now they are glad they made the sacrifice. They're proud. Their son is a high school vice principal now. But I'm a little puzzled, to be frank. I want to challenge you to think some more about your goals. You do so well in your studies. Don't aim too low. A bright mind is a terrible thing to squander. Especially a bright *black* mind. People like Justice Marshall and Dr. King and the generation after them have worked hard to pave a road of opportunity for you. There are a lot of people in addition to you rooting for you to take advantage of the opportunity."

Maybe that was the problem. Wherever he went, people reminded him that he had to live up to something—his teachers' expectations, the sacrifices his parents had made—because he was a black kid who had had extra advantages. Charles just wanted to be Charles—not the black kid with the white parents.

In the mid-1960s, Florida had chartered a fifth public university in the state in Boca Raton, just two towns and a few exits on the interstate south of Boynton Beach: Florida Atlantic University (FAU). Since FAU was within easy commuting distance, Charles saw it as an opportunity to continue to live in his parents' home, which was not at all an unpleasant prospect, and earn a degree at the same time. Charles didn't have the usual eighteen-year-old's impatience to move out of his parents' home. He got along well with them, and his father, who had seemed to age a lot during Charles' senior year; though his father didn't say so, Charles knew he could use his help with the grass and other outside work.

Some of his teachers were disappointed that he didn't aim higher but, at the same time, they felt rewarded that a black student had graduated successfully and continued on to college.

The first time he saw a certain girl was in a huge classroom amphitheater that was one of the few classrooms that could accommodate the freshman psychology classes. She was standing in the aisle waiting to find her way to a seat in a row of seats a few rows below his. In that era before students carried their books and just about everything else in a backpack, she was holding her books and notebooks in her arms to her chest. Charles was smitten immediately.

She was listening to a handsome, athletic-looking white male student whom Charles didn't know but had seen in class at least once before. She was smiling at her interlocutor but seemed to be taking his measure at the same time.

The girl had beautiful raven hair that flowed smartly down over the back of her collar and almost to her waist. Like many teenage girls that year, her fashion icons seemed to be Cher or country crooner Crystal Gayle with their long, black hair that seemed to have been ironed straight. This girl's hair, Charles noticed, seemed alive with a smooth gleam like the young women in shampoo commercials on television.

Charles had a sudden and, unusual for him, stab of jealousy toward the white student. Would this girl even see him? He suddenly regretted that he hadn't ever done much to develop whatever athleticism he had. He was at one disadvantage already: being black; he didn't feel he could compete with the muscular, athletic physique of this nameless suitor for this very attractive young lady's attention.

Charles concluded from the demeanor he observed that this fellow was not at all her type. Of course, Charles hadn't introduced himself to her or spoken a word with her. It just became apparent to him that the seeming self-confidence this fellow might have, in fact, exceeded the limits of mere self-confidence to the point of self-absorption. He appeared to be talking to the girl as though he considered what he had to tell her was the very thing she needed to know, and that his stabs at humor were the most charming phrases and sentences she would ever hear.

The girl's friendly smile began to shine less brightly as his one-sided soliloquy droned on. They were too many rows away from him for Charles to overhear the monologue, but he judged by her diminished smile and the metaphorical rolling of her eyes that she was having none of his efforts to impress her and flirt with her. She had a bemused look on her face as though he were a Fuller Brush salesman trying to fast-talk her into a much too expensive purchase.

A satisfied smile broke over Charles' face as it appeared that the fellow had lost the first round. The girl coolly walked away and took a seat down the row about five or six seats to the right. It suddenly struck Charles that he himself might have a chance—perhaps not a big one—but a chance he was willing to take. With her sumptuous raven hair, intelligent face, and endearing friendliness, this girl was simply too perfect to pass up.

Things progressed quickly after that. The next week Charles took an empty seat in the lecture hall right beside hers.

"Hi. This seat taken, or are you saving it for a friend?"

"Yes, if you are a friend."

Charles was almost bowled over by her clever answer. His initial nervousness abated.

Make sure you don't talk just about yourself. Ask her some polite, innocuous questions about herself. She'll be flattered by my interest in her.

"How are you enjoying Psychology 101—I'm sorry I don't even know your name," Charles said.

"Hi, I'm Dana—Dana Miller. And yes, I am enjoying this class. How 'bout you?"

"I think I'll begin to enjoy it even more now that I actually know someone else in the class, Dana. I'm Charles Wilkerson." He held out his right hand to shake hers.

The professor stood at the podium at the front and signaled that he was ready to begin.

Dana managed to squeeze in a couple of words before the class quieted completely.

"I'm glad to meet you, Charles. I look forward to seeing you here again."

AT CLASS A WEEK LATER, THE SEAT BESIDE Dana was unoccupied again.

"Again, Dana Miller, this seat's just empty or are you saving it for a friend?"

"Sure, it's reserved for a new friend I met last week. Take the seat, Charles. Good morning."

As the class was dismissed, Charles didn't rise from his seat. Dana stayed put as well. They sat together in silence.

"I sense you've got something to say," she said to Charles without any shyness.

"Something to ask you, actually. A couple of my buddies from my old high school are having a little party on Friday night up in Pompano. Their semester hasn't started yet at Miami. They're really a good bunch of guys. It'll be fun, but I don't think there will be any wild stuff. I'd like to invite you to come along. Interested?"

To his relief and never-ending gratitude, she said yes without any further questions or a second's hesitation.

"I'm way up on the tenth floor of the Glades Park Towers. I'll come down to the lobby at the entrance on the first floor. Any idea what time I can expect you?"

"Seven-thirty work for you?"

"You've got a date."

IT WAS JUST A SHORT DRIVE BACK from Roddy's apartment to the FAU campus. They hadn't been on the road back very long at all before Dana initiated a conversation.

"Thank you, Charles, for inviting me this evening. I really enjoyed meeting your high school buddies."

"I was pretty sure that you'd like them and vice versa," Charles said, delighted.

"When I was growing up," Dana said, "my parents always used to tell me that you can know a lot about a person by the quality of the people he hangs out with."

"Interesting. My parents used to say much the same thing. So, Dana, tell me, what did you learn about me by seeing me with my friends?" he asked playfully.

"Well, for one thing, that you use good judgment in choosing who to be friends with. They're kind of a serious bunch—like *you*, for that matter."

"Oh, tell me more."

"I heard your answers when Roddy and the others asked you about college. You told them about your courses, and how much you enjoyed your American Lit, and why."

"Isn't that what Roddy wanted to know?"

"You know him better. That may be what he wanted to know. But someone else might have boasted about skipping classes and homework and telling about all the hottest girls in their classes."

Charles chuckled good-naturedly and asked her, "You mean they didn't really care what I had chosen as the topic of my fall semester paper about Walt Whitman's *Leaves of Grass*?"

"Somehow I doubt it. They seem to know you well enough that they weren't surprised or thrown off by your obvious anticipation of writing a nerdy paper on Whitman. They knew you wouldn't regale them with your thrill at the physical features of hot girls around campus, at least not in the hearing of a female guest on your first date. I appreciate that quality in you, and your friends."

"How about your friends? How would they have replied to Roddy's question?"

"Oh, I suspect that one or two of them would talk about guys they've seen around. But Nancy or Carol would answer much as you did. They'd talk about what is challenging to them intellectually or academically."

They were pulling off Interstate 95, just a few short minutes from the FAU campus.

"I really enjoyed being with you this evening, Dana. I hope we can do this again soon."

"Yes, I would like that, too."

"How about a movie?"

"Sure, unless it's something like *Beware the Blob* or *The Bride of Frankenstein.*"

She chuckled. She was pretty confident that they wouldn't be Charles' cup of tea, either.

"Oh, for sure. Not violent or gory enough for me," Charles agreed. They enjoyed a moment of laughter together.

"Maybe we can find a half-decent romantic comedy," Charles amended. "I know that *Butterflies are Free* with Goldie Hawn is playing in town. Or, if you want to venture down to Fort Lauderdale, we have a ton to choose from, like *Pete and Tillie.* Walter Matthau always makes me laugh."

"You seem sensible. I'll let you choose. Next Friday or Saturday night?"

"I choose Saturday night. I'll pick you up at the same place as tonight."

AFTER A COUPLE OF DATES, CHARLES and Dana were practically inseparable. Other students began to see them as an "item." They spent many evenings and hours together on weekends in Dana's dorm room, reading, studying for tests, and completing homework assignments. Charles would try to answer Dana's questions about Nathaniel Hawthorne or Melville's *Moby Dick,* which Dana found absolutely baffling. Dana would check over Charles' trigonometry sheets to catch his careless errors.

One evening Charles asked her where her roommate Imelda had disappeared to. He hadn't seen her for many weeks, and suddenly he noticed that the top of Imelda's dresser was without the usual bottles of lotion, various kinds of make-up, and her combs and hairbrushes.

"She decided to move out—and move in with her boyfriend Alvaro. He has an apartment off-campus in town. They're like us. They spend all their free time together, and I guess they figured, why not just move in together?"

"That's bold, don't you think?" Charles asked a little tentatively.

"They're pretty serious about each other."

After a while, he asked, "I wonder what her parents think."

"I don't know if she's really talked to them about it," Dana answered.

"Honestly, I'd be afraid of how my parents would react. Not very favorably, I think."

"But you've said that your parents are no longer very religious."

"No, they aren't. They used to be when I was very young. I think it's just a generational thing. But I judge from things I've overheard them say over the years that they wouldn't be jumping up and down in joy were you and I to decide to move in together."

"I don't think they really have to be worried about that happening."

"No? Didn't you dream of it when the Beach Boys sang about it when we were in high school? Remember: *Wouldn't it be nice if we could wake up In the morning when the day is new? And after...*"

Charles stopped, grasping for the next line.

Dana caught on and added the next line: *"And after having spent the day together hold each other close the whole night through?"*

"Yeah, that's it. Wouldn't that be nice? I wouldn't have to kiss you and say goodnight and get on the interstate to my parents' place?"

Dana smiled at him but didn't say anything right away.

"It'd be a lot less expensive than your paying for a dorm room and my moving out from my parents' and renting an apartment for us."

"Charles, of course, it sounds good in the song. But is that reality?" Dana asked.

"Well, I wouldn't venture to move in together before we're married anyway. I don't want to risk my parents' disapproval."

"Imelda won't be able to wear the pure white wedding dress I think she dreams of. At least if she's really honest. I think they do more than just play Tiddlywinks in the evenings," Dana continued. "I have that dream, too, and have had since I was a little girl. It's how good Catholic families do weddings."

"And I gather that the Millers are a good Catholic family?"

"Yes, they are. And I'm a good Catholic girl or trying to be. I want a wedding in the Catholic church in Winter Park where I made my First Communion as a little girl and was confirmed by the Bishop. I want to hear the familiar Catholic prayers and be blessed by Father Duffey, who I really like."

"And you want your parents and the rest of your family witnessing the wedding with their wholehearted prayers and encouragement?"

"That's spot-on, Charles."

"So do I regarding my own parents."

Dana leaned over the desk and gave Charles a relieved kiss on his cheek. She thought about it again right away, and kissed him on the lips passionately.

"I think we've talked our way out of moving in together, don't you think?" Charles said.

Dana gave a gentle laugh in agreement.

"At least for the time being," Charles added and chuckled.

DURING THE SCHOOL BREAK about a year after they met, Dana told Charles that her parents wanted to invite him over to their Winter Park home. Charles became silent when she informed him.

"What's the matter, Charles?" she asked. "You seem upset."

"Not upset, really. Just a little anxious."

"About what? It's only my parents, not a Justice of the Supreme Court. They don't bite."

"You've told them that your boyfriend is black, right?"

"Of course, I have."

"And they still want to have me for dinner? This isn't going to be one of those *Guess Who's Coming to Dinner* moments, is it?"

"Naturally! Why wouldn't they? Oh Charles, you're going to have to meet them and spend time with them sooner or later," Dana reasoned. "Haven't you had this happen with your white friends' parents before?"

"No, not exactly," he said. Yes, there had been times when he felt he had to meet a greater set of expectations for behavior and attitudes than his other white friends had to when meeting parents. But this was different. This was the girl he wanted to marry.

"But you've got to realize that any guy I bring home will have to meet my parents' standards—whether he's white or black. I'm their precious daughter," she said with a little laugh. "They want to be satisfied that the man is deserving of me. You'll do just fine, Charles. My parents trust me and respect my judgment. They know I wouldn't bring home a loser."

Charles was comforted by Dana's assurance. Once he had been introduced to them, and the Millers' initial questions to him about where he lived, where he had come from, and what he intended to study at FAU were over, Charles relaxed. He told himself to stay loose and enjoy the evening, for his own sake and for Dana's as well.

After dinner and a delicious dessert, Mr. Miller asked, "Anybody up for a board game?"

Charles glanced over at Dana. She nodded her head quietly.

"Charles, what game do you like to play?"

Charles' family didn't play board games as a rule. Charles didn't know how to answer.

"Ever played Rummoli, Charles?" said Mr. Miller.

"If not, you'll learn quickly enough," Dana reassured him, sensing his sudden loss of self-confidence. "Daddy suggested it, I suspect, because he usually wins, and it makes him feel like a real poker champ."

They proceeded to play the card game for about an hour. Remembering what Dana had said about Mr. Miller's desire to win, Charles didn't have to lose on purpose out of politeness. The fact that he was learning the strategy of the game by the seat of his pants took care of that.

When the game was finished, Dana gathered the cards and poker chips and put them neatly in the package. She gave Charles a subtle, surreptitious wink of her eye.

"I think I'd better get on I-95 and drive back to Lantana. Thank you, Mr. and Mrs. Miller, for a lovely dinner and pleasant evening."

Mr. Miller lowered his voice in a mock warning to Charles. "You take care of our precious daughter, ya hear, son?"

"Please come eat with us another time. I'm sure Dana will see to that," her mother added.

Dana joined Charles on the driveway. Her hand was holding Charles by the crook of his arm.

"See? I told you that you had nothing to be anxious about. They loved you as I knew they would."

"Thanks for reassuring me. I enjoyed the evening.

Charles drove to Lantana, hoping he could maintain such enjoyable harmonious relations with Dana's loved ones for a long time.

CHAPTER 4

JUNE 1976

DANA INSISTED THEY HONEYMOON at Disney World. In fact, her strong preference for the Orlando amusement park was the first time in their relationship that she had insisted on anything. Usually, she deferred to Charles.

"But you grew up in Winter Park," Charles said. "Surely you've been in the Big Mouse House at least a hundred times. Are you sure that's what you want?"

"I'm sure. The last time was Senior Night when I was in high school. But it's just such fun every time I've been there. There's no place like it. It really is the happiest place on earth."

Always ready to please his new bride, Charles made reservations for them at the Polynesian, the more romantic of the park's two hotels. He was always up for a happy place. They met several other honeymooning couples at Disney World, some of whom had traveled from as far away as western Canada and places in Europe. A rather introverted and private person, Charles was happy to leave the role of social coordinator to Dana. Charles was in awe of her gregariousness. She met new people and made easy conversation with them the way most people breathe. She pulled people to her, coaxed even the shyest out of themselves, and embraced them with all their flaws as newfound friends. She clearly enjoyed being with them as much as they did with her, and Charles beamed with unqualified pride.

Charles always found her alluringly beautiful. He was still transfixed by her magnificent hair. It was long and thick, dark and heavy, healthy and strong. She had a part-time job filing at an office in Palm Beach County lined up even before graduation and the wedding. They developed a ritual when she came home to their apartment after a long workday that Charles would not miss for anything. Dana claimed that their ritual lowered her blood pressure and smoothed over any bumps she might have inadvertently brought home with her from the office. Dana would sit on the floor in front of their couch. Charles would perch behind her on the sofa, brushing her hair all over, rhythmically, first to one side and then the other until she was so relaxed that her head dropped to her chest and her long hair covered her face.

He loved seeing her rich mane of hair blossom on her pillow each bedtime, framing her face. When they were invited by friends once on a boat ride with them on the Intracoastal Waterway, he found it irresistible when her hair blew uncontrollably in the wind created by the speed of the boat. When they arrived back on land, she tried to wrestle her hair back under control. She gave up the fight, gathered her locks, and shaped them into a long black ponytail, which didn't suit her any less.

At a Miller family gathering one day, one of her cousins told Charles that her great-grandmother had been from Spain and had jet-black hair and deep blue eyes. Charles thought that wherever her physical beauty came from, he was grateful that her ancestors had bequeathed to her their rich dark hair, warm olive skin, and angelic blue eyes from heaven.

In time, Charles found a job as well. During his junior and senior years at FAU, he was hired at a Winn-Dixie grocery store on Lantana Road. The manager noticed Charles was about to graduate and offered him a job to start as a foreman in the produce department, with the opportunity to work his way up over time to assistant and, eventually, to manager of the department. That was worth aiming for. He would switch to full-time work. FAU isn't going away. He could always go back and finish his degree anytime. All kinds of time for that.

"I'm pleased, of course, that I was offered the position," he told Dana when he got home from the interview. "But I'm surprised at the same time. I could have been hired for the housekeeping department or as a stock boy. The housekeeping staff occupies the storage area at the back of the store. It looked like almost all of the housekeepers in the storage room were black. I wonder if any other black employees are on the management track as I will be."

"Oh honey, you're not just another run-of-the-mill black employee from the wrong side of the tracks. You deserve the job. Don't overlook your strengths. The manager who hired you didn't."

"You'd be surprised by the number of real-life stories I've heard of blacks being hired for positions lower in the pecking order than jobs awarded to lesser deserving whites."

Dana had a disbelieving look on her face.

"You don't believe me; you think that I'm exaggerating. Maybe it's hard for even well-intentioned white folks to appreciate how discouraging that is to blacks, even me. True, my job as foreman is better than working in housekeeping, but for a young black man, being foreman is probably the highest I can aim for."

"But you said the manager told you that you can work your way up to be the assistant manager—manager even."

"True. But it's too early for me to judge whether he really means that."

"I'm sure he does. He wouldn't say that if he didn't mean it."

I guess white kids are raised to trust what their authority figures say. How different from the experience of black people, for sure.

It wasn't the first time that Charles realized that even though Dana wasn't personally prejudiced—she'd never even seemed to notice the difference in their skin, even when they first met—her experience in the world growing up as a young, white woman in the South had been quite different from his as a black man. Her experiences had misled her to believe that everyone was judged by their abilities, not the color of their skin.

BY 1981, HOWEVER, CHARLES had advanced through the ranks of the large produce department to assistant manager. When Roy Oswald, who had been the manager of the department for over twenty years, had to retire because of his aging knees, Charles stepped into the manager's role.

At the same time their marriage was progressing smoothly if conventionally.

"Charles, we'd better talk. I'm not 100% sure yet, but I think I'm pregnant."

She was disappointed by Charles' initial reaction. He became mute. She couldn't tell whether he was overjoyed by the news or disappointed. Or angry.

"I don't know what your sudden silence means, Charles."

"I'm sorry I wasn't as excited as I'm sure you wanted me to be at first," he apologized. "I'm really happy for you, for us. I just wasn't expecting it. It's just that I suddenly realized we have to look for a decent house right away where this new ball of joy will have room to grow up."

"I'm glad I've got a husband who thinks of such practical things."

Grateful that he had landed the managerial job to put on their application for a mortgage, even if produce foreman was just a step above a regular employee, they were approved quickly and, with a realtor's help, located a three-bedroom ranch house on a quiet street near his Winn-Dixie store in unincorporated Palm Beach County. The house had a large backyard and was adjacent to a vacant lot. The lot was overrun by tall thistles, other unattractive weeds, and bothersome melaleuca seedlings. But the realtor assured them it would remain that way for their child to be able to explore. And, the realtor said, the lot would provide a level of privacy and security.

When the Wilkersons moved in, neighbors stopped by their house and received Dana's cordial welcome and "How do you do's?" Though they tried not to be too obvious, some seemed a little taken aback when the very pregnant lady of the house introduced her black husband. Charles took notice of it and wondered if Dana caught the subtle signs. But if there was any surprise or discomfort about a new neighbor, Charles chose to overlook it. In fact, everybody pretty well ignored Charles. They preferred to ask Dana about the baby— questions about when was the baby due, did they know if it was a boy or a girl, and at which hospital would it be delivered.

It was at Good Samaritan Hospital in West Palm Beach that Dana gave birth to Travis in the first week of a very tropical-feeling August 1983.

"How about that?" Charles remarked. "We almost timed it so that Travis and I share a birthday."

Charles and Dana didn't have much time in the minutes after Travis's birth to consider things like that. Their obstetrician came into the new mother's room to inform the baby's parents that Travis wouldn't be able to go home with them until a week or two later.

"I'm sorry to say that the neonatal staff noticed a slight irregularity," the obstetrician reported empathetically. "The doctors are in agreement that young Travis has a hole in the wall separating the two ventricles in his heart."

"What does that mean?" Charles asked, suddenly fearful for this tiny new child who had already captured his heart.

"It's not the best start, but it can be addressed eventually by open-heart surgery."

"Eventually?" Dana queried, still unbalanced after the shocking news.

"Normally, it's a serious enough surgical procedure that a newborn wouldn't survive. The surgeons prefer to wait until the child is at least three years old or weighs at least thirty pounds."

"That's over three years from now. What are we to do in the

meantime?" Charles asked.

"One of the surgeons will be by to check on Travis's vital signs and give you instructions about caring for him until he's at least three."

THE FOCUS OF THEIR MARRIAGE suddenly changed. While they were grateful for each other and for the addition of a child to their family, every moment of their lives was now dominated by concern bordering sometimes on fear for Travis's health and well-being. They became very anxious about the demands of Travis's medication schedule and the daily struggle to keep him alive. They learned to measure their days by every one of Travis's doses of medicine.

The pediatric nurses who made twice-weekly visits at their home always reassured them that they were very vigilant parents, and that Travis was progressing and growing as well as could be expected. That comforted Charles and especially Dana. But even with her deeply rooted Catholic faith, neither she nor Charles were able to feel at peace, knowing that they could lose Travis with just one small misstep, one forgotten dose of medication, one careless moment when they weren't being wholly attentive to the baby's needs.

They were young, excited newlyweds, but some days or nights they felt they carried the weight of the whole world on their sagging shoulders.

CHAPTER 5

JULY 1986

WHEN THE PHONE CALL CAME FROM the head of pediatrics at John F. Kennedy Hospital in West Palm Beach, Charles had to sit down for fear that he would faint from anxiety.

"Hello, Charles. Dr. Lawrence here at JFK. How are you?"

Charles chuckled self-consciously.

"A little nervous, to be quite frank, Doctor."

"Well, it appears that you and Dana have done such a crackerjack job of tending to Travis that we are sure we can proceed with the heart surgery for him even a few weeks before he turns three years old."

"Really?" he said, as excitement warred with panic.

"The people at Jackson Memorial tell me that the surgeon will be up in North Carolina on vacation all of August. So they recommend we proceed now while he's still in Florida. What say you?"

Charles put his hand over the telephone receiver and spoke quietly with Dana, who had come into the room when she heard the telephone ring. "Dr. Lawrence wants to know if we're ready to go forward with Travis's surgery."

"I don't think I'll ever be ready to put him through such a potentially dangerous operation. But this is what he needs so—" She nodded. "Let's go ahead."

Dr. Lawrence was pleased with their agreement. He instructed them to be at Jackson Memorial Hospital in Miami by 7 a.m. on July 30 and check into their accommodations the previous evening. He told them not to be concerned about making hotel reservations in Miami because the pediatric surgery department at Jackson Memorial would take care of that and, furthermore, absorb the payment, thanks to a generous grant from the American Heart Association. The hospital would send papers to sign, authorizing the surgeon to conduct the operation and any follow-up that might be required,

"But I know these guys and their work. I wouldn't expect any complications. You can be sure of that."

The doctor's words were reassuring at the time, but by the time they loaded the car on the morning of July 29 and settled Travis into his booster seat for the drive to Miami, Charles and Dana's comfort and confidence had pretty well eroded. Since Dr. Lawrence's call, their days had been a beehive of activity as they arranged to have time off work, informed the families, and received the well wishes and encouragement of their neighbors.

Dana settled into an attitude of positivity on the drive down I-95, but Charles was on edge, cursing at other drivers, blaming them for being on the road at all when he had a toddler in the car who was facing life-threatening surgery.

"Come on, Gramps. You drive more slowly than molasses in January in Buffalo. Move over!" he barked.

"Charles, honey. We're not really in such a hurry. The surgery isn't until tomorrow," Dana said in an effort to calm him down.

Calm down is what Charles did. He swallowed his anger and frustration.

"I'm sorry, Dana. I'm a ball of nerves wound tightly. You're right as usual. I know I'm driving that way, and I will try to do better."

Jackson Memorial had them staying in a small boutique hotel built in traditional white stucco Mission style a few blocks away from the hospital. They gave Travis a dose of the melatonin that Dr. Lawrence had recommended to help him sleep soundly.

"Charles, maybe you could use a dose yourself," Dana said, then smiled to make sure he knew it was a joke.

They distractedly scarfed down the hotel's breakfast in the morning and headed immediately to the hospital. The volunteer at the reception desk was so helpful in directing them to the pediatric surgery unit in the huge hospital that they arrived with Travis in tow almost a full hour before they were expected. The unit nurse informed them that the surgeons were on their way but might not be there for at least another half hour.

Charles was too high-strung to be embarrassed.

When he arrived, Dr. Eugenio Lopez, the lead surgeon for Travis's procedure, came by the small waiting area near the entrance into the surgical unit and met briefly with Charles and Dana. He was the epitome of serenity and spoke with them very empathetically. He pointed them to the main surgical waiting area not far away and tried to reassure them.

"Anything I am able to do for Travis's healing using my skills and experience I can do only in the power of the source of all healing."

Dana didn't try to hide her tears of gratitude at the doctor's spiritual sensitivity. His words were exactly what she needed to hear. Charles, for his part, was not accustomed to such a frank and open expression of faith by a professional. *It's in the surgeon's skills that I will choose to put my faith,* he thought to himself, but he knew better than to say that to Dana. Instead, he put his arm around her shoulders and led her to the surgical waiting room down the hall.

The waiting room was filled with young parents and presumably the siblings of children who were having surgery. While the children played with toys or read books they had brought from home, some of the parents held private conversations in muffled tones. Dana made eye contact with a young Hispanic woman and exchanged nervous smiles with her. The man sitting next to the Hispanic woman nodded politely to Charles at the same time. Charles accepted the man's nod as an invitation to exchange a nonverbal greeting.

Charles hoped that the peaceful, quiet in the room would continue. Sometimes in these kinds of settings and circumstances Dana would initiate a conversation. She knew from Charles' body language that morning that he would not welcome her attempts to violate the silence in the room and thereby burst his safe and comfortable bubble of introversion and privacy. She knew this was not the time nor the place to engage him in conversation. She was sensitive enough to Charles' needs not to turn to any of the other anxious parents for companionship or small talk, or even ask about what kind of surgery or procedure their son or daughter was undergoing.

Instead, Charles' womb of silence and privacy was transgressed by a seventyish gentleman wearing a string tie who sat beside a woman of about the same age who was sitting directly opposite Dana and Charles.

"Y'all look a little anxious," the man addressed Charles.

Charles looked away pretending he hadn't heard.

"Don't waste your nervous energy worrying about your loved one in the surgical theatre behind this wall here, son. The surgeons here are the best ones in Dixie."

Charles continued to look in any other direction but the man's who had run roughshod over his clear desire for nonengagement. He had violated Charles' privacy by revealing his anxiety to all in the room, despite Charles' best efforts to appear calm and composed.

The string-tie man raised his already loud voice. "I'm talking to *you*, son. Perhaps you didn't hear me."

Charles could sense the blood running to his head and turning his face red. He felt his heart pounding faster in his chest. He clenched his fist. He silently cursed this invasive man for not having the sense to decipher his clear signals that he would prefer to be left alone with his thoughts. What else did he have to do to communicate to this boorish oaf his desire for seclusion?

"Our grandson has had a pain in the ass since he was a wee one. I don't mean that he *was* a pain in the ass to us. Anything but, in fact. What I mean is that he was born with an anal fistula."

It was as if her husband's loud voice and laughter at his own joke caused his wife to come awake.

"Bud, I don't think everybody at Jackson Memorial needs to know that. Just wait quietly like the rest of us."

"Come on, Noreen. I'm just trying to be friendly to this guy. He looked so down in the mouth when he came in."

"My apologies, friend." he boomed at Charles. "My name is Bud Norris, and this here's my wife, Alice—or should I say my better half?"

Dana stepped in to try to rescue Charles. It wouldn't be the first time, or the last, when Dana intervened just at the right moment.

"We're the Wilkersons. My husband is Charles, and I'm Dana. Glad to meet you, Bud and Alice."

"So glad to meet you, Charlie and Diana. I'm getting the impression that you two are the only other people in this room who can converse in English. Ah, the way Miami *used* to be before Castro took control of Cuba. Spanish practically became a second unofficial language. In Miami, shit, I think Spanish is really the *first* unofficial language. 'Will the last real American remember to turn off the lights as you leave Miami.' Where y'all from? Not from Cuba, thank the Lord, I can tell."

Dana fielded Bud's question

"I was raised in Winter Park myself. My husband came with his family from upstate New York. We live between Lantana and Boynton Beach now."

"You call Charlie your husband? You a married couple? What's your daddy say about that?"

Dana looked over anxiously at Charles. Charles didn't even try to hide that he was rolling his eyes, which was his way of saying, "Here we go again."

"I mean, you ain't the same skin color," Bud explained in case Dana and Charles didn't catch the drift.

Dana straightened her posture in her seat. She glanced again a little anxiously at Charles.

"I guess you never know who you'll fall in love with. Or who will fall in love with you. Our life has been delightful, believe me, since we married just about ten years ago."

Her voice contained a hint of apology in it. Charles was a little surprised—and disappointed.

"I guess your old man is more tolerant than I am, Diana. If our daughter had brought home a colored man and introduced him to us as her fiancé, I'm not sure what I would have said to her. It wouldn't have been pretty, you can be damned sure. But, of course, she knew better than to test our patience."

Charles had been trying to ignore the conversation, to block it out of his hearing as much as Bud's loud, intrusive voice would allow. But Dana could sense that he was seething. Bud had trespassed into dangerous territory.

"First of all, Bud. Her name is Dana, that's D-A-N-A, not like Lady Diana. Mine is Charles, if you please, not Charlie. Charlie sounds like some field hand's name, and I'm not that. I'm a manager."

Dana reached over to put her palm over Charles' to plead for patience.

"And that we have a mixed marriage is none of your damn business. Orange County in Florida gave us a marriage license, which makes our marriage legal in the eyes of the law if not in the closed minds of some of its citizens. And we would prefer to wait until our son's surgery is over and not hear any more of your—" Charles thought of describing Bud's ignorant racist dribble with some colorful expletive but held back and checked his tongue for Alice's sake. He was certain she heard plenty of indelicate vulgarity from that cretinous husband of hers.

Charles held tightly onto the armrest of his chair, and Dana could hear that he was snorting subtly like a bull that had seen red. He was silently replaying in his mind a fantasy to which he returned from time to time in which the black hero of the story finally explodes and unleashes a torrent of his pent-up anger and frustration at the white man's undisguised racial animus against him in particular and his black race in general.

Alice must have heard the snorting, too.

"Come on, Bud. Let's go for a walk out in the corridor, shall we?"

"Noreen, I don't think *we're* the ones who need to go for a walk in the corridor. Doesn't it sound to you as though this colored fellah needs to get ahold of himself and bite his tongue? Jesus. Trust the blacks to make a federal case of every conversation that includes race, even if the speaker doesn't intend any disrespect."

Alice took Bud's arm by the elbow. "Come on, Bud. Do as I say."

Alice rose from her chair, and Bud got up, albeit resentfully and very reluctantly. Dana looked up at them, trying to reach for Alice's hand.

"I'm sorry, Alice. It's been a tense time at our house the last week or so ever since the doctor scheduled this surgery."

Charles couldn't believe what he was hearing his wife say. An apology! For what? For protecting him from such unexamined intolerance and bigotry?

Alice led Bud out the door to the corridor. The Hispanic family seemed to comprehend by the angry tone of Charles' voice and the rapidity with which Bud and Alice stormed from the room the meaning of the conversation, even if they might not have understood the words. Dana looked down at the floor before sneaking in a friendly smile toward the young mother across the room to indicate that, though some passions were aroused, things were okay.

"Why did you do that, Dana? Apologize to them, I mean. That's not really like you. *We* are the ones who are owed *their* apology, at least his."

"Charles, honey, you're allowing this man's ignorance to distract your attention from Travis just when he needs us to be with him wholeheartedly. There will always be a Bud Norris or people like him in every crowd. They don't say anything you've never heard before—or anything you won't hear again."

CHAPTER 6

PALM BEACH COUNTY, FL, AUGUST 1986

CHARLES' ANXIETY WASN'T ALLEVIATED much after his encounter with Bud Norris; Travis was still on the operating table. But the moment he and Dana first saw their child after the four-hour surgery, all of Charles' worries evaporated. He and Dana embraced in utter relief. For the first time in Travis's life, he was a beautiful, luminous pink.

"I love you, Dana," Charles said while exhaling his breath. "Our boy is going to be okay."

Exultant, they drove back to Lantana two weeks later. Dana had called their neighbors—the O'Neills and the Buckleys—from the hospital to report the good news. When Charles pulled the car into their driveway, the two families gathered around to see the beautiful, healthy boy and congratulate the fortunate parents. Alicia Echeverria, another neighbor, was there, too, but her husband, Armando, was at work.

Charles and Dana felt so joyful and full of gratitude for the success of Travis's surgery—and that they had such loving neighbors.

"We're so blessed," Charles said to Dana after they'd closed the front door behind them and entered their living room. Dana was not accustomed to Charles' uncharacteristic choice of this devout phrase. But she shared the feeling.

By the next day Travis was racing around in the backyard with some of the neighbors' kids and playing as hard as any of the others. He savored every moment of it. Charles and Dana sat in lawn chairs thoroughly enjoying the spectacle of their son playing actively with the others without turning a shade of blue from exhaustion. And they were thrilled with not having to hover over their son while feeling the protective impulse to call him to withdraw from the fun and games to rest and catch his breath.

"We made it, Babe," Charles said contentedly. "It's great to see Travis playing like any healthy child. His future and ours seem much brighter now," Charles said, his arm around Dana's waist.

"Isn't this the perfect birthday gift, honey?" Dana smiled at her husband.

Her sentiment reminded Charles that the day after next was his thirty-second birthday.

"What else can a father wish for his birthday?" he asked, sure that the answer was "Absolutely nothing."

"Let's all go out on your birthday to celebrate: your birthday, the health of our son, and a new beginning as a family. My treat."

"Now you're talking," Charles responded. "I think a big, juicy steak at the Okeechobee would be just the thing, don't you? I wonder if they have a child's menu."

"I'm sure they do, but I'll ask before I make the reservation," Dana replied.

THE NEXT DAY, SUNDAY, Dana called the Okeechobee Steak House in West Palm Beach to make a dinner reservation for Monday evening. Dana and Charles were familiar with the establishment and its massive and filling thirty-ounce steaks, and the restaurant did have a child's menu. They hadn't been back there since their dating days more than a decade earlier when Charles had taken Dana there to celebrate the one-year anniversary of their relationship. Now, having a healthy Travis in tow gave an additional joyous dimension to the event. Though it was Charles' birthday, he was more than happy to share the spotlight with Travis.

The Buckleys had volunteered to babysit Travis at their home so that Dana and Charles could enjoy a romantic birthday dinner together. The Wilkersons thanked their neighbors but declined their thoughtful offer. The truth was that they wouldn't have considered the evening complete if they could not spend it as a threesome.

When the hostess led them to their table, Charles requested a highchair for Travis. He took the adult menu as well from the hostess's outstretched hand.

"I don't think I'll be needing this," he remarked to Dana across the table. "I'm pretty set on what I'm going to order for myself."

After reading the menu, Dana put in an order for the small filet mignon for herself and a child's cheeseburger and French fry platter for Travis. Charles ordered the jumbo steak and two glasses of red wine.

"We're so proud of you, Travis, for what a big boy you were at the hospital," Dana said. "Dr. Lawrence and Dr. Lopez were so impressed with how brave you were."

"And how quickly you have recovered from the operation,"

Charles added.

"They cut me open and fixed my heart. It didn't even hurt," Travis commented.

"Yes, honey, they fixed your heart, and now you can run and play with the other children," Dana said. "Isn't it wonderful to be able to do that now without getting tired?"

"I can beat Danny in a running race," Travis boasted.

"That makes you a very fast runner, Travis," Charles complimented him.

Charles and Dana clinked their wine glasses together, and Travis took a deep sip of water from his sippy cup, which he was just learning to use.

"Travis is behaving as though he's an old hand at dining out in a snazzy restaurant," Dana remarked through her smile.

Charles basked in the light of her smile. He hadn't seen Dana this happy for a long time. "This evening is going to get nothing but better," he said as he winked suggestively in Dana's direction.

CHARLES RECALLED THE FIRST TIME he and Dana celebrated his birthday together. They were not yet married. What occurred was a surprise to him. It hadn't entered his plans for the day at all. He wasn't certain, though, whether what followed had been in Dana's mind as they returned to her dorm room that afternoon. But looking back, it seems it had.

They had gone over to Red Reef Park on the Boca oceanfront to do some snorkeling. It was near the end of the summer term. The August sun was brutal.

"Don't you think it's too hot to stay in this unfiltered sun?" Charles said to Dana as they raised their heads out of the shimmering water. "We'll be burned to a crisp. Even a few inches underneath the surface the ultraviolet rays can reach our skin."

"I gather you want to leave."

"No, I don't *want* to leave. This is a great way to celebrate my birthday. It's just that if we don't get out of the sun, we'll regret the sunburn we'll suffer from tomorrow.

"You're probably right. Let's go back to my room and get out of our wet bathing suits. You brought a change of clothes in your gym bag, didn't you?

"Yes, of course."

"Perfect. I've got a surprise for you back at my dorm. I baked a lemon meringue pie last night. It's meant to be dessert, even though we haven't had dinner yet."

"But life is short, so eat dessert first. Isn't that what they say?" Charles quoted.

"Let's do it."

"Okay, let's."

Charles detected the possible double entendre of what Dana said: "Let's do it." and "I have a surprise for you." But it was just his passing thought, an innocent coincidence.

As they walked hand in hand from the parking lot toward Dana's residence hall, Charles asked, "We can't just barge in and take over the whole room, can we? Doesn't Imelda have a say in that?"

"Silly, remember me telling you that Imelda is home in Davie? She's not enrolled in the summer term."

"Oh, I'd forgotten."

"Mr. Birthday Boy, no worries. We have the whole room to ourselves."

As soon as they arrived in Dana's room, she excused herself to the bathroom to get out of her wet swimsuit. When she came out, she had just the beach towel wrapped around her. She approached Charles so that he would wrap his arms around her. He did so and kissed her on the lips passionately as though he'd never kissed her before. Dana took two short steps backwards toward the sofa, and he followed as though they were dancing. She fell backward without warning onto the sofa. Charles had no choice but to let himself fall on her supine body.

She kissed him fervently on his neck several wet times while she ran her fingers through his hair. Charles was aroused by the kisses and took his turn to kiss her greedily on her neck. Charles wasn't at all certain where this was headed. They had embraced and exchanged passionate kisses many times before, but this was the first time they had done so in this more stimulating position. She was practically naked. He was hungry for her, for more kisses, for the exciting feel of her lithe body beneath his, for her ample, white breasts barely constrained by the towel.

He held off moving his hands to any part of her body. He was unsure of how she would react. *But she has been leading this dance up to now. This is the time for me to follow the leader.*

"Oh, Charles. I love you so," she whispered into his ear as she continued to kiss him. She pulled off his t-shirt and kissed him on his nipples.

"Charles, I want you inside me."

Charles was caught totally off guard. Suddenly, he ceased the erotic movement of his hips against her. She could feel the bulge in this bathing suit against her groin.

"This is our chance, Charles. No one's around. Haven't we been waiting for a time like this?"

"Dana, are you sure? I don't have any protection, no condoms. Are you sure you want to risk becoming pregnant?"

"Oh Charles. Where do you pick up your information? A girl doesn't get pregnant *every* time she has sex. Come on, I can feel you want this as much as I do. Show me what you've got underneath that bathing suit."

Charles had read that there is more that needs to happen to prepare him for intercourse. *But she's right. We'll be married in less than a year. Go ahead. Just let it happen, Charles.*

She helped him remove his damp swimming trunks. When it was time to slide the trunks over the bulge at his groin, she stopped and allowed him to finish the task lest she hurt him in some way.

The act was completed awkwardly like a couple unaccustomed to dancing as a pair. After he had come, they separated wordlessly, she into the bathroom while Charles scooped up his bathing suit off the floor and wondered what had just occurred. *I can't believe this happened.*

Charles had a difficult time looking directly into Dana's face.

"There, we've done it, Charles. I feel so much closer to you. This was good, but I am sure the next time it will be more comfortable. My mother told me the first time is always special but a little awkward and maybe painful. She was probably just trying to prevent me from doing it."

"Did I hurt you?"

She wrapped her arms around him. "No, dearest, it was good. I've heard of couples who celebrate their birthdays this way every year. Don't you think that is a good idea?"

"I can think of less pleasant ways." As soon as he had answered her thus, he wanted to take the clumsy response back. *I'm missing an opportunity here.*

"Yes, let's do that. But Dana, until we're married, I think I should use a condom. We don't want an unplanned baby so soon, do we?"

"You're in charge the next time. Consider it a date for next February 18, my birthday, and then again next August 12—if not sooner. I'm not sure I can wait that long. After all, like they say, practice makes perfect."

AT THE OKEECHOBEE, CHARLES was still radiating happiness as he helped Travis down from his highchair while Dana paid the tab. He couldn't remember when he had last been this content with his life. He didn't know how long he had been lost in his pleasant and private recollection of that new birthday ritual between them that they had established. He was aroused again by the memory and the potential for more later that night.

As the three of them walked across the parking lot to their car, Travis walked between his parents, holding Charles' hand with one of his own and Dana's hand in the other, and began swinging his body back and forth and breaking into a gleeful squeal.

When they arrived home, Dana started to put Travis to bed. She read him his favorite story about the Berenstain Bears.

Meanwhile, Charles turned on the television in the living room. President Reagan's press conference was just ending. Reagan fielded the reporters' questions about the ending of *apartheid* in South Africa, the tearing down of the Berlin Wall, and other issues that seemed so very important that night, but which would quickly fade from Charles' mind in the following hour.

At that moment his only thoughts were about romance and sex. The good feeling of the dinner and Dana's lustrous smile from across the dinner table both served to stimulate his imagination and his appetite for intimacy.

In anticipation of that intimacy, the day before he had stopped on his way home from work at a small video store and picked up a soft porn movie. Turning on the TV, he inserted the cassette into the VCR, then pressed "play" to check that he'd brought home the video he wanted. When he sat down on the sofa, he overheard Dana coming to the end of the Berenstain Bears story.

Dana came out from Travis's room into the living room and saw the blanket that Charles had spread out on the carpeted floor in front of the fireplace. She smiled at her husband and plopped down on the blanket.

Charles got up from the blanket and fetched them both a glass of wine.

"Oh, thanks, honey," she said, taking a small sip. "That's good wine. But I'm warning you: If I drink any more of this, I'll be asleep in less than a minute. Tonight was a very good evening but I'm totally exhausted." She lay her head down on the blanket.

She raised it again not long afterward. She looked at the video that was running on the television. There were several shapely young women running on a beach in topless bikinis. A couple of young fraternity-type males were eyeing the women from their beach blanket and breaking out into manly cheers. "Charles, what in the world have you brought home?"

"It's nothing you haven't seen before, Dana. Just something that might get you in the mood, I'm hoping."

Just then they heard the pitter-patter of small slippered feet on the carpet in the hallway. Travis had awakened or else hadn't really fallen asleep in the first place.

Dana wasted no time getting up off the blanket. "I'll take care of it, honey," Dana said, and headed down the hall to Travis's room.

In the days and weeks to come, Charles would look back on this incident with regret and embarrassment. *How could I have been so insensitive? I had the whole day off for my birthday, but she worked all day and now was taking care of an active, excited toddler. What was I thinking?*

Before Dana returned to the living room, Charles lay down on the blanket on the floor where Dana had been lying.

When she came back, Charles could read the exhaustion on her face. Nonetheless, he took her into his arms as they lay together and caressed her in the hope of triggering a little romantic interest. Instead, almost instantly, he began to hear her familiar soft snoring. Feeling sorry for himself, Charles got up, swallowed the rest of the wine in his glass, and headed back to their bedroom, leaving Dana on the blanket on the floor.

Alone in their queen-size bed, peeved at what he saw as a missed opportunity, Charles allowed himself to fall asleep. He hardly stirred from his sleep when, a few hours later, Dana came to bed, curled around him, and whispered into his ear, "I'm sorry, honey. Maybe next time, Babe."

CHARLES WAS ALREADY AWAKE WHEN the alarm rang at 5:00 a.m., the same as on every workday. He stepped into his familiar rigid morning routine—showering, dressing, downing a bowl of cereal, and leaving the house for work by 5:30. Neighbors had commented to him jokingly that they could set their watches in the morning because his time of departure for the fifteen- or twenty-minute commute to the Winn-Dixie was exactly the same every other morning.

This morning, however, still smarting from what he felt was Dana's rejection the night before, he did one last thing before he left the house. He glanced at Dana sleeping soundly on the bed and then left a note for her that, like much of this fateful morning, would haunt him for the rest of his life:

Dear Dana, I know you didn't mean to, but you made me feel really unwanted last night. Even after such a delightful meal, the moment we got home, you started to binge on the rest of the cookies. Then, while I was caressing you lovingly, you dozed off to sleep. I had been hoping for the kind of action that has been a tradition between us on my birthday since before we've been married. I'm not mad this morning. I just wonder how you might have felt if you had been left hanging on your birthday or our anniversary. Have a good day. ILY. Charles.

Charles propped the note against a bottle of hand lotion on the counter by the bathroom sink where she would be sure to see it, got in his car in the garage, and went to work.

CHAPTER 7

AUGUST 12, 1986

THE SCRUFFY MAN, PERHAPS IN HIS early forties, watched silently from the window of his green van as Charles pulled his car down the driveway and into the street at 5:30 a.m. *This son-of-a-bitch certainly is as prompt and predictable as a Swiss train. He's right on time.*

From the front of the house, where he entered his garage, the rear of the house was totally out of sight. Charles would be oblivious to the green van and the man inside it.

Before he stepped out of the van that had been parked near the construction zone behind the house all night, he waited to make sure that Charles' car had turned right onto the street toward the exit from the subdivision. He smiled when he saw that no lights were on in the house, especially in the area he surmised was the bedroom.

"That's it, Ma'am," he whispered to himself. *"Stay asleep for a little while longer."*

He was a big man; his full, reddish, lumberjack beard made him look even more massive. He was dressed in a badly wrinkled, green work shirt with the name "Ernie" sewn in white stitching over the left breast, and the words "Palm Beach Carpets" stitched in cursive on the back. Tufts of unruly long red hair peeked out from underneath his mesh baseball cap. He crouched down and peered through the overgrown prickly thistles in the construction zone behind the Wilkersons' home. He also looked behind him and to both sides to make sure he had not been seen.

After waiting for a tense quarter hour, he was confident that Charles was close to his workplace and would not return to the house. He was growing restless to get on with this morning's task. He was so hyped from adrenaline and distorted sexual energy that he thought he would explode. He rose from his crouched position, still keeping his head low to avoid being noticed. After glancing warily to his right and left, he crept cautiously toward a gate in the fence, minding the sharp spines on the leaves of the thistles, the broken remains of construction materials, and the used coffee cups and soft drink cans discarded carelessly on the ground.

The gate was locked, in a manner of speaking, but the locking mechanism was no obstacle for the man. He simply reached down and manipulated it until he could open the gate toward him and step into the backyard. *Bingo! We're on our way to paydirt!* he rejoiced, his heart pounding in his chest with lecherous anticipation.

He hoped he would find the sliding glass door at the rear of the house just as easy to open. The sun had risen so he had no trouble locating the door. He stepped up to the door quietly and deliberately. Before he tried to slide the door open, he put on a pair of red gloves he carried in his back pocket. He placed his hand on the space cut into the aluminum to serve as a handle and slid the door slowly to the left until it was open. The door had been left unlocked!

He pushed the sheer curtain aside. Before him was the empty den. On his way through the den, he picked up a stout piece of firewood from the grate next to the fireplace. He made his way without turning on the overhead lights through the corridor that his familiarity with these kinds of suburban ranch houses told him would lead to his destination: the bedroom.

He tiptoed into the bedroom. The woman was still asleep on the bed. When she sensed that she was no longer alone, she sat up and called the name "Charles!" The man swung the firewood with all the sexual adrenaline he could muster. He was certain that the first blow to her head was sufficient. But his perverted lust for blood caused him to strike her again and again.

He pulled his bandana from his hip pocket and held it over the woman's face to smother her. Pretty well unconscious, the woman made a desperate attempt to strike back. He wrapped the bandana around his fist and struck her with it several times. Finally, she quit struggling.

His distorted sexual energy satiated, he used the bandana around his fist to wipe the sweat off his forehead. Then he shoved it carelessly into his back pocket.

The man was not totally alone with the corpse, however. The killer didn't notice that a little boy about four years old had been awakened by the noise and his mother's muffled screams and was watching from the bedroom doorway. In a desperate panic, the boy couldn't scream, though he tried. For a few seconds he was frozen. Then he backed away in abject fear of the strange hostile monster in his mother's bedroom, and silently ran back to his own room and hid in the closet.

The man found the bathroom across the hall. He took off his dirty clothes and stepped into the shower to wash the blood off his hands. The boy left the closet when he heard the shower running and peered around the corner to catch a glimpse of the trespassing monster. He went back into the closet to hide.

The man turned off the shower and found the towel on the rack on the wall. He sorted through his pile of clothes and put them on quickly. He went back through the den and stepped out through the sliding glass door. He crossed the vacant lot next door toward his green van. He pulled the bandana out of his pocket to wipe the stubborn sweat that continued to secrete on his forehead. He returned the bandana to his rear pocket.

But as he stepped over the tall weeds in the lot, before he got to his van, the sweaty, blood-stained bandana fell from his pocket onto the weedy, sandy ground.

CHAPTER 8

PALM BEACH COUNTY, AUGUST 13, 1986

As Charles drove east along Hypoluxo Boulevard toward his Winn-Dixie store, he replayed in his mind the events of the previous day. Though he had gone to bed alone and frustrated the night before, he was surprised that much of the resentment he had felt had dissolved like mist in the dawn of a new morning and no longer bothered him as it had just a few hours earlier. Instead, his new regret was leaving the rather petulant and whiny note for Dana. *What a way to greet your wife first thing in the morning!*

Charles didn't think of himself as the grousing kind, the type of self-centered guy who complained to others, especially his wife, about how bad things are. Rather, he thought he was very adaptable and accommodating, easygoing, willing to accept matters. He was usually ready to forgive imperfections and adjust his expectations accordingly. "We all make mistakes," he would remark, either out loud whenever Dana apologized to him or silently to himself when he realized his expectations of the other had been unrealistic.

Maybe it was the fact that yesterday had been his birthday that gave him permission to be bolder and more upfront about his own desires. The fact that Dana was treating him to the special dinner, which, in fact, had been her suggestion in the first place, emboldened his sudden sense of entitlement. *Didn't I as a husband deserve the right to insist on my marital prerogative to enjoy sexual pleasure with my wife?*

When he arrived in the produce department receiving room in the back of the Winn-Dixie, Charles savored a quiet, uninterrupted cup of coffee. As the six o'clock hour approached, one by one the other employees arrived. Cassandra, a Hispanic college student adorned as usual with far too much eye shadow, was almost embarrassingly attentive to him on the day after his birthday.

"D'ya have a good birthday, boss? I hope your lucky lady was good to ya."

Charles hoped that the other employees in the room hadn't overheard the barely camouflaged sexual innuendo in her question.

Derrick, who was about all things outdoors, chimed in, "Did you at least get to dunk the end of the fishin' line in the water?"

"No, Derrick, I just rolled around on the living room floor and played with my son. then we went out for a birthday dinner in the evening."

"Where d'ya go for dinner?"

"Just the Okeechobee Steak House up there where Palm Beach Lakes Boulevard merges with Okeechobee Boulevard. You know the place?"

"Oh, yeah. I know it. But never eaten there, though. Too pricey for the likes of me. Maybe when I get to be the manager of the produce department I'll be able to afford it." Derrick laughed heartily at his own joke.

"Will that be after you buy the big fishing boat you've been wantin' or before?" Charles joined in the laughter. He looked down at his watch.

"Well, the meter is running, folks. Let's get the produce department in shape for the opening bell."

The group of employees let out a good-natured groan of mock protest, then scattered dutifully among the aisles of fruits and vegetables. Contrary to his own command, Charles retreated to the back of the storage area and found a seat on a box of Washington apples. He grabbed the telephone mounted on the back wall and dialed his home number. He was surprised that he hadn't heard from Dana yet, teasing him about the note he had left for her or telling him off for it. Maybe even apologizing for her inattentiveness to their birthday tradition. But nothing. Neither was there an answer to his attempt to call her. The phone at the house just kept ringing until Charles hung up.

She's probably in Travis's room helping him get ready to go with her to the babysitter's or in the bathroom getting herself ready, he rationalized. *She may be reading the note right now. I'll go do something on the floor and try calling again in a few minutes.*

He waited for almost ten minutes to call back, after giving some last-minute instructions to Barry to straighten up the grapefruit display.

He reentered the storage area that was devoid of any of the other employees. He dialed his home number again. He tried to be patient as he waited for Dana to get to the phone in their kitchen and pick it up. But again, all he heard was the succession of rings in his earpiece. Dana didn't answer.

His conscience pricked him. *Is she giving me the silent treatment because of my note? It's not like her to be pissed off by something like the note and bear a grudge all the next day.*

Charles hung up the phone. He was irritated that she wasn't picking up the phone. *"Dammit, Dana. Pick up the receiver."*

He approached Glenn by the potatoes.

"I'll be back in a few minutes. I'm just going to run over to our son's babysitter's in the next subdivision off Hypoluxo. I'll be right back."

Glen didn't ask any questions. He nodded that he had heard and understood the message. Charles let himself out to the parking lot by the employees' door.

He had an eerie sense of foreboding as soon as he pulled his car into Guadeloupe's driveway and approached the front door. When Loupe came to the door, she had an odd, befuddled look on her face.

"What are you doing here? Travis isn't here today, Mr. Wilkerson."

"What do you mean, not here? Wasn't he supposed to be here a quarter hour ago?" Now Charles had the odd, befuddled look on his own face.

"Usually, yes," Loupe answered. "Mrs. Wilkerson didn't bring him. I was expecting him. But she didn't call to tell me that she wasn't bringing Travis today."

Charles could feel his heart beginning to pound harder in his chest and the blood run to his face. Dana was very efficient and responsible. Almost to a fault. She would never have failed to inform him of a change of plans. She wouldn't neglect to warn Guadeloupe, either. Often she remarked to him at the end of the day how valuable Loupe was. She wouldn't risk offending Loupe or seeming to take her for granted by failing to inform her that Travis had to miss being babysat at Miss Loupe's. *Something is wrong here.*

He asked to come in and use Loupe's phone to try to call Dana again.

"Of course, Mr. W."

Again, the receiver at the other end just rang and rang. Charles let it ring a long time. Even though Loupe didn't stand right by him, her presence in the kitchen reminded him to remain calm and not exhibit any impatience in front of the babysitter. He held the receiver at arm's length from his eyes as though it might be malfunctioning and not permitting his call to go through to Dana.

He shook his head in frustration at the lack of an answer. He was about to hang up when he heard the ringing stop suddenly. The call was being received. *"God Almighty, Dana, finally!"*

But it was an unfamiliar male voice that answered the phone, not Dana. Charles was confused. The voice identified himself as Sheriff Buck Davidson. Charles suddenly felt nauseous.

"Is this Mr. Charles Wilkerson?" the Sheriff asked.

Charles gave an automatic positive response to the question. "Sheriff, has something happened to our son, Travis? Has he been hurt?"

"There's no one else here right now except your wife. I think you had better come home right away. ASAP," the Sheriff added in a direct and emotionally neutral voice.

Charles was almost out of Loupe's house when he stuck his head back in to explain to Loupe that the Sheriff was at his home and he had to go to see what was the matter. "Sorry that I'm rushing out in such a hurry. This may explain why Travis didn't come today."

"What's going on, Mr. W.? Please keep me in the loop."

"I'll call, Loupe, as soon as I find out myself."

Charles sprinted to his car, jumped in, and ignored the seat belt. He backed out the driveway maniacally. Straightening the wheels, the tires let out a squeal of protest as he stepped on the gas to rush out of Loupe's subdivision.

His mind was racing and his hands were shaking, even as he grasped the steering wheel. As he focused on the cars parked on the street, he reminded himself to be careful not to hit any of them. An oversized delivery truck entered the subdivision, slowly moving up the street in Charles' direction.

Charles cursed as he was forced to slow his vehicle and steer it to the right side of the road to allow the wide truck to pass.

In just these few seconds, Charles was able to comprehend and accept that something tragic had happened at his house. *Why else would the Sheriff of Palm Beach County be there? Had the house caught on fire? Had Dana become sick suddenly? The Sheriff never answered my question whether Travis was okay. Shit, what has happened, for God's sake?*

When Charles turned onto his street, he saw what he had been fearing. His home was surrounded by yellow crime scene tape. Sheriff's department sedans, at least a half dozen of them, were parked on the street.

Groups of neighbors were standing on the front lawn. When Charles careened to an abrupt stop in the driveway and stepped outside the car, they all turned their eyes toward him, watching curiously, watching his house intently, some of them pityingly, whispering conspiringly to each other so that Charles would not hear.

Sheriff Buck Davidson strode out through the front door as though he had been waiting for just the right time to make a dramatic entrance onto the stage. The rail-thin man was adorned in a huge white Stetson hat. He swaggered toward Charles and stepped in front of him to stop him in his tracks. "Are you Mr. Wilkerson?"

"Yes, yes, I am, sir. Charles Wilkerson."

"Just stay put right here, Mr. Wilkerson."

He said no more. He gave no explanation of what was going on, why he was there, and what the crime scene tape and all the sheriff's deputies were all about. He took Charles' measure, looking him up and down silently from head to foot as though he was making some kind of assessment of him.

Charles was confused and increasingly angry. *Am I the only person here who doesn't have a clue what has happened?*

He couldn't hold back anymore. He blurted out, "Is Travis okay?"

"Yes, he is. He's with one of the neighbors right now."

"Good," Charles said and breathed out. "Is Dana sick? Is she okay?"

"That's your wife?" Davidson queried.

"Yes, Dana, my wife. She okay?"

Davidson looked intently into Charles' face and didn't respond right away. "I can't say much more. But Dana's dead. She's been killed."

Dana's dead? Been killed?

Charles stood helplessly on the front lawn, lightheaded, unbalanced, weaving slightly, about to collapse. He watched Davidson in utter disbelief as the sheriff reentered the house without any further word. He had to repeat the sheriff's bald, blunt words to make them sink in.

Dana's dead. She's been killed. In our own home? Today? By whom?

Charles felt as though he were falling, falling down, falling apart, breaking into little pieces under the weight of the Sheriff's words, unable to put himself together again—with no effort whatsoever by

Davidson to hold him together. He gasped for a breath of air. He was in free fall to the bottom of the deepest, darkest ocean in the world.

James Luther Adams

Raiford, FL, 1984

An investigation after the trial uncovered the existence of exculpatory evidence involving both the testimony of witnesses and specific crime lab findings. This information was withheld from Mr. Adams' defense team by the prosecution before and during the trial.

In 1976, the Florida Supreme Court upheld Adams' conviction and execution. The United States Supreme Court refused to intervene and to reconsider the case.

James Luther Adams was executed in the electric chair at the Florida State Prison in 1984.

CHAPTER 9

PALM BEACH COUNTY, FL, AUGUST 13, 1986

SHERIFF DAVIDSON WAS BACK OUT IN the front yard in just a few minutes. To Charles, they felt like hours. He stood on the grass not knowing what to think, or even how. Nobody, least of all the top law enforcement officer of the county, had even tried to tell him what had happened to Dana.

Jacobson motioned with his hand for Charles to approach the front door of their house and come inside. Charles took a few steps toward the door, each footstep feeling more unreal than the previous one. He was oddly weak. His legs felt as though they were made of glass. He feared that they would shatter at any moment. He was surprised that he could walk at all. He stopped at the door. He was unsure whether he really wanted to enter the house. He feared what he might see.

Finally, he pushed the door open. He was totally perplexed. The house that had become so familiar, the home of which he and Dana both had been so proud, no longer belonged to him. The realization was underscored by the way that Davidson was treating him—as though he were an unwelcome stranger off the street that the sheriff was forced to invite reluctantly into his office.

It seemed to Charles as though his house had become a veritable satellite of the sheriff's department. The rooms were teeming with officers, some loitering and chuckling with others while they smoked cigarettes. A few more were going through cabinets and allowing the cabinet doors to slam shut when the deputies didn't uncover anything that would help them in their investigation of the crime. Two men, whom Charles assumed were plainclothes officers, were covering the walls and door frames with a dirty black powder as he had seen on crime television shows when they dust for fingerprints. One officer seemed to be looking intently at the cache of firewood in a pile leaning against the wall in the den.

A male voice coming from the kitchen called out happily to no one in particular that he had found some ice in the freezer above the fridge to chill their soft drinks.

Stepping guardedly into the corridor leading from the living room to the bedrooms, Charles became aware of the sounds of other people in this part of the house walking and murmuring, going through things. Every now and then one would call another over to take a look at some kind of discovery. The deputies were accompanied by the constant clicks of camera shutters. Bright flashes of light repeatedly bounced off the walls of the hallway.

Charles judged from the sounds coming from his and Dana's bedroom that Dana must still be in there. He fought off a sudden urge to go into the bedroom to see Dana again, to try to shake her back into the land of the living.

"Dana! Dana! Don't leave me! Come back! This is just a bad dream!" Charles was overcome by tears. *"Dana. Open your eyes."*

But again, the fear of what he would see in the bedroom kept him in the hallway. From overheard conversations among the deputies, he concluded that Dana had been beaten to death. Charles shuddered. His whole body trembled uncontrollably as though the deadly impact was just beginning to sink in. "Beaten to death?"

Charles couldn't summon the nerve to step into the bedroom. Aimlessly, he retreated back into the living room.

Sheriff Davidson sat on an easy chair overseeing the activity of his deputies. He was close to being a caricature of the clichéd Southern sheriff. He was over six feet tall when he stood—even taller whenever he rested his gigantic ten-gallon Stetson hat on his head. He wore a couple of matching gun belts over his slim hips. The tie clip sported a tiny pair of handcuffs. The sheriff gave orders to his deputies every now and then in a thick drawl that revealed that he was an old Florida Cracker. When he spoke to Charles, his booming voice had no hint of empathy or emotion in it.

Charles chose to sit down at the table in the dining room. He got the sheriff's attention and nervously asked if it was permissible for him to go into the dining room and sit there.

"As far as I'm concerned, it's your house. Go ahead."

It didn't feel to Charles like his house in the least. *A house that has been invaded by forces from the sheriff's office that may be friend or foe.*

As soon as Charles had a seat, Sheriff Davidson came in and launched into tersely reading him his Miranda rights. Charles hadn't been expecting that. He had seen plenty of movies in which law enforcement personnel informed a suspect under investigation that he or she had a right to remain silent and to have a lawyer present during the questioning. *A suspect*—he wasn't a suspect, was he?

The sheriff thinks I'm a suspect in my own wife's murder. My own wife. My own precious wife. I can't believe it. How can he possibly suspect me of such a heinous thing? But isn't that what cops always assume about the black man?

Instinctively, Charles pushed his chair back with aversion from the table, and thus from Davidson. It was as though the sheriff had built an invisible but impenetrable wall in the space between himself and Charles.

Another uniformed sheriff's deputy with two stripes on the cuffs of his shirt at his biceps came in and looked for approval from his boss.

"Go ahead, Chet. He's all yours for the time being."

"Mr. Wilkerson, I'm Sergeant Chester Ramsden," he said, holding out his right hand to shake Charles'.

The sheriff added, as if to explain, "I've appointed Sergeant Ramsden here to head the investigation on my behalf. He has a few more questions for you."

"But Sheriff, I don't have an attorney present. I'm not sure I should be answering any questions without legal advice."

Charles made a mental note to find a lawyer ASAP.

"No worries, Mr. Wilkerson. I can put off some of those questions for now. All I have is a form for you to sign."

Charles preferred this sergeant's polite and respectful demeanor to Davidson's more bellicose approach. *But I wonder if Ramsden really heard my concern about having to answer questions before I have a lawyer here.*

"What am I signing?"

"Mr. Wilkerson, this form gives me and my assistants permission to enter and search your car."

"I'm not sure that I should sign that document, or anything else, for that matter, before my attorney is present."

"Son, you refuse to allow Sergeant Ramsden to inspect your vehicle? Are you sure you want to do that? That might not be looked upon favorably by a jury in a courtroom. Certainly not in your favor."

"Mr. Wilkerson, to inspect the vehicle of the person who was probably the last to see the victim of a murder alive is standard police procedure," Ramsden added.

Charles was beginning to feel confused. He didn't know how to decide. *I can't think rationally or logically. I feel rushed, backed into a corner, to make a decision immediately about signing the document. I don't know all the repercussions if I sign it. How will it look if I refuse or ask for more time? They'll probably use it against me no matter how I choose. What should I do, Dana? Dear Dana. God, I wish you were here so you could set me straight. The sheriff already assumes I'm guilty of the crime. I don't want to fortify his prejudicial judgment.*

Charles looked at the consent form on the dining room table and signed it, even though his gut urged him to request a delay of a day or two.

CHARLES WAS GROWING EMOTIONALLY exhausted. Sheriff Davidson made no effort to disguise his frustration.

"Son, you seem to be making a big deal about answering our questions without an attorney present. They're routine."

"But isn't that my right? You yourself read me my Miranda rights. I'm sure it's not the first time you read the words that I have a right to have an attorney present. Surely, you know them well."

"There's no reason for you to get hot under the collar and impudent with me, Mr. Wilkerson. I'm just doing my job."

Charles thought better of continuing to criticize the sheriff.

"I haven't seen my son, Travis, since last night. I'd like to see him now."

"Would you excuse us for a moment?"

Davidson and Ramsden stepped away from the dining room table and recessed together into the hallway, leaving Charles there alone.

That infuriated Charles even more. *Doesn't a father have the right to see his own son, for God's sake?*

Davidson and Ramsden came back to the dining room.

"Sergeant Ramsden will take you to see your son. He's with a neighbor a few doors down and across the street."

Then to Ramsden: "Remember what I told you, Chet. Take him by the backyards."

By now, vans from several West Palm Beach and Fort Lauderdale television stations had parked in front of the house. Cameras were positioned on the sidewalk and aimed at the front door. Ramsden stepped over to the back sliding glass door in the den at the rear of the house. He slid open the door and signaled for Charles to follow him.

Charles led Ramsden out the gate of their yard into the

neighbor's. There was no gate out of that yard but Charles had vaulted the fence several times before. He took a firm hold of the top of the six-foot wooden fence and with one foot found the fence's two-by-four cross member.

Ramsden stood and waited for Charles to clear the fence. He struggled to get a hold on the top of the fence and place his foot on the cross member. When he finally reached the top, he wobbled slightly and then hurled himself over, landing hard and awkwardly in the neighbor's yard. Charles could see Ramsden's difficulty and was about to offer his help. But he thought twice about it, not wanting to embarrass the young sergeant. *Jesus, this man has been given power over my life or death.*

They moved to the front of the neighbor's house in order to cross the street. Davidson would not have appreciated their timing, Charles and Ramsden couldn't cross the street until waiting for a grey hearse to make its mournful passage out of the neighborhood.

So that's why we took the route through the backyards. They removed Dana's body from the house and didn't want me to witness it. Compassion? Or some other motive?

When Charles finally got to Travis, the poor little guy was wearing some other kid's shirt and even his diaper. Travis was disheveled. Charles could see immediately that Travis had been weeping—a lot, and probably for much of the morning and afternoon. He looked so alone and upset.

When Travis saw Charles at the front door, they ran to each other, collapsing together against the wall and weeping in each other's arms. They cried and huddled together for a long time, holding on tightly to each other and to all that was left of their once happy family.

Chapter 10

Palm Beach County, FL. - August 14, 1986

Charles had no idea where to begin searching for an attorney. Until that point in his life, no one in his family had ever had a need for a criminal lawyer. Charles had limited experience with lawyers, and he certainly didn't know a criminal attorney. *Where to start?*

He knew from sitting in on management meetings at Winn-Dixie that the company had good relations with a man who represented them in various legal matters. Dick Bartley had always been cordial with the heads of the store's various departments like himself, even though they seldom had legal problems that had to be addressed.

Charles decided to give Dick a call.

Dick was very approachable on the phone. Charles recognized that Dick might be curious about why Charles was in need of a criminal lawyer but he was a paragon of discretion.

"You're looking for someone to counsel a friend who may be under investigation for a capital crime, is that right?"

"Yes—*falsely* accused."

"Oh dear, that doesn't sound good. But I know it happens. I can't think of anyone who knows that phenomenon better than Steve Shillington and his partner. His office is up in West Palm, right in the center of town."

Charles leafed through the Bell Telephone yellow pages as soon as he hung up with Bartley. He applied a little pressure on the woman who answered the phone in Shillington's office, trying to impress upon her that he would like to see Mr. Shillington as soon as possible. Sheriff Davidson had told Charles at the house that he would have more questions for him tomorrow.

"He's in court in West Palm Beach as we speak, Mr. Wilkerson. But he never goes directly home from the courthouse without checking in with me to see if I have messages for him. When he calls, I'll ask him if he can see you sometime during the day tomorrow."

Charles figured that in case Shillington was unavailable the next day, or if it's too late in the day before Charles can see him, he'd better call Davidson to give him a heads-up.

Davidson was his gruff self when Charles called him.

"That would delay our investigation. It's for your own good, not just my convenience, that we want to move forward as fast as we can. Be sure to call me as soon as you know when we can proceed."

...*for your own good and not just my convenience*.... Charles didn't believe it for a second. Davidson wouldn't be so considerate.

LATER THAT DAY AT SHILLINGTON'S office, Charles was introduced to Shillington's partner, Bryce Nelson.

"Bryce assists me with most capital cases," Shillington said.

Judging from their appearance and wardrobe, Shillington and Nelson were foils for each other. Shillington wore his curly brown hair long enough that it flowed in the back over his collar. He had a fu manchu mustache to emphasize his more unorthodox image. Nelson had close-cropped hair and wore a white shirt and tie beneath his stylish sport coat. Shillington's desk was disorderly and covered by unruly piles of papers, which suited his careless and wrinkled shirt and trousers. He clearly had no ambitions to be promoted to the position of judge.

Shillington inspired confidence in Charles, however. He had served as a prosecutor in Dade County before switching to defense attorney. He knew the ups and downs of criminal court. He spoke slowly and thoughtfully. Each of his statements was delivered with a world-weary authority. It impressed Charles that when he listened to the unique particulars of Charles' case, he seemed to care about Charles; what happened to Charles mattered to him. In the days and weeks ahead, Charles would discover that Shillington's good heart was outshone only by his fierce intellect.

"Be circumspect when talking to the sheriff," Shillington advised. "That is *our* job from now on." Shillington nodded his head toward Nelson to indicate he meant that he and his law partner would take care of relations with Davidson.

Charles raised his eyebrows at that comment.

"Obviously, Davidson has his own agenda. You need to know, if you don't already, that he has ambitions to be more than Sheriff of Palm Beach County. He will probably announce soon that he is a candidate in the next election for the office of Palm Beach District Attorney. He's had several setbacks in the courts recently. He boasted a few years ago that he had convinced Henry Lucas to confess to the murder of a stripper in Riviera Beach. The community and fellow attorneys were congratulatory. But he was deflated and embarrassed when Lucas confessed to 360 other murders around the country. What a farce. That served to discredit Lucas completely. The judge threw out the confession and then ruled a mistrial. Lucas is still loose and free. And Davidson is still wiping the egg off his face."

CHAPTER 11

PALM BEACH COUNTY, AUGUST 15, 1986

CHARLES COULDN'T REMEMBER A DAY in which he felt more relieved that it was almost over. By the time he helped Travis gather his things at the Buckleys' and answered the absolute minimum of their questions about what was going on and why the fleet of the Sheriff's Department Ford LTDs was parked outside his home, he was absolutely done. Charles thanked them for stepping into the breach when he himself could not care for Travis. Other than brief answers that he hoped would satisfy them, Charles wasn't in the mood to say any more.

Mrs. Buckley placed a baggie of candy in Travis's hand as they said goodnight.

Charles looked down at his son and asked, "Travis, what do you say?"

"Thank you, Mrs. Buckley," Travis responded almost automatically.

"And thanks for stepping up and helping today," Charles added. "I felt that Travis was safe here with you. That's especially important to me right now. Have a good weekend."

"I must admit that I was pretty rattled when I went to open the front door and there was little Travis standing with a sheriff's deputy," Mrs. Buckley said. "Amalia Echeverria told us about having found Travis outside his house wandering about aimlessly."

"Amalia also told you about finding Dana's body in our bedroom?"

Charles couldn't keep his eyes on Mrs. Buckley as he waited for an answer.

"Yes, she did. What a shock for Amalia, and what a shock for us, too. Are you going to be okay for the night at home?"

"I'm still in total shock," Charles managed to get out. Then, shaking his head, he added, "I don't know which way is up and which is down. But yes, I've got to face our home without Dana in it sometime. I guess it might as well be this evening."

As they came down the walkway toward the street, Charles held out his hand for Travis to hold on. Charles was surprised at how tightly Travis clung to it.

"Daddy, I'm afraid."

"Of the dark?"

"A little bit."

"Travis, you don't need to be afraid of the dark because I'm right here," Charles tried to reassure him.

But Charles understood that Travis was afraid of more than the dark right then.

"Is Mommy ever going to come back to us, Daddy?" Travis asked nervously. "Will I always have you as a Daddy?"

"I'm afraid I can't promise for sure, Travis, that I will never die or be killed. But you don't need to be afraid of losing me because I'm here with you now and will try my best to be with you always."

"That's why I am holding onto your hand real tight, Daddy. Maybe if I had held more tightly onto Mommy's hand, she wouldn't have left us."

Charles was surprised and deeply troubled. *God, my innocent little toddler is blaming himself for his mother's unexpected death. The child thinks Dana abandoned us by her own will. Help me, God, to know how to teach him otherwise.*

CHARLES WAS GLAD THAT THE NUMBER of Sheriff's Department vehicles at his house had diminished to just a couple and the TV cameras had been packed away into the back of vans. With every step toward their house, however, he stuffed down the anxiety and fear that Travis would ask to see Dana. Then he remembered that the hearse had driven Dana's corpse from the house.

Looking as they walked at the other houses on their street and the familiar cars parked in their driveways was surreal. This was his street, for sure, and the scene was familiar. But the neighborhood felt strange and irretrievably altered. The loss of his familiar neighborhood made him hopelessly sad. Charles realized that he was relying on his little son to lead him home by his hand, a reversal of roles that heightened his longing for things to be what they were just a few days prior.

"Dad, what's the matter? You're walking so slow."

Charles was lost in his own neighborhood.

Once they were in their house, Travis sat down on the living room floor to examine the baggie of goodies Mrs. Buckley had given him. Charles plopped down in sheer exhaustion on the sofa.

The doorbell rang. Charles got up slowly off the sofa to answer it. The McKinleys, new occupants of the little two-story Cape down the street, along with their daughter, Kaylee, a little older than Travis, stopped in to express their condolences to Charles. Kaylee regarded Travis's teary eyes with curiosity. Charles felt immersed in his pain and disbelief and tired from the day's activities. He tried to be attentive to the McKinleys as they talked with Charles about their dearest memories of Dana. Later that evening Charles tried to remember what they had said about Dana. He remembered that each memory that they referenced produced bitter tears in Charles' heart. Though he wasn't able to focus on what was being said, he knew he was deeply grateful for his neighbors who came by, trying to provide comfort.

When the McKinleys stood up to leave, Charles took special note of how unusually tightly Steve McKinley seemed to be holding Kaylee. *Are they shielding her from me? In spite of the warm and pleasant late summer evening, the McKinleys must feel that a dark sinister mist has descended on their safe, comfortable neighborhood. I'm sure that they have heard from Amalia about the bloody state of Dana's body when she found her. I can see that the McKinleys comprehend that any pretense of their personal safety or that of their daughter has been stolen from our close-knit subdivision. Something evil has infiltrated our neighborhood, broken into this very home, killed a person we all love, and then slipped away.*

After he closed the front door behind them, he wondered, *do they wonder if the "something evil" that has done such a grisly thing just a few doors away on the street from their cozy home was me?*

Charles looked at Travis with the most poignant love he had ever felt.

"Bud, it's just the two of us now," Charles said on the verge of a flood of tears. He lifted Travis into his arms and together they wept tears of gratitude. "Daddy is so thankful to have you."

Chapter 12

Palm Beach County, August 15, 1986

Charles thought it rather puzzling that now on the third day since they learned of Dana's murder, her parents, Ruth and Dwight, had not come down from Winter Park. Charles had called them during that horrid afternoon after his birthday to inform them their daughter had been found bludgeoned to death in their bedroom sometime after Charles had left for work. Their very emotional response was not at all unexpected. They vowed that they'd drive down Florida's Turnpike the next day to comfort him and Travis. Nonetheless, two whole days had passed and no phone call to inform Charles that they were delayed in departing.

Charles felt some relief when Dwight's Lincoln pulled into the driveway. He scooped Travis up from the floor to greet them after their four-hour journey from Central Florida. Charles was in particular need by that day to be with people he knew were on his side. Charles was aware of how much they loved Dana and how much she loved them.

After Ruth stepped out of the car, she hurried in Charles' direction and wrapped her arms around him in a sympathetic embrace.

"Oh, you dear boy," she said to Charles through tears that had been pent up inside her since his call three days earlier. "What you have lost! I know how much you loved Dana and how dearly she loved you. This is just downright terrible—incredible."

Ruth released Charles from her embrace and moved to her left as if to make room for Dwight. But Dwight didn't come up the walkway toward a waiting Charles. Instead, he spied Travis playing in the garage and joined him there. He picked up his grandson, hugged him tightly, and kissed him on the cheeks and forehead.

"We can't replace your mom, Travis," said Dwight. "But we know you're a strong boy and will do all right. She was one of a kind, but I know she has taught you well. And those lessons will help you thrive during this difficult time."

Travis looked sad and confused and turned to his dad for his reaction.

Charles was struck by the odd and formal way Dwight spoke to his grandson, who, after all, wasn't even in kindergarten yet.

Ruth went over to Travis and gave him a grandmotherly hug as Dwight continued to stand awkwardly in the middle of the garage floor, a spectator of his wife's affection for her grandson. Only then did Dwight make a move over toward a confused Charles and greet him.

"I suppose there have already been some significant changes around here. I can't imagine your family without our dear Dana."

"No, Dwight, I can't either. I've been trying to make sense of what happened—to try to figure out how we will go on without Dana." Charles said tearfully "All I do is cry and do what I can to shield Travis from the worst of the tragedy."

"The Sheriff called us at home last night and told me he has tried to keep an eye on you to make sure the two of you are doing okay. I felt comforted by that."

Charles didn't know how to react to that news. He didn't want to add to Dwight and Ruth's burden of sadness and worry by getting into all the ins and outs of his tense relationship with Sheriff Davidson. *Yeah, I just bet it was to "make sure I was doing okay" that Davidson's keeping an eye on me. More like checking me out for any more suspicious behavior that would confirm that I'm the murderer.*

But almost instantaneously, a new thought occurred to Charles. *Sheriff Davidson called Dwight and Ruth? Why? They couldn't tell him anything about the murder. So why the phone call?*

Charles had observed enough of Davidson's modus operandi to know that, more than accurate forensic information, he valued relationships that might be advantageous for him in some way. Even in interviewing Charles, Davidson had never given him the impression that he was interested in his version of the events. He had such an incredulous look on his fat face when Charles tried to speak. Charles was sure that Davidson already possessed all the information about Dana's murder that he wanted. *So Davidson wasn't pumping Dana's parents for new information. It was something else.*

Davidson, Charles reasoned, might have intuited that, like many fathers-in-law, Dwight could have had some serious unspoken doubts about Charles' worth as his only daughter's husband. Davidson might have had a sense that Dwight was a man after his own kind. Did he hope he had found an ally in Dwight? Had Davidson divulged to Dwight and Ruth his own premature bias that Charles indeed was Dana's murderer? *Wouldn't he know that to do so was unethical?*

Dwight hadn't approached him when he and Ruth got out of the car. Of course, he was concerned about his grandson, but Charles had perceived unusual brusqueness and distance from Dwight ever since they had arrived. While Charles stood in his front yard and pondered what Dwight's coolness toward him might mean, Dwight and Ruth had taken Travis into the house. Dwight was sitting on the sofa and holding Travis on his lap. Then he passed him over to his wife, who continued to shower the boy with kisses.

Out of the blue Dwight said, "Well, we're going to shove off to the motel."

Ruth averted her eyes. Clearly, she would have preferred to stay longer.

"But Dwight, you just got here less than twenty minutes ago," I said. "Travis has been asking when you'd be coming for a couple of days now. He's been looking forward to it."

"Well," Dwight responded, "we just wanted to stop in right after we arrived to check in with you, to let you know we're in town. It's a tiring and boring drive through orange country down the Turnpike. I think we'll go to the motel to put our feet up and get some rest."

"If you really feel you must go so soon, I guess I can't stop you. But do come back tomorrow for lunch."

"Tomorrow's Saturday, you know, Travis," Ruth offered. "You can watch your favorite cartoons all morning, and then I'll make us all some French toast for brunch. How would that be?"

"Yummy!" Travis exclaimed enthusiastically, realizing now that his grandparents were not limiting their time at his home to this briefest of appearances.

CHARLES' HEAD WAS SPINNING FROM his in-laws' hasty exit. He tried to hide his displeasure from Travis. But after his recent dealings with Sheriff Davidson, he was downright pissed off at Dwight and, more particularly, at Davidson if Charles' suspicion about his sharing privileged information about the case with Dwight was accurate.

Charles was so irritated and emotionally depleted by the events of the last few days that he felt tempted to suggest to Travis that they go and stay at a hotel themselves rather than spend the night in the house where Dana had been murdered. He was angry that Dwight's hasty decision to leave for the motel had put him and Travis in the position of having to make a decision.

Yet, it was because this was precisely the house where Dana

spent her final hours that determined Charles' decision for him and Travis to stay home. Charles' restless, overactive mind was groping for what to do and where to go. He resolved to remain at home in spite of the surreal feeling. Now that it was only Travis and he, he had a profound sense that Dana was still in the house as well. There were hints of Dana everywhere. Charles thought he caught the aroma of traces of the perfume she wore the evening they all went to Okeechobee's for dinner. *Oh, Dana. We're lost without you. I beg you, please come back!*

By staying at the house another night, Charles and Travis could commune with Dana just a few hours more.

CHAPTER 13

PALM BEACH COUNTY, AUGUST 15, 1986

"WELL, BUD, WHAT SHALL WE HAVE for dinner?" Charles asked Travis, then broke out into a wide smile. "How about a bowl of Fruit Loops?"

"No, Daddy. You're silly. Fruit Loops are for breakfast, not dinner. Mommy always says we're supposed to have something salty for dinner."

"Oh, I see we have some pretzels here in the pantry. They even have little chunks of salt on them. Do you mean something like that?" Charles was enjoying his game with Travis. It took his mind off his apprehensions about the rest of the evening. He had seldom spent a whole evening alone with his son without Dana. She had served as a familial lubricant that kept the father-son relationship moving along smoothly.

How we miss you now, Babe.

"No," Travis said decisively, almost angrily. "You can't have just pretzels for dinner. You have to have something with them. Like a bowl of soup or a sandwich. That's what Mommy would make."

Charles was amazed how matter-of-factly Travis was able to mention his mom, almost as though he had forgotten Dana for the time being, or that she had been killed.

"Well, let's look together for something else that's salty for dinner," Charles suggested, trying to transform the search for dinner ingredients into some kind of treasure hunt. "I'll go rummage through the freezer in the garage and see if I can find something."

After a while Charles came back into the kitchen empty-handed.

"How did you make out, bud? Find anything in that cupboard?"

"Just soup, but the thin kind Mommy used to make for lunch."

"No, we need the chunky kind of soup since it's for dinner," Charles sighed. "You know, 'how do you handle a hungry man?' as the guy sings in the commercial. 'With Manhandler.'"

"I guess we don't have anything here for dinner," Travis concluded.

"No, you're right. Mommy didn't have time to do any grocery shopping this week or call me to bring something home from Winn-

Dixie." Then Charles remembered that Dana had intended to go to Publix on the afternoon after Charles' birthday to pick up a few things to make him a belated birthday cake, along with ingredients for dinners the rest of the week. But then....

Travis was quiet in the way children are when they are waiting for the grown-ups magically to suggest a solution.

"No, you're right, Travis, we don't have much here today," Charles restated. "But there's the McDonald's just a mile away on Dixie Highway."

Travis's eyes, which had been overcast with concern about no supplies for dinner, lit up.

"Do you think a hamburger and fries, or a Kids' Meal would be salty enough to qualify for dinner?" Charles inquired, trying to look serious but with his tongue thoroughly in his cheek.

THE DINNER AT MCDONALD'S helped Travis perk up a bit and become a little more talkative. But when Charles' car pulled into the driveway, Travis became withdrawn. He wasn't crying, just aware that something was wrong, terribly wrong. The closer they got to their home, Charles noticed he himself became more uneasy as well.

When they were in the house, Charles said, "Well, bud, suppose you find me one of your favorite books, and I will read it with you. Then it will be time to turn in and go to sleep."

Travis got more energized and ran to the bookshelf in his room. He brought out Charles' old copy of *Mike Mulligan and His Steam Shovel,* complete with the book's ratty corners and faded red cover.

"You brought out my favorite book when I was a little boy," Charles said as he smiled at his son. "Is that the one you want to hear again, Travis?"

"It's my favorite book, too, tonight, Daddy."

"Tell you what. I'll begin reading it to you, and we'll take a breather and do your teeth and go to the bathroom, and then finish the story."

Travis gave his reluctant approval of the plan. He followed his father to the sink to brush his teeth. He always liked it when Charles was in charge of that nightly duty because he was significantly more lax about the process. Dana had always forced Travis to continue brushing until she was satisfied that he had covered every square inch of his teeth and gums.

They finished and returned to the floor in the living room.

Charles picked up the story of Mike Mulligan about where they had left off. Charles invited Travis to lay his head on Charles' outstretched arm.

Before Charles had read a few sentences, he noticed that Travis had fallen asleep. Charles lay still until he was certain that Travis was in a sound sleep. Then he gently took his son into his arms; he risked waking him by lifting him off the floor and carrying him to his toddler bed in Travis's room. He lay Travis down gingerly on the mattress.

CHARLES HAD BEEN BOTH EAGERLY waiting for this moment when Travis was asleep and at the same time dreading it. He desperately needed to go into the bedroom and get a fresh change of clothes. He hadn't changed since his shower on the morning when Dana was discovered murdered.

But more urgently, he knew that he now had to do the achingly difficult thing that he hadn't had an opportunity to do before then.

Quietly, he walked out of Travis's room into the hallway. He turned toward their bedroom. He switched on every overhead light on the way as he passed. Charles could see that someone had left a light on the nightstand beside their bed.

Charles took his miniature jack knife from his pocket and cut through the yellow crime scene tape the sheriff's department had used to close off the bedroom as an evidence site. He stood in the doorway without going in, not even breathing as he looked inside.

By the faint light provided by the bedside lamp, Charles saw that the bed was stripped. As his eyes moved over to their dresser, he saw that some of the drawers had been sloppily pulled out and turned upside down, the contents emptied haphazardly on the floor. Likewise, in front of the dismantled dresser was a random pile of clothing and accessories such as belts and scarves. Dana's shoes were laying helter-skelter among Charles' dress shirts and neckties.

Charles moved over to flick on the overhead light. He was sickened immediately by the sight.

The ceiling was flecked with brownish spots, which had been red just days and hours earlier. The headboard of their bed was spattered with blood and pieces of what Charles surmised were human tissue of some kind—*Dana's* tissue.

Charles moved about the room as though he had never been through it before. The amount of blood stains on the carpet and floor were overwhelmingly heartbreaking. Charles collapsed on the floor and cried uncontrollably. Even through the misty lens of his tears he could make out more splatters of blood everywhere he looked. They arched up the walls to the ceiling. He rose to his feet when he spied the framed family photo that sat inside the headboard bookcase. Its face was covered by the same deadly shower of dark red blood so that the casual observer would not be able to recognize the three figures in the picture. Charles picked it up to get a better look. His legs gave out on him, and he collapsed again on the mattress, folded into a fetal position, and wept some more.

After a few minutes Charles got up again and roamed around the bedroom as if exploring an alternate universe. Everything was so unreal. He found the blood-splattered book that Dana had been reading sitting on its side on the headboard shelf. He looked intensely at the book, *If Tomorrow Comes*. He had to touch it with his hands and see it with his eyes, just to reinforce the increasingly distant and unreal fact that the book actually had belonged to Dana, that she had read it when she was still alive.

He put the book back and moved aimlessly into the master bathroom. He turned on the tap to wash off the fingerprint dust and the ashes the sheriff's deputies had left in overflowing ashtrays. He also wanted to wash away, if he could, the horrific sight of the bedroom in total disarray and the splotches of blood from ceiling to floor.

Before he turned from the sink, he caught a glimpse of the note he had written and left for Dana to see after he left for work. He burst into bitter tears again for having written it, for not being able to turn back the clock to before he wrote the note. He could only pray that the murderer had completed his grisly business at the house before Dana ever had a chance to read it.

CHAPTER 14

PALM BEACH COUNTY, AUGUST 15-16, 1986

CHARLES RETURNED TO TRAVIS'S ROOM, still shaken by what he had seen in the bedroom. He curled up on the carpeted floor beside Travis's bed. He stayed there about ten minutes, then got up, walked again through the brightly lit house to the bedroom, then back to Travis and lay down again on the floor—and then did it all over again.

Again and again.

All night long, he glided like a ghost through the glowing house, looking for what? Looking desperately for someone he knew wasn't there anymore nor would ever be again but looking all the same for anything to help him wrap his brain around the explosive device that had gone off in their lives without warning.

The morning sun shone through the kitchen windows. Charles was still wandering about the house, aching with grief and a lack of sleep. He had to pull himself together soon for Travis's sake. He brewed some coffee, sat down, and began making a list of the telephone calls he never dreamed of having to make, which emotionally he hadn't been able to make earlier.

He hadn't given any thought yet about making initial inquiries with the funeral director's arrangements. All he knew was that Dana would want a Roman Catholic priest to officiate.

It's so ironic, so cruel, that those most hurt by the sudden death of a loved one have to swing into immediate action and make big decisions. God, I don't think I'm up to that, especially not now.

At 8 a.m., Charles' parents arrived at the house. Charles' tight nerves felt immediate calm and hope when he saw his parents getting out of their car in the driveway. Richard and Eileen had always been a great source of comfort for Charles. Now at the lowest point in his life, they were a welcome distraction. He badly needed anything other than the enveloping darkness and the growing despair within him.

Richard and Eileen began to squire Travis around, playing with him for hours, asking him to show them the presents he had received after his surgery. Eileen made sure that both Charles and Travis were dressed and fed and moving forward. Otherwise, they understood that they needed to let Charles just be.

Dana's older brother, Doug, and his wife, Cheryl, came also. Richard and Eileen had only met them once—at Charles and Dana's wedding—but everyone seemed to be comfortable with one another.

"MY DAD CALLED ME ABOUT DANA'S murder, and we came here as soon as we could," Doug said, placing his hand softly on Charles' shoulder.

"I'm so sorry for you and Travis," Cheryl added, hugging Charles.

Doug had barely been seated in the kitchen for five minutes before he asked to see the room where Dana had been murdered. Doug had served many years in the Orange County Sheriff's Department. He and Cheryl were now in the middle of a move to Oregon where he had been offered a better position.

Charles had no reservations in granting Doug's request. *Maybe Doug would have some insight into the ghastly crime.*

The three of them—Doug, Cheryl, and Charles—stood awkwardly around the empty bed. Doug launched immediately into forensic work. In his own mind, Charles tried to envision just where the murderer had stood. What had he been looking for in the drawers of the dresser? What had been taken? *He doesn't seem to be blaming me for his sister's murder. His father must not have spoken to him about it.*

"Doug, I have a .45 pistol in a vinyl pouch on the shelf at the top of my closet. I kept it just in case of a break-in. Dana knew it was there for her own protection."

"Did you tell the Sheriff about the gun?" Doug asked.

"Yes, at least I entered the information on the sheet of missing items they wanted me to fill out."

"The gun has disappeared?"

"I'm afraid so. But the sheriff's department has ruled out the possibility that Dana was shot dead in her bed."

"Let me guess: The Sheriff assumes you're the guilty party, right?"

"Why yes. That seems to be his assumption. I can't believe it."

Doug grimaced. "I'm not in the least bit surprised. The damn Palm Beach County Sheriff's Department doesn't have the best reputation. I wouldn't want to work for them. I mean, what have they done to explore the possibility of someone else having murdered

Dana? Were they out here yesterday? Have they come yet today? Did they just investigate you and leave it at that? I'm really disappointed that they haven't taken it further and deeper than the conventional thinking that it's always the husband."

Charles was relieved that Doug didn't settle for the "conventional wisdom."

Doug moved over to the window that faced the backyard. He told Cheryl that he was going to try to get inside the killer's head. Walking around the room, he began to act out what he believed would have been the logical approach the killer would have used to get in and out of the bedroom. Then he traced by steps the most likely path the killer would have traveled to make his getaway.

"I'm going out back to have a look around. Knowing the Palm Beach guys, I am sure I can find some other small piece of evidence out there that those monkeys overlooked."

Cheryl walked by Doug's side through the house to the den. She had obviously accompanied him before on such unofficial investigations. They opened the unlocked sliding glass back door where Doug was sure the killer had entered. They walked through the small backyard toward the faded wooden fence.

"Charles, did you notice any vehicle parked on the street behind the vacant lot when you went to bed the night before the murder?" Doug asked. "Or did you see anyone when you left for work the next morning?"

Charles felt inadequate as he answered, "No, I hardly ever look out into the partially wooded area behind the house. In the morning I entered the garage by way of the front entrance to the house. I can't see to the back from there. That's not much help, is it, Doug?"

"Just hang on. We may be onto something here, Charles."

Doug quickly climbed the fence and jumped down to the vacant lot. He walked over to the lot beside it where the new house was being built. The frame was up but all the inside work was waiting to be resumed.

"Wait, Charles. I think I see something," Doug shouted over the fence.

A few minutes later Doug jumped back off the fence and into the Wilkersons' yard. With two fingers, Doug was carefully holding a square of dusty blue cloth.

Initially upon seeing it, Charles was underwhelmed. *So that's all? A lousy piece of dirty cloth? Part of a blue western bandana perhaps? One of the construction crew could have been wearing it. What does it prove?*

Doug asked Cheryl to find and hand him two twigs off the ground. He put the piece of cloth on the ground gingerly, then picked it up by the corners with the twigs as if with a pair of chopsticks without touching the cloth again with his hands.

Without being ordered to do so, Cheryl ran into the kitchen to retrieve a clean plastic baggie as though she lived there and knew just where Dana would store such things.

Meanwhile, Doug held up the cloth with the twigs so that Charles could take a good look at it.

"See anything interesting on the cloth, Charles?" he asked.

"Well, just those little brown speckles."

"What do you think they are?"

Charles felt a little like a schoolboy being quizzed in a science lab. *I wish Doug would just tell me.*

"Dried blood spots, I guess." Charles finally replied.

"You've got it, brother-in-law. Dried blood spots. Maybe from the killer's hand or something like that. Maybe not. But we're going to keep it uncontaminated in a baggie, call the sheriff's department, and ask them to come by and see what the monkeys missed—or didn't think was significant."

"Come on in the house, Sherlock, and have a beer," Charles said, putting his right arm over Doug's shoulder. For the first time in days, Charles felt a fresh wave of renewed hope.

CHAPTER 15

WEST PALM BEACH, AUGUST 16, 1986

SKIP HENDERSON, A PROSECUTOR for the Palm Beach State
Attorney's Office, sat nervously at his table in the diner waiting for
his former father-in-law, Buck Davidson, to arrive for their breakfast
meeting. He was nervous because since he and Buck's only daughter,
Debbie, divorced, Skip detected an attitude of disapproval from Buck.
Buck was a big man; if Skip were frank, he'd admit that he was a
little intimidated by Buck.

Skip scanned the diner and noticed several pairs of deputies from
the Palm Beach Sheriff's Office scattered about the room, along with
a tall carafe of morning coffee placed halfway between them on the
Formica-covered table.

Judging from her familiar way of chatting with them and teasing
them, the waitress seemed to know them from previous visits to the
Farmer Girl Diner. That was to be expected since the Farmer Girl
Diner was just a couple of blocks south on Dixie Highway from the
sheriff's department complex. Sheriff's deputies were regulars.

Skip wasn't eager to have the deputies catch sight of him at his
table some twenty yards away from them. He especially hoped that
once Davidson arrived to join him, the deputies would not hear a
word they had to exchange with each other. The Farmer Girl was by
no means an elegant place for breakfast. But people who were looking
for a location to have a private conversation could find it there. There
was enough ambient noise from the shouting of orders by the
waitresses to the short-order cooks in the kitchen and the banging of
ceramic plates and bowls as the busboys emptied them into the plastic
tubs to drown out conversation beyond the other person at the table
with you.

Skip and Buck met regularly here for ham, eggs, and toast and to
talk over details of cases Buck was passing on to the State Attorney's
Office for prosecution. When Davidson called Skip's office to set up
the breakfast, Skip had a good idea that Davidson would be especially
eager to discuss the Charles Wilkerson case.

"Mornin', Skip. How's my son-in-law the prosecutor doin' this
mornin'?"

"Fair to middlin', Sheriff. But remember it's your *former* son-in-law."

"Maybe so, but it's the fact that you've been assigned by your boss as prosecutor in the Wilkerson case that interests me this mornin'."

"So I'm told I am. Let me ask you, Buck. Did you intervene with the State Attorney to request that I be the one in the office assigned the case?"

"Oh, I admit I may have bragged about your ability to him at a party sometime and made a friendly suggestion to him."

"Buck, you realize that doing so violates state legal ethics. It can be seen as tampering in the case. That could lead to the whole case being thrown out."

"Oh, God forbid, Skip, that I would do anything illegal or unethical. You know me better than that. Friends and colleagues like Morgenthau and me talk all the time. We're colleagues aiming for the same goal, after all. By 'intervening,' as you call it, I admit I may have been stretching ethics a bit. But it's nothing that doesn't happen out on the golf course whenever two or three attorneys and a judge or prosecutor are present."

Skip decided to overlook the doubts and red flags that he had been sensing ever since Davidson has requested this breakfast tête á tête.

"You seem to have a sense of urgency about this particular case. All I know about it at this point is what I read in *The Palm Beach Post*."

"Skip, you know it's been a coon's age since Palm Beach County has won a high-profile case. The Wilkerson case is way beyond high-profile. It may be the biggest case we've had in these parts in a couple of decades. When do we ever get a premeditated domestic murder case? When are we not just trying to straighten out some petty infraction by the blacks? CBS News has asked for passes to cover this trial. The eyes of the nation, and certainly the legal community, will be on Palm Beach County in the next few weeks."

Davidson attracted the curious glances of customers at nearby tables when he banged his fist down on the table in front of him. "We must *not* lose it. We just can't."

"Buck, please keep your voice down. Why do I have a distinct feeling that your urgency for us to win this case is part of your strategy for November's election for District Attorney of the county?"

"You bet your ass it is. I can't go into the campaign in a couple months with almost zero convictions in the last six months. The opposition would laugh me off the stage. And so would the voters."

"You're probably right."

"The people of this county—any county in the United States, for that matter—are tired of the crack cocaine heads walking all over the law and getting away with it. I've got to make the point that in Palm Beach County, if you break the law, you will pay with years behind bars."

"I gather that this Wilkerson fellow looks a lot to the untrained eye like those crack cocaine heads?"

"Perception, as they say, is reality. In point of fact, Wilkerson is black, but he has the cleanest record this side of Wong's laundry. He's actually went to college—didn't graduate, though; he's a manager at Winn-Dixie and a responsible citizen, husband, and father."

"But he's African American, right? And people are afraid they've taken over the system?" Henderson asked.

"The case against him is tighter than an oil drum," Davidson exulted a bit too loudly. "It's precisely what we need: an open and shut case, good ol'-fashioned case of a wife who is white and her murder by a black husband. It's made for TV, don't you think? And just the kind of thing that elicits the fears of the public."

"And brings instant notoriety and favor to the sheriff who arrested him and eliminated him from the streets," Henderson added.

"You're catching on, son. Arranging for you to prosecute the case is doing you a favor as well, I hope you realize. Your winning a high-stakes case like this could raise you a couple of rungs up the pecking order in the State Attorney's Office, wouldn't it? Perhaps to the level of an Assistant State Attorney someday?"

Henderson was listening but chose to make no reply.

"You need to know in confidence that yesterday Wilkerson's brother-in-law, an officer on the Orange County Sheriff's Department, called to tell us that outside the Wilkersons' home he found a blue bandana that our guys missed. He suspects that the brownish spots on the cloth might be blood—either Wilkerson's or his victim's. He gave it to us, the nosy meddlin' bastard, and asked us to have some tests run on the bandana to determine whose blood it might be—if it's that of anybody connected to this case."

"Or the blood of some other individual who may have committed the murder."

"That's not what happened, Skip. Wilkerson had the perfect motive and the perfect opportunity to rape and off his wife. For the time being, that piece of cloth is going into the safe at my office for safekeeping, and any word of its existence is not going to Wilkerson's legal team anytime soon."

Henderson was taken aback.

"I wish I hadn't heard that, Buck. That's withholding evidence, possibly exculpatory evidence, from the court and the defendant's legal representatives."

"You can interpret it that way," Davidson rationalized. "But I just think of it as 'keeping it simple, stupid.' We're so close to closing this case that it would be a damn shame to complicate it with new, potentially irrelevant 'facts.' You know how juries work. They can only handle a limited amount of evidence before they're all confused to hell."

Henderson remained silent and deep in thought. After a moment he seemed to gather the strength to counter his father-in-law.

"*Potentially* irrelevant, I suppose," he mused. "But at the same time a fact that could doom the case against Wilkerson's guilt. You're playing a dangerous game, Buck. If Wilkerson has a lawyer worth his law degree, he'll spot the violation and accuse the county of violating not just legal ethics, but the laws of the United States."

It was Davidson's turn to be mute and pensive.

"How's a lawyer going to know that a piece of evidence—if that's what the scrap is—is being withheld if he never knows we have it in the first place? I just thought that before you launch the prosecution you ought to know, that's all. I've got enough help and cooperation at my department to get around that kind of accusation. Now I am relying on family, my daughter's ex-husband, in fact, to provide the right kind of assistance and support, too. I can count on you for that, right, Skip?"

CHAPTER 16

WEST PALM BEACH, AUGUST 16, 1986

CHARLES OPENED THAT MORNING'S issue of *The Palm Beach Post*. He saw that, in addition to whomever else Sheriff Davidson had talked to in the course of his work, he had addressed members of the media. Of course, the nature of the modern world is that a reporter's job necessitates approaching political and civic leaders to get their statement on current issues. It had probably been on the initiative of some card-carrying reporter for *The Post* that the story outlining details of Dana's autopsy appeared in the newspaper.

Then again, knowing as he did after his visit with his attorney Shillington that Davidson had aspirations for higher office than just Sheriff of Palm Beach County, Charles figured that Davidson would not have discouraged the reporter's interest in the autopsy and would have welcomed it, in fact, as just the kind of publicity he coveted.

Among other things, Davidson informed the media that the Palm Beach County medical examiner had pinpointed the time of Mrs. Wilkerson's death as approximately 6 a.m. on the morning of August 14.

That made sense to Charles. He had left for work at 5:30 a.m., which he'd told the sheriff. Charles also knew that it was a well-known fact, a source of humor actually among his neighbors, that he never left later for work than 5:30.

There you go, sheriff. You said it yourself: 6 a.m. or so, a whole half hour after I left for work. I also told you that I took one final look into the bedroom before I left and saw Dana comfortably asleep on our bed. She was still alive at 5:30 a.m. Therefore, I couldn't be the one who killed her. Whoever did it had to have committed the crime after I had gone to work.

Charles called his attorney to inform him of the article in *The Post*. Shillington had seen and read it already.

"How do you react to it, Mr. Wilkerson?"

"Very positively," Charles affirmed. "It pretty well gets me off the suspect hook, doesn't it?"

There was a silent pause on the other end of the line. After a moment Shillington spoke.

"Well, we're not going to request that the autopsy be repeated, that's for sure; the medical examiner's estimate of 6 a.m. or so is a positive for our case. We wouldn't want them to have some other medical examiner do a second autopsy and perhaps come up with a different conclusion about the estimated time of death. You need to know, Mr. Wilkerson, that the estimated time of death is a subjective finding. It's quite possible, likely, in fact, that another medical examiner could estimate a time that is less advantageous for our case. That is why we should let sleeping dogs lie, as it were, if we can."

"If we can?" Charles asked, surprised.

"All I am saying is that *we,* the team for the defense, will be satisfied with the Palm Beach medical examiner's report. But I suspect is the prosecution will find that report not to its liking and will ask the court for a second autopsy in the hopes of getting a different result."

Charles was disheartened.

"Oh, I didn't realize that things can be so flexible. We'll just have to wait, I suppose, and hope for the best."

"I'm afraid that's all we can do for the moment. I'm sorry to burst your balloon, Mr. Wilkerson. We've had this good news for the time being. But I just wanted you not to be too naïve. I'm sorry to use such a strong word as 'naïve' for how you are feeling today."

"I don't suppose this will be the last time I feel that way," Charles acknowledged.

"That's why you have retained Bryce and me, isn't it? We're supposed to be the ones who are realistic, maybe even suspicious at times. 'Flexible' is one word you can use to characterize the legal process to determine guilt in capital crimes. But those of us who have been working to try to reform the system have chosen to use the word 'arbitrary' to describe it."

CHARLES HUNG UP THE PHONE FEELING EMOTIONALLY deflated. What had sounded so favorable when he read the report in the newspaper was not necessarily a positive thing after all. *The learning curve to understanding the legal system is a little more steep than high school civics made it sound.*

Charles knew, however, that he couldn't afford either time or emotional energy to dwell on Shillington's attitude toward the legal system in capital cases. For one thing, Shillington implied that there would be more unexpected setbacks, so it was better not to let one blow knock you out but to get up and be prepared to deal confidently with the next reversal.

He recognized how much he was reeling from loss, even without concerns about an alternative coroner's findings. He woke up that morning feeling an acute vacuum in his life after Dana's death. He had been so concerned about Travis's well-being that his mind hadn't been free to allow him to think a lot about Dana, or his life without her. Now Dana's sudden absence left a gaping hole in his world, a shrieking emptiness that he had never known could exist.

He thought about marriage for the first time since before the wedding. He had been told by Dana's priest during the premarital sessions at the church that being married is very much like becoming one person. Dana had been a part of him for ten years—a vital organ, a limb, a function that he needed to stay alive. With her gone, Charles felt that he was only a half, at most, of who he had been. He felt that he was dying himself.

He recalled what he had heard about classmates who were shipped back home from Vietnam—how they claimed to feel phantom pain in their legs, even after they had lost a leg and been paralyzed totally below the waist. When Charles sat on the couch, he could almost feel her beside him. Whenever he walked into the kitchen, he could practically hear Dana laughing and making dinner. When he went out the front door, he thought he could see her bending by the flower beds tending her pansies.

Her absence was so powerful, like a palpable force. He spent time in his head talking to her, telling her about his day, and reporting on Buck Davidson's latest outlandish theory about the killing.

THE TELEPHONE RANG, AND WHEN Charles picked it up, even before he had said the customary "Hello," he heard Davidson's now familiar booming Southern drawl.

"Mr. Wilkerson, are you free in the next hour to come up to the station in West Palm? I'd like to chat. I have an update for you about the investigation."

Instantly, Charles ran through his mental Rolodex to see whom he might be able to call to provide care for Travis at such short notice. Plenty of neighbors had offered their assistance with childcare in the past few days.

Charles was hopeful and excited about an update on the investigation. What he wanted—no, what he *needed*—most of all now was answers. Do they have any other suspects? Any new leads? New evidence? What is the sheriff's thought about the bandana that Doug had found near the construction site? Charles was certain that it was the Sheriff's Department that was obligated to provide answers and was confident that eventually they would.

When Charles arrived, there was no one at the door to direct him to Davidson's office. By trial and error, he managed to locate it. Davidson was sitting waiting for him behind a massive wooden desk. Surrounding the sheriff's workspace was enough Western memorabilia, Charles thought, to be able to open a museum: horseshoes on the wall, gun belts and handcuffs hanging on pegs, and Davidson's signature wide-brimmed Stetson.

Charles sat down in the old-fashioned oaken office chair after Davidson motioned to the chair with his eyes. Charles' face reflected his high hopes for some answers.

Once Davidson launched into a conversation, however, it became clear to Charles that Davidson was not going to be the one who would share information. Charles was expected to do that.

Almost immediately, Davidson led Charles painstakingly through every detail of Dana's final hours of life on August 13. He also questioned every one of Charles' own movements and actions that afternoon and evening. Charles was accustomed to this grilling from his first encounter with Davidson. Charles paused a couple of times to try to recall an answer after Davidson had volleyed a question.

"Come on, boy. I'm asking a question about a time only a few days ago. It's not that long ago. Just answer with the truth without stalling for time like that to make up an answer."

Suddenly, Charles remembered Shillington telling him on his visit to the lawyer's office to leave the conversations with Davidson to him or Bryce.

"I didn't realize I would need an attorney to be present for this interview," Charles said to Davidson. "I'm supposed to let them handle the questions."

Davidson looked as irritated by Charles' objection as he was the first time Charles refused to answer questions without a lawyer present.

"Come on, boy. What are you trying to hide?"

"I'm not trying to hide anything, Sheriff. I'm just insisting on proper legal protocol that is customary and well-established, which I am sure is familiar to you."

"You continue to resist questioning, boy. That could get you into shitloads of trouble with the law."

"I don't think my attorney would advise me to stop answering questions by the authorities and to leave that job to my legal team if he knew it would get me in trouble with the law. Now, if you have more questions, I'd like permission to call my attorney to join us."

Davidson made no effort to hide his frustration and disappointment. He could see that he and Charles were at the same impasse a few days ago.

"I believe that when you called me about coming up here, you had an update for me about the investigation," Charles said.

"I do. But before I say anything about it, I need to get someone else in here to witness that I did not try to withhold anything from you."

Davidson picked up the telephone receiver from his desk, punched in a few numbers, and waited.

"Hello, Chet, are you in the middle of something? I need you here in my office for a second to witness my conversation with Mr. Wilkerson."

In less than a minute Chet was knocking at Davidson's door.

"Just come on in, Chet."

Davidson looked at Charles with a look of victory that said, "Two of us can play this game, boy."

Then, he added, "The county medical examiner has issued a report on your late wife's autopsy. He gives an estimated time of death as about 6 a.m."

Charles' frustration abated some.

"Thank you, Sheriff. I did see the article in this morning's paper. 6 a.m. or later sounds right to me."

"That's his preliminary judgment, of course," Davidson said, now in a calmer voice. "Frankly, I find these estimates of the time of death a royal pain in the ass. They can be updated at any time. The estimate is subject to change in light of any new information or evidence that is brought forward."

Charles nodded to indicate he understood. *But what new information or evidence?*

"The medical examiner has another question," Davidson said as if Charles had not objected to more questions without legal counsel. "He wants to know what your late wife had for dinner on the evening of August 13. You have already told us you remember her having a small filet mignon. That's correct, isn't it, Mr. Wilkerson?"

Charles nodded.

"Can you recall what side dish she had with the filet? That's what the medical examiner wants to know."

Charles remained silent since he had not been given permission to call Shillington and invite him to come join them.

Just then Chet Ramsden leaned over on his chair, raised his body over a report on Jacobson's desk, and pointed to a sentence.

"Oh yes, Thanks, Chet. I see you had said broccoli and cheese sauce. Mr. Wilkerson, do you still stand by your original report to us?

Again, Charles was mute. *If you have the original report in front of you, why the hell do you ask me again? Or call the damn restaurant if you don't believe me? They'll have a record of what Dana ordered. You're just trying to catch me in a lie, you fucking incompetent country bumpkin, if I say something other than what I had said in our first interview.*

"The medical examiner wants to know because a meat product digests in the stomach at a different rate than vegetable matter. It seems his estimate of time of your late wife's death was based on the decayed remains of the filet she consumed. He wants to go back and examine the remains of the vegetable dish to make another estimate, if necessary."

Charles did not want to hear that, and he was sure Shillington wouldn't receive it as good news either.

Charles said gruffly. "The answer to your question is, 'Yes, I still stand by what I said on August 13.' Now, if you would excuse me, Sheriff, I believe we're finished."

Chapter 17
Winter Park, FL, July 1986

Charles trudged across the funeral home's baking-hot asphalt parking lot. He was in Winter Park now, where Dana had spent her childhood and would be buried. Charles knew this was where Dana had wanted her funeral to be held. Her parents knew the funeral director and had made almost all the arrangements. They consulted with Charles about a couple of minor things, but otherwise they had just taken over and planned the event, as if what he wanted didn't count.

"This is our final act of love for our dear daughter," Ruth told Charles on the telephone when she informed him that he would have no say in how his wife was buried. "Having the funeral in Winter Park will be a source of peace for Dwight and me. We want to know that Dana will always be here close to us."

Now, as Charles entered the funeral home, he felt an urgent need to see Dana. He desperately longed for conclusive proof of her death, something real and tangible. He fiercely hoped that the funeral would be a critical moment that allowed him to let Dana go, that would force him to concede to himself that Dana wasn't coming back. He had realized in the days since her death that he was unable to decide how he and Travis would move on into a different, unplanned-for future until they started to lay Dana to rest—literally and metaphorically.

In the August heat his steps slowed; now he seemed in no hurry to get inside the funeral home. He wanted that sense of closure. But at the same time he wasn't altogether sure that he could endure seeing her lifeless body in the casket and face the stark truth that he couldn't, no matter how determinedly he tried, turn the clock back to the night of his birthday. Here everything was soft and serious and terribly sad. Melancholy music meant to anesthetize the guests whimpered weakly from the speakers of the public address system. The funeral director had met him at the entrance with obsequious concern and carefully rehearsed grief.

"Sir," Charles said to him, "I'd like to see my wife, Dana, if I may."

The director was nonplussed and suddenly flustered. "Oh my,

I'm afraid Mr. and Mrs. Miller and I hadn't planned for that. The members of the Miller family had a private moment to pay their respects to their daughter before all the guests arrived."

"I'm sorry, sir. I couldn't get here earlier. The drive from Palm Beach County took longer than expected, and I had to drop our son at his grandparents where he would have childcare from one of their neighbors. Is there any chance I can pay my respects privately before the service itself begins?"

The funeral director had an uneasy, embarrassed look on his face. He clearly wasn't prepared for Charles' request.

"The deceased is your wife, you say?"

"Yes, she is. I'm Charles Wilkerson."

When he heard this, the funeral director's stance came to sudden attention as though he had heard a command from a superior officer. It was as though he remembered suddenly that he was on duty.

"Mr. Wilkerson, I am sure that can be arranged. I'll ask Mr. Miller quietly for his permission. I'm confident he will be amenable." Then he left the anteroom quietly.

About five minutes later he returned from the main salon and motioned for Charles to come and follow him. At the double doors, which opened into the salon where the guests were silently waiting for the service to begin, the director stood aside so Charles would have room to pass.

The salon was filled to capacity. Ruth and Dwight occupied the formal upholstered chairs at the front closest to the steely grey coffin. Their daughters, husbands, and children sat several seats away. Charles quickly scanned the room and caught sight of his own mom and dad, Eileen and Richard, a couple of rows behind the Millers. Eileen lifted her hand slightly to greet him with a wave, and Richard signaled with his sympathetic eyes. *You'll get through this, son.*

The only unoccupied seat was in the last row of the salon in the back. The funeral director ushered him to it and whispered, "Whenever you're ready, Mr. Wilkerson. You can approach the casket. Take as long as you need."

From his seat, Charles was able to see the coffin that was open at the front but could not see Dana.

He glanced at the funeral director for a sign that he could stand up and approach the front of the room.

Charles' steps toward his wife in the casket were slow and muffled. A curious and somber air descended upon the guests. A few women leaned in their chair toward the person in the neighboring chair and whispered a few words very quietly.

Charles continued his slow approach to the open casket. The closer he got to the front, the deeper he could see into the coffin. Not Dana's body right away, but the creamy silk fabric that nestled her, and the handles on the side of the casket that would help the pallbearers perform their task. Charles knew that if he continued his forward progress, he would see Dana at any second. He felt his heart beating faster in his chest. He sensed the damp perspiration underneath his suit.

Charles flinched slightly to the right as he got closer to the casket. *My God, I'm not ready. I thought I was, but I'm not.*

Dana's head came first into Charles' view. He stopped at the foot of the casket to steady himself. He swallowed the lump in his throat.

Charles was moved when he saw the long strands of her beautiful hair that he had combed for her many times when she sat on the floor in front of him. He could almost feel them in his hands one more time. He took one more small, tentative step so that he could reach into the coffin and stroke her hair. He needed to touch her. Silent tears rolled down his face. His body trembled as he wept, but he made no sound.

Dana's body was lifeless. The funeral director's staff had tried to add some tint of color to her face, but there was only so much they could do to give her the appearance that she was comfortably asleep.

Charles regarded her face intently. The violence that had taken her was still evident. Even cradled as she was by silk and dressed in her Sunday best, with her long locks combed carefully, her hands delicately clasped together in a pose of devout prayer, it was clear that death had changed her irreversibly. Her skull had been crushed, shattered, and left slightly concave by what Charles knew were repeated blows by the killer.

My dear Dana, my beautiful, beautiful Dana, is now just a cruel and grotesque semblance of who you were—how stunningly beautiful you were. Ruth and Dwight should have ordered the casket to be closed.

Charles' knees buckled and began to shake uncontrollably as he knelt on the kneeler by the casket. The roar of something that sounded like escaping steam filled his brain. His eyes were blinded by his bitter tears. His breathing came in gasps. The salon tilted. He pushed himself up from the kneeler and had to hold onto the edge of Dana's casket to maintain his balance. His senses were under siege. *I can't stand it any longer. Dana, I'm sorry. This is too difficult. I've got to get out of here to get some fresh air.*

He bolted suddenly. One of the funeral home staff reached out his hand to help steady him but Charles was already out the door.

Chapter 18

Palm Beach County, August 1986

As Sheriff Davidson rushed to his car in the parking lot, his progress was halted when he heard someone calling his name.

"Sir, Buck, Sheriff Davidson!"

Davidson stopped to see who it was who was delaying his departure. It was Sergeant Chet Ramsden.

"What is it, Chet? I'm about to shove off for the Wilkerson funeral. I've got at least a four-hour drive ahead of me to Winter Park. Whatever it is, make it quick."

Ramsden had been running in the sheriff's direction. "I just wanted to update you briefly on our investigation," Ramsden said, catching his breath.

"Can't it wait until I've returned from the funeral, Chet?"

Ramsden thought it was unusual for Davidson to be going all the way to Central Florida for this particular funeral. Not for a political dignitary or a fellow sheriff, just an ordinary woman from suburban Palm Beach County.

"Well, of course, sir, I'll have a full report for you then. I just wanted to give you a heads-up now that a squad of us under my command will be canvassing the Wilkersons' neighborhood."

"That sounds pretty routine, Chet. You don't need my permission to do that. I didn't order you to do a canvass since it's a standard part of an investigation. I don't tell you how to do your job."

Then Davidson looked Ramsden directly in the eyes and said to him, "Who knows? Someone may blurt out his own misgivings about Williamson or give you a report of his having acted strangely the day before the murder. Have your ears open, especially for that kind of thing, Chet."

"Will do, boss. I'll have a report on your desk when you get back. Have a safe trip."

Ramsden divided the eight deputies into four pairs and assigned each pair four or five houses to canvas.

He put Barilko together with Templeton.

They had no luck getting a brief at-the-door interview in the first two houses. No answer to their knocking. At the third house a timid grandmotherly woman cracked the door open. When Templeton introduced himself and Barilko as deputies of the Palm Beach County Sheriff's Department, she looked at them, shook her head, and took a step back into the foyer. "No speak Inglés. Sólo hablo español." Then pointing at her chest with the palm of her hand, "I from Cuba." She smiled shyly. "Sorry."

Templeton thought of asking if there was an English speaker in the home with whom they could talk, but he figured that the old woman wouldn't understand the question. Barilko and Templeton smiled politely at the woman, nodded their heads, and said, "Gracias."

They proceeded to the next house. They knocked on the front door. A forty-something woman, an Anglo this time, answered.

"Yes."

Templeton gave his rote introduction. "We are officers Templeton and Barilko of the Palm Beach County Sheriff's Office."

"How do you do? I am Edna Bascom. My husband is Henry but he's still at work. How can I help you?"

"You are aware, I'm sure, that on August 13 a neighbor of yours, Dana Wilkerson, was discovered murdered in her home."

Mrs. Bascom's face became downcast, and she shook her head lamentably. "Yes, unfortunately, I am aware of that. Such a sad thing."

"As part of our investigation, we are canvassing neighbors and asking them if they happened to notice anything amiss in the neighborhood, any behavior by anyone, even by your neighbors, that was suspicious in any way, or out of the ordinary, particularly on August 12 or the morning of August 13. Or at any time in the recent past."

"Officers, please come in and have a seat in the living room."

When Barilko and Templeton were settled in easy chairs, Mrs. Bascom offered them coffee, which they declined. "Oh, I'm sorry. What am I thinking? It's a hot day in August. A cold drink instead, perhaps?"

"No, thanks, Ma'am. We won't be here long enough to drink it. We don't want to take a big chunk of your day."

Mrs. Bascom smiled. "I understand, gentlemen."

"As we were saying, we are contacting neighbors of the Wilkersons to explore if they can point to some unusual behavior by anybody in the neighborhood. Particularly Mr. Wilkerson,"

Templeton said.

Mrs. Bascom pondered the question briefly.

"I knew both Dana and Charles. It's terrible and unbelievable what has happened."

"Yes, Mrs. Bascom. But did Mr. Wilkerson give any indication to you in the days before his wife's death that he was having strange thoughts?"

"No, I saw them in their driveway the afternoon before. He was his usual quiet but friendly self. He told us they were going to have dinner in West Palm Beach. They all waved goodbye as they backed their car out onto the street, even the little one."

Barilko broke his silence and asked, "I presume that their home was vacant for several hours while they were in West Palm. Did you notice anyone stopping by the house, knocking at their door, or trying to gain entry in some way?"

"As I recall, they returned to the house at about 9 p.m. That's about five hours. I might have looked out at their place from our front window once or twice, but that's all. I don't remember seeing anyone. But there was a lot of time during those five hours when I was busy and couldn't look out the window."

"No, of course not." Barilko said. "We just thought you might have by chance seen some activity in front of their house, that's all."

Barilko looked at Templeton and shrugged to indicate his opinion that there wouldn't be more new information from Mrs. Bascom and that they might as well say goodnight and thank her for cooperating with the investigation.

Templeton got the point. He closed the small tablet of paper on which he had written a few notes and put it in his breast pocket.

The deputies rose as if to head to the foyer and the door.

"But there is something else that's been on my mind. I want to tell you about it before you leave," Mrs. Bascom said.

Templeton stopped in his tracks and took Barilko's arm to ask him to hold on, too. Templeton took the little notepad from his pocket again.

"I've talked a little about this with a couple of other neighbors but no one else says that they saw the same thing. I think they think I'm hallucinating, that the stress of the turmoil on the street has me seeing things. But I swear I'm not hallucinating."

"What did you see, Mrs. Bascom?" Templeton asked.

"Well, on several mornings before Dana's body was discovered, there was a dark green van parked on the partially paved street behind our row of houses. It doesn't have a name yet. I didn't notice the van in the daytime, but I saw it early in the mornings when Henry, my husband, was leaving for work."

"Did you see anybody in the van?" Templeton asked.

"The first morning I didn't see anybody. But later that night, after it was dark and I was doing one final check on the locks in the doors, the green van was back. I noticed a small fire, probably a campfire, in the vacant lot where the new house is being built. But I didn't see a person."

"Were there any markings on the van, any sign identifying it?" Barilko asked.

"It's hard to see what's out in the back because of the tall weeds in the vacant lot and, as I said, it was getting dark. When I looked back there the next morning, all I could make out was the word "carpet" printed on the side door of the van. I figured there were more words than that, but I couldn't see them."

"Did you see the van after that?" Templeton quizzed her.

"It was there again on the morning of August 13. But then later in the day it was gone. It hasn't been back ever since. Or, to answer your question, at least I didn't *see* it after that morning."

Templeton was writing in the small pad.

"My first thought was that perhaps they were installing carpets in the new house. But when I told Henry, he said the house wasn't ready enough inside for carpets yet."

"Mrs. Bascom, I have made a note about what you've seen. I will include it in our report to Sergeant Ramsden, who will include it in his report to the Sheriff. Thank you, Mrs. Bascom, for coming forward with this. In this kind of investigation, no detail is too small or insignificant. It may lead to something more important," Templeton said to her. "If you recall anything else about the van, like the full name of the company on the door, make sure you call us."

Mrs. Bascom looked gratified that she had done her civic duty. She loved the Wilkersons, especially Dana.

"I feel so bad about that family. I hope perhaps I have been of some help."

RAMSDEN DID MAKE MENTION IN his report to Davidson of the information shared by Mrs. Bascom. But instead of congratulating his deputies for the new potential lead, the sheriff looked downright irritated.

"Anyone remark about Wilkerson? About any strange or suspicious behavior?" he asked Ramsden gruffly.

"Nobody our team interviewed made any remark about that at all. Except that many of the neighbors liked Wilkerson and felt horrible about Mrs. Wilkerson's fate. Do you think, sir, that this reported sighting of the green van has anything to do with the blue bandana that was given to us?"

"God dammit, Chet. There's no way to prove that it belonged to whoever was driving that van. It probably was dropped on the ground by some other workman at the empty house. Don't get sidetracked by either the green van or blue bandana. They'll lead us to a dead end."

Ramsden listened to Davidson but was a little disappointed. Now that they had the investigation's first new lead in weeks, he was eager to proceed and explore the presence of the green van. But he relented.

"I guess you're right, sir."

CHAPTER 19

WITH THE FUNERAL BEHIND THEM, at least chronologically, Charles and Travis tried to find a new kind of normal. Since Charles had not been charged with a crime, he returned to Winn-Dixie, which had preserved his produce manager's job. Once he got home after work, his life revolved around Travis's needs and wants.

His mother, Eileen, came over from Boynton Beach to provide day care for Travis while Charles was at work, and to keep house and their lives on the rails. Eileen was no substitute for Travis's mother but was a generous and loving grandmotherly presence. She took Travis to the playground at the elementary school on the next block, kept the refrigerator well stocked, especially with popsicles for Travis, and made sure his toys were put back in their proper place and out from under Charles' feet when he got home. She cooked meals, did the laundry, and kept Charles and Travis moving forward.

Charles felt that going back to work was imperative. There were the usual bills to pay. They were without Dana's income now, and her small life insurance policy provided little in the way of replacement income. Besides, he had used most of that to retain his lawyers. Now there was the added burden of the inestimable attorneys' fees. Sheriff Davidson had given no indication that he would back off his insistence that Charles was still the prime suspect, or any sign that they were close to pursuing another possible one, or even that the department was interested in exploring that.

Charles felt a need to visit his attorneys again. Shillington and Nelson tried to maintain a positive outlook and to encourage Charles to believe the best about his future.

"Look, Charles. You have no previous record of a felony," Shillington said. "That will mean something to a jury, should there be a trial. The prosecution has not a single shred of physical evidence that you are even remotely guilty of your wife's murder. I know there aren't any other suspects at this time. But that's out of your control. It's up to the D.A. and his team to deal with that."

"You do make me feel more confident, Steve. I don't feel that on many days."

"A judge worth his salt would look at the facts of this case, and if you were the only suspect left, he'd throw the whole damn case out the window."

"I appreciate that you believe in my innocence, Steve."

"Bryce and I have concluded that our strategy is to convince the prosecutor's office not to accept the sheriff's recommendation that you be charged."

Charles relaxed visibly in his chair.

"Really? Is that even a possibility?"

"Charles, you haven't even been arrested yet so the prosecutor can't charge you."

"That's reassuring. But I don't want to forget to tell you that a few weeks ago one of Dana's brothers, Doug, a former Orange County sheriff's deputy, came over to the house and did his own investigation of our property. There's a vacant lot behind our house, and a new house is slowly being erected in the lot beside it."

Shillington was the picture of patience as he listened to Charles.

"Well, Doug found a scrap of blue cloth, possibly part of a handkerchief or, as Doug thinks, an old, discarded bandana. He showed me the brownish spots on it that could possibly be blood. He picked it up with makeshift tongs, placed it in a baggie, and then called the sheriff's department to report it and to ask them to come by the house to pick it up. The deputy said he'd give it to the sheriff."

"Sheriff Davidson still has it?"

"I don't know. What he's done with it is anybody's guess. I know that's not much help to you."

"It gives us a lead to follow, though." Shillington said, glancing over at Nelson.

"It's unclear if the bandana was just dropped by any one of the crew working on the house," Nelson appended. "But if we can get our hands on it, we might be able to see if it is connected in any way to the crime."

CHARLES RETURNED HOME BUOYED by his visit with Shillington and Nelson. Because Eileen had some things to do back home in Boynton, she left Charles and Travis to fend for themselves. Charles cooked a special dinner. Nothing gourmet, just macaroni and cheese with salad and a burger. Travis was upbeat because his Dad was preparing one of his favorite dinners. He danced around the kitchen, doing his best to help Charles, as his father rinsed, chopped, simmered, and stirred. They laughed together when Charles admitted he didn't know where the grated cheese was kept, and Travis was able to show him. For the first time since Dana's death, Charles felt at home.

As he stood minding the pots on the stove, he heard a knock on the front door.

"Let's go see who it is." He scooped up Travis into his arms and carried him happily to the door. Charles opened the door wide, still holding Travis.

There standing on the two steps that led into the foyer was Sheriff Davidson. Sergeant Ramsden and a handful of other deputies stood silently behind him along with an official-looking young man and a woman unknown to Charles, wearing light grey uniforms that he couldn't recognize.

"Charles Wilkerson" he announced flatly. "By the authority vested in me by the citizens of Palm Beach County, I am here to arrest you for the murder of Dana Miller Wilkerson."

Charles stood frozen and stunned. He had thought about this moment but now it was happening. Just a few hours prior, he and his attorneys had spoken about his possible arrest but that had been a theoretical and hypothetical discussion. This was real. He found it difficult to speak.

"Sheriff Davidson, I have pots on the stove. Just a minute. I need to go back in the kitchen and turn them off."

Charles turned back toward the kitchen before Davidson could respond.

Suddenly, Davidson reached into the house and grabbed Charles tightly by his elbow.

"Just a second, Mr. Wilkerson. Where the hell do you think you're going? I didn't give you permission to move. You can face the added charge of resisting arrest." Then Davidson nodded at Ramsden to enter the house and escort Charles to the kitchen.

"I don't want you trying to escape by the back door," Davidson barked at Charles. "And you better let me hold your son. I've made arrangements with one of your neighbors to watch him and keep him overnight. He'll be safe and fed. He can't come where you're going."

"Daddy, where are you going? You said you'd always be with me." Travis started to cry.

"Your daddy will be safe, son," Davidson said in a not particularly comforting voice.

"Mr. Wilkerson. Put your hands behind you," Ramsden

instructed.

One of the other deputies took the pair of handcuffs from the belt around his waist and proceeded to snap them on Charles' wrists.

Seeing his father with his hands manacled behind his back, and hearing the barbarous snap of the handcuffs, Travis shrieked and clung fiercely onto Charles' leg.

Charles tried to smile for Travis's sake, but the boy did not respond. He had lost his mother; now they were taking away his father.

Davidson tried to take Travis by his hand. Travis pulled back his hand emphatically. Davidson signaled for the neighbors, the O'Neills, to step forward to try to lead Travis by the hand out of the door and toward their home a few doors away. Travis intensified his loud shrieking.

Charles was undone by his son's fearful squeals.

"It's going to be all right, Travis," he tried to say through his own tears. "You've been at their house before. They'll take good care of you."

But as he saw Travis being taken by the O'Neills, Charles broke down in uncontrollable sobs.

Chapter 20

West Palm Beach, FL, September 24, 1986

When Davidson's deputies led Charles by his right elbow to the cruiser parked in the driveway, Charles saw the crowd of neighbors gathered in small groups gawking and whispering behind their hands. One neighbor raised a fist to Charles, as if to tell him to stay strong—or to go to hell; it was hard to know for sure which. Charles had lived on the same street for years; now they looked at Charles as though they had never seen him before.

His senses, in overdrive since the sheriff's party had arrived, combined with Travis's unbearable shrieking, were now blurry. A dispatcher's voice was almost indecipherable over the ceaseless crackling of the police radio. Ramsden picked up the transmitter and calmly responded to whatever had been the dispatcher's question.

"This is Badge Number A147153 in Lantana. Apprehended suspect. Departing now for the Palm Beach County Jail. Over."

Charles looked out his window. His familiar neighborhood went by in a bleary flash. Nobody in the cruiser said a word either to him or to one another.

Is this what it's like riding in a hearse? Or being broadsided by a fist to the face in a fight you weren't expecting?

Before Davidson ordered Charles' humiliation in front of his neighbors, he had given him permission to make one telephone call. He called his parents. As Eileen answered, Charles realized he didn't know what to say. He hadn't rehearsed what he was going to tell them or how.

"Mom, are you sitting down? The sheriff came to the house and arrested me. They are transporting me right now to the Palm Beach County Jail."

"Oh, my God. The sheriff really went through with it?"

"I'm afraid so. In a strange way I'm kind of relieved. Waiting for what seemed like the inevitable was becoming too much. Maybe this will get the ball rolling for me to prove my innocence. I wasn't getting anywhere trying to convince the sheriff."

He could hear Eileen's motherly sobs. "I hope so, son."

"Listen, Mom, one more thing. The sheriff has appointed the

O'Neills, neighbors in the little Cape Cod house a few doors down and across the street from ours, to take care of Travis. I don't know if it's just for today or for more time than that. Can you or Dad or both of you call Sheriff Davidson and ask if you can step in and take over? It's not that I don't trust the O'Neills. It's just that I know how much Travis loves you. Can you do that?"

"Of course, dear. We'll do our best. Can we call you at the jail? Or, vice versa, can you call us to keep track of things with Travis?"

"This is uncharted territory for me, Mom. I'm not sure."

"Charles, take care of yourself, please," Eileen said tearfully. "Don't do anything to resist the orders of the guards. You know that you have at least one strike against you already—you're black."

IN THE DARK SILENCE IN THE CRUISER, Charles was numb, angry, and scared. Scared of the unfamiliar place they were going. Scared of what was waiting for him there.

The Palm Beach County Jail was an ugly, antiquated, overcrowded, and forbidding two-story building. Charles had read in the newspaper that there had been discussion among the county's powers-that-be for as long as he could remember about the need to construct a new facility to replace the existing jail. In recent decades the population of West Palm Beach had grown tremendously. The courts had ruled that the old jail was much too small, uncomfortable, and unsanitary to handle the bulging inmate population. The county was in danger of violating the eighth amendment prohibition against "cruel and unusual punishment."

In a word, the process of getting booked was awful. It was hot and crowded and loud. The booking area was an open space with little privacy and quite integrated into the rest of the jail. The sounds of arguing and shouting, the stuttered jokes of the half-deaf and the completely drunk, the impatience and fatigue of the guards and deputies—all of it together formed an ugly cacophony.

When it was Charles' turn, he obeyed as his mother warned and did whatever the staff ordered him to do. He stood where they pointed, waited for them when they ordered it, and answered every question that they asked politely and promptly. He posed for a mug shot in a small room off to the side, not knowing where to look or *how* to look. How to look trustworthy for the picture? Innocent? Normal? *What is normal anymore?*

Charles could overhear Sheriff Davidson on the other side of the door of the room where the photographs were taken. He was answering questions from a party of reporters that had followed them to the jail. He entertained them with details of his latest arrest, a man who was the "cold-blooded murderer of his wife." He tried to impress them with the skills he had exhibited in cracking the case, and the evidence that convinced him that the man they arrested was the guilty party.

You flock of unthinking sheep! You believe this fraud? Evidence? What evidence did he have to conclude that I am the killer? I'd like to know myself. Everyone who reads the newspapers or hears the television news in the next few days will be told Davidson's skewed version of my story.

Charles was ordered to wait while he sat on a bench in the booking area. It was ghastly hot.

Is there no air conditioning in this world's worst hotel?

He was led by two guards down a hallway. He could see into the cells lining the corridor—a seemingly endless row of stalls housing young black men lying languidly on the single bed. One or two of them looked up curiously and regarded the new "guest."

Charles was dripping in sweat until the guards escorted him into the elevator.

What is this? A damned meat locker making its way to the Arctic Circle?

They turned to the left out of the elevator. Charles was handed a well-used mattress, a threadbare blanket, a deteriorating sheet, and a change of clothes. Soon he was shown into an empty cell. He stepped in. They stood outside the cell and locked the metal door.

Looking around his new domicile, Charles saw essentially nothing. The light green walls were bare, there was the toilet in the corner, and the metal bed attached to one wall. No radio, no television, nothing to read except the few obscenities scrawled on the walls by previous guests of this "suite."

Charles tried to straighten and fold the pieces of clothing he had been given. The inmate uniform had once been white, Charles figured. But after too many washings with cheap detergent and too many years of hard wear, the uniform looked like a lot of the inmates' uniforms Charles had seen in their cells on the first floor—worn out.

He unfolded the thin mattress and flopped it onto the noisy springs of the steel bunk. He slumped his body on top of the mattress and, against his better judgment, wrapped the practically useless blanket around himself. He closed his eyes, tried not to think of whoever had slept there the night before, and fell asleep.

Sleep was the only way he was leaving this place that night.

WHEN CHARLES AWOKE HE DIDN'T KNOW how long he had slept. The fluorescent light on the ceiling was still on, just as it had been when he fell asleep. After he wiped the sleep from his eyes, he could hear voices and running water nearby. Strangely, or so he thought, the door into this cell was wide open. Charles stuck his head out into the corridor to look in the direction of the racket.

"The boys is having breakfast in the dayroom," a friendly inmate in the cell across the corridor said to Charles. "The door is open so you can walk down the hall and have some grub."

Charles was unsure and confused. "You mean I can just walk out of this cell?"

"If you're going to the dayroom, yes. You wouldn't get very far if you try to wander off anywhere else, though. You'd be tackled by the guards in a minute, or worse."

Charles shrugged and took a few tentative steps into the corridor.

"Go ahead, brother. I swear it's okay. Enjoy your chow."

Charles continued walking cautiously to the dayroom. The place was abuzz with inmates using their plastic forks and knives to cut into what looked like French toast and teasing their tablemates loudly.

"Wonder Bread this morning, brothers. I'm surprised they feed it to us. Aren't they afraid that it'll make our bodies strong twelve ways?"

"PJ, you're the only dog at the table old enough to remember that old commercial," and then laughed heartily. The other men joined in the good-natured revelry.

Charles noticed a vacant chair and took the seat. He greeted the inmate beside him on the right with "Good morning." The young man, an African American, seemed unsure if he ought to respond.

"The guys around here don't usually greet one another like that. They only know two ways to talk to others: joking and teasing, or else threatening them."

"I'm new here. I just came in late last night. I've got a lot to learn about this place."

Charles' lack of the customary inmate bravado and his unusual vulnerability seemed to alleviate the young man's anxiety. He looked at Charles, smiled in a friendly manner, and reached out his hand.

"Hi, I'm Dexter Wright. I haven't been here very long either. Nobody is until they move you on to a more permanent placement."

"Glad to meet you, Dexter. My name is Charles, Charles Wilkerson."

"What are you in for?"

"I have been arrested and charged for the murder of my wife—and in case you're now worried for your own safety, I was *falsely* accused and arrested."

"Boy, Charles. That's a hot one. All I did was go out with a bunch of buddies who I *thought* were my friends and then woke up in here with a wicked hangover and a charge of attempted robbery of a convenience store. No memory of it, though. We had been drinking, and I was told we went to the convenience store to steal another couple of six-packs."

"The other guys here, too?"

"No, the guards tell me that they disappeared like a fart in the wind, took the six-packs, and just left me there as a sitting duck for the cops."

"Just suckered you, eh? You must feel very much alone and abandoned."

"A little lonely. And fucking angry, too."

"Well, Dexter, I've been there, too. It's an awful feeling, isn't it? How about your family? Are they nearby?"

"Shit! They aren't worth a whole lot to me. My father's a wino who's probably drunk already this morning. And my mom just takes all kinds of crap from him and then sticks by him like glue." Dexter was shaking his head.

Charles felt deeply sad for this youngster, probably under twenty years old, who didn't have anybody. If Charles hadn't had good trustworthy friends as he did and a loving, responsible family, Dexter might be an incarnation of himself in his teens.

"I'll still see you here later today and tomorrow morning for breakfast?"

"I've got nowhere else to go."

"Well, let's meet tomorrow for breakfast. Cool with that? I appreciate the company and conversation. Right now I've got to shove off and find the office here where I can get information about bail and see how much it'll take to get me out of here."

For Charles, this brief encounter with Dexter was a temporary cure for his own frustrations, a welcome distraction from the constant awareness of his own dire situation.

Chapter 21

West Palm Beach, September 1986

A SHORT, MIDDLE-AGED MAN in an ill-fitting plaid sport jacket came into the wing looking for Charles' cell. A guard directed the man to it.

"Mr. Wilkerson? Charles Wilkerson?" he asked as he stood in front of the metal bars that made up Charles' "door."

Charles confirmed who he was.

"You have a phone call. If you follow me to the offices, you can take the call in one that is vacant."

Charles had intended to call his parents but didn't know the procedure. He also wanted to touch base with Shillington.

He was ushered into an office only slightly more spacious than two cleaning closets. An old government-issued desk was against one wall with a matching chair. A flashing telephone waited on the desk.

"Hello. This is Charles Wilkerson."

"Charles, how have the days and nights been at that palace?" the caller chuckled. "This is Steve Shillington checking in on you."

"It's kind of strange here, frankly. But day by day, I'm getting accustomed to things."

"We want to make sure that while we wait for the court to set the date for the pre-trial hearing, you aren't cooped up in the big box—. unless you're so comfortable there you'd like to stay."

"No, I've got no particular attachment to this place. What have you got in mind?"

"We'll request the court for a bail reduction hearing. That way you can be in your own home to help us piece this puzzle together. The prosecutor has recommended an unrealistically high bail for you. North of $250,000."

"Man! I don't have that kind of money just hanging out doing nothing in a bank account somewhere. I'm sure my parents don't either."

"I didn't think so. Understand, though, that the inmate is not responsible to raise the full amount, just ten percent of it."

"But even then—"

CHARLES HAD NO SOONER RETURNED to his cell when a guard informed him that it was the visiting hour, and he had visitors. The guard shackled him and the several others from the wing who also had visitors. He led them in single file downstairs to a large room. One wall had tall windows made of thick pane looking into a room adjacent to the visitation room. The space by the glass windows in the visitation room was lined with empty, individual counters. Facing the counter was a single plastic chair. A telephone was mounted on the wall beside the window.

He was ordered to sit on the chair provided and to cool his heels until his visitor arrived. The inmate wasn't informed of the identity of the visitor.

Finally, the sharp ringing of a bell signaled for the visitors to enter the visitation area. Charles was relieved to see his parents standing just inside the door, scanning the row of inmates on the other side of the glass. They looked perplexed by the process. Clearly, they and the other visitors had not been given more than the most rudimentary instructions. Meanwhile, Charles seemed to understand the procedure instinctively. He rose up from his chair when he saw them and started to wave his arms eagerly to catch their attention.

"Inmate in stall number 21," a guard said over the loudspeaker, "you are not permitted to rise from your seat. Please resume sitting."

Charles was so happy to see his parents that he didn't pay the guard's instruction any heed. The guard, looking irritated, grabbed a clipboard urgently, looked through the list of names and stall numbers, and said, "Inmate Wilkerson. You must not have heard me. Please resume your seated position in the chair. The prison regulations stipulate that you not rise from your chair until we are done."

Feeling chided like a disobedient kindergartener, Charles sat down again. Meanwhile, his parents had approached the counter on their side of the glass window. Richard picked up the telephone receiver and waited for Charles to do the same with the phone on his side of the glass divider.

"Dad, Mom. I'm so glad to see you. I didn't know you were coming."

The scene was so surreal. He and his parents were separated by a glass wall, speaking on a telephone when they were within unaided speaking distance from one another.

Eileen took the receiver from Richard. "Of course we would

come, honey. You are all we think about at home. We had to come and see you—frankly, for our own sake as well as yours. How are they treating you? Are you getting enough to eat?"

"I wouldn't pay much in order to eat here. But they allow seconds, so I've been getting enough. But I never imagined that I'd end up spending time in a place like this."

"Good Lord! Frankly, neither did we," Eileen declared.

Even though he had not committed a violation of the law to deserve imprisonment and he knew that she didn't mean it the way it sounded, Charles felt a jab of guilt course through him.

Richard took the phone from Eileen again. "Son, we brought you something. We didn't know we can't place it in your hands personally. Prison rules, you know?"

Charles rolled his eyes in agreement. "I'm learning about those."

"It's a carton of cigarettes. We left it at the front desk, and they assured us that you will get it."

Eileen's turn on the phone: "I reminded your father that you don't smoke. You never did that I know of. Not the most practical gift for you, is it?"

Charles looked gratefully at his dad. "Actually, I think it is, Mom. I'm learning among other things that cigarettes are a valuable form of currency in the prisoner economy. A few cigarettes may just get me something I need but don't have. Ingenious gift, Dad."

"Do you know what's next, son?" Richard asked.

"You're probably asking the wrong guy. The inmate is often the last to know. Probably, hopefully, a bail reduction hearing next. Mr. Shillington, my defense lawyer, said he is going to apply for one for me. I told him I don't have $250,000, or even $2,500, laying around the house, and how you don't either."

Aghast, Eileen asked, "Is that what they expect you to come up with? Good God!" She glanced over at Richard. "I haven't cleared this with your father yet, but I am sure we can help."

"I wasn't going to ask you but thank you. I've made some decisions, and they have an impact on my financial situation. I've heard about court-appointed public defenders. They are good, compassionate people, I'm sure. But I've read horror stories about how they are swamped with all these cases. I'm sure there's no way they can prepare adequately for all or even most of them. I've declined a public defender and have chosen to find my own legal counsel. Shillington and Nelson have some experience with capital cases like mine. But it's not cheap, as you can imagine. I scraped up enough resources to be able to retain Steve and Bryce, but it has pretty well drained my account."

Richard and Eileen looked at each other as if reading each other's mind. Richard said, "We think you've made a good decision, Charles. As Mom says, we will be on standby in case you need help."

AFTER HIS PARENTS LEFT AND THE OTHER inmates were finished with their visits, the group was escorted back, handcuffed, to their cells on the wing. Charles looked at the other inmates, most of them uplifted by having seen loved ones just as Charles was, but at the same time tired, discouraged, and bedraggled.

Charles knew nothing about their circumstances but guessed that they lived their lives in the prison to the beat of a melancholy soundtrack. Despite all that had happened to him since Dana's murder, he considered himself fortunate. He thought of Dexter, the young black dude with whom he had had breakfast, who was deprived of so much, especially the love of a stable family. Charles' parents probably did have the means to help bail him out of jail. They cared enough to find ways to pull him through. He had enough savings, in addition to Dana's life insurance payout, to be able to afford a good defense team. He knew Dexter did not, and dared to surmise that neither did many of the guys he'd been living among during the past week, especially his African American brothers.

CHAPTER 22
WEST PALM BEACH, SEPTEMBER 1986

SHILLINGTON AND NELSON MANAGED to get a substantial reduction of Charles' bail to a much more reasonable and manageable level. The bail was paid. He was told he was a free man again. For how long, he didn't know; he just knew it was not a permanent state.

His father came to pick him up from the prison and take him back home. He was as free as anyone can be when trailed by television cameras, sheriff's cruisers, and a procession of lies that he was powerless to counter.

At the press conference he gave when Charles was being released, Sheriff Davidson was in his election campaign mode. He presented Charles as a lower life-form, a sex-mad, selfish monster without redeeming qualities. A subhuman who was clearly guilty of the crime of murder.

One of the reporters had asked Davidson, "On what evidence does your department base your case against Mr. Wilkerson?"

Davidson had replied in short order. "I will leave that up to the prosecution, of course. I am certain that once a jury of Palm Beach County citizens hears and weighs the facts, Mr. Wilkerson will be found guilty and justice will be served."

Instead of celebrating and enjoying his moment of release, Davidson succeeded in propelling Charles into a precipitous descent of fury. The next morning he ventured outside into the neighborhood. Neighbors he encountered on his walk around the block looked away, even when he greeted them with a "Good morning." Outside to fetch his mail, neighbors were as cold as ice, formal but unfamiliar. Charles sensed that they regarded him as a scary intruder into their safe neighborhood. Women who lived close by stared at "the monster" on their street and whispered to one another. Charles could tell that instead of the friendly man they thought they knew, they had come to believe in the fictionalized character they had seen on TV. If their husbands were home, they would accompany their wives to the mailbox back into the house. They feared that their wives might be attacked by a man who beat his own wife to death while she slept, simply because she wouldn't have sex with him on his birthday.

What a creep. I wouldn't like that guy either. My arrest has changed everything. The life I have come back to after just a week in the Palm Beach County bucket is not the one I had before I was locked up.

His grief over Dana's death had dominated every single day for almost two months. Now, after only a brief taste of life behind bars, he realized that survival did override everything else. He had to learn to compartmentalize his sorrow over Dana from his battle to stay free for Travis's sake.

I'm fighting for my life, my freedom, my future as Travis's father. If I fail to survive in one piece somehow, I will not be able to raise him as my son or protect him and support him. I won't be able to see him grow up, get married, and have children of his own. I will lose everything I have to live for.

Each of his actions was instantly suspected. A patch of marigolds that Dana had planted beside the house died from Charles' inability to find time to water them. One morning he went out to clean up the ravaged flowers. It became fodder for backyard gossip about Charles' guilt. He was "killing Dana all over again."

Some of my neighbors don't want to be seen socializing with a murderer. But it's as though they have been warned by their spouse not to do or say anything to offend a dangerous criminal with nothing to lose. "Who knows what would happen if you insulted him somehow?"

Charles went back to Winn-Dixie to announce his desire to return to work.

"Frankly, I need the income," he explained to the general manager. "I have new expenses I didn't have before."

"I'm sorry, Charles. You were a good produce manager. But we can't hire you back. I'm sorry. People have seen and heard the coverage of the murder of your wife. To have you here would hurt business seriously. I am sorry I can't do better than that."

"With all due respect, Mr. Osborne, I was a good employee for over eleven years. I had a good record, didn't I? I got along well with the other managers and with the people in my own department. If I got my old position back, I'd be department head. I wouldn't have much contact with the public. Besides, Mr. Osborne, those reports that you and customers have heard are nothing more than a pack of lies."

"That may or may not be. But I can't be the judge of that,

Charles. All I know is the public perception. We can't risk it, I'm afraid."

"But, Mr. Osborne, I haven't had my day in court yet."

Charles' argument was in vain. In the court of public opinion, he had already been convicted and judged guilty.

Shillington and Nelson sent a letter to Osborne to advocate for Charles. They pleaded for Winn-Dixie to reconsider their decision, at least until after Charles' trial, but to no avail. Fortunately, the attorneys also contacted the employees' union, which took on the case and pressured their management to keep Charles on the job until the trial was complete. Charles wasn't, in fact, a member of the union so the union's advocacy for him surprised and humbled him. The company caved. It was the first time Charles received unsolicited help from someone without having to be paid but on just a matter of the principle of justice.

It wouldn't be the last.

Having a job was a godsend to Charles. It gave his life some semblance of normalcy. He and Travis were back in a familiar pattern. Many of his former colleagues in the produce department gave Charles the benefit of the doubt, at least until after the trial.

Charles tried to cope with the rumors and blatant lies about his guilt with a mischievous sense of gallows humor. One day while ferrying some paperwork to the front office, a customer pulled him aside.

"Excuse me," he began. "Where is that guy who beat his wife to death? I've heard he works here. You know him?"

Charles stopped, leaned over toward the man, and spoke quietly in his ear. "You want to see him?" Charles asked conspiratorially.

The man had glee written all over his face. He could hardly hold back his excitement.

Charles motioned with his head for the fellow to follow him. He took the man on a complicated, circuitous route through the store to the far side of the building. They stopped at a tall mirror against the wall that served partly for advertising, partly as a shoplifting prevention tool. Charles looked warily around the corner to add suspense and mystery. The curious customer came and stood beside Charles, looking ahead into the mirror.

Charles said nothing for a few seconds so that the man had a chance to recognize what was happening. When he came to the realization of Charles' black comedic strategy, his eyes grew wide and his mouth gaped open.

"Look. There he is." Charles pointed into the mirror. "One of these two characters before you is rumored to be the gruesome murderer. I'll leave it to you to figure out which one."

The man's horror was eclipsed by his fear and embarrassment. He bolted from the store. Charles felt little guilt or shame.

ATTORNEYS SHILLINGTON AND NELSON were working as hard as they could to piece together a defense for Charles but it was difficult. They simply had nothing to go on except the estimated time of Dana's death, the fact that Charles was at work at that time, and Charles' reputation as a decent guy who loved his wife—and even that wasn't holding up well now.

Charles felt badly that he couldn't be of more help to them. He told them again the same stories, the same details, the same memories. One day Shillington offered to take Charles out on his boat. Perhaps a day on the Intracoastal Waterway would lift his client's spirits. Maybe a change of scenery would prompt new memories.

Shillington drove the boat out toward the inlet to the Atlantic Ocean where the waves became higher. He turned the boat back toward the shelter of Hypoluxo Island, where they dropped the anchor and began conversing.

"You know, Charles," Shillington began. "Don't misunderstand me. I say this to prepare you. In a capital case like yours, an innocent man is often next to useless to his defense team."

"I certainly feel that way, Steve."

"An innocent man is the hardest kind of defendant to represent. He usually knows nothing about the crime because he wasn't there. He has no explanation for the atrocity. He customarily can't name others who might be suspects. It's as if the defense team is up the creek with no paddle."

"As I say, Steve, I wish I could be more helpful. I'm grateful that you and Bryce believe in my innocence. But I'm not going to make up a story just to have something new to report to you."

"No, no, Charles, I'm not suggesting that you do. I just wanted to alert you to our difficulty. We're doing our best. But you need to know that we're near the bottom of a long, steep hill that we have to climb. All we can hope for is that the prosecution makes an error and maybe we can capitalize on it. Skip Henderson doesn't make many mistakes, mind you, but he's only human like the rest of us."

BRADY V. MARYLAND

John Leo Brady of Maryland, and a companion Donald Boblit, were tried for the murder of an acquaintance William Brooks. They were convicted on June 27, 1958 and sentenced to death. Brady acknowledged that he was involved in the murder but claimed that Boblit had done the actual killing, and that they had stolen Brooks' car ahead of a planned bank robbery but had not planned to kill him.

The men were tried separately. In Brady's trial, the prosecution withheld from Brady's defense team any information about private testimony given by Boblit in which he confessed to having committed Brooks' murder by himself.

The Maryland Court of Appeals, however, affirmed the conviction of Brady and remanded his case for a retrial on the question of punishment only. Hoping for a new trial for Brady, his defense team appealed his case to the United States Supreme Court in 1963. SCOTUS ruled that withholding exculpatory evidence from the defense violates due process "where the evidence is material either to guilt or punishment."

The ruling of the SCOTUS was that Brady deserved to receive a new hearing regarding punishment but not a new trial for the murder. Brady was given a new sentencing hearing at which his death sentence was commuted to life in prison; he was ultimately paroled. He relocated to Florida, worked as a truck driver, started a family, and did not re-offend.

In 1985 in the *United States v. Bagley,* the SCOTUS stated that the suppressed evidence is exculpatory if there is a reasonable probability that a defendant's conviction or sentence would have been different had the withheld evidence been disclosed.

As a result of *Brady v. Maryland,* when a defendant or his/her defense teams requests "Brady disclosures" or "Brady materials," they are referring to the requirement that the prosecution disclose to the defense any evidence in its possession that might exonerate the defendant. "Brady evidence" includes statements of witnesses or physical evidence that conflicts with the prosecution's witnesses. Also included as "Brady material" is evidence of false statements by the prosecution's witness(es) or evidence that a witness has been paid to serve as an informant against the defendant.

Wikipedia

CHAPTER 23

WEST PALM BEACH,OCTOBER 16, 1986

STEVE SHILLINGTON CALLED CHARLES on the telephone.

"I regret that I don't have any news of progress in your case. It's a damn hard nut to crack. But I do have news. The date for your pre-trial hearing has been set for November 7."

"Pre-trial hearing? Not the trial itself?"

"The pre-trial hearing is not the same as a trial in which your guilt or innocence is judged by the jury. The judge appointed for your trial calls us all together for a powwow: Bryce and me, you, Skip Henderson, and whoever else he has on the prosecution team. The judge will suggest a date for the trial itself and talk about the selection of the jury. We'll have an opportunity, if we choose, to file a petition for a reduction of the charges and so on."

Charles felt his stomach tightening as Shillington described the process. *My God. It's really going to happen. This isn't a game anymore. We're playing for real stakes.* He wiped the beads of sweat from his forehead.

"Since you can't leave the county, I want to ask a couple of attorney colleagues of mine from Miami to come see you at FSP to put you through some witness training. You'll like them. They're tough, but they know the procedures of capital trials as well as anybody. They're consultants who will instruct you on how to testify on your own behalf at the trial."

A week later two attorneys named Lauren and Cindy from the firm Dunn and Mansfield in Miami paid a half-day visit. They put Charles through a series of mock interviews and pretend cross-examinations.

"Charles, be warned. A good prosecutor might grill you mercilessly to establish a motive for the crime. Of course, they already have the note Steve told me about, the one you left for your wife on the morning when she was murdered. They'll use that to argue that her murder was a crime of passion committed by you. But they'll try to pile it on to build a more compelling case. For instance, did your wife have a life insurance policy?"

"Yes, we both had policies with a payout of about $200,000."

"That could be mighty tempting to get your hands on, couldn't it?"

"No, it never entered my mind until I needed to scrape enough money together to retain Steve and Bryce as my defense team."

"So you cashed in your wife's policy pretty early in the game? That sounds suspicious," Lauren said.

"Are they actually crazy enough to argue that I would murder my wife out of both passion and greed?"

"We'll have to wait and see. But you need to be prepared for any eventuality. Charles, nothing presented in court needs to be reasonable. It just has to resonate emotionally for the jury," Cindy added.

"First rule of defendant testimony: Only answer the question you are asked. Add nothing. No mentioning that you used the proceeds of your wife's life insurance policy to retain attorneys. They didn't ask you that. It's none of the court's business. Offer no reasons. Reveal no weaknesses. Don't say a word about any marital scrapes with your wife. If you're asked if you and she had any, however minor, just answer their question directly and concisely; offer no further details. They might come back to bite you."

For lack of more evidence, Shillington arranged for Charles to take a lie detector test. The attorney knew full well that the results would not be admissible in court. But he thought if Charles passed the test with flying colors, even the unofficial results might be enough to compel Skip Henderson to back down from his insistence on a first-degree murder charge against Charles, or cause the judge to order Henderson to do so.

Charles did pass the test with flying colors. For good measure, Shillington ordered a second forensics service to perform an additional lie detector test. No problem. Charles aced it, too.

Shillington took the sheet of results personally to Skip Henderson.

"You know better than that, Mr. Shillington," Henderson told him. "You know that the results are inadmissible in court so I just discount such things. Besides, you controlled the tests, and we didn't."

"Not a problem, Mr. Henderson. You can test him. Use whatever certified lab you choose."

Henderson shook his head and uttered an emphatic "No" and then, without any further discussion, turned and walked away.

CHARLES RETURNED TO HIS CELL feeling discouraged and more than a little anxious. In the sessions with Lauren and Cindy, he felt he couldn't do anything right. While he was relieved that both lie detector tests pointed to his innocence, he was frustrated at the legal system for not admitting those results in court. Henderson didn't budge but maintained the charge of capital murder against Charles.

He was looking forward to spending the evening at home with Travis.

After dinner Charles announced that it was high time for him to clean the bathtub and shower area.

"Can I help, Daddy?" Travis asked.

Charles knew that he could clean the tub faster and more efficiently if he did it himself, alone. But Travis's eagerness to help him with such a mundane task won him over.

"Sure, buddy. Let's do it together and make it twice as clean."

Charles got on his knees beside the bathtub. Travis followed his example but discovered he was too short to clean the tub while on his knees. He stood beside Charles and watched intently.

"Daddy, who was that monster in the shower the morning when Mommy died, the one in the green shirt taking a shower with his clothes on?"

Charles gaped at Travis, stunned beyond words. A thousand unpleasant images ricocheted inside his head, images of that morning, images of Dana bloodied and beaten, images he didn't want to revisit. Charles sidestepped Travis's question and waited in silence, hoping that Travis would say more.

"I asked Nana, too. She didn't know who it was but wrote things down on a piece of paper. I told her I saw a monster in the shower. His hands were all red. He tried to wash them in the shower. But he didn't see me."

"What did Nana say?"

"She just asked if I recognized the monster and if you were there, too. I told her you were at work. She said she would tell the police about what I said."

The next day Charles visited Shillington at his office. Shillington invited Nelson into his office for a second pair of ears to hear Charles as he reported to them what Travis had shared with him.

"Probably the real suspect," Shillington said.

"Not probably," Charles amended. "*That's* the guy."

"The trouble is your son is only three years old, probably too young to testify and be 100% credible. And if we try to bring it up, it will be ruled as 'Hearsay' and therefore inadmissible."

"I don't know it for a fact if my mother-in-law followed through and informed the sheriff."

"If she did, we can add that to the list of pertinent information that is in the sheriff's possession that he hasn't informed us about."

"Yeah, like the mysterious blue bandana."

"I'm discerning a definite pattern in the sheriff's behavior, aren't you?" Nelson asked his partner.

"Those may be only the tip of the proverbial iceberg," Shillington said. "Makes you wonder, doesn't it, what else is the sheriff keeping to himself? And does the prosecution have access to what the sheriff may be withholding without saying a word to us?"

Nelson moved to sit on the edge of his chair. He seemed to be on the cusp of an idea.

"Is this a possible door to a defense strategy for Mr. Wilkerson, Steve?" Nelson asked.

"A possible Brady violation, you mean? Or, better said, perhaps a series of them?" Shillington inquired.

They lost Charles in the conversation. To him, it was as if the attorneys' dialogue were in ancient Greek for all Charles could understand.

"It's certainly worth pursuing. We have very few alternative strategies, right?" Nelson asked.

"It may not be easy," Shillington said. "But it may be the first light at the end of this tunnel."

Charles wanted to know but delayed his question about the Brady violation to another time. He might not have understood who Brady was, but he felt encouraged by the renewed energy of his defense team.

CHAPTER 24

CHARLES DIDN'T REMEMBER MUCH about the pre-trial hearing. He didn't sleep the nights before. His mind was consumed by the unwelcome question his father had asked when his parents had come to visit him at the Palm Beach County Jail a few months ago: "What becomes of Travis after the trial if the court sends you back to jail for a long time?"

Charles didn't have a better answer now than he did back in November. Though Ruth and Dwight Miller hadn't communicated with him directly—in fact, they hadn't made contact with Charles since their abbreviated visit at the house after the murder was discovered—he did hear through one of Dana's sisters that someone from her family would petition the courts to hand Travis's custody over to them. After Charles heard about that he was in a deep funk for days. That was not what he wanted. With the exception of her brother, Doug, who was way out in Oregon starting a new job, Charles couldn't think of a single person in Dana's family who was even the least bit open to his claim of innocence. But if he was declared by the court to be guilty of murder, he would have no say in Travis's placement. Even as the father he would be disqualified from any legal parental rights.

Steve and Bryce embraced Charles at the end of the pre-trial hearings to congratulate him on enduring another step in a long process. The actual trial would begin February 7.

Charles was in strict custody for the pre-trial hearing and jury selection of the Sheriff of Palm Beach County beginning that night. He was back in the Palm Beach County Jail. After yet another practically sleepless night, Charles was awakened by guards who placed handcuffs on his wrists. They wanted to ensure he was ready for the ride to the Courthouse in Sheriff Davidson's cruiser.

Davidson led him by the arm through the noisy, roiling mob alive with shouted questions, the whir of overworked camera shutters, and the presence of TV station cameramen adept at shooting while walking backwards. Shillington and Nelson met him and Davidson at the entrance and nodded "good morning" to them but remained totally mute, their faces hard and set as though preparing to face the lions in the Roman coliseum. Charles was tempted but did not venture to answer a reporter's question: "Mr. Wilkerson, do you still maintain your innocence of this crime?"

Charles and Davidson ascended the stairs inside the front entrance with the gaggle of reporters and camera crews following in step. They grew increasingly frantic as they neared the wooden door into the courtroom, beyond which the cameras could not follow.

Charles felt like an outsider who was just learning the ropes on the first day at a new school. He was apprehensive.

Shillington and Nelson took their places in seats at the defense table. Davidson led Charles to that table. An officious bailiff appeared and asked the gathered people to rise as he introduced Judge Julius Erskine.

My goodness. The judge's got to be at least seventy-five years old or more if he's a day.

During the first break in the proceedings, Steve told Charles that Erskine had been on the bench for decades. Palm Beach County, in deference to his diminishing hearing, had installed a microphone stand next to the witness stand. Still, Charles noticed that during the proceedings Erskine requested several times for the prosecutor and his attorneys to repeat themselves and for their points to be made again— only louder this time.

If the judge needs this much help hearing even with a microphone, what are the odds that he wouldn't miss more of the trial than anyone knew? I hope to God he doesn't suffer from diminished reasoning or memory, too.

Across the aisle from the defense table sat Skip Henderson and Sheriff Davidson. Even in his chair, Davidson dwarfed the diminutive prosecutor. In Henderson's appearance, there was very little that would intimidate a defendant: His light brown hair was thinning in the front and his rumpled suit looked a little too unkempt for a prosecutor. Shillington had warned Charles not to be misled by Henderson's physical appearance. "It's when Henderson winds up and prepares to deliver his pitch that his real strength begins to show."

Henderson looked so cozy with Sheriff Davidson at the table. If they experienced any tension in their relationship as ex-father-in-law and ex-son-in-law, it didn't show. They looked as tight as members of a small-town bowling team. They looked confident and exuded power. As Charles looked at them sitting side by side, he felt intimidated and anxious. *They are in charge, and they are against me. That's all that matters.*

The first group of potential jurors was escorted into the courtroom by the bailiff. He asked them to take a seat in the area reserved for the jury. They waited anxiously while the bailiff shuffled a stack of index cards, each containing the name of a potential juror. He made a random decision about which local would be interviewed first.

A game of cards? Are they stacked against me?

Charles' suspicion was confirmed almost immediately. As one woman was questioned by Charles' legal team, it was revealed that the distinguished-looking woman was actually the manager in the prosecutor's office.

Is the pool of potential jurors so small and provincial that it included someone so close to Henderson? I'm in deep trouble.

After a series of follow-up questions from Shillington when the woman acknowledged her position in Henderson's office, Shillington looked up at Henderson, smiled at him sarcastically, and shook his head in disbelief.

"Your Honor, this situation is patently absurd," Shillington rose from his chair to object. "With all due respect, this woman has no business being qualified to sit on this jury. Her close connection to the prosecution disqualifies her completely. Your Honor, we move for her removal from the jury panel for cause."

Judge Erskine looked sheepish as he allowed the defense team's motion for removal with cause.

A new group of potentials was ushered in. Shillington, looking angry and flummoxed, asked the group, "I'd like to ask, ladies and gentlemen, for a show of hands by any and all individuals with any kind of link, *any* kind of prior relationship—by marriage, employment, friendship, family ties, or church membership—to the prosecutor's office, Sheriff's department, or anyone else connected to the case."

About half of the potential jurors raised their hands. Shillington stretched out his arms in frustration and turned to the judge.

When Shillington had returned to the defense table, he said to Charles, "There were only two African Americans in that bunch."

"Yes, I noticed that." He waited for Shillington to say more.

"I plan to do something about that. We'll see if there are more in the next group of potentials. We aren't going to let you have to face an all-white jury, don't worry. I know how those turn out."

Again, the bailiff shuffled the index cards and led in a new group of prospective jurors. Eventually, Henderson and Shillington whittled the group down to a smaller pool for closer individual questioning.

Everyone had heard of the case through newspapers or television news, or else by way of conversations with neighbors or at church. One by one, they were called to the front. Several voiced concerns about their ability to remain fair in judging the case. One woman told the courtroom, "I'd like to do my civic duty and all that. But I wouldn't want to be responsible if he was innocent and we judged him guilty."

Henderson commented that he hoped "everyone on the jury panel felt exactly like you do, Ma'am."

Charles looked over at Shillington as if to say, "Isn't that exactly what we fear most?"

Charles watched as a couple of other conscientious folks worried about convicting an innocent man to be sent to Raiford to die. Other less scrupulous men made the cut. *My hopes for a fair trial just dwindled.*

"Ladies and gentlemen," Shillington said, "if you don't mind, I have a few follow-up questions."

Henderson looked irritated but made an exaggerated gesture with his hands that bordered on sarcasm for Shillington to take a turn.

"Let me ask again for a show of hands, ladies and gentlemen, on a different question this time. Would any of you who have ever been a victim of a crime please indicate so by raising your hand?"

Surprisingly, almost half of the group of twenty-five or so prospective jurors raised their hands.

Shillington paused to take an informal count. "I am relieved for those of you who have been fortunate enough to have been spared the violation and misery of being a victim of a crime."

He was looking at a middle-aged white woman who had raised her hand. "May I ask your name, Ma'am?"

"It's Rose Gaffney, sir."

"Now let me refine the question a little and ask for another show of hands. If you have been the victim of a crime, and the perpetrator of that crime has been discovered and apprehended, and if this individual was of the African American race, please raise your hand."

"I object, Your Honor," Henderson inserted. "We're here to try this defendant. Whatever crimes some of those people have endured are in the past."

"Objection overruled," Judge Erskine pronounced. "Given the race of the defendant, the Counselor's question is quite relevant. I think I see where he is going with this. Proceed, Mr. Shillington."

No diminishment of reasoning power there on the judge's part, thank God.

Henderson looked anxiously at Davidson beside him.

"I think I see where this nigger lovin' son-of-a-bitch is headed with this, too," Davidson mumbled under his breath to Henderson.

The potential jurors looked at each other with uncertainty. Who would be the brave one to be the first to acknowledge such an experience? One by one, hands started to go up until a good percentage of the persons had their hands up.

Shillington addressed the group. "Thank you, ladies and gentlemen. I have just one more question for those of you who have been a victim of a crime committed by an African American."

"Let me just ask you, Mrs. Gaffney. Do you think your negative experience of a crime perpetrated by an African American individual might affect your decision about the guilt or innocence of the defendant in *this* case, who, as you can see, is an African American male?"

Rose looked at the judge, for assurance or perhaps protection from the question. She hesitated before she answered.

"Mrs. Gaffney, I hate to have put you on the spot but this is very important."

Judge Erskine added, "Indeed, it is, Mrs. Gaffney. Mr. Shillington is not asking a question that is unusual in these circumstances. I encourage you to provide an answer."

Mrs. Gaffney was disappointed that she wasn't let off the hook.

"Since our garage was burglarized in 1979 and most of my husband's tools stolen by a black man, I have to admit it has made us regard any black person seeming to be wandering in our neighborhood with suspicion. Seeing all those reports on the TV news about crime and mug shots of black men as the suspects hasn't helped."

"Thank you for your honesty, Mrs. Gaffney," Shillington said. "I'm afraid you haven't answered my question directly. That is, would your experience prevent you from being impartial in the trial of the defendant, Mr. Charles Wilkerson?"

"I'd have to think long and hard about it. I'm not sure."

"Thank you, Mrs. Gaffney. You've been most helpful."

Then addressing Judge Erskine, "Your Honor, I'm afraid that given Mrs. Gaffney's uncertainty, and with all due respect for her willingness to serve the state, we of the defendant's defense move that Mrs. Gaffney be removed with cause from the pool of possible jurors."

"Your motion is sustained, Counselor," Erskine replied.

Henderson started to rise from his seat in anticipation of the judge's excusing the current crop of potential jurors.

In fact, Erskine looked as though he was about to do so when Shillington interjected, "Your Honor, excuse me. We aren't quite finished yet with these ladies and gentlemen. I have a few further questions for several of them, if I may."

"Surely," Erskine replied reluctantly. "Be my guest, please."

"I'd like to ask Mr. Randall if he might respond to a question or two."

A tall, slender, greying black man rose self-consciously from his chair.

"Now, Mr. Randall. I recall that you were not among those who raised their hand when I asked who had been the victim of a crime perpetrated by an African American person. Am I recalling correctly?"

"Yes, you are."

"But you raised your hand to indicate you had been the victim of a crime, is that right?"

"Again, yes, it is. Our car was broken into in our driveway, but the perpetrator was never apprehended, to the best of my knowledge. So I couldn't say for sure if the perpetrator was a white or black individual."

"Thank you, Mr. Randall, for withholding your judgment. Does it make any difference to you, Mr. Randall, whether the perpetrator, who is still at large apparently, was white or black?"

"No, sir. Whether it was a white man or a black man, it wouldn't undo the damage to our car or to our peace of mind."

"So can I extrapolate, then, from your answer that you feel confident that the race of the defendant would not influence your ability to judge him guilty or innocent separately from the facts as presented in *this* trial?"

"That's accurate, sir. I'm here to try my best not to let it influence my decision."

Bryce Nelson gave his partner a nod of approval and congratulations. All it takes, he knew, was *one* person on the jury who was sensitive to subtle racial dynamics to prevent a majority white jury from a lynching disguised as a legal proceeding. Just one, he knew, would be enough to neutralize any potential blindness or implicit prejudice in the white members of the jury that might influence the outcome of a verdict.

BY THE END OF THAT FIRST DAY, they had a jury of seven men and five women in place, and two alternates in addition, including Mr. Randall and one black woman who was part of the next cohort of prospective jurors. Charles was relieved and impressed with Shillington's handling of the potentially divisive racial issue. Yet, he was also simultaneously anxious. These fine, middle-class folks, be they white or black, admired and trusted law enforcement and believed that the prosecutor represents their interests. To them, Charles conjectured, he was just another uninvited Yankee who had moved into the area in recent years, making South Florida a more congested and a more dangerous place.

Chapter 25

West Palm Beach, FL, February 8, 1986

"Ladies and gentlemen of the jury. We are elated that yesterday, on the very first day of this trial, without any further delay, we have been able to find twelve citizens of Palm Beach County who are willing to perform their civic duty by being part of this nonpartial jury, or their alternates, in the capital trial of Mr. Charles Wilkerson. We are glad that all twelve of you have returned prepared to serve and hear the facts of this case," Prosecutor Henderson opened the trial the next morning.

"I won't delay the beginning of this trial more than I need to in order to address you. You will also hear from several witnesses today. I am sure that their testimony will be very congruent with what I have to tell you in this opening statement. The brutal crime of the beating and murder of Dana Wilkerson, the wife of the defendant, was a horrendous act of violence, committed as we will show, by her husband, the defendant Charles Wilkerson."

Charles sat absolutely still in his chair and did not allow his eyes to wander over to the jury box or make eye contact with a single member of the jury.

"By committing such a deviant crime within his own marriage, Mr. Wilkerson has proved himself to be essentially lower than the lowest form of humanity. Consider yourselves fortunate, ladies and gentlemen, for not having been privy to the sickening scene in Mrs. Wilkerson's bedroom when her mutilated and deceased body was discovered by a neighbor, as you will hear from a witness later this morning. You will hear the medical examiner testify that the victim's face had been disfigured beyond recognition by a vicious beating with a blunt object."

Henderson paused to allow the picture he had painted to sink into the minds and hearts of the members of the jury. Charles' eyes filled with tears.

"Miraculously, Mrs. Wilkerson's body had not been violated in the sense of rape by her husband. I say 'miraculously' because, as you will see not much later in this trial, Mrs. Wilkerson had declined sexual intercourse with her husband, which set him off on a vicious bout of fury, as displayed in an exhibit you will see in time: a note scribbled by the frustrated husband and left for his wife ostensibly to discover and read. Of course, she would never be awake to read it. He had gone to their bed thoroughly foiled, his sexual appetite unsated. He awoke during the night in a heightened mood of dissatisfaction and sexual fury and proceeded to commit the crime of passion."

Again, Henderson paused and looked each member of the jury directly in the eyes.

"I am sure that this lurid behavior on the part of the defendant violates your personal beliefs about the sanctity of the marriage bond and human life, as it does, I'm certain, of the collective values of the population of our fine county. As the grisly and lurid details of the crime are revealed to you in the course of this trial, I am confident that you will vote for a guilty verdict in accordance with the evidence we present to you."

"Mr. Shillington, do you have an opening statement to the jury?" Judge Erskine asked. "If so, please proceed now."

Shillington rose from his chair and adjusted his suit jacket. "Yes, Your Honor, I do."

"Ladies and gentlemen of the jury. What you have just heard is not a summary or preview of the prosecution's case against the defendant at all, which is what we expect. Rather, it is a blatant assassination of the defendant's character. The prosecutor has given a statement filled with stark and extreme language meant to shock and prejudice the court and jury before we have even begun the trial itself. He has belittled your intelligence, ladies and gentlemen, by taking away from you your right to use your own independent judgment and reason to reach a fair conclusion about Mr. Wilkerson's character and the charge against him.

"Why does the prosecution infantilize you so? Is it perhaps, I ask you, because in the end he will not have sufficient credible evidence to present to you for you to make such a judgment? We suspect that Mr. Henderson and his colleagues are able to present additional evidence to the jury than we of the defense team are aware. For unless he can present to the jury more than he has thus far, I would venture to say that a case with such a paucity of credible evidence linking the defendant to the crime is risking being thrown out due to a lack of evidence. I am confident that as intelligent and responsible citizens, you will come to the same conclusion and render a verdict of not guilty for Mr. Wilkerson."

"Thank you, Mr. Shillington. If we are finished with the opening statements, Mr. Henderson, you may proceed to call the first witness."

"I call Mrs. Ruth Miller to the stand."

Dana's mother rose and anxiously approached the witness stand. After swearing on the Bible that she will tell the truth, the whole truth, and nothing but the truth, she sat down without looking at Charles.

Henderson began, "Thank you, Mrs. Miller. Just to establish your credential to the jury: You are the mother of the deceased, Dana Wilkerson. Is that correct?"

"Yes, sir. She was our eldest daughter." She swallowed to suppress her tears.

"Thank you. Mrs. Miller. I know this is difficult for you so I only have a question or two. I wonder if you could describe for us the nature of your daughter's marriage to Charles Wilkerson."

"Well, things began very well. My husband and I shared Dana's excitement about Charles as her husband. He was always very nice and respectful toward us as Dana's parents.

"But after a couple of years, Charles seemed to withdraw a little from us during their visits. We didn't understand why. We didn't think we had said anything offensive to cause him to withdraw from us. We tried not to treat him any differently than we would have treated a white man if Dana had chosen one for a husband. We asked Dana about it. She just said that sometimes he gets quiet, that's all."

"Interesting, Mrs. Miller. Did you notice the same kind of withdrawal by Mr. Wilkerson from your daughter?"

"Well, sometimes when they arrived at our house, he wouldn't take a seat beside her the way he used to. It's as though they had been having some kind of quarrel on the drive over from their house."

"Thank you, Mrs. Miller. Your witness, Counselor."

Shillington stood up and approached the witness stand.

"Mrs. Miller, you say it was as though Mr. and Mrs. Wilkerson had been having a quarrel in the car before they arrived at your home. Do you know this for a *fact*? Did you approach your daughter in private and quietly ask her if they had quarreled?"

"Well, no. I figured it was none of my business. My husband and I try not to trespass into our adult children's affairs. Charles just looked angry. That's what led me to believe they had quarreled."

"Mrs. Miller, did your daughter ever make reference to her husband's anger?"

"No, not directly. As I said, we didn't intervene in our children's affairs, and they don't tell us everything going on in their marriage."

"Mrs. Miller, that sounds like a wise, hands-off policy."

Henderson stood up to speak. "Before you dismiss Mrs. Miller from the stand, Your Honor, I have one question to follow up if I may."

Judge Erskine didn't object.

"Mrs. Miller," Henderson began, "can you tell us what impact the tragic loss of your daughter has had on your family?"

Ruth paused as though unsure if her words would be allowed in court.

"Yes, I just need to say—"

She found it almost impossible to continue because of the tears she had been holding back.

"We have not been able to accept that our Dana is dead. I know I will not be able to accept it ever. She will always be a part of our family."

With that, Ruth broke down in tears. The bailiff came over, put his hand on her shoulder, and led her from the stand. She whispered something to the bailiff and waited for his response. He ushered her not to her original seat beside her husband, but rather to the empty chair immediately behind Charles.

Charles thought her choice of seat was strange. Shillington passed him a slip of folded paper. "Just consider what the jury sees every time they look at you."

Then Charles understood. They would see the weeping mother-in-law. The more empathetic of the jury members would feel the urge to relieve Ruth's pain. *Another reason for the jury to hand out a guilty verdict.*

Who had arranged for just that one particular seat to be open?

CHAPTER 26

WEST PALM BEACH, FEBRUARY 8, 1987

AFTER THE LUNCH RECESS, EVERYONE took his or her place in the courtroom.

"Mr. Henderson," a tired-looking Judge Erskine said. "Your next witness?"

"We call Mr. Adolfo Esteban to the stand."

A middle-aged, distinguished-looking Hispanic gentleman approached the stand.

"Mr. Esteban, would you please inform the court of your office," Henderson began.

"Yes," Esteban answered in a thick Hispanic accent. "I am the Chief Medical Examiner of Palm Beach County."

"Thank you, Mr. Esteban. I am presuming that the autopsy you performed on the deceased body of the victim, Mrs. Dana Wilkerson, was not your first?"

"No, by no means, sir. I have performed over 7,000 autopsies."

"Excellent, Mr. Esteban. And this autopsy of Dana Wilkerson, which you performed. Would you judge that the condition of the corpse was better or worse than the more than 7,000 you have examined?"

"Objection!" Shillington interjected. "A simple description of what Mr. Esteban found during the autopsy, which I anticipate Mr. Henderson was going to ask Mr. Esteban about, should suffice, Your Honor."

"Objection sustained. Mr. Henderson. We are not interested in a ranking of the worst mutilations of bodies in autopsies."

"All right. Let me ask, Mr. Esteban," Henderson said, "that you provide the jury with a description of what you found when you began the autopsy of Dana Wilkerson."

"She was in very bad shape. On her forehead, there was a six-inch wide cut through which brain matter, blood, and bits of skull bone were exuding. Her face had been so badly battered that I had difficulty making out the color of her eyes."

That elicited an audible whimper from Ruth Miller. She looked at Charles with red-hot hatred.

After an appropriate period of silence, Henderson continued. "Would you kindly continue, Mr. Esteban."

"I counted eight different blows to her head. She had a fractured nose, and some of her teeth had been knocked out."

Esteban seemed to feel he had said enough. Having heard the horror of Dana's death, there was absolute silence in the courtroom except the sound of Dana's mother weeping. No one in the jury dared look at Charles.

What I saw in the bedroom later was the cleaned-up version. Esteban had seen her as the killer had left her.

"Mr. Esteban," Henderson continued, "can you tell us your opinion of the time of the victim's death?"

"Yes, I can. Mrs. Wilkerson probably died up to four hours after her meal on the night before. That would be at 1:15 a.m. or so. Based on my experience, no later than 1:15 a.m."

"Mr. Esteban, is my calculation correct when I say that's over four hours before the defendant was due at work that morning?"

"Yes, that would have left four hours between the time of the victim's death and the time he was expected at his job."

"Thank you for your expert witness, Mr. Esteban."

Judge Erskine said to Shillington, "You may cross-examine the witness if you wish, Counselor."

Shillington and Nelson were still conferring animatedly. When Nelson rose to cross-examine, he had a puzzled look on his face.

"Mr. Esteban, we are a little confused. I'm afraid your answer to Mr. Henderson's question about an estimated time of death differs by a matter of hours from the initial report from your office that the estimated time of death was closer to 6 a.m. Can you explain the discrepancy?"

"I cannot, except to say that the time of 1:15 a.m. is based on my final examination of Mrs. Wilkerson, not my initial one."

"Mr. Esteban, help the jury understand. In any autopsy, is not the estimated time of the death of the deceased always a rather *subjective* decision? That is, is it not possible that another coroner, perhaps just as experienced as you, could come to a very different conclusion about the time of death?"

"I suppose that's possible."

"Not just possible, Mr. Esteban," Nelson raised his voice. "But very *often*, isn't that more accurate?"

"Perhaps, sir. We coroners each have our own methods as we

perform the autopsy. A different method could possibly lead to a slightly different conclusion about the time of death."

"In fact, Mr. Esteban, in spite of the common notion on the street of the accuracy of autopsies, determining the time of death is not an objective decision based on actual *science*, is it? There is plenty of legal precedent for a coroner's estimated time of death being inadmissible in a trial because the process of coming to certain conclusions is based on *pseudoscience* at best."

"My estimate of the time of death is based on the latest forensic science as I understand it," Esteban said with a noticeably growing defensiveness.

"With all due respect for your vast amount of experience performing autopsies, Mr. Esteban, the revised estimate of the time of death, which, as I say, might be discarded and replaced by an estimate provided by another coroner is not very reliable, not at all reliable, in fact, in helping determine the guilt or innocence of our client."

Then, addressing the judge, Nelson continued, "I respectfully appeal to the bench to strike the testimony of Dr. Esteban from the record, and for the jury to strike it from their memory."

All eyes were on Judge Erskine. "I rule that as a germane request. I will consider it and provide a ruling on it when the court reconvenes tomorrow."

Charles heaved a sigh of relief. The defense team had no idea that the medical examiner had revised his estimate of the time of Dana's death. They had been broadsided. The new time of 1:15 a.m. meant that Dana had been murdered while Charles was still in the house. *Even if the judge rules in favor of the request to strike Esteban's testimony from the record, the jury had heard it. The damage was done.*

Shillington's face became an angry shade of crimson as he considered what had transpired. "Your Honor, related to our request to have Dr. Esteban's testimony struck from the record, we want to have put in the record our objection that the prosecution did not turn over to the defense a summary of Dr. Esteban's revised estimate as required by the Rules of Criminal Procedure."

"As I have said, Counselor," Erskine replied testily, "I will render a ruling tomorrow. I will consider your objection in coming to a decision. Proceed, Mr. Henderson."

Henderson thanked the medical examiner again. He called Amalia Echeverria to the stand. Amalia, her husband, and their little son had lived next door to the Wilkersons for about a year. Amalia was the person who discovered Dana's dead body.

She told the jury that on the morning of August 13, she had seen Travis sitting alone on the single front step to the Wilkersons' home. "He just kept getting up and going back into the house, and then shortly coming out again. Occasionally, Travis would peek around our car in the driveway to look at me while I was working in the yard. I said hello to him but I didn't think anything was amiss."

"What did you do then?" Henderson asked.

"At about noon, it was getting too hot to work in the yard. It suddenly struck me that Travis had been alone and that I hadn't seen Dana with him at all. I thought that was unusual. Dana usually kept her eye on Travis when he was outside."

"Did you talk to the boy at that time, Mrs. Echeverria?"

"He seemed to be unusually shy that morning. So I walked over and picked him up. His diaper was rather heavy and needed changing. Dana never let Travis go long with a dirty diaper. I tried knocking on the front door, but there was no answer. I just pushed the front door open with my foot and walked through the house, holding Travis, and calling for Dana. Again, the only response I got was total silence. I changed his dirty diaper in Travis's room and then walked through the living room and kitchen a couple of times. Then I took Travis over to our house to play with Luis, our son, while I came back and looked further for Dana."

"Did you see anything amiss at that point?"

"Not right away, not until I saw some dresser drawers dumped on their bedroom floor. I didn't stop to think much about it. Perhaps Dana had been cleaning her drawers. But then I saw the bedcovers pulled all the way around the bed and tightly packed in. I knew that was not how either Dana or Charles made the bed.

"I began feeling around the base of the bed through the bedspread. I was very nervous. I didn't know what I might find. Finally, my hands could make out under the covers what to me looked like the shapes of feet and ankles. I went over to the side of the bed and lifted the covers slowly. I saw a wrist. I'm a nurse so the first thing I did was check for a pulse. Nothing. In fact, the wrist was very cold."

"Did you call 911 at that point, Mrs. Echeverria?"

"No, not right then. I was in shock. My heart was pounding out of my chest. I didn't know what to do. I ran out of the room and the house. I ran home and then called the sheriff's department. I was trembling. When they arrived, they removed the bedspread and found the beaten, dead body. I couldn't look at what they uncovered. I still have nightmares about it.

"They also found a handwritten note on the vanity in her bathroom and asked me about it. They gave it to me to read and asked if I knew anything about it."

Henderson seized the opportunity. "Can you tell us what the note said?"

"I was so shocked by what I read that I had to read it a second time. I was still shaking with adrenaline. The note was from Charles to Dana in which he said he was disappointed that he and Dana had been unable to have sex the night before. That's when Sheriff Davidson told me that Charles was the prime suspect in Dana's murder."

"Objection, Your Honor. The witness's testimony here is based on hearsay."

"Objection overruled," was Erskine's judgment.

Henderson stopped in front of Judge Erskine's bench. "Your Honor, I would now like to enter into evidence Exhibit A, which is the original note to which the witness refers."

Henderson placed the note, sealed in a plastic baggie, in front of Erskine on his bench. The clerk of the court picked it up and handed the baggie to the judge.

"I request permission to have this note read aloud so that the members of the jury can hear it."

Erskine responded, "Yes, I grant permission," Holding up the bag containing the note, he said, "I request that Sheriff Davidson appoint one of his deputies who discovered the note to please read the contents to the court."

There was some commotion as Davidson signaled authoritatively to Sergeant Ramsden. Ramsden stood up and approached the witness stand. He took the note from the clerk of the court and read it very slowly and mechanically. The eyes of a few of the jurors grew into wide circles of disbelief as they listened. Charles sat still, too embarrassed to look at any members of the jury directly. The note was only a few short sentences long, but hearing it read aloud felt to him to take an hour or more of painful torture.

Henderson remained totally silent after the reading so as not to interfere with the shocked silence of the jurors.

It was Judge Erskine who finally broke the silence. "We have about an hour until time for dismissal. Mr. Henderson, do you have any more questions for this witness?"

"Yes, Your Honor, if it please the court, I have one and perhaps another follow-up question for Mrs. Echeverria."

"If you can make it brief, Mr. Henderson, proceed."

"Thank you, Your Honor. Now, Mrs. Echeverria, you mention that the Sheriff revealed to you that Mr. Charles Wilkerson was considered the prime suspect in his wife's murder?"

"Yes, he said it just that plainly."

"Were you at all surprised by his statement?"

"Well, I was taken aback at first, not knowing if I was supposed to be given such information about the crime. But, no, when I got home again and thought about what the Sheriff said, it made sense to me."

"Objection, Your Honor," Shillington interjected. "What the witness thought of the sheriff's conclusions is irrelevant."

"Sustained. Mr. Henderson, can you reword your question to Mrs. Echeverria to help her provide an answer that is relevant?"

"OK. Let me ask the question in this way: Mrs. Echeverria, have you ever observed anything in Mr. Wilkerson's behavior toward his wife that indicated the state of their marriage?"

"I had observed occasionally that Charles—Mr. Wilkerson—had a temper. He would bark at her sometimes about where she chose to plant a bush, for instance. I remember how one night a group of us neighbors, including us, were sitting at their outdoor table in their backyard, and seemingly out of nowhere, Mr. Wilkerson raised his voice and said to Dana, 'Bitch, go get me a beer.' I couldn't believe— none of us could—that he would speak so unkindly to his wife."

At that, Charles' hand went up instinctively as though he wanted the judge's attention to refute the witness's testimony.

Judge Erskine noticed it and said, "Please wait, Mr. Wilkerson. Anything you say now would be ruled out of turn. You will get your turn to speak when your attorneys call you to the stand, should you choose to testify. For now, you'll just have to be patient. Mr. Shillington?"

Charles turned immediately to Shillington and quietly spoke a few words that were inaudible.

Shillington nodded his head in agreement. "No further questions for the witness, Your Honor—for the time being. I want to give notice to the court and to the prosecution, however, that we reserve the right to call her back to the stand at a later time. We have some uncertainty about her testimony."

CHAPTER 27

WEST PALM BEACH, FEBRUARY 9, 1987

JUDGE ERSKINE WELCOMED THE JURORS back and addressed those assembled.

"In reference to the motion by the defendant's attorneys to remove the testimony of Mr. Esteban from the official record of the trial proceedings. I have reread the *Florida Rules of Criminal Procedure.* Rule 16 (a)(i)G allows for a testimony to be removed from the proceedings by the judge if he or she rules that the testimony contains 'redundant, immaterial, impertinent or scandalous matter.' I have considered the motion, and I rule that since the witness testimony did not contain any such material, the motion is denied and the testimony remains in the official proceedings."

Nelson didn't try to hide his disappointment and turned to look at Shillington, and then Charles. Shillington raised his open palms off the table to indicate to Charles, "Well, we tried. We'll have to find another way to deal with the revised estimated time of Dana's death."

"As I recall, we left this trial with many kinds of unfinished business," Erskine continued, "among them the incomplete cross-examination by the defense of Mrs. Echeverria. If the prosecution and defense counsels agree, I'd like to propose that we pick up the proceedings at that point. Is that agreeable to you, Mr. Henderson, and are you prepared to continue your cross-examination of the witness, Mr. Shillington?"

Henderson nodded affirmatively.

Mrs. Echeverria was called back to the witness stand.

Shillington took over the cross-examination. "Mrs. Echeverria, during the recess between yesterday afternoon and this morning, we had further conversations with our client, the defendant. You may have noticed that he was quite anxious yesterday after your testimony, and Judge Erskine rightly counseled him to withhold his objections, if he had such, until it was his turn to take the witness stand. As his defense team, Mr. Nelson and I wanted to investigate his discomfort with your testimony.

"Our client felt that since you made mention of an incident in the Wilkersons' backyard and quoted Mr. Wilkerson speaking in what you described as a surprisingly rude manner, Mr. Wilkerson wanted to put his utterance, which he does not deny, into its proper context so that there is no misunderstanding.

"Mrs. Echeverria, the defendant is not accusing you of fabricating the quote. He acknowledges that it's true that at least once he did say to his wife at such an occasion, 'Bitch, bring me a beer.' What you didn't say, Mrs. Echeverria, or perhaps didn't realize, was that Mr. Wilkerson's remark to his wife was delivered in jest. He had a smile, not a scowl, on his face as he said those words. He and his wife had a running inside joke ever since they were at a restaurant years ago and heard a brutish man call his female guest that evening 'bitch' and demanded in all seriousness that she fetch him a bottle of beer from the bar. They thought it was very funny, even though they didn't approve of the way the guy spoke to her, and ever since that incident, they would playfully imitate that boorish behavior and call each other 'bitch' and order each other to bring a cool beer.

"Mrs. Echeverria," Shillington said, "I think it is important for the jury to hear the comment between the defendant and his wife delivered in the proper tone and with the proper intention of humor. It makes all the difference."

"Let me ask you, Mrs. Echeverria, do you still stand by your earlier testimony that from time to time in your relationship with the Wilkersons, you heard Mr. Wilkerson, quoting your own words, 'bark' at his wife?"

Mrs. Echeverria seemed somewhat chastened by Shillington's cross-examination thus far.

"Perhaps, as I think about it, I would take back my word 'bark' if I could and just say that he stated his preferences *strongly*, for example, about the placement of bushes. "

"There was an obvious difference of opinion? Did that seem unusual to you, Mrs. Echeverria?"

"On reflection, I have to admit that it was an example of the run-of-the-mill difference of opinion that even close married couples experience."

"That he expressed with respect, not undue anger or violence of any kind, is that correct, Mrs. Echeverria? In fact, can you honestly claim that in the year since they have been your neighbors, you have ever witnessed an occasion when Mr. Wilkerson spoke to his wife in any way other than with respect?"

Mrs. Echeverria was defensive. "No, I can't say I did. That's why that evening his address as 'bitch' struck me. He had never spoken like that to her before in my hearing."

"Thank you, Mrs. Echeverria. That helps to clarify what might have been confusing to the jury. You are excused from the stand."

She stepped away. On the way to her seat, as she passed the prosecutor's table, Henderson pulled her closer and whispered something to her. She nodded and resumed her return to her seat.

I'm grateful Steve pushed for that acknowledgment. But it may be too late. Hasn't the damage been done already?

Henderson said, "Your Honor, we call Sergeant Chester Ramsden."

Ramsden took the oath of truthful testimony and settled into the chair in the witness stand.

Henderson began the questioning. "Sergeant Ramsden, please tell the court your role in this case."

"I was appointed by my boss, Sheriff Davidson, to be the chief investigator of the crime."

"Sergeant Ramsden, please tell us in chronological order the major aspects of your investigation of this case, beginning with the day of Mrs. Wilkerson's murder."

"Well, that morning I was called to the scene by several officers after they had received a call from a neighbor about having found a body."

"And, after that?"

Ramsden fidgeted. "I went into the bedroom and inspected the crime scene—took it all in."

"Was the body of Dana Wilkerson still there?"

"Yes, it was still in the bed."

"When did you first encounter the defendant, Mr. Wilkerson?"

"It was later that afternoon. I was at the kitchen table conferring with Sheriff Davidson, who told him that his wife was found killed."

"And how would you describe the defendant's reaction to such news?"

"He was surprisingly controlled and stoic. He simply asked Sheriff Davidson and me how his son was."

"No reaction of any kind to the fact that Mrs. Wilkerson had been discovered killed? No tears? No hysterics?"

"Not that I saw. It was as though he already knew she was killed. He just asked about his little son."

"Objection, Your Honor," Shillington said, almost in a shout.

"The witness is adding his own gratuitous interpretation. He could not possibly know what the defendant did or did not know already."

"Objection sustained," Erskine announced immediately. "Please strike from the record the witness's comment that he thought the defendant already knew that Mrs. Wilkerson was killed. And members of the jury, please disregard the witness's words to that effect."

"At this point, Your Honor, I yield the floor and defer any further questioning to the defense."

Shillington had waited eagerly for this moment. "Sergeant Ramsden, what were the names of the officers who were at the crime scene when you arrived that morning?"

"One was Watkins, I remember. But I really don't recall the names of the others—in specific detail, I mean."

"Then let me ask you: What did the officers tell you when you arrived?"

"Again, sir, I don't honestly remember offhand what they told me."

"But surely, Sergeant Ramsden, you have notes about the names of the officers and what they told you at the beginning? As part of your investigation, would you not have made a record of these things?"

"Oh yes, I always do that as a matter of routine."

"Good, Sergeant Ramsden. Then you would be able to provide answers to my questions if you referred to those notes of the investigation?"

"I'm sure I could, sir."

"Well, Sergeant Ramsden. Then would you please refer to those notes now to answer the several questions I have already asked you, and the additional ones that I intend to ask a little later?"

"Sir, I cannot refer to them right now."

"Oh, and why is that?"

"I didn't bring them with me."

"But surely you have the habit of bringing your investigation notes with you to a trial for a crime in which you have been the chief investigator?" Shillington was looking directly at Henderson and Davidson as he asked this.

"But I don't have those notes, or any of the rest of the report of the investigation. At the end of each day, the procedure was that I handed my notes and report of the investigation to my boss."

"By whom you mean Sheriff Davidson?"

"Yes, Sheriff Davidson."

"Would you say, Sergeant Ramsden, that all these notes and reports are detailed and extensive and contain an accurate report of your investigation?"

"Yes, sir, I would."

"And so, to the best of your knowledge, Sheriff Davidson is still in possession of your notes and the report. Is that correct?"

"All I know is that I did as I was ordered by my superior. What happened to the notes after I surrendered them at the end of each day, I have no way of knowing. I presume that he handed them on to Prosecutor Henderson before the trial, although I don't know that for a fact."

"Thank you—for the moment, Sergeant Ramsden. You've been more helpful than you know, perhaps."

As Ramsden passed the prosecution table, Davidson tried looking at him but Ramsden didn't return the gaze. But if looks could kill, the look of anger, almost rage, on Davidson's countenance was committing manslaughter.

"Your Honor," Shillington said, "it's becoming apparent that there is a body of material, including possible evidence, that we on the defense team have not been shown. We have never received either a copy, or even an executive summary, of Sergeant Ramsden's report of his investigation after the crime, whereas the prosecution has direct access to that material through its relationship with the Sheriff's Office of Palm Beach County. That places our client and his attorneys at a distinct and unfair disadvantage as this trial continues. I request a sidebar conference with you and Mr. Henderson at the bench, or preferably in your quarters, to discuss this aberration that in our opinion borders on a violation of the Jencks Act requirement that notes of the investigation be shared. In fact, should there be exculpatory evidence contained in those notes, it adds up to a violation of the Brady rules."

"Mr. Henderson, are you amenable to this request?" Erskine asked, looking a little flustered.

"We have no reason to be anxious about Mr. Shillington's concerns, and so, yes, we are."

"Therefore, I announce that for today, the court is adjourned and will resume on Monday morning at 9:00 a.m." He slammed his judge's gavel with emphasis.

"YOUR HONOR," NELSON BEGAN ONCE he was satisfied that all the pertinent players in the case had arrived at Judge Erskine's chambers. "We wish to give advance notice that the defense intends to file a motion concerning several potential Brady disclosure issues that the prosecution has failed to correct, or even acknowledge, either to our satisfaction or according to the terms of the laws of the State of Florida."

"Whoa, hold on there, Counselor," Erskine responded. "That's an accusation of a serious violation of procedure by the state. I am sure we can resolve such an issue without a formal motion that would lengthen this trial. Isn't that why we are conferring here in my chambers?"

Nelson looked over at Shillington, who nodded decisively. Then he rose to assume the lead defense lawyer's role from his partner.

"Your Honor. We argue that ever since the commencement of this trial there has been an irregular, if not a technically illegal, pattern in the state's deliberate attempts to place the defendant and his defense team at a distinct disadvantage in this trial. It began, for instance, with the fact that the prosecution never communicated with us about the fact that the medical examiner had revised his estimated time of the victim's death. I am sure that an experienced prosecutor like Mr. Henderson is aware of how the medical examiner's new testimony is not favorable to the defendant. And yet the very first we, the defendant's attorneys, heard of the change in estimated time of death was not until Mr. Esteban was testifying on the witness stand. That left no time for Mr. Nelson and me to assess the new testimony and plan for the defense of the defendant. Your Honor, we protest. But we add that apparent withholding of vital information is only the beginning."

Henderson allowed no visible hint on his face that he was in any way embarrassed by the oversight or feeling guilty of a deliberate pattern of lack of communication with the defense.

"Only the *beginning*, Mr. Shillington?" Erskine asked.

"Yes, wasn't it as clear as day when Sergeant Ramsden hemmed and hawed his way through his testimony? He didn't even bother to bring his notes of the murder investigation along to a trial that will determine the fate of the defendant."

Shillington paused and looked with disdain at Henderson and Davidson. "We find it suspiciously *convenient*, if you will, that the deputy sheriff testified without his notes of the investigation, especially since his superior, Sheriff Davidson, has possession of those notes and has not provided the defense access to them. We can't be certain if Sergeant Ramsden failed to bring his copy of his notes on his own initiative, or, as we suspect, he was instructed to leave them at home by either the sheriff or prosecutor, or maybe both. But in any case, it amounts to a violation of Mr. Wilkerson's right to due process. According to the constitutional principle established in the wake of the United States Supreme Court's decision in *Brady v. Maryland,* the defense has every right and reason to expect full disclosure by the prosecution of any material that has the potential to exculpate a defendant."

Shillington continued the defense team's appeal to the judge. "Your Honor, we dispute the state's determination that notes containing the statements made by the defendant to law enforcement officers such as Sheriff Davidson on August 13 should be withheld from the defense. That action by the prosecution violates Rule 16 of the *Rules of Criminal Procedure.* We look to you, Your Honor, for a ruling that we are rightfully entitled to the sheriff and prosecution's records of these statements."

Shillington was looking accusingly at Henderson and Davidson beside him as he spoke. Henderson was shaking his head during Shillington's appeal to the judge. Charles noticed that Davidson had a defiant scowl on his face.

"Your Honor, we respectfully request not only those specific statements by our client— who, I should add, was pressured to make those statements without an attorney present, yet another in this series of violations of prosecutorial ethics—but, in addition, that the state turn over other documents that the state might have in its possession that could be judged as Brady material."

Judge Erskine looked at Henderson. "Mr. Henderson, let me ask you right in the beginning before we continue, do you have in your possession any material that could qualify as Brady material in this case?"

"No, sir, we do not," said Henderson.

Charles thought Henderson was almost too quick to reply.

Shillington and Nelson shot Henderson a look that could cut ice.

Henderson supplemented his reply. "Your Honor, if it please the court, I am well aware of our Brady obligations in this case without a paternalistic lecture by defense counsel, as I am in every other capital case in which we participate. You know that I have made Brady material available in the past. Furthermore, Your Honor, I object to the defense's contention that any of the statements made by the defendant to law enforcement officers constitute Brady material. I have reviewed those statements, and I can tell you categorically that they do not qualify."

Judge Erskine responded, "Nonetheless, I instruct the prosecution to provide my office, no later than 5 p.m. today, the contents in full of Sergeant Ramsden notes and reports on the investigation, and any notations entered subsequently into the reports by Sheriff Davidson, for my *in camera* review of them over this weekend. Mr. Henderson, please allow *me* to be the judge of whether anything you have allegedly withheld but now are instructed to supply qualifies as Brady material."

Erskine adjourned the meeting, and the participants departed until they were to report to Judge Erskine's chambers on Monday morning before the trial continued. Henderson and Davidson retreated to Henderson's office where he began to gather the material and documents that Judge Erskine had requested for his *in camera* inspection. He put a few files and papers into an 8-inch by 11-inch Manila envelope and at 4:50 p.m. ordered his clerk to walk to Erskine's office and hand the envelope to the judge.

ON MONDAY MORNING, THE Judge opened the meeting in his chambers. "I have reviewed the contents of this Manila envelope over the weekend, and I find that I must agree with Mr. Henderson that none of what I have reviewed qualifies as Brady material."

Henderson tried not to make the slight smirk on his face too obvious. "Thank you, Your Honor."

"I will now surrender this envelope and its contents to Misters Shillington and Nelson of the defense team for the defendant. I am grateful, Mr. Henderson, for your cooperation with the court in supplying the material as instructed."

Henderson nodded his acknowledgment of the judge's recognition. He had a victorious smile on his face.

"But at the same time," Erskine continued, "I must issue for the record a reprimand for the late date on which you made this material available for perusal by the defense. It should have been made available to the defense team at the outset of the trial. Do not let it happen again, Mr. Henderson."

CHAPTER 28

AS RELIEVED AS CHARLES' DEFENSE ATTORNEYS were that at last they had access to material that may or may not have the potential to provide a new perspective on the case, Shillington was visibly disappointed.

"Is this all?" he wondered out loud as he and Nelson conferred. "This envelope is skimpier than Twiggy in a bikini."

"Henderson and Davidson are still hiding something, I'm sure," Nelson agreed. "This is very much short of a full disclosure."

Rejoined Shillington: "We'll just have to find another way to insist on a more transparent divulgence."

Charles listened to his attorneys' disappointment, read their body language, and felt the noose tightening around his neck. He tried to chase the sensation away. He mined inside himself for the positive emotions he had stored there. He knew that he was innocent. He continued to hold on to the hope that somehow the criminal justice system would work and that his attorneys would find a way to get him vindicated. *Isn't that how the system is supposed to work?*

A deputy of the sheriff's office double-checked the handcuffs around Charles' wrists, took Charles by the arm, and led him out of the courtroom for the night.

"YOUR HONOR," SHILLINGTON PROTESTED first thing the next morning in the courtroom. "It is clear that this is a major criminal investigation and trial. All the prosecution has supplied the defense team thus far—and not at all on their own initiative or will—is an extremely thin envelope that contains more than 108 photographs taken at the scene of Mrs. Wilkerson's murder, which we have already seen. and the pages containing the notes of only the initial interview of the defendant conducted on behalf of the Palm Beach Sheriff's Department by Sergeant Ramsden on August 13. There are no results of Sergeant Ramsden's investigation in the days and weeks subsequent to that date. No formal report by the investigator. No material in any way helpful to the defense team."

"I'm sorry you feel that way, Mr. Shillington," Erskine lamented. "That's what I was given to examine *in camera* this past weekend. As I say, none of that qualifies as Brady material as you have contended."

"Still, our client remains at a significant disadvantage in this trial. His defense team is convinced, perhaps even more so since the prosecution's shoddy provision of material thus far, that there remains a substantial quantity of material germane to the case that has not been made available to us. The defense team has become hypervigilant to further episodes of incomplete divulging of information, or none at all, by the prosecution."

"The court is so advised. In the meantime we proceed with the trial."

It wasn't until now that the jury was escorted into the jury box.

"Mr. Henderson, do you have further witnesses for the prosecution?" Erskine asked.

"Yes, Your Honor, I do. I call Sheriff Davidson."

Sheriff Davidson approached the stand in full cowboy costume and swagger. He took the seat, a lanky, lean lawman with three decades' experience as a serious, dark-eyed character who carried the burden of dealing with the county's tragedies, protecting its citizens from the villains, the good guys from the evil. Davidson carried himself as though he was all that stood between the good folks of Palm Beach County and the horrible kind of fate that Dana Wilkerson had met.

Henderson stood up and approached the stand with a broad, friendly smile.

"Sheriff Davidson, can you tell the jury when you first met Mr. Charles Wilkerson?"

"Surely, Mr. Henderson. I met him in the front yard of his residence late on the morning after his wife's murder. At that time I told him that his wife was found murdered in a bedroom in the house."

"How did Mr. Wilkerson respond to such shocking and horrible news?"

"I thought maybe he hadn't heard me or allowed the news to penetrate. Because he simply asked about his son, Travis, and how he was, that's all."

"No questions to you about his *wife?* No outward sign of deep emotion? That's rather unusual, isn't it in your experience, Sheriff?"

"Not always, Mr. Henderson. Sometimes the husband already knows the fate of his wife and so doesn't respond emotionally at all."

"What did you conclude from Mr. Wilkerson's lack of emotion?"

"Once I thought about it, I came to the conclusion that Mr. Wilkerson already knew of his wife's murder by the time I met him."

"Someone else, one of your deputies at the house perhaps, someone other than yourself had informed him?"

"No, my deputies are well trained and know that it's not *their* responsibility to provide any information. That's *my* responsibility. They know that."

"Then how do you think, with all your experience as a sheriff, that Mr. Wilkerson would know?"

"There could only be one source of such information, Mr. Henderson."

"And that one source, you surmise, is what?"

"That he committed the actual murder of his wife *himself.*"

The members of Dana's family looked at each other with satisfaction. The husband of one of Dana's sisters made an enthusiastic fist pump. This is what they wanted to hear.

"Objection, Your Honor," Shillington exclaimed. "The witness's statement is irrelevant and constitutes an impermissible lay opinion."

"Objection sustained," he said.

Henderson continued. "You interrogated Mr. Wilkerson further at that point?"

"Yes, surely, since I had a very strong feeling that Mr. Wilkerson would be the prime and perhaps only suspect. It was too early to arrest him there on the spot, but I was pretty confident that we had found our man. I became even more certain of it when one of our deputies told me that he had found a cassette of a pornographic movie in the living room."

Henderson turned to face Judge Erskine. "Your Honor, I request permission from the court to show Exhibit B to the jury, the pornographic movie in question."

"Objection in the strongest possible terms, Your Honor! Again, the prosecution made no effort to inform the defense or make the video available to the defense for inspection in advance. Let me remind you, Your Honor, that this is a blatant violation of Rule 16 discovery."

"Overruled. I will permit the viewing of the video if it is germane to the case."

"I assure you, Your Honor, as you will see, the film is germane, *very* germane. It helps to explain Mr. Wilkerson's lascivious state of mind on the evening of August 12."

Shillington and Nelson glanced at each other in disbelief at the judge's ruling.

The audio-visual technician had the video ready on the VCR to show on a television monitor, which Henderson proceeded to place right in front of the jury. He stepped back to the VCR.

"We are ready for the audio-visual, Mr. Cartwright."

Cartwright started the VCR and images of topless women running on a beach appeared on the screen. The males in the jury watched the movie with a modicum of interest. Several of the female jurors looked away from the screen as though they were averting their eyes from footage of a grisly crime scene.

Charles could not look any of the jurors in the eye. He felt as though he were standing in front of the court with his pants down. He felt most awkward because his parents were in the courtroom. His pride, his privacy, and any remnant of honor was being stomped on in public.

When Cartwright turned off the VCR, no one spoke a word. There was a long, restless uncomfortable silence in the courtroom. No sound of trucks or car horns from the street outside. All one could hear was the steady hum of the ceiling fan, and inside Charles' head, the loud shouts of "Shame! Shame!"

Charles was hoping for a crack of lightning and the roll of thunder to break the sheer, excruciating silence.

Charles realized that a threshold had been traversed, a taboo had been committed, and that anything could happen now.

"Ladies and gentlemen of the jury. As you can see, these are the images that saturated Mr. Wilkerson's thoughts as his wife returned to the living room. His mood was—how do I put it? Highly stimulated sexually, to say the least. Anticipating sexual gratification from his wife. When he didn't get it, he was enraged. Enraged enough to beat her to death."

"Objection, Your Honor. Once again, the prosecution is giving an impermissible lay opinion."

"Sustained," Erskine agreed. "Let's move on to the next witness."

"Your Honor, the prosecution rests."

"Mr. Shillington?" Erskine asked.

"We call the defendant, Mr. Charles Wilkerson, to the stand."

He heard his name being called to the witness stand. Charles had known that this moment was coming. He had looked forward to the chance to tell his own side of the story. But after the soft-porn film, he started to dread the moment. But the time had come.

As he walked to the stand, Charles caught a glimpse of Henderson, who watched him approach the stand with an almost theatrical disgust on his face that Charles should be breathing the same air as the good people of Palm Beach County.

Charles' time on the stand started easily enough with his attorneys leading him through his life with Dana and the difficult years when Travis had been so sick after his birth.

Charles reminded himself of the witness coaching he had received from Cindy and Lauren in Miami. *Just answer what you're asked. Answer in short, declarative sentences. Don't overshare, and most importantly of all, hide nothing.*

Shillington continued. "Mr. Wilkerson, you heard Sheriff Davidson's testimony that he was surprised by what he described as your underwhelming emotional response when he informed you of the murder of your wife. Let me ask you: Do you have a comment now about the sheriff's testimony?"

"Yes, Mr. Shillington, I do. When I was informed by the sheriff of Dana's murder, contrary to the sheriff's impression, I did collapse, but not there on my front lawn. I had indeed fallen apart quickly, instantaneously, but quietly. Completely on the *inside.*"

"But," Shillington asked, "you would say that the way you reacted, collapsing privately, was typical of how you react in times of crisis such as that?"

"Yes, it was typical of *me*, Mr. Shillington. I have always compartmentalized my life and feelings. A part of me focused on caring for Travis. Another part of me was attentive to my work. Another part budgeted our finances and paid the bills. And a big part of me is still grieving deeply the loss of my wife. Please understand that, especially after I no longer had Dana, so this was the only way I could cope with it all. I had to erect walls between the different compartments of my life to prevent having to handle more than one or two at a time. If I didn't do that, I'd be consumed by a tsunami of despair and fear and anxiety."

"On the afternoon after the murder that the sheriff was describing, when he informed me of Dana's death, I felt terribly threatened and in danger."

"You felt yourself to be in danger or under threat?" Shillington asked.

"Yes, not by the real murderer, but honestly, by the sheriff himself." Charles looked over at Davidson, "He was very intimidating. His manner was gruff and brusque. It was accusatory almost right from the start, even though I protested over and over again that I was not guilty. I felt the whole time that he was terribly suspicious of me, almost as if he had already tried and sentenced me for the crime. So I didn't have much time to devote to my grief before I felt in his presence that my whole future was at stake. It felt very much like a matter of life or death to me and, of course, it does now more than ever."

Charles' voice trembled slightly.

"At that moment I decided to concentrate my attention for the time being on the perceived threat and get back to my grief when I could be home and do it in private."

Shillington nodded toward Henderson to indicate that he could proceed with his cross-examination.

Henderson rose from his seat almost threateningly.

"Mr. Wilkerson, your testimony sounds like the infantile jabbering of a juvenile."

"We object, Your Honor. The prosecution is using objectionable argumentative language with our client."

"Mr. Henderson," Erskine said, "please reserve your remarks about the defendant for your closing statement to the jury. Please do not do so during your cross-examination."

"Yes, thank you, Your Honor. To excuse your less than normal emotional response to the news of your wife's murder by claiming fear of the sheriff's intimidation is a complete chucking of your own responsibility. It leads me to ask you: Are you a grown-up human being or are you not?"

Charles was taken aback by the question. "Why, yes I am."

"Well, then, start acting like one before this court," Henderson roared. "Don't keep attributing your immature behavior to your fear of the sheriff. Stand up and be a man!"

"Objection, Your Honor. The prosecutor insists on badgering the witness."

ERSKINE LOOKED AS THOUGH he hadn't heard Shillington—or pretended not to. Charles looked at a loss as to how to proceed. Since the prosecution hadn't really asked a question, Charles chose to remain silent.

"To what do you attribute your decision to beat your defenseless wife in a rage—again and again and again?" Henderson contorted his whole body to demonstrate how he imagined the murderer had killed Dana. "You were reacting in a typical juvenile way to your wife's declining your invitation that evening for sex, were you not, Mr. Wilkerson? A grown man would have been able to accept his wife's feelings that evening and gone on with his life. In fact, ladies and gentlemen, what the defendant went on to do after he brutalized his wife to death was to masturbate, to pleasure himself, with the dead hand of his wife."

Charles shook his head demonstrably. A woman in the courtroom let out an instinctive gasp, "No!"

Henderson concluded his accusation. "Have you ever heard of anything more outrageous than such a selfish, perverted act?"

Shillington's face reddened in anger. "Objection, Your Honor. Such an improper theatrical exhibition as the prosecution has just now displayed has no place in a murder trial. The prosecutor is making a serious accusation against my client for an offense against decency without a shred of evidence. He's throwing accusations against the wall and seeing if any of them might stick."

"Sustained. Mr. Henderson, there's no need for such theatrics in my court."

Then a stunned silence descended on the courtroom once again. Charles was flabbergasted, horrified, helpless.

Henderson replied immediately. "Your Honor. But there is evidence. The forensic team discovered remnants of semen on the sheets."

Shillington was incensed. "Did the forensic team—from whom the defense team for the defendant has never seen even a trace of a report—estimate the age of the semen sample? Because it would not be at all unusual for a remnant of semen to be discovered on the sheets of just about any bed used by a married couple in the United States."

"Your Honor," Henderson said very sheepishly, "I retract the remark and am ready to pursue a totally different direction in my cross-examination."

"I instruct that the prior remark be struck from the record and the jury ordered to disregard it."

Charles was grateful but concerned that the jury had heard the baseless accusation and fortified their belief that he was some sort of sexual pervert.

So it went for the rest of Henderson's cross-examination of Charles. In almost a breathless, staccato fashion, Henderson launched again into a merciless onslaught of verbal invective and accusations. Charles' attorneys continued time after time to object to Henderson's abuse of his power to hit Charles inappropriately when he was pinned down and hopelessly backed into rhetorical corners. In some cases, the objection was sustained by the judge, but in others, it was denied. *He's got all the cards. I am just the latest joker.*

When Henderson finally ceased his barrage, Charles was shell-shocked and utterly exhausted. He didn't verbally respond to all of Henderson's wild accusations, but the unremitting bombardment of baseless allegations enervated him and drained his energy.

CHAPTER 29

"YOUR HONOR, I AM PREPARED NOW to make my closing argument," Henderson said.

"Then please proceed, Mr. Henderson," Judge Erskine permitted.

"Ladies and gentlemen, this crime was a gruesome, hideous, terrible one. During this trial the prosecution has demonstrated beyond a reasonable doubt that Dana Wilkerson was killed by her husband, the defendant, in a fit of rage because she refused to watch a pornographic movie with him and have sex with him on his birthday. He cold-bloodedly killed her by bludgeoning her to death while their three-year-old son lay asleep in an adjoining room. After the bloody murder, and still several hours before he was due at his job, he callously left the house, leaving no one to care for their son, who had seen her dead mother and was found by their neighbor several hours later wandering alone in the yard, distraught and fearful.

"The defendant, of course, has been denying this killing up and down, claiming that he is innocent of the crime and maintaining defiantly that some anonymous intruder is the guilty one. To make it look like that's the way it was, before he left for work the next morning the defendant pulled out a series of dresser drawers in the bedroom and rummaged through them, tossing things willy-nilly onto the floor. He was trying to outsmart the law enforcement officers that he knew would be on the scene as soon as someone discovered the victim's dead body. But there was no way he was going to outsmart a county sheriff who has over thirty years' experience on the job and whose instincts about the perpetrators of crime, especially in murder, are finely tuned.

"You have heard expert testimony, ladies and gentlemen, from the medical examiner who estimated the time of Mrs. Wilkerson's death to be no later than 1:15 a.m. That left the defendant more than four hours to arrange the evidence to make it appear that someone else, again this fictitious intruder, committed the horrible act.

"Ladies and gentlemen, you've also heard the testimony of a neighbor who testified that the defendant and his wife had a contentious marriage in which he would from time to time speak to her in a rage calling her by vile names.

"You have heard the facts. In performing your duty as citizens of this fine county, you will have no choice under the law other than to find Charles Wilkerson guilty of first degree murder in the death of his wife, an innocent victim. This county must be assured that the perpetrators of such vile acts are removed from our midst. Thank you."

"Mr. Shillington, are you prepared to offer your closing argument?" Erskine asked.

"Yes, Your Honor. I am." He looked down to his notes. "Ladies and gentlemen, thank you for serving on this jury and paying close attention to the testimony. Yours is an awesome responsibility, and I know none of you takes this responsibility lightly. An innocent man's life, that of the defendant, hangs in the balance.

"I see that you have been paying close attention to the evidence. But I ask you: Has there really been *any* evidence presented by the prosecution? Have you been told of a single shred of physical evidence that ties the defendant to the murder of his wife? Oh, to be sure, we've heard a lot of *conjecture* from the prosecution and his former father-in-law, Sheriff Davidson, about Mr. Wilkerson's guilt. But the laws of Florida do not permit a man to be condemned to death because of conjecture—only by *evidence* that leaves no room for a reasonable doubt. But there hasn't been such evidence whatsoever."

The courtroom was absolutely still. You could almost hear the jurors breathing.

"If there ever was a case when reasonable doubt is compelling in requiring a verdict of not guilty, this is surely one. It is the obligation of the prosecution, of the state, to prove guilt beyond reasonable doubt. Ladies and gentlemen, has the prosecution done this in this case? They haven't even come close.

"Where is the murder weapon with the defendant's fingerprints on it? I haven't seen it, that's for sure, and neither have you been shown such evidence. Ask yourselves why that is, ladies and gentlemen. That's because the defendant did NOT commit the murder. The defendant may be right that another intruder committed the crime and took the murder weapon with him. I ask you: Don't you have at least a shred of doubt now about Mr. Wilkerson's guilt?

"Then we have this pesky issue of the time of death. I repeat: As we presented during Mr. Esteban's testimony, the forensic scientific literature is almost unanimous in holding to the opinion that determining the time of death by analyzing the digestion of the stomach contents of a victim is not credible science and therefore not to be trusted in a murder trial. The medical examiner, on whose testimony the prosecution's case depends, is not trustworthy, plain and simple. Aren't the words "reasonable doubt" written across this so-called evidence in bright red letters, ladies and gentlemen?"

Charles glanced quickly at Mr. Randall in the jury box, the sole African American member of the jury and the one friendly face in the jury box. Charles thought Mr. Randall looked particularly engaged as he listened to Shillington. Charles could see that Shillington was appealing to the idea of reasonable doubt and aiming, at the very least, for a hung jury.

"Lacking any credible physical evidence, the prosecution has tried to replace evidence with witness testimony detrimental to the defendant. That he and his late wife had a contentious relationship, for instance. Are disagreements in a marriage, even about sex, all that unique to the defendant's marriage to his wife.? Such disagreements do not necessarily lead to murder, do they, ladies and gentlemen? Watching a soft porn movie together is no proof of who committed a murder. Remnants of seminal fluid from a man who slept every night for over ten years in a marriage bed with his wife is only a sign that they enjoyed marital relations from time to time, not proof that the defendant murdered his wife and then used her hand to pleasure himself. That is all the distorted conjecture of minds that are accustomed to scraping the bottom of the gutter."

"Objection, Your Honor," Henderson rose from his seat and declared. "There is no need in a legal argument to characterize the prosecution like that. Talk about conjecture!"

"The objection is sustained," Erskine responded. "Mr. Shillington, I am warning you."

"I retract that last statement. It is only a symptom of my serious frustration with the questionable conduct in this trial. Ladies and gentlemen, I am sorry that I had to interrupt my presentation. Allow me to continue. There is also the note that the defendant left for his wife to see as he left for work on the morning of August 13. It expresses his disappointment at not having sex with his wife the night before. How can it possibly be interpreted as some kind of cover-up for the crime? Does that make any sense? It can be taken at its face value, can it not, as an attempt by the defendant at reconciliation with his wife? The prosecution conjectures otherwise, however. *Chooses* to conjecture differently.

"You've heard the sheriff's testimony that he thought the

defendant didn't display sufficient sorrow and shock at the news of his wife's murder. That's rather presumptuous on the sheriff's part, isn't it? How can anyone of us, ladies and gentlemen, a neighbor, or even a sheriff, pry into the privacy of a grieving man's heart and presume to speculate how that person should grieve?"

Shillington pulled out a handkerchief from his trousers' pocket and wiped the beads of sweat from his forehead. He told himself he was doing fine, but he had to slow down, especially now that he was about to finish.

"In fact, ladies and gentlemen," Shillington pressed on, "I considered asking the judge for a directed verdict. What that would mean, should the judge agree to grant such a verdict, is that the defendant would be considered not guilty based on the fact that the prosecution has failed to prove its *prima facie* case. But you have heard the testimony yourselves, ladies and gentlemen, so you understand the lack of evidence that would be needed to convict the defendant as guilty beyond a reasonable doubt. You have made a commitment to follow the law here, and it can and should result in no verdict other than not guilty. Thank you."

Judge Erskine was beginning to raise his gavel in anticipation of any further objection from Henderson, but Henderson remained silent. Apparently, he was pretty sure that he already had the jury convinced of Charles' guilt.

ERSKINE HANDED THE CASe to the jury with his instructions before lunch. "Then, since we have heard the closing arguments," Judge Erskine announced, "I judge that we have sufficient time still this afternoon for the jury to be excused to begin its deliberation or possibly even arrive at a determination of guilty or not guilty in this case. I adjourn the proceedings until such time as the foreman of the jury is prepared to announce the verdict."

As they filed out of the courtroom, the members of the jury made no eye contact with Charles. He sat alone in the empty courtroom. He hadn't gone to lunch during the whole trial because he couldn't eat. He saw the rest of the world as a monstrous enemy now that was out to get him so he didn't want to be in a cafeteria that effused more hostility. He chose the solace of solitude instead. He paced the floor of the courtroom, looking out the windows, astounded that people on the street were going on with their lives while inside a catastrophic mockery of justice was unfolding.

THE JURY WAS OUT ONLY TWO HOURS.

As they returned to the courtroom, they seemed to be struggling to appear stoic, unemotional, and impartial.

The foreman of the jury rose when acknowledged by the judge. "Have you reached a verdict in this case?"

"We, the jury, find the defendant, Mr. Charles Wilkerson, guilty of the crime of first degree murder as alleged in the indictment."

The spectators gasped. Charles' mother cried out involuntarily.

Charles rose and looked pleadingly into Ruth Miller's eyes behind him. "I didn't do this! I didn't kill Dana. I swear," he mouthed the sentence silently.

Ruth's mouth formed a thin, tight straight line. She looked hard at Charles and then turned coldly away. That was to be the last time that Charles saw his mother-in-law.

"The state thanks the members of the jury," Judge Erskine announced. "But we will convene once again in the near future for the sentencing phase of this trial."

Charles saw Sheriff Davidson rise triumphantly and heard him taking the handcuffs from his belt. Then he heard the snap of the cuffs on his wrists.

Charles' knees buckled, and Shillington struggled to hold him up.

It seemed to Charles as though the word "guilty" was ringing through the courtroom. His mother, Eileen, reached out for him and held him as close as she could. His father stood beside her but looked rattled, not knowing what he should do, overcome, and teary-eyed.

Dana's sisters stood nearby wordlessly. They offered nothing in their stony expressions except righteous rage and an almost palpable disgust and then turned their backs and walked out of the courtroom.

Ramsden accompanied Davidson as he led Charles down a series of echoing stairwells to the ground floor. They flanked him as they stepped out into the overcast afternoon and marched past the crowd that had gathered. The onlookers gaped at Charles as though they were seeing Hannibal Lecter in the flesh, a man too dangerous to be in public without an armed sheriff and his deputies.

Someone from the crowd yelled encouragement to Davidson. "Good luck in the election, Sheriff."

Television cameras jammed into Charles' face, and the reporters waved microphones and fired off questions to Charles that felt to him more like thinly veiled taunts: "How do you feel about going to death row?" and "Why did you do it?"

Charles didn't answer any of the shouted questions from what felt like an angry mob. But he had come upon a single statement that summed up what he wanted the world to know. He repeated over and over again. "I didn't do it. I am innocent."

He was still saying it when Davidson put his big hand on Charles' head and pushed it down so that he could shimmy into the back seat of his cruiser.

It was over. He felt the weight of his crushing new reality. For the foreseeable future, death sentence or life in prison, either way, somebody else will be in charge of every decision of his life, what he ate and when, where he could lay his head down at night, when he lived and when he would die.

Charles had nothing. He felt like a nothing. The rest of the world felt that he deserved nothing.

CHAPTER 30

As Sheriff Davidson drove Charles the few blocks to the Palm Beach County Jail, Charles noticed that the sheriff made a detour through the business district of West Palm Beach. It was obvious that Davidson was in no particular hurry to get the convicted passenger in the back seat of his cruiser to his destination. It dawned on Charles that the Republican primary was scheduled for the following Tuesday. Like a Roman general parading his war loot through Rome, Davidson was driving a victory lap so that the citizens of the county could catch a glimpse of the "law and order" sheriff who had successfully apprehended a brutal wife-killer and made the county safe for the law-abiding residents. Charles was Davidson's living election advertisement.

At last, the longest possible journey to the nearby jail came to an end. Charles saw the ancient building out his window. It was familiar but triggered no particularly fond memories for him. This time Charles was escorted by two guards not to the general holding area but to a different part reserved especially for inmates who were on their way, eventually, to one of the more than fifty institutions operated by the Florida Department of Corrections.

As he entered the wing, Charles was given a Department of Corrections (DOC) uniform—not white this time but an orange jumpsuit, the unofficial uniform for death row inmates. He was ordered to empty his pockets before he changed and to surrender everything he had of value—his wallet, his watch, a large portion of his pride, and it occurred to him later, his prior identity. He was now Charles Wilkerson, soon to be identified by DOC number 0637095, as a convicted murderer.

One of the guards handed him what the DOC called a "mattress," which resembled a long, very worn-out, not-quite-filled pillow. Charles was directed to carry his shabby cushion to the "tank," two massive rooms holding ten or twelve prisoners. The tank was dark, dirty, and littered with gum wrappers and empty cigarette cartons. Charles managed to make out a kind of dayroom, a single shower, a sleeping section, and a communal toilet in the corner. The cramped space was packed. All the bunks already had mattresses on them, or else a sleeping body.

An older black inmate walked over to Charles as soon as the guards slammed the door shut behind them. Charles stepped back, on guard, defenses up. The older inmate, who said he was named Alphonsus, told Charles that there was an informal seniority system for doling out bunks. As soon as someone left, Charles would get that guy's bunk. He advised Charles to drag his mattress over to the wall in the common area and make a temporary sleeping spot for himself. Another inmate chimed in to say that he had claimed the space already. "Only had to sleep three nights so far on the concrete floor."

The older man who gave Charles the friendly advice was known as the "shot caller" by the others. He seemed to be deadly serious about his role and helpful, which Charles appreciated. The man seemed to know his way around the jailhouse rules and rituals. Later, Charles found out that he was an "institutional professional," having served time in Texas and Alabama as well as in a multitude of other facilities throughout Florida.

Charles would soon come to see that veterans of the system like Alphonsus were invaluable in keeping the jail running, if not smoothly, then at least predictably. Charles determined that his job was to pay heed to what Alphonsus advised and learn to adapt.

Charles slept fitfully that first night. He tossed and turned uncomfortably on a woefully thin pad on a concrete floor in a crowded room filled with violent, and violently snoring, men. The fateful announcement by the jury foreman earlier that day—"we find the defendant GUILTY of the murder of his wife"—the whole trial, and the entire six-month saga since losing Dana. played in a continuous loop in his feverish mind. He was stuck in a macabre theatre that showed the same heartbreaking film over and over again.

The next morning Alphonsus showed Charles the way to the shower. "The suits from Tallahassee were here a couple of days ago for inspection. They weren't pleased with some of the things they uncovered. For one thing, there was no hot water. We've been freezing our asses in cold showers every morning for weeks. We've complained about it to the guards but they haven't been in the mood to be helpful to a bunch of criminals like us. But the suits gave the order to the superintendent to turn on the fucking warm water. So today we're in for a treat."

There were several inmates already under the weak spray, soaped up and with shampoo in their hair. They were taking an icy shower just like the morning before. But then the scalding water hit.

Anguished cries of "What the fuck?" and "Shit!" rose out of the showers stalls. One man flung himself desperately out of the shower and onto the concrete floor with a scream and a bone-cracking landing. The man received first-degree burns on his upper torso. Neither Charles nor anyone else wanted a shower after that. Three days went by with no one bathing.

It had now been at least twenty-four hours since Charles had last seen Travis. At the time Charles did not know that it would be almost a full year before he would see him again. Now Travis would go on to be raised by a family that completely and thoroughly despised Charles. During a recess in the trial, Shillington told him that Dana's younger sister, Danielle, and her husband, Randy, were applying to the courts to assume legal custody of Travis. He learned from Shillington that the judge who would rule on custody was the same one who oversaw Charles' conviction, Julius Erskine. Small world.

Because Charles was in the custody of the Florida Department of Corrections, he was not permitted to attend the custody hearings. On the morning that Judge Erskine would announce the results of the custody hearing, Charles would be on his way to the FSP.

Every morning, a guard would walk up to the bars of the tank with a clipboard and read off the names of inmates who would be transported to Raiford on that day. Charles listened until he heard his name called. He approached the bars and asked the guard at what time he should expect the bus to be ready to take him and other prisoners northward.

"Shit, man. I don't have a clue. They don't tell us such things. Just be ready to get your black ass out of here at any time of the day."

A fortyish white inmate approached Charles. "Don't ask too many questions, friend. Just be glad you're getting out of this hole."

"Glad about going up the river to a more high security joint?" Charles asked, surprised.

"Yeah. It's nothing but just sitting on your ass around here, doing nothing. No TV, no radio, no newspaper, no make-work projects, no visitors. Just sitting around and waiting on their schedule."

Without warning, a guard came over to Charles. "You've got a visitor: the Sheriff of Palm Beach County and a couple of newspaper reporters."

"Damn it!" Charles was concerned that these unexpected visitors would cause him to be late or to miss the bus to the FSP.

"Will the bus wait for me while I take this visit?" Charles asked the guards with some urgency.

"They'll be pissed off if you're late, but the bus can't leave until every inmate on the list is on it and ready to go. Be quick with your visit."

Charles was self-conscious with the eyes of many of the others waiting to be transported peeled on him. He remembered that he had been told that only he and the sheriff were permitted to make any public statements about the trial or his conviction. Charles could speak with the press only with the sheriff in the same room. Sitting in a tiny, windowless room, dressed in his orange jumpsuit with Sheriff Davidson just a few feet away, Charles was eager to tell his story. "My trial was a total farce where the prosecutor merely threw inflammatory accusations at me in place of any real evidence. It was quite a diva act, shouting at me, pounding the table, crying crocodile tears, overwhelming the jury with his emotions."

Sheriff Davidson remained mute but all the time was rolling his eyes. *Fuck the sheriff. What can he possibly do to me now? I don't give a rat's ass what he thinks of what I am saying, the God damned cretin. He's probably had plenty of opportunity to retell the lies he has sprouted before. Or if he hasn't, he'll have these reporters all to himself to poison their curious minds with exaggerated lies about the now notorious wife-killer he has gotten off the streets. This interview is perfect timing for the Republican candidate to be the next District Attorney of Palm Beach County.*

The reporters gave the impression at least that they were writing down what Charles was saying, but Charles doubted that any of it was sinking in. *They probably think that here's another run-of-the-mill black convicted pervert. They probably conclude that every statement I am making is little more than evidence of a sick, twisted criminal personality now trying to gain sympathy for his selfish, sick cause. Davidson must be loving this. Seeing me lose the argument all over again. I'll never give another interview again, I swear.*

CHAPTER 31

WHEN THE VISIBLY PERTURBED CHARLES arrived at the location to board the bus, a guard angrily put his legs in shackles. "It's about fucking time, Wilkerson. You kept us all waiting."

As he stepped onto the bus, he heard the mumbling of some of the inmates.

"I'm sorry, fellas. I got a last second visit that held me up. The visit was useless. If I had known in advance, I would have refused it and we would have been on the road by now."

One of the older inmates on the bus answered back. "Now that's something you should never do. Never refuse a visit. It's one of the few ways you can get a break from the endless routine of death row."

"I'll try to remember that advice. Thanks," Charles replied to the fiftyish, maybe sixtyish, passenger. His black face etched with lines of wrinkles showed that he'd been around the block a few times and knew what he was talking about. *A part of my education into the unfamiliar ways of death row.*

About a half-hour drive from the Diagnostic Unit to which Charles and all other inmates entering Florida prisons needed to report for a medical evaluation, the bus turned onto another highway. Neat but utilitarian bungalow homes with huge yards lined both sides of the highway, homes for some of the higher ranking officers of the various prisons in the vicinity and their families.

The bus went around another turn in the road. "There she is, the infamous Rock," shouted one of the inmates near the front who stood and turned to face the rest of the passengers. He looked a little older than the other peach-fuzzed men on the bus. He was an obvious returnee to the Raiford collection of prisons and knew the sights enough to serve as a self-appointed tour guide.

The "Rock" looked right off the set of a 1920s vintage crime movie—a huge, mountainous, intimidating brick edifice built in 1913. It stood alone, separate from newer buildings nearby.

"Don't be concerned, gentlemen," the "tour guide" assured the passengers. "Notice that the windows are all boarded up. The place has been abandoned. All the prisoners have been transferred elsewhere. A few years ago the Florida legislature finally surrendered the Rock to the rats, who were winning the war for possession of the place anyway. It's been condemned. Those of you fortunate enough to have long enough sentences may still be here when they start destroying the place and mercifully putting an end to its misery. Of course, like everything else the state of Florida does, it will take a while. They say there will be a new state-of-the-art correctional facility built in its place."

The bus driver continued for about another mile eastward toward Starke. "Take a look on your right, fellahs. Look first at the one-story part of the building closest to the highway. I hope none of you will have to spend any time in the few cells in that wing. They're reserved for 'death watch' for those inmates to whose death warrants our illustrious governor has attached his signature. 'Old Sparky" sits in the room at the end closest to the road, the room that has the double doors so that the undertaker can wheel the poor dead bastard out of the prison. After Texas, ours is the second-busiest electric chair in the United States. Believe it or not, a lot of people are proud of that, especially the politicians."

Charles took a quick glance but couldn't look too long. The thought of possibly ending up on Old Sparky for a crime he hadn't committed suddenly sent a shiver down his spine.

The bus turned off the highway. With the bus windows open because of the heat, Charles could hear inmates calling to each other through the open windows of the prison, sometimes hurling violent threats. *The noise inside must be unbearable.*

The bus stopped by a walkway leading into the prison. Charles looked at the entry door and beheld the portal to his new life.

The motley crew stepped off the bus. The ones ticketed for death row could be recognized by their telltale orange jumpsuit.

Charles' name and that of a few others in orange jumpsuits were called out, and their names were checked off on a list. They were directed into a cage made of chain-link fencing. It was then that Charles saw the threatening rounds of razor wire that formed the perimeter of the prison complex, glinting in the late-evening sunshine. Tall, imposing towers were positioned every twenty yards or so, each with two or more guards stationed on top, rifles at the ready to fire at anyone who had managed to escape from the inside as far as the razor wire impediment.

For what seemed to Charles like an hour, his group of inductees to death row sat on the austere wooden bench inside the cage while groups of the other inmates were led into the prison. *This must be how my ancestors felt waiting on the dock in Charleston to be sold into slavery. I'm just a piece of state property to be sold up the river.*

Though he was careful not to stare at anyone else, Charles took a quick visual inventory of the group. This prison was built and intended for the hardest nuts to crack in the Florida penal system: the murderers, the bullies, the rapists, and occasionally, Charles surmised, an innocent man, wrongfully convicted, not belonging there at all, mixed into the collection. Some of the guys had messed up at some other institution by attacking staff, attempting escape, or behaving in a way that made the prison administrators bent on making their lives more miserable as payment.

Unlike everyone else, my days here will be relatively few. This hellish nightmare will be cut short. The whole mess and confusion will get straightened out. I just have to learn the ropes here for a little while and stay alive until the truth emerges and, in a flood of guilt and shame and remorse, the judge who sent me here will set me free.

At long last a guard escorted the death row inmates into the huge main building. Charles almost tripped. The chain linking his two feet together was so short that if an inmate didn't reduce the length of his step, he'd be lying flat on his face on the hard concrete sidewalk in no time.

Within a matter of a few steps inside, another guard led the men one by one through a metal detector. The detector made a hellish, piercing sound because of the handcuffs and manacles. The guard ignored the alarm. Once the inmate had passed through that, another guard frisked his body thoroughly. *Do they really think we've gotten this far into the prison carrying a weapon?*

Inmates were separated one by one from the group and escorted by other guards to other wings. Charles was given the familiar half-assed pad the DOC insisted was a mattress. He was led into a cell block and ordered to haul his mattress three floors up to his assigned cell, C1-3-13T. When he got there, no one was home. The bunk in the cell appeared to have an owner, however. So he dragged his mattress back down and informed the guard that the cell was already occupied.

"C1-3-13T? No, that's your cell, boy." He held up his clipboard for Charles to see. "Look, it says so right here. Go back up and take the mattress already on the bunk and bring it down here. Then make the bed with *your* mattress."

Charles obeyed and did as he was ordered. He made his bed and lay down on the bunk and, in short order, fell asleep. He was awakened in the dark a few hours later when he felt another man trying to get under his blanket.

"What the hell?" the other man uttered. "Who the fuck is in my bunk? What's going on here?"

Charles, still groggy from sleep and alarmed from being awakened without warning, explained to the agitated man that he had been ordered here to this bunk and to replace the mattress and blanket that were on the bed with his own. "No hard feelings, brother. Just doing what I was told."

"Man! They're always fucking up things like this. Their right hand never knows what their left hand is doing. As long as they don't confuse matters like this when it's time to be called to death watch. Well, it's too late to get this straightened out now. I'll have to see what they can do in the morning. I'll just sleep here in the corner on the floor for now."

Charles realized that he had dragged the guy's mattress and blanket downstairs to the guard. "Here," he said to the man while sliding out from on top of his mattress, "take mine for the night. Here, take the blanket, too. I'll be all right."

The man did take the mattress and blanket and laid them down on the floor for a makeshift bed. Not a word of thanks to the newbie, however.

Again, though he was tired, he had trouble falling and staying asleep. He could hear a faint melancholy sound from the cells down the line. He listened more carefully. It was the haunting sound of a grown man crying, calling for his mother. "Mama, mama, help me. I can't make it."

In these battered cell blocks, built of concrete and steel, men every bit as hardened as that concrete and steel were weeping in the dark. Captivity does brutal things to a man, no matter what he's done to lose his freedom.

He wished he had come equipped with an on-off switch for his brain when his mind was racing in overdrive. *What I would give. For the soft bed in our bedroom. To have my old life back. For a way to turn the calendar back to the days before my birthday. To caress Dana and hear her sweet voice assuring me that I would be able to survive in this God-forsaken hell.*

He lay on the bunk staring at the ceiling in the dark, crying silent tears for himself, for Dana, for Travis, for whatever lay ahead for him.

Chapter 32

Florida State Prison, Raiford, Florida

BY NIGHT, CHARLES WAS PREOCCUPIED with thoughts of his survival, fully focused on the novel dilemmas he faced every day, the decisions he had to make on his feet. He was surrounded by violent men, and their almost universal ignorance about the world beyond the walls of FSP. How could he stay alive? How could he get out of here?

By day, he kept his head down and his mouth shut, worked at the few cleaning jobs that staff assigned to him, and waited to hear from his attorneys, who were preparing the automatic appeal that the state mandated for inmates found guilty of capital crimes.

One morning Charles was told he had a telephone call from his attorney.

"Hello, Charles. It's Shillington. First, how are you faring at the Florida State Prison?"

"Oh, I don't know. It's not easy to get adjusted here. But I'll find a way."

"That's good to hear, Charles. I'm sorry you have to be there. We haven't forgotten you."

"That's reassuring, Steve. But I'm afraid I will have to let you go as my attorneys. 'No money, no funny,' you know how it goes. I've drained my resources in order to retain you and Bryce, and I don't feel comfortable asking my parents to pick up the legal tab for whatever is next."

"Don't worry about that, friend. After that phony showpiece of a trial, Bryce and I are more certain of your innocence than ever. We've agreed to keep your case and represent you *pro bono*."

"*Pro bono*? You mean, no cost to me? Wow! That's generous of you. I don't know if I can accept that."

"Oh, sure you can. I don't need to buy another Porsche. I really feel energized and challenged right now to take on Henderson. I also really want to unveil Davidson's corrupt practices for the public to see so that he doesn't get elected as the Palm Beach County District Attorney. The county deserves better. To have the opportunity to accomplish both those goals, man, I'd pay for the privilege."

Charles listened with tears in his eyes. "Thank you, Steve. Your faith in my innocence means more to me than you can know."

"Just know that now that the stakes are higher after your conviction, nothing good will be automatic or easy. We'll have to fight harder than ever to overturn a guilty verdict or get an amendment to it in some way. We'll start with the appeal."

SHILLINGTON CALLED BACK TO the prison just a few days later.

"Hello, Charles. I'm floating ten feet off the floor! Something unexpected has come up in your case."

"To make you fly that high, it must be good news."

"Potentially so. It's a traditional practice in capital cases in Florida for both sides, the prosecution and the defense, to meet with members of the jury after the verdict and the sentencing to review the procedure. We want to gain some insight into what aspects of your case led the jurors to reach their verdict. These are usually inconsequential pro forma meetings that don't interest me a lot. Except *this* time. We received a call from a Jennifer Lipkus, an assistant prosecutor in Henderson's office. She said she would share some new information that we might want to hear as we prepare the appeal."

"New information?"

"I don't know what it is until we show up for the meeting. But I have heard this from a trusted colleague: He told me over lunch the other day that immediately after the trial Miss Lipkus tendered her resignation from Henderson's office effective at the end of this month."

"Resignation? Interesting timing."

Apparently, she was pissed off that she was given a minor, almost invisible, role in prosecuting your case. She was pissed at Henderson for stealing all the thunder to further his own career. So she feels under no compunction to keep quiet about a few things in which Henderson took a short cut with the court."

"A few things?" Charles remarked. "How about *most* things? What's that old saying? That 'hell has no fury like that of a scorned woman?'"

Shillington chuckled at Charles' joke. "It will undoubtedly be an interesting meeting. I'll call again after the meeting."

HENDERSON DIDN'T EVEN CONSIDER attending the confab with

Shillington, Nelson, and a few members of the jury to be worth his time, so he gave Lipkus permission to represent the prosecution.

She opened the meeting. "I've been looking forward to this session since the actual trial for your client, Mr. Shillington. This is probably my last duty in the employ of the District Attorney's office. Mr. Henderson sends his regrets that his schedule precludes his being present. Frankly, Mr. Shillington," she lowered her voice and confided to Steve conspiratorially, "it may be just as well."

Shillington looked into her face with his eyebrows raised.

"I'm aware," Lipkus continued as she rearranged herself on the chair, "that the defense protested several times during the trial that they suspected there was pertinent material missing from what the prosecution supplied to the defense."

Shillington's ears perked up. "Yes, Miss Lipkus, we did. It was terribly difficult, to say the least, to build our case in defense of the defendant with only bare skeleton information."

"Mr. Henderson chose not to be present. But I have to say that during the trial I attempted several times to ask Mr. Henderson about the trove of information that the deputy at Sheriff Davidson's office provided to the prosecution. I saw the file containing all the notes from his interviews and his investigation of the case." Making a hand gesture displaying the three or so inch gap between her index finger and her thumb, she said, "It was at least *this* thick."

Shillington was floored at her gesture and looked at Nelson and nodded. Neither was surprised.

"That file was certainly thicker than the lean little envelope of notes Mr. Henderson supplied the court and us."

"Exactly, Mr. Shillington. I hope that explains why I am resigning as assistant prosecutor. I don't want to be a part of such shady practices, nor do I want my career thrown off course and jeopardized by any association with them."

Nelson asked, "Miss Lipkus, do you know if there was any exculpatory evidence buried in that inch-and-a-half-thick file? Because Mr. Shillington and I theorized that certainly, there must have been because Mr. Henderson seemed so intent on keeping the full contents of the file hidden from the court."

"I can't swear that there was for a fact. I never had an opportunity to inspect the contents." Her voice waxing sarcastic, she continued, "I'm just a *female* assistant prosecutor. Mr. Misogynist Henderson would never share such a key strategic file with *me*. But knowing how Mr. Henderson often behaves in court, it would not at all surprise me if there was."

Shillington and Nelson nodded their heads in agreement.

"I find I must apologize on the prosecution's behalf to the court in some way," Lipkus said sadly, "and to you, the defense. Hiding an offense file containing evidence favorable to the defendant is not just inconsiderate and very unprofessional. As you know, it is also purely illegal."

SHILLINGTON TELEPHONED CHARLES a third time."Well, Charles, I wish you could have been there. Henderson never showed up but sent a helpful assistant prosecutor instead. She was nothing short of fantastic. She told us how there was a thick file of Sergeant Ramsden's notes and Lord knows what else not included in the scrawny envelope Henderson surrendered to the judge. She thinks there might have been material in the file that was favorable to your case."

Charles felt a wave of elation. "The bastard was caught with his hand in the cookie jar."

"We have this invaluable information now, but we have to be careful to use it prudently," Shillington said soberly. "Bryce and I made an appointment right away with Judge Erskine to report what we had heard. We told him that, in light of the new information, we were requesting a new trial. He said he would sleep on it and consult with a few other judges and inform us the next morning."

"And did he?" Charles wanted to know.

"Yes, he did. The news is not all good, mind you. But I think you will be happy with at least a part of his answer."

"Give me the bad news first," Charles said.

"Erskine wouldn't grant a new trial. We even made a motion to dismiss the verdict based on the failure of the prosecution to turnover Brady material. Erskine wouldn't budge. Judges seldom do. It means his admitting that somehow he did a bad job overseeing the first trial."

"But he called us back into his office later that afternoon to inform us that he had been advised to modify your sentence."

"Modify it?"

"Yes, change it significantly. Revise it. Reduce it. Erase the former sentence. Enter a new one. Declare that you will have life in prison instead of the death penalty. A lifetime behind bars is no picnic. But just think, Charles. No execution hanging over your head!"

"And I was always skeptical about miracles. Suddenly, I'm more open to them now. I would never in a million years have expected this."

"I wish I had a bottle of champagne and glasses for you and me to toast this one."

CHAPTER 33

A FEW DAYS LATER CHARLES WAS ordered to take off the orange jumpsuit and surrender it to one of the guards. In exchange, he was given a tight, white, t-shirt and grey casual slacks and told that the administration was arranging for a new cell for him because he was moving off death row to "the general population." He'd stay in his current cell on the row for a few more nights.

When the overhead lights were turned off down the wing at 10:30 p.m., Charles climbed into the bunk. He stared again at the ceiling above him and waited to fall asleep feeling cleansed, even though it had been several days since he had been able to take a shower. He underwent a baptism. It felt as though a former identity that besmirched him for a relatively brief time had been washed off his back and shoulders. A dark stain had been scrubbed off his forehead. He was no longer Charles Wilkerson, condemned murderer with an address on death row.

I heard news today of a miracle that will change my life for the rest of my days. I'm still confined to this prison, but I suddenly feel as though I can fly. Is there any reason why I can't expect some other miracle while I'm here?

With those thoughts Charles fell asleep.

HE WAS AWAKENED BY THE SLAM of the door at the end of the corridor. *Just the guards doing the count at the end of the day. Sixth count this day. Do the numbers really change from hour to hour?*

Charles had been in a deep sleep. His eyes were heavy. He closed his eyes again.

Not for long. He heard the guards. "Odom, what number did you say is Wilkersons'?"

"I told you at least twice, you moron. It's C1-3-3T."

"It's fucking hard to read the numbers in the dark."

"Well, moron, use your fucking flashlight."

Charles shut his eyes tight when the guard turned on the industrial-strength Streamlight they carried and shone it at the head of his bed.

"Voilà, fellahs! Here he is."

In the contrast between his dark cell and the intense light from the flashlight, Charles could only make out the figures of four or five men but was too blinded by the light to see the features on their faces.

"Good evening, Wilkerson. Sorry to interrupt your sleep. But we were talking tonight and realized we'd never given you a decent welcome to death row. We thought that just wouldn't do. So we're here to do that now. We wouldn't want you to think poorly of our hospitality. We Union County folks are a friendly bunch, aren't we, fellas?"

Four voices joined together to chant, "Yes, we are."

"Now, come on down out of your bunk, boy. Down *here*. Do you hear me?"

Charles was confused by the order. The rules and regulations were that once the lights on the wing were turned off, the inmates were to be and remain on their bunks.

The guard sounded impatient. "I guess you didn't hear me. I ordered you to come down out of that fucking bunk. Come on, boy. On the double. It's an order."

One of the guards had run out of patience. He stepped up the metal ladder and reached up into the top bunk. He grabbed the blanket and threw it angrily off Charles and down onto the floor.

"Don't you know to obey orders, boy? That's one of the most basic rules of prison life. The sergeant ordered you to get down out of your bunk to the floor where we can get a good look at you."

Charles heard some moaning and grunting from the neighboring cell. "What the hell's going on out there? Some of us are trying to sleep."

"Just mind your own fucking business, Cooper. That's the second most basic rule of prison. You've had your black ass on death row long enough to know that."

Cooper must have learned the first rule very thoroughly. There were no more questions from that cell.

Charles decided to risk coming down out of the bunk to floor level.

"That's more like it, boy. We can't very well do the welcome for you if you stay in bed."

Charles was very wary. These were four or five guys much bigger and heftier than him. If they decided to beat him now, he wouldn't stand a chance. He kept his eyes wide open for any sudden actions by the guards.

The apparent leader of the pack (it must have been Odom) took a tight hold of Charles with the biceps on his left arm and said, "Follow us, Wilkerson. We're going to give you a tour of the rest of the wing you never get to see."

He gave Charles a rough shove, and Charles felt one of the other guards grab his right arm.

The guards shoved him through the door at the end of the corridor. Charles saw a corridor almost identical to the one they just left.

"Just keep going until we tell you otherwise, Wilkerson. Consider this our complimentary rehearsal for your long walk down these corridors one day in the future to the cells on death watch."

"Actually, gentlemen, this is not necessary. My sentence has been changed to life in prison. The death sentence has been reversed. You haven't been told?"

Suddenly, he felt a bony fist smacking against his right cheek. Charles lost his balance and pummeled to the floor of the corridor.

"Did the sergeant order you to speak, boy? Don't get smart with us. We do all the talking on this tour, understand?"

Charles lifted himself off the floor. He shook the dust off his clothes. He scanned the faces of the guards but it was too dark in that corridor, too. With his tongue, he sensed a warm, salty liquid inside his cheek. He ran his hand along the outside surface of his cheek to check for external bleeding. He still tasted the blood on the inside of his cheek. He began to roll his fist into a ball, but then thought better of it. *They have all the advantage. They'll beat me to a pulp.*

"Just keep walking, like I told you, until we give the order to do likewise."

Charles progressed straight ahead toward the brown metal door at the end of the corridor.

"Just stop in front of the door and wait."

When Charles arrived at the door, he read the sign affixed to it. "Staff only beyond this point."

Odom sorted through the numerous keys on the chain on his belt. He picked one and inserted it into the keyhole in the door. He pushed the door open and ushered Charles through it. The other guards followed.

"You're in the inner sanctum of the prison now, Wilkerson. Once one of you has been led to one of the cells in this wing, they seldom get back out. These are the death watch cells reserved for wife-killers like you."

One of the guards behind Charles pushed forward so that Charles almost tripped.

"The next stop is the death chamber. No inmate who has ever been led there has ever walked out. He's been rolled out on a gurney into a waiting hearse."

One of the guards grabbed Charles' t-shirt at his chest and pulled him closer to his face.

"That's what you have to look forward to, boy!"

Two guards grabbed Charles, one by each arm, and forcibly lifted him into the electric chair.

"Your skinny black ass fits perfectly into this old chair. Are you comfy, boy?"

"I told you fellas that my death sentence has been dropped. I won't be brought here."

One of the guards reached up and walloped Charles on the cheek. "Didn't we tell you that *we* would do any talking that's needed? Your job is to shut your fucking mouth, you insolent black son-of-a-bitch."

Another guard struck Charles on the other cheek for good measure.

Odom intervened. "I'm sorry, then, that we won't be seeing you much in the future. So we want to leave you a farewell gift to remember us by as you move into a new wing with all your jungle bunny friends. You ought to feel at home there with all those young dudes from Colored Town, or whatever the hell they call it now."

"I think you mean Overtown, Odom."

"Shut the fuck up, McGriff. I don't need you to correct me, you smart ass. He knows what I mean." Odom retorted. "Don't you, Wilkerson?"

Charles tried to respond. "Yes, sir. I know what you mean."

"Get out of that chair, Wilkerson, and stand up on the floor tall and straight." Odom ordered.

Once Charles was down, Odom landed a heavy punch on Charles' stomach. Charles panted for breath. Before he was able to get air, the next guard struck him from behind in the small of his back with his fist. Charles bent his body forward at his waist from the force of the blow.

"Now guys, not in the face, you hear?" Odom shouted at the others. "Don't mess with his face. If the superintendent sees any scars or wounds on his face, there'll be no end to the questions."

A third guard swung his fist and punched Charles squarely in the stomach again. Charles crumbled helplessly to the concrete floor. A trickle of blood oozed out of his mouth.

"Don't forget our kindness to you for showing you around the place, Wilkerson, when you move to that other wing," Odom said. "The guards on the other wings are too afraid of the inmates to give you a proper welcome as we have."

Then Odom kicked the prone body on the floor mercilessly, again in the gut. On the strength of Odom's boot striking him, Charles' body snapped back and caromed off the wall.

Their mission for the evening accomplished, Odom and the guards caught their breath and gave Charles a few short minutes to recover from the blows. Then they led him, limping and favoring his stomach, out of the death watch wing and back to his cell.

CHAPTER 34

"Here's your mail, Wilkerson."

For inmates in a prison, just as for college students living in residence halls on campus, those are the best words of any day. Mail is a living connection with the outside world.

The bigger Manila envelope was from the First District Court of Appeals in Tallahassee, Florida. Charles had already been informed by Shillington of the failure of the appeal, but he ripped open the envelope anyway, and devoured the sheets of paper inside the way a starving man would eat a juicy steak. He lay on his bunk in his cell, trying to make heads or tails of the legalese. All he understood from the letter was that Shillington and Nelson were on his side, and the judges on the panel reviewing the application were not.

He also knew, however, that he had never read words on a page that held such power. His very life hung in the balance—his freedom and his chance at a future.

As an inmate in the general population now, Charles suddenly had the freedom to walk down the corridor to the library, with a pass, of course, to see what he could learn in the law books there.

Charles also knew that at FSP there was an underground cottage industry of "jailhouse lawyers." One of them would probably have read for him the letter from the court of appeals and given him an opinion about the worth of his appeal—for a fee, of course. But since he already knew the result of the appeal—and because in the short time he had been locked up, he knew that most of the "jailhouse lawyers" were not worth the price of their fee—he declined to use one despite the fact that he was propositioned for business several times as soon as he was seen leafing through a law book. Most of the so-called lawyers were known to use their "expertise" as a way to scam the uneducated or unwary out of the little money they had.

So he decided to learn something by himself. He joined the "legal eagles" in the library, reading and endeavoring to comprehend opinions and arguments, case laws, and the odds for an appeal like his.

The library was a good, relatively safe place to pass a few hours in the middle of a day. Unlike the cells, the library was air conditioned. Every now and then he would interrupt his reading to ponder his options inside the prison for finishing the college education he began at FAU years ago.

Meanwhile, his education in the particular mores of prison life continued apace. Privacy, he learned, was a monumentally valued commodity. Not that real privacy was ever possible in prison, but prisoners developed small courtesies that afforded at least the *illusion* of privacy. Like the others, Charles learned when to look away, when to put on his SONY Walkman headset, and when to yield room to the others. There was an unspoken rule among the inmates that they were never to look inside another man's cell as they walked by in the corridor. That was considered highly disrespectful, even dangerous.

There was, for instance, an inmate named Hector, who either didn't know about the unspoken rule or chose to ignore it. Whenever he passed a row of cells, especially if they were empty temporarily, he would stop, turn, and gawk inside. A few of the inmates warned Hector about his habit but it did no good. Hector just kept on gawking.

One afternoon he was waltzing toward the dayroom to join the others watching TV—invariably, the TV was set on the channel that showed NBA basketball games or World Wrestling Entertainment (WWE). On his way, Hector took his time. He walked slowly down the row of cells, pausing to stare into each empty cell. Eventually, he went on to inspect the *wrong* cell. The inmate who lived there was waiting for him. As soon as Hector stepped into the cell, he got a cup full of urine thrown in his face.

"This is what a pisshead deserves," the resident inmate said.

After that, Hector learned the lesson.

CHARLES HAD WAITED an entire year to see Travis. The other envelope in the morning's mail delivery had the return address of the Florida Department of Child Protective Services. It informed Charles that his son and his legal guardian, Danielle Brooks, Dana's older sister, would visit him on the upcoming weekend.

Charles was too full of adrenaline to finish reading the complete letter. He was so eager to be with Travis again after such a long time. But as soon as he savored the feeling of joyful anticipation, he was nagged by fear. *Does Travis even know who I am? What has he been told about his father by Dana's family? Does he imagine me now as some kind of monster who would kill his mother? What does he remember of me? Will he even still recognize me?*

The night before their scheduled visit, Charles lay sleepless on his bunk, trying to pull himself out of the day-to-day grind of prison life. For the first time in ages, he treated himself to the luxury of thinking about his son. He hadn't before because thinking about Travis always made him sad. The smile on his face would vanish as he thought of all that he had lost.

But on this night Charles fully conjured the sensation of holding his little boy. He could almost feel him in his arms. The way Travis used to drape himself around Charles' neck, and how Travis would lay his sleepy head on Charles' shoulder, or dig his heels into his father's side to hold on tight. He recalled the way Travis's soft hair always seemed to smell of baby shampoo, and the way Travis's face would light up when Charles returned from a day at Winn-Dixie. *This is what I will be thinking of as I sit in the waiting room before they arrive.*

But once again, reality would turn out to be more complicated than daydreams.

Judge Erskine had awarded custody of Travis to Danielle and her husband at the time. But she and her husband had divorced not long afterward. She was now single and living in a small, one-bedroom apartment in Fort Lauderdale with no other children. Perhaps Judge Erskine overlooked, or more likely, had *chosen* to overlook that in the past Danielle had had extended stretches of unemployment and being adrift. She had lived briefly with Dana and Charles during one of those blue periods. But after Dana's death, Charles had felt Danielle pulling away from him, and they had been estranged ever since.

Now twelve months after his conviction, Charles had not heard from Danielle or learned anything about Travis's day-to-day life. *Who would babysit him if Danielle had landed a job again? Was Danielle dating someone, and was this new guy nice to Travis?*

There was no legal requirement for Danielle to share that kind of information with him. The custody arrangement simply ordered that after this first year Danielle bring Travis to visit Charles in prison every six months until Travis turned eighteen years old. Before the custody hearing, Charles had written to Judge Erskine, stating his preference that custody of Travis be awarded to his parents. But apparently Charles' preferences were ignored or overruled. *Is this Palm Beach County's way of rubbing my powerlessness in my face?*

Still, Charles' parents had been seeing Travis regularly. Despite their estrangement, he trusted that Travis was safe with Danielle. He knew she loved Travis, as did the rest of Dana's family. However, Charles still remembered the loathing in the eyes of her parents and siblings during the trial. They were convinced in their hearts beyond a shadow of a doubt that he had mercilessly killed his wife, their daughter and sister. He feared that as Travis grew up, Charles would see the same look of anger and disgust on his face. *Travis is spending a lifetime with people who hate me. This does not bode well for my relationship with Travis. All I have with which to try to neutralize their toxic influence on Travis are these twice-yearly visits. I must make them as meaningful as possible for him, starting today.*

Charles checked in at the central desk in the visiting area, as did the other inmates who were expecting family visits that morning.

The officious guard behind the desk outlined the ground rules for the visit without much warmth or compassion. "You will be sent in a few minutes to either the contact or noncontact visiting area. Contact means just what it sounds like: The inmate is free to touch the visitor—within reasonable limits, of course. No hands up the blouse or down in her pants. He may kiss the visitor, hug, or hold hands; a child may sit on the inmate's lap, a husband can cradle his wife's face. There just may not be any exchange of items—food, drink, paper, cigarettes, or drugs, of course. None of that shit. The noncontact visit is different. No touching the visitor because you will be separated by a plexiglass screen.

Other inmates had described the procedure to Charles. He knew that contact visits were worth gold. The opportunity to hold and be held by another human being was like a heavy rain in the dry desert. Those being disciplined for some infraction didn't get the contact visits. They would go months, if not years, without any human touch. Sometimes it meant the difference between survival and being dragged down by the pressures of prison life. The noncontact visiting room was split down the middle by a thick sheet of plexiglass and a room-length table. Inmates sat on one side of the plexiglass, families on the other, communicating through a black telephone.

The noncontact room was open so that there was absolutely no privacy for the inmate. The other inmates could hear what the inmate next to him was saying to his family. In that room, voices were often loud, crude, and occasionally angry and ugly with husband-to-wife rage. This is where inmates would get heartbreaking brush-offs from a girlfriend who had tired of making the long bus ride from Miami or

Broward County. Every now and then an inmate would learn that his wife was pregnant, and the inmate would be reminded that he was stuck in prison and could have had absolutely nothing to do with making his wife pregnant.

The guard sent Charles to the noncontact visit area.

"But Judge Erskine had ordered a contact visit with my son," Charles protested. "Let me run back to my cell to get a copy of their order from Judge Erskine."

"It probably won't do an ounce of good but what the hell, go on."

Charles was panting for breath when he got back. The guard handed the document to the captain, who unceremoniously shot the paper back across the desk.

"I don't give two shits for what some judge in West Palm Beach ordered. You're here in down-home Raiford now. We have our own orders. And they are that you get a noncontact visit today. Or no visit at all. Is that understood?"

Charles felt he had no choice but to accept these restrictions. He wondered if Danielle and Travis had seen him leave the room. He caught a glimpse of Danielle. As expected, she had Travis on her lap and looked impatient that not only did she have to drive up to such an awful place but then had to wait for Charles to be ready.

Charles entered the noncontact room looking upset and angry. Danielle sat quietly with Travis on the other side of the plexiglass. The plexiglass divider had generations of handprints on it. Charles began his conversation by warning Travis not to touch the glass.

"Hey, big guy! You've grown to be so big. I'm so glad to see you. How are you?" Charles said into the telephone receiver.

Travis was holding the other receiver behind the glass. He was confused by the telephone. He seemed not to hear Charles and didn't respond to his question.

"Travis, tell your Daddy how you are," Danielle said, trying to help.

Travis looked up at Charles when he heard Danielle say the word "Daddy." Charles thought Travis looked as if he had some vague memory of Charles' face but the telephone distorted and changed his voice too much to sound to a four-year-old like someone he remembered.

He handed the telephone receiver to Danielle, looked down, and started playing with his miniature cars.

Charles could see that Travis, though a year older than the last time they saw each other, was still too young, too confused by where he was, and too unmoored to know what was going on.

Charles and Danielle engaged in some small talk about her life, her parents, and her siblings. Charles could discern that she was very uncomfortable being there.

"Well, Charles, Travis and I have a long drive back to Fort Lauderdale."

"I'm so grateful you made the drive. It's been over a year since I've seen Travis. I'm disappointed they assigned us to a noncontact visit but your bringing Travis so I can just see him today means the world to me. Tell me, honestly, how is he doing?"

"He's about as happy as any four-year-old boy. He makes me very happy, too."

She leaned over to rub Travis's cheek affectionately with the palm of her hand. She tousled his blond hair. Charles felt a stab of jealousy.

"That's good. I'm happy for you and him. Is Travis in preschool now?"

"He'll be starting in the fall at the Episcopal Church on the next block."

"Oh, that's good. He's always been such a curious boy. Some schooling now will be good for him. Can you do me a favor, Danielle? Can you stick a picture or two that he draws in preschool in the mail to me to help me decorate my house?"

"Your house?"

"Yes, that's what we call our cell. Our house."

"We have to go now," Danielle interjected before she could respond to Charles' request.

Charles glanced at the clock on the wall. There were still forty minutes in his scheduled family visit. But he didn't say anything except "Goodbye, Danielle. Until the next time. I'll make sure I get a contact visit so that I can hug my little guy. Have a safe drive back."

He knocked on the plexiglass and waved goodbye to Travis and tried to smile but Travis didn't seem to comprehend. Charles could see Danielle instructing Travis to wave back.

He watched as they left the visiting area and went on their way to Danielle's car. Charles wiped away a tear from his eye before he turned to leave the room and walk back to his house.

CHAPTER 35

CHARLES ARRIVED BACK AT HIS CELL and threw himself down dejectedly on his bunk. He brooded over the very real possibility of the loss of his son and the powerlessness of his new life. He realized that Travis was in the same boat he was—an innocent victim of circumstance, bad luck, and overwhelming loss.

The only solace Charles could find was in the friends he had made during the year at FSP. Many of them shared the same frustrations and anger; as a fellowship of the weak, they shared just about anything else—the criminally bad food, the arbitrariness with which the administration made changes to the routine, and the dull-witted guards who unfairly meted out discipline, especially, Charles lamented, when the offender was black.

Charles was surprised, in fact, by how overwhelmingly many of the inmates were black. He had heard about the phenomenon of "mass incarceration," which was just beginning to characterize the court and prison systems all over the United States. The American public had begun to feel overrun by the explosion in drug crimes as the "crack cocaine" epidemic erupted in the 1980s. The public voted in politicians who took what appeared to be a stance of being "tough on crime." When Charles read about that phenomenon, he thought immediately of Sheriff Davidson.

Charles also knew that the primary consumers and dealers of crack cocaine were black youth and young adults who could not afford the more stylish powdered cocaine used by more affluent whites. It stood to reason that the majority of those convicted and sentenced to prison for the possession of the lower-caste crack cocaine would be black. In fact, in 1980 more inmates were convicted and imprisoned for possession of crack cocaine than for any other crime in the country's prisons.

For some reason that puzzled the guards, Charles found more affinity with the fewer white inmates such as Billy DeLisle, for example. Charles and Billy became immediate and fast friends way back on the school bus ride from the Diagnostic Unit to their current digs at FSP. Charles learned that Billy was a former police officer in Jacksonville whose wife had been beaten to death. He was given a sentence of twelve years in prison. He was scheduled to be released in

1997.

What bonded Charles immediately to Billy was that at the Diagnostic Unit, they noticed that Billy and Charles were the only inmates being processed without a tattoo on their nude bodies. That, along with the interesting fact that what mitigated Billy's sentence was the fact that after his trial, it was uncovered that the prosecution had withheld exculpatory evidence in the case.

That sounded totally familiar to Charles.

Billy's cell was right across the corridor from the dayroom. Every day and every night, Billy had to endure the cacophony blasting from two TV sets always tuned to different channels at full volume. There was the relentless shouting and bellowing bombast from opinionated and often ill-informed sports fanatics. There were angry verbal confrontations and the occasional inevitable outbreaks of violence.

Compared to Billy, Charles now had a veritable penthouse suite on the third level of cells, far above the clatter and chaos of the first floor. Billy always felt that he had been assigned the cell he had because of his "bad attitude" toward the guards. He loved making fun of their "southernisms" and constantly correcting their speech and grammar. Billy thought the guards and administration were "getting back at him." Who knows?

Billy and Charles had studied just enough psychology to be dangerous. They used to sit around the dayroom quietly analyzing their fellow inmates and identifying the issue that they concluded bedeviled them. They fancied themselves as the intellectual giants of the dayroom.

Since both Billy and Charles had at least a smidgeon of college education, they were lucky and experienced enough to be assigned to the "Typing Pool," the Records Conversion Facility. They were in charge of entering state paperwork digitally, and they photographed and developed microfilm. It was boring, routine work.

But then again, it beat being across SR 16 and banging out new Florida license plates in an un-air-conditioned warehouse for eight hours every day. Or sewing together an unending number of shapeless uniforms or boxer shorts for the new inmates who would be arriving into the embrace of the state. The work on the inmates' clothing was hopelessly crude. But what would the DOC expect from a group of indentured tailors forced to stitch together the most visible evidence of their status as prisoners? The inmates' uniforms were handmade for angry people by resentful people.

Like Charles, at least Billy had family on the outside who might visit occasionally and deposit a little money in his commissary account. They often talked together about other inmates who had nothing—and sadly, nobody to care about them.

Some inmates, for many reasons, were particularly vulnerable to attack or exploitation. FSP did have a "protection wing" for men who would not fare well in the general population. There you would find the child molesters and the convicted police "snitches"—both of whom were on the lowest rung of the human totem pole as far as the prisoners were concerned. So, too, were the "out" gay men who, without the protection of living apart from others, would be savaged by other inmates. There were more suicides on the "protection wing" than on any other. Even if an inmate was isolated from the others for his protection, being denied the small freedoms and camaraderie of other human beings could crush him.

That's not to say there wasn't homosexual behavior in the general population. Often it was by men who described themselves as "straight." Charles had met several inmates who introduced another male to him as his "girlfriend" or his "wife," but the inmate would immediately insist that he's not gay because he always "pitched" and he's never, ever "caught."

Prisons are notorious, at least in the movies, for rapes. They do happen. But like sexual assaults out in the wider world, they are almost always acts of power rather than sexual desire. Early in his time at FSP, Charles had to learn to fend off an attempted rape. He had overheard a couple of inmates remarking to each other, "Look, Tyrone, here comes new booty." Charles immediately braced himself and fisted his hands. He had learned that your best chance to avoid molestation was to maintain your ground the first time you are confronted. When one inmate tried to grab him from behind by the arm, Charles reached up and slugged the guy in the face. The guy stepped back in surprise. He tried to massage his face to rub away the pain.

"Try something like that again, Motherfucker, and I'll put my fist right *through* your face the next time until you're unrecognizable."

Charles was never bothered in the same way again. He shocked himself with his uncharacteristically violent speech and his courage— or was it folly? The guy might have had a hidden shank on him that he was prepared to use to slice the "new booty" on the wing into pieces.

That precisely was another of the mores of prison life that he had to learn. An illusion that it seemed all inmates work to maintain was strength, at least in some form. Some joined a gang for strength in numbers. Others formed alliances with other inmates in the wing who had an aura of strength. Strength in brute force was most important. Charles had a year under his belt when he could observe other inmates carefully. To survive and avoid the fate of a character in *Rambo,* an inmate needed to be direct with the others and give the impression of supreme self-confidence. (Charles had called it brashness or cockiness before his days at FSP.) Any potential attacker needed to feel the other's self-confidence palpably in the air between them or he wouldn't remain just a "potential" attacker.

Charles was reminded of that lesson one morning when he was working in the darkroom developing microfilm with Rudy. Rudy had already been working in the Typing Pool when Charles was assigned to it. Like Charles, he was sentenced to life in prison. Unlike Charles, Rudy had served prison time twice before.

Rudy and Charles were in the darkroom getting ready for the day. Another inmate, unknown to Charles, entered the small darkroom. Charles could see from the sudden transformation of Rudy's face and his almost catatonic body language that Rudy and the intruder knew each other from some previous encounter. Charles tried to ignore the stranger and went back to work on a microfilm. Before Charles recognized that anything was wrong, the intruder whipped out a shank—a kind of homemade knife fashioned surreptitiously by the inmate from a piece of metal. He held the point of it against Rudy's throat. Rudy stood about eight inches taller than the stranger.

The intruder spat out an insult in Spanish that Charles deciphered as saying something about Rudy's mother. Rudy balled up his fists, glared down at the guy, and leaned slightly but menacingly toward the blade. Charles was frozen in place, unsure of how he could help Rudy. Rudy uttered a few obscenities at the intruder. *This is not Rudy's first rodeo.*

The guy made the mistake of retreating a few steps from Rudy while Rudy matched his steps backward with several of his own toward the stranger.

In this terrifying battle of wills, Rudy said defiantly to the attacker, "Come on, you yellow bastard. Go ahead and try to cut me.

Big man with that shank, aren't you? But afraid to use it, you shit!"

At the time Charles thought Rudy's challenge was insane. Rudy took another two steps in the guy's direction. Instead of slashing the shank at Rudy, however, the intruder kept backing up a few more steps as Rudy was taking as many steps toward the attacker. The two men kept repeating the steps as though they were performing some treacherous, choreographed dance.

It suddenly dawned on Charles where Rudy was leading the man. *Out of the darkroom.* Charles tiptoed behind the intruder and opened the steel door leading from the darkroom out into the corridor. He suddenly realized that he hadn't breathed since the guy had intruded into the darkroom and whipped out the shank.

Raising a metaphorical white flag, the man timorously slipped the shank back into his pants' pocket. Finally, he backed out through the open door and vanished.

"Rudy, are you all right?"

"Yeah, the fucker's a pussy," Rudy muttered and went back to work.

In the FSP you had to risk dying in order to stay alive.

CHAPTER 36

WITHIN ONLY A FEW MONTHS AT FSP, and certainly after his first year there, Charles understood in his bones what every inmate does.

Prison is not just a place, not just a stack of cells with bars for walls, not just a collection of buildings where everyone is angry. Prison is a different planet, its own universe turned inside out and upside down. It has its own kind of oxygen and gravity. Prison has its own ruthless masters and its own pathetic slaves. It's a warehouse filled with broken men who don't want to live in such confining proximity to others whose addictions, defects, and rage they need to be protected from.

The Florida State Prison is where the state of Florida puts its problems, its rejects, and its mistakes. In Charles' case, the mistake is that he was there at all. They all see it happening, and we hear it coming. There is nothing anyone can do to make it stop happening. Violence, abuse, and racism are everywhere. Whatever form the violence, abuse, and racism take, they are just part of the natural habitat. There is very little the guards can do to stop them—especially since they are often the source of the problem.

Many of the guards were what were called "state raised." Their families had lived off the prison system in Union County and adjacent Bradford County for generations. The prisons were the primary employers in the region. The fathers of the guards had been guards before them, and the sons and often daughters had grown up with the expectation that they, too, would become guards.

As little boys and little girls, they were regaled with stories of the power their fathers and grandfathers had over some of the toughest convicted criminals in the state. Too often they looked at inmates as props to be bullied and demeaned around the clock, a source of entertainment and perverse validation of their power.

One day as Charles and his fellow typing pool workers were making their way from the main building to their job in one of the converted warehouses closer to the perimeter of the grounds, one guard took the opportunity to show the inmates who was boss.

The inmates had to make their way down a narrow sidewalk flanked by a chain link fence that extended upward to form an escape-proof ceiling for the walkway. As they began the trek, it started to rain lightly. At Charles' suggestion, the group broke into a jog down the walkway. They came to a stop midway down the walkway at a gate where they had to wait until the guard in the high tower above them buzzed to unlock the gate and let them through. One inmate made the mistake, when he saw that the gate was locked and the rain strengthening, of shouting up to the guard, "Open the gate!"

No guard likes to be told what to do by a lowly inmate, especially a black one. It was clear that the guard had heard and that he could see the darkening of the sky from his perch atop the tower. The group had to stand there unprotected while the guard asserted his authority. They were unprotected and trapped as the rain grew stronger and the wind whipped into their faces.

Some of the incensed inmates started to yell upwards to the tower while others cursed. Two other guards came to the side of the first to see what the ruckus was all about. They were enjoying the spectacle below. The inmates had nowhere to go and no way to avoid getting drenched to the skin. The guard stood smiling in the tower, looking down dispassionately and holding a rifle as the inmates huddled together in the downpour.

The guard finally must have felt that he had had enough fun for the time being and buzzed to unlock the gate. The inmates shuffled through. There was no point in jogging or running now. Charles remembered feeling well-nigh homicidal. *Why did the guard do this? Simply because he could. He was reminding us again that we are powerless, that he has all the power. Just another in an endless series of demonstrations of how this God-forsaken place is a hate factory. We come into this place as "bad people," and if we ever come out at all, we come out as enraged people.*

Charles, however, was determined to try to come out—if he ever did—as a smarter person. He read everything he could get his hands on—all the books in the library he had intended to read, all the books he learned he should read, and all the books he would probably never have even thought of reading if he were not in prison.

A group of other inmates joined Charles in what they called the "world's roughest, toughest book club." *You practically had to have killed someone to be able to join it.*

As a regular in the library, Charles requested the inmate librarian to get permission from the administration to order new books that the book club might explore together. They devoured classic Stephen

King novels. One inmate introduced the others to Scott Turow and John Grisham legal thrillers. *To Kill a Mockingbird* by Harper Lee about the murder trial of a young black sharecropper in Depression-era Alabama sparked a tremendous amount of discussion for several weeks. Charles was particularly fascinated by the novel in that Atticus Finch was drafted to defend an *innocent* man against the false charge of raping a white woman.

The members of the book club passed each ripped and dog-eared copy from cell block to cell block, bunk to bunk. As quickly as an inmate finished one book, he was handed another one. The men became surprisingly informed in critiquing each author's reading style and understanding of the plot. If the men ever took a vote for a favorite, they would have expressed a strong preference for the novels of Ernest Hemingway.

Reading was the only means of escape available to the inmates unless they were satisfied with old *Gomer Pyle* reruns. With a book, they could climb over walls, even ones crowned with rolls of barbed wire; they could walk on a beach, they could meet new friends, and they could mourn the loss of someone they had gotten to know. Charles was no longer starving intellectually, and each new read was a veritable feast.

Charles' parents made the five-hour drive from Palm Beach County to visit him as often as they could. They also sent small amounts of money for his commissary account that enabled him to buy the occasional self-indulgent "luxury" such as shaving cream or a pint of ice cream.

In Charles' first weeks at FSP, his mother, Eileen, had been terrified. Now the fact that he was still alive over a year after his conviction and sentencing helped calm her down. On one of their visits, Charles happened to mention that he had seen a fellow inmate in the shower with tattoos on every inch of his body. His small-town churchgoing mother was shocked. But not so shocked that she didn't ask, "Even down there?"

"Yes," Charles replied with a smile, "Even down there."

Eileen's eyes were as big as jumbo dinner plates. "What'd it say?"

"Good God, Mom! I'm trying to stay alive in here. I couldn't just bend down and read it."

Seeing my parents, or anyone else from my old life, is so

bittersweet. I love having visitors from the free world. But then they have to leave and drive home. Then I feel more alone than ever.

Charles hugged his parents tightly as they were leaving. As he watched them walking down the corridor toward the parking lot, he began to weep and reflected again: *God, I've lost everything in my life that I value: my wife and marriage, many of my former friends, my job, my car, my savings, my freedom, and my reputation. And now I fear I may be losing the most precious thing I have left in my life: my son.*

Six months after Travis's first visit with Charles, Danielle brought him again to the FSP. It had now been a year and a half since father and son had touched each other, since they had last had a real talk, since they had hugged and played together.

By that time Shillington and Nelson had applied pressure on the powers-that-be at FSP that the institution needed to abide by the judge's orders to let Charles have contact visits with Travis. The three of them sat outside at a wooden picnic table behind a double chain link fence topped with razor wire, All the inmates and their visitors were under the watchful eye of several guards milling about them cradling rifles.

Charles tried to engage Travis in conversation. *He really feels no connection to me.*

Danielle excused herself and left them by themselves as she retreated to the smoking area, a recent addition at FSP.

One year in the life of a little five-year-old boy is an eternity. I'm no longer even a distant memory for him. Just a disheveled man in an ill-fitting white t-shirt, desperately trying to make conversation by asking far too many specific questions about the boy's Hot Wheels collection.

Charles didn't know what Travis was feeling that day. As for Charles, he held on for dear life to every word Travis said. Charles was fascinated by Travis's every move and gesture, how Danielle had chosen to dress him, and what he chose to have him order for their lunch from the snack bar in the visitors' area. Charles could see that the boy was growing. *I wasn't there for his birthdays. I have missed all his milestones. I haven't been there to help make new memories. I wasn't there to fall asleep with him on the sofa while we watched Sesame Street together on TV. I wasn't there at all, ever. He's growing away from me.*

To Danielle, looking at us from afar, it might look as though father and son are having a deep, meaningful conversation. But really this is just a charade. He is my son, but he doesn't know me. I haven't been a part of his life for so long. Does he still remember Dana? Or are both of his parents now forgotten and gone forever?

CHAPTER 37

DECEMBER 1989

One of the chaplains stopped in front of Charles' cell one afternoon. Charles was surprised to see a person in street clothes at his cell asking to see Charles Wilkerson specifically. He couldn't remember a time when he'd seen someone in civilian clothes since his trial, in this case a young man in a black suit, black clerical shirt, and a white dog collar.

The chaplains and their approved volunteers were the few personnel at FSP who could "roam" freely in the wing and carry on a conversation with an inmate at the front door of his house. One of the chaplaincy team members would stop by from time to time but ceased doing so after Charles told him once, "Father, I appreciate your friendly visits, but I'm afraid you're wasting your breath with me. I've never really had much use for religion."

This chaplain named Father Macomb, however, came on another errand, He reminded Charles that he had checked off a box for "Further my education" on an interest survey that the Chaplaincy Department had distributed to all the inmates.

"Oh, I remember now," Charles said after a silence. "I checked the box because I'm interested in exploring if there are any options to continue my college education here at FSP."

"Well, I see I came by your cell at just the right time, Charles." He opened a file he was carrying and dug out a colorful brochure. "Up to now there haven't been any good options at FSP. An inmate whose sentence expires is released without much education at all. You probably know that some of the more ambitious fellas take some of the classes that qualify them to take the GRE exam and hit the streets with at least a high school-equivalency certificate. But I gather you are looking for something more."

"Yes, Father. I did a year plus a few courses at FAU before I got married, a long time before I started here at FSP. I'd like to complete my undergraduate degree if I could. I know that nowadays a B.A. or B.Sc. degree is the minimum to be considered for many jobs when I get out of here—*if* I get out of here."

"There are academic departments at the University of Central

Florida (UCF) in Orlando that are willing to convene such classes. I'll leave it to you, Charles, to see if there are any other inmates who might be interested in the same thing you are."

CHARLES ANNOUNCED THIS OPPORTUNITY at the book club meeting. He tried to temper his enthusiasm to prevent his hopes from getting too high. But several inmates were interested, and they knew of some other inmates who were possibilities. A couple of the members stated their preference for a remedial class in mathematics. Charles pointed out that the small education department in the prison offered those kinds of courses regularly.

"I was thinking more of a course we could do together on the contemporary American novel," Charles said.

"You mean a professor would come way up here to help me understand what the hell Kurt Vonnegut means?" one asked. "I never could figure out the novel about the guy obsessing about that damn white whale."

"Yes, *Slaughterhouse Five* is a contemporary American novel," Charles assured him.

"So it would be like having our book club meeting but we'd get college credit for it? Then let's go for it!"

CHARLES FOUND THE THREE-HOUR CLASSES every Tuesday evening to be a real treat. For several of the inmates, who should surely have been diagnosed as having Attention Deficit Hyperactivity Disorder, by an hour and a half into the class, their focus would begin to wander elsewhere. They'd be doodling purposelessly in the inside cover of their book or their eyes would become vacant.

But for Charles, the classes were an oasis of sanity in an intellectual desert. Occasionally, two opposing worlds would collide during a discussion, and the language of the two opposing students devolved into what Charles felt as an embarrassment. Once the instructor got accustomed to such emotional outbursts either defending or attacking Norman Mailer or Barbara Kingsolver, he began to find the juxtaposition of higher learning and threats of violence morbidly funny.

Many of the inmates were emotionally needy, always feeling inadequate yet proud of being in an academic class right in the heart of "the joint" and wanting affirmation by the professor. Once one inmate asked the professor how their work compared with that of students on campus in Orlando. The prof said, "Honestly, often you inmates come better prepared for class than the kids on campus. You inmates do your homework, read the material before the class, and come prepared to talk about the book, sometimes rather intensely. I can tell that you care about the novels and their plot and characters. I tell them about you in my classes down in Orlando, and the students feel shamed, as they should."

Charles was embarrassed by the men's undisguised begging for affirmation. *But when is the last time any of us received even such a brief testimonial of our worth and hard work? Never here at FSP, I'm sure.*

Charles was proud of his classmates.

The men were all "double-dipping." While analyzing novel plots, at the same time they were getting their PhD in penitentiary life, the unique rules, rituals, and phrases of what they called "Slammerland." Charles chuckled to himself as he observed how the men were able to teach a little bit of "prison patois" to the instructor.

Charles was living a dual experience. A part of him was succeeding at adapting to life in prison, while another part of him fought the insidious creep of prison slang and victim mentality into his personality. He struggled mightily against the crudeness that comes from living in a state-sanctioned internal exile. He took no small amount of secret pride when another inmate asked him, "What the hell are *you* doing here?" Charles was reassured that even an inarticulate inmate who was not the sharpest knife in the drawer could see that Charles didn't belong in a place like FSP.

Yet, in spite of everything that Charles tried and despite the best of his intentions, prison life wore down his resistance. Things came out of his mouth that made him cringe. The casual curses, the prison vocabulary, and the hateful posing all oozed out if he didn't watch himself.

On one of his parents' visits, his mother told him to be sure to do everything he could "to stay out of trouble." As is the prison way, Charles lit into her and nearly tore her head off with his reaction.

"Don't tell me how to behave! You don't have the slightest clue of what life is like in here!"

Charles was aware that his mother could see that he was changing, and so could Charles. Neither one liked the change. His rough edges had become a way to cope with his harsh environment at

FSP.

Another change in himself that bothered Charles was his occasional tendency to craft carefully planned fantasies of how he was going to take revenge on each and every one of the people who was responsible for putting him behind bars. During sleepless nights he enjoyed the fantasizing and was strangely energized by it. He saw exactly how he would arrange it so that Buck Davidson and Skip Henderson would be killed. He had elaborate plans for taking down Judge Erskine, and how he was going to get away with the murder. *I want the bastards to hurt the way I did, to feel firsthand how they made me feel.*

No one else knew about Charles' fantasies. But he knew that just about all of his fellow prisoners, even Calvin Shank the Mennonite, had similar plans for the people out on the street who had crossed them. Plotting revenge was a common way to stay warm in a cold cell in February, a kind of sweetener for the bitter drink of everyday existence behind bars.

THERE SEEMED TO BE NO LOGIC that Charles could understand for the system, if there was one, of stocking newspapers in the dayroom. If the inmate was lucky, he could peruse a copy of the previous day's edition. But for some reason, if you looked around more thoroughly, you could find older issues, too. The editions would seldom be complete, the sports section and comics almost surely taken and missing.

Charles had gotten tired of having to fight for supremacy with the TV remote control. Every evening when it was time for the evening news, the "Liberty City Gang" of prisoners from that notorious section of Miami had absolute control of the remote and therefore the channel that was blaring on the TV. It was usually set to a station that broadcasted a seemingly endless diet of mindless game shows. No news.

One day Charles picked up an issue of the *Miami Herald* from on top of one of the tables. It was the issue of November 7, 1988, a full year ago. At first Charles was disappointed and tempted to show it by slapping the newspaper back down on the table. But then it struck him that with everything coming down in his life at about that time a year ago—his sentencing, his introduction to his new domicile in Raiford, and his initial, difficult adjustment to rules and rituals at FSP that were completely unfamiliar to him—he couldn't remember what else was going on outside the past year. He kept the newspaper and opened it to see what he had missed.

There on the first page of the local section was the headline, "Palm Beach County Sheriff Elected District Attorney."

Well, wouldn't you know it? The cowboy lawman got what he was pining for. God bless the people of Palm Beach County. God bless anyone who gives even the appearance of breaking the law if the new District Attorney has made up his mind that you're guilty.

Over in another column on the same page was an introduction to the man Davidson would be replacing. This was a total surprise to Charles, perhaps to Davidson as well. Skip Henderson was so admiring of his work as prosecutor for the county—particularly, he said, in securing the guilty verdict in the trial earlier that fall of the brutal murderer of his wife—that he had been encouraged by the governor of the state to consider an appointment to a vacant judge's seat in the Fifth Circuit Court. Henderson accepted and was appointed for an initial one-year term until he was ratified by a countywide vote.

Charles chuckled as he read the brief notice. *So much for the rhetoric about the integrity and impartiality of the courts. I ought to receive at least a gratuity from both of the bastards. After all, it was my conviction that each used as a handy stepping stone to higher office. But back to prison for you, boy.*

CHARLES GOT THE IMPRESSION THAT MANY of the men at FSP, even his classmates in the college class on Tuesdays, had grown up with parents who built their nests for their family in precarious places. Most of the parents, at least those who weren't overcome by the disease of alcoholism or addiction, didn't realize until too late that their children didn't stand a chance in this world. Many of the men had been badly scorched early on by traumatic experiences from which few of them would recover. They suffered from inattention and abuse, their own substance abuse or their parents', or just plain ignorance that seemed to be part of their inheritance. They had been taught few other strategies on how to handle differences except physical force and violence. When they grew up, it's as if they had no place to go but FSP.

And Charles was there with them, every minute of every day. That was underlined for him in December 1988 when the district appellate court rejected his attorneys' motion for a retrial for him.

A year later, in December 1989, he was still there with the others when the Court of Criminal Appeals gave Charles his final rebuff. Being turned down by the courts was becoming routine by now so it no longer sent him into a downward spiral of resentment and despair.

"A conviction is like coming up against a stone wall," Shillington said when he called Charles with the bad news. "To have a chance to climb over it, we have to keep trying to find the places in the wall where you can get a strong foothold. We haven't found one yet but this court decision won't stop us from looking."

Charles was gratified by his attorneys' commitment to him. But he could see that getting out of FSP was going to take longer than he had thought. His prospects were growing bleak.

Chapter 38

January 1991

ONE DAY, EVEN ONE YEAR, AT FSP was pretty much like the next. Charles had lost track of the passage of time. But when he saw a calendar for January 1991 above a guard's desk, he realized he had been at FSP for almost five years.

He thought immediately of Travis, who would be nine years old this year. Charles was relating to his son on the installment plan with a visit every six months. Each time Travis was brought to FSP, Charles felt it was like meeting a different child. Travis would be taller or rounder or more talkative, or often less so. He would share bits and pieces of his life with Charles, or he wouldn't.

In the early years after his sentencing, 1987 and 1988, Charles could entertain Travis with lemon drops and with questions or observations about his toy cars. As Travis grew older, however, Charles noticed that his son would look around the visitation area as they were talking. It was clear Travis didn't like all that he saw. Charles could no longer convince him that the inmate with an eye patch and full beard was a pirate. Charles found it more difficult to distract Travis in the visiting room when some of the inmates' families' visits dissolved into tears or anger. Travis knew that the fathers of none of his schoolmates lived in a prison.

Charles couldn't help but sadly wonder what Dana's family, especially her parents, had told Travis about his father and why he was locked up in prison. Charles assumed it had to be bad. He began to feel he had become more and more distant and more diminished in the boy's eyes. After Travis and Danielle left FSP on their visit in the previous year, Charles had the definite sense that coming on a long car ride to Raiford to see the man who kept insisting that he was his dad became a distasteful task he was being forced to carry out.

Charles realized that if he didn't get released from FSP soon, he was in danger of losing Travis entirely.

June 1995

A guard shouted out in the dayroom: "Wilkerson, you've got mail."

Charles leapt out of his bunk as though he were being shot out of a cannon. He had only a couple of minutes to catch the guard who delivered the mail before he moved on to the next wing and another inmate eager to be remembered by the United States Postal Service.

An envelope with an inmate's name and address on it was a reminder that he was still among the living, tangible proof that someone out there knows that he still existed. The mood in this wing was always elevated on days when the mail delivery happened.

Charles was waiting for word from Shillington or Nelson about whether or not their petition to the court for a writ of habeas corpus for him had been accepted. If the petition was approved, Shillington and Nelson would finally be granted access to the thick file of evidence that the disgruntled assistant district attorney in Henderson's office, Jennifer Lipkus, had told Shillington about.

But there was no envelope from Shillington's practice. *The petition's probably been denied—just as I expected.*

But there was an envelope with Danielle's return address on it. Charles opened the envelope casually. *Danielle must have a question for me to answer.* But on the paper inside the envelope was a letter in a child's hand, specifically Travis's hand.

Charles liked believing the illusion that Travis wrote to him regularly. But he knew when a letter did come from Travis, it was probably not by his own initiative. Over the years Travis had signed his name to a birthday card, or scrawled his name at the bottom of one of Eileen's letters to FSP. Whatever mail from Travis there was came with Charles' parents return address on the envelope.

That Travis had chosen to write and send this letter from Danielle's address now puzzled Charles. When Travis was at his paternal grandparents' home, they always encouraged him to write something to his dad. *Perhaps the fact that he wrote and posted this letter from Danielle's home was a sign that he was growing up. He's fourteen years old now. Maybe he's chosen to reach out to me on his own.*

Charles returned to his cell to read the letter. Whether he was getting good news or bad, he wanted to absorb it in private.

Charles opened the envelope carefully and began reading. But the youthful imperfections of Travis's spelling and penmanship could not soften the hostility of the message.

"Charles," Travis began.

Charles couldn't remember if Travis had ever addressed him by his first name instead of "Dad."

"I have decided to write to you before I am skeduled to come visit you soon to tell you that I don't want to come to the prison to visit you anymore. I'm tired of the long trip to talk with someone I hardly know. I'm tired of waiting through the long check-in process where they treat the visitor like a prisoner.

"Maybe Danielle has already wrote to you to tell you that she has met a man, Gary. Gary is a very nice man. He and Danielle got married last month and have decided to adopt me as their son. That means Danielle is now my Mom and Gary is my Dad. Gary takes me to football and basketball games at the university which is cool. We are moving soon to a real house where I can have my own room. Gary knows about you in prison but Danielle has told him not to talk with me about you. Thank you for buying me the burger and fries for lunch last time. But I won't be coming again the next time."

Travis's letter stung Charles. It cut like a knife slashing at the meager measure of pride he had left. It cracked the brittle belief Charles had in the future. Travis's rejection of him mocked the glimmer of hope that he had been nurturing that someday, somehow, something decent would come out of this nightmare.

Travis was all he had left. He was all Charles had been living for. Travis was the only remnant of his life with Dana. In the succession of all his losses in the last nine or ten years, Charles had always been able to recover by telling himself he still had his son, even if everything else was gone.

He crumbled in his bunk. He lay there, clenching and unclenching his fist, feeling hot tears forming and then falling down his cheeks. He clutched Travis's letter close to his heart as though he were trying to squeeze all the hurt out of it. He was crushing the letter as though he could change the contents of the letter by doing so. Then he did as he always did when things got too difficult for him to handle—he thought back to Dana and the way she could calm him and could make everything suddenly better.

"Oh, Dana, princess. I love you. I miss you. I am grateful for you. I am thankful for the boy we produced together."

THE INNOCENCE PROJECT

The Innocence Project, founded in 1992 by Peter Neufeld and Barry Scheck at Cardozo School of Law, exonerates the wrongly convicted through DNA testing and reforms the criminal justice system to prevent future injustice.

Our mission is to assist the staggering number of innocent people who remain wrongfully incarcerated, and to bring reform to the system responsible for their unjust imprisonment.

The Innocence Project is working to pass laws tackling police misconduct through greater transparency and accountability. Police officers committed misconduct in 35% of exoneration cases since 1989, according to a recent report by the National Registry of Exonerations. When such abuse and misconduct goes unchecked, it not only leads to wrongful convictions.

Police disciplinary records are currently confidential in 21 states. Keeping these records hidden from the public contributes to wrongful convictions in two major ways. First, the secrecy around these records makes it difficult for there to be public or external oversight of how complaints and allegations against officers are handled. Without this transparency, law enforcement's internal affairs departments can avoid disciplining officers for illegal and unethical behavior, which means these harmful behaviors will not be corrected. And, because officers are not being held accountable for past wrongdoing, they may continue to engage in misconduct in the future.

Prosecutorial misconduct: As the pace of DNA exonerations has grown across the country in recent years, wrongful convictions have revealed disturbing fissures and trends in our criminal justice system. Together, these cases show us how the criminal justice system is broken – and how urgently it needs to be fixed.

In each case where DNA has proven innocence beyond doubt, an overlapping array of contributing factors has emerged – from mistakes to misconduct to factors of race and class.

Only a fraction of criminal cases involve biological evidence *that can be subjected to DNA testing, and even when such evidence exists, it is often lost or destroyed after a conviction. Since they don't have access to a definitive test like DNA, many wrongfully convicted people have a slim chance of ever proving their innocence.*[1]

---

[1] Quote from Innocence Project website www.InnocenceProject.org

CHAPTER 39
APRIL 1995

CHARLES' LIFE WAS THROWN INTO considerable upheaval when he received the letter from Travis. Charles' mind was consumed by thoughts about Travis. He was paralyzed by grief at losing Travis's twice-yearly visits, even though they were often awkward and brief. What hurt Charles perhaps more than anything was that the decision to cease the visits appeared to be 100% Travis's own. Surely, Dana's family had not done much to discourage the boy from making that decision. But Charles could also see that his decision had not been the result of a momentary feeling but a choice brewing inside Travis for quite some time.

Strangely enough, after the emotional cataclysm, Charles found that the routine of prison life was a source of comfort. After a pause of a few weeks during which Charles could not muster the energy or desire to attend the college class that he and some of the book club inmates initiated several years ago, Charles resumed participating again. He was promoted in the library to a position of a volunteer with more responsibility. At first he wanted to decline the promotion. But one morning a couple of weeks later, he awoke with a curiosity about the new duties and responsibilities and showed up at the library to inquire. Just being in a room full of books again energized him. Besides, he felt he owed the volunteer senior librarian, a retired clergyman who drove to Raiford from Yulee, north of Jacksonville, a debt of gratitude and respect for his having bestowed this honor on him.

Nothing else had substantially changed for Charles. In many ways daily life in FSP remained the same tragicomedy it had been since Charles arrived there eight years earlier. But the carnival was moderately entertaining at times, and it gave Charles a place to hide the emotional turmoil he felt.

Still, there were moments when a random sound or scent would take him back to the life he used to have.

One day he was resting on his bunk and listening to the hissing of the prison sprinkler system outside his window. He closed his eyes and immediately was transported back to his backyard in Palm Beach

County. He could feel the familiar lawn chair where he used to sit on his deck after mowing the lawn and running the sprinkler. It was as though he could reach down beneath the chair, grab the cold bottle of Miller High Life, and feel the cool, refreshing sweat on the bottle. To his left, the young Travis was playing on the swing set Charles had erected for him earlier in the spring. To his right, he could see a flash of movement from inside his house—Dana was walking past the glass doors of their bedroom. She had gone inside to change into a bathing suit. Charles watched as Dana removed her blouse and let it drop to the bedroom floor. Looking up out the window, she saw Charles watching her and gave her husband a delightfully wicked smile, and then faded away.

Charles missed her terribly. He missed their son. He missed the man he used to be and the life they used to live.

There were still the occasional fruitless reports from Shillington and Nelson about yet another setback for Charles in the courts.

He felt like a drowning man whom those in the justice system who had authority and power to save him were looking the other way.

Charles had reached the sad realization that even in these United States of America, probably in Canada, too, it was perfectly legal to imprison a man for a crime he didn't commit. Even when his attorneys had crossed every t and dotted every i, no higher court could—or would—intervene to correct an injustice of a prior court, particularly with a young African American defendant, in the Cracker State of Florida.

I have to find some other way. There has to be some evidence somewhere to help me.

As it happened, at the very point of Charles' most profound despair, things were about to change for the better.

In the spring of 1995, the trial of retired football running back O.J. Simpson was "must-see" television in many, if not most, homes in the United States. The same was true in the dayroom on Charles' wing in FSP. Every day—all day on some days—inmates, including Charles, spent their idle moments glued to the television to watch the bizarre proceedings of the murder trial of a popular sports celebrity. After each surprising development in the trial, the group of viewers in the dayroom would break out into loud animated discussion.

"Shit, man. Look at that F. Lee Bailey prancing about in that damned full-length fur coat. The fucking show-off! But if I had had him as my defense attorney in my trial, I wouldn't be rotting here in Raiford."

After attorney Johnnie Cochran's creative defense of Simpson, another inmate would chime in, "That nigger lawyer's going to get Simpson off for the crime, just you wait and see."

Charles asked to be excused from his duties at the library on those days. He arrived early in the dayroom before most of the others and found a good seat where his view of the television was unobstructed and made mental notes. He was particularly captivated by a young defense lawyer—Barry Scheck—when he gave a presentation on something called DNA and how the new technology of DNA testing could affect murder investigations and jury trials with more definitive clarity—near-certainty, even—than ever before.

Even then, watching and listening to the self-assured Jewish New York attorney, Charles could see that DNA technology was not quite the unambiguously "secret bullet" of murder investigations Scheck boasted that it was. Day after day, Scheck disputed the reliability of DNA tests performed on Simpson.

"Blood evidence is only as good as the people collecting it," Scheck told the court. He pointed out irregularities, incidences of mishandling of DNA samples, and the improper mixing and contamination of blood and DNA samples, which led him and others on Simpson's defense team to suspect a conspiracy by the Los Angeles Police Department to frame him for the murder of his ex-wife and male friend.

Nonetheless, Scheck cited examples of the acquittal of numerous inmates in several jails through the use of DNA tests since 1992 when he and a fellow lawyer, Peter Neufeld, had established what they called the "Innocence Project." Charles' ears perked up when he heard Scheck say the word "exoneration."

It was a challenge for Charles to contain his surprise and elation that there was an organization such as the Innocence Project dedicated to the difficult work of defending and advocating for inmates like him who were wasting away in prison, even though they were innocent.

"It's not just the Innocence Project," Scheck acknowledged in a television interview one evening during Simpson's trial. "I can name a dozen or fifteen others doing the same work."

Charles sent a letter to Shillington reporting on the excitement and hope that Scheck inspired in him. He asked Shillington about the procedure of DNA technology. "Have you ever heard of Scheck's outfit? Would it be a good fit for me?"

A reply came from Shillington within a few days, a quick turnaround for prisoner mail.

"Dear Charles, You sound in your letter as though you are on the verge of a new lease on your life. Yes, as a matter of fact, I do know of the Innocence Project. It's a small world after all. I attended a conference for lawyers in Atlanta last month about the proper use of DNA evidence in capital trials. Who should be the keynote speaker but a bright young graduate of the law school at the University of California-Berkeley named Ilona Lawrence? It turned out that Ms. Lawrence had been a classmate with Barry Scheck.

"Scheck invited Ms. Lawrence to serve on the staff of a new initiative that he and Neufeld were establishing called the Innocence Project. As she spoke about the work of the Innocence Project and described some of the success that they had enjoyed with the help of DNA tests, I thought immediately of *you*, Charles. She could have been describing you and your case.

"So after one session of the conference, I approached Ms. Lawrence and made an appointment to meet her during a coffee break to explore whether the Innocence Project might help in your particular case. She agreed, even though keynote speakers at law conferences are often swamped with requests for private tête-à-têtes with attendees.

"We did have coffee. I outlined some of the details of your case. I started to give a list of the outrageous irregularities, incompetence, and malfeasance of Henderson and Davidson, even Erskine in the trial. I had just gotten started when she opened her folder, dug out Barry Scheck's calling card, and gave it to me.

"'Sounds like you have a classic case of wrongful conviction. Call Barry. He salivates when he hears about one like this,' she had said.

"As soon as I got back to West Palm, I did call him. The guy is an off-the-charts extrovert, as garrulous as they come. We spent almost two hours on the phone talking about the specifics of your case.

"'Our problem now," I told him, 'is that we are almost out of legal remedies. We still haven't been able to get our hands on most of the pertinent evidence, some of it exculpatory we have very good reason to suspect.'"

"'There are proven ways to deal with that,' Scheck assured me. "The evidence must be somewhere. They presented so little of it in your client's trial.'

"'The Innocence Project sounds expensive to me, what with all the tests, many of which have to be repeated.'

"'Don't let that get in the way. We survive on donations mainly. Your client is one of the unusual lucky ones: He had a decent defense lawyer. If you can find an equally committed and suitable lawyer to work up front for us in Florida, we'll do most of the work *pro bono*.'

"'Today may finally be Charles' lucky day.'

"'I'm afraid that the local capital case lawyer I mention cannot be you or your partner. I'm sure you've been doing a great job. But we're going to need to go back to some of these nincompoops you describe for some of that missing evidence, and they're accustomed to turning you down. We need to have a new face and voice dealing with them.'

"'Gotcha.'

"'There are a few steps you or that local capital case attorney near you in Florida need to take: applications, background reports, and such, and then, Voilá, we're in business.'"

SHILLINGTON AND NELSON COMPLETED the necessary application forms to the Innocence Project on Charles' behalf. Barry Scheck telephoned them several weeks later to tell them that his case sounded like one that they would accept and have the experience and expertise to provide help.

Charles was like an excitable little child on Christmas Eve when Shillington called to give him the news. In fact, in addition to feeling like a Christmas wish come true, to be taken on by the Innocence Project was also a Christmas hope and bedtime prayer to the Tooth Fairy rolled into one.

Charles became aware once again of the miraculous, transformative power of *hope*. Suddenly, he had a heart full of it. He began to greet inmates who on normal days were irritants to him with a smile and "How ya doing?" and actually meant it. He felt he got more than twice as many of his tasks at the library finished than before. He stopped in the corridor to chat about last night's football game with a guard who had the reputation for being among the meanest and angriest of them.

Scheck had warned Shillington that the Innocence Project was the victim of its own success and had a backlog of cases to process and work through the courts. It would probably be months, if not years, before they could get to work seriously on Charles' case. With his replenished storehouse of hope and joy, however, any possible delay would not discourage Charles.

"What's another three years in jail? I've survived this far. I can make it a few more."

Shillington did say that once the Innocence Project assumed leadership in Charles' case, Scheck and another Innocence Project (IP) attorney would become his defense attorneys. Shillington and Nelson would "retire" from the case. They would remain available to the IP attorneys, however, as repositories of the history and idiosyncrasies of the case, but when Charles received a call from his attorneys from then on, it would be either Scheck or an associate such as Ilona Lawrence on the other end of the telephone line.

Scheck instructed Shillington and Nelson to rummage through their mental Rolodex of names of lawyers who could serve as the IP's local contact to perform some groundwork and represent them in court when neither Scheck nor Lawrence was able to travel to West Palm Beach. Shillington and Nelson had a few ideas but hadn't approached anyone yet.

The hope engendered in him by Scheck and the IP would help him survive at FSP. Though Charles realized it was dangerous to put all his eggs into one basket, he knew from seventeen years of experience in prison that getting through the day was easier if you believed that help was on the way. He *chose* to believe.

CHAPTER 40

SUMMER 1995

IT WAS GRADUATION DAY AT FSP; twenty-three years after he left Boynton Beach High School, Charles was finally receiving his undergraduate degree in American literature. The graduation ceremony was a troubled Florida prison system production. Every inmate graduating from anything was brought together in a non-air-conditioned chow hall where the graduates could sip punch, chew on store-bought cookies, and sweat with their lucky guests.

A motivational speaker was hired to stroke the inmate grads' egos, telling some of the least disciplined people in the world: "If you put your minds to it, you can be anything you want to be."

Charles snickered secretly at that sentimental pap and supposed the other inmates did, too. But then again, many of them had already reached their goal in life: They had wanted to grow up to be "tough guys," and here they were.

Guys who had struggled to get their GED made up the largest and rowdiest group of graduates and were the reason FSP had extra guards on hand that afternoon. Some of them had gone through the GED program two or three times before they achieved it—but they *had* achieved it. The state had a new requirement that any inmate who passed the high school equivalency program be granted parole. Every inmate wanted parole, even if it meant they would have to endure the pain of learning or relearning to read and do basic math.

After the ceremony Eileen and Richard came over to Charles and overwhelmed him with congratulations. Like a high school adolescent, Charles ushered them to where this instructor from UCF was standing stiffly with several other B.A. recipients, and proudly introduced him to his parents.

"Charles was a delight to have in our weekly class all these years," he told them, then patted Charles on the back in gratitude and with congratulations.

Charles returned the gracious compliment. "We owe you our gratitude for sharing your love for literature with us. Thank you."

Later Eileen said, "Oh, Charles. Wouldn't Dana be so proud of what you've accomplished?"

Charles knew Eileen meant well, of course, but the mention of his late wife altered the mood of celebration. Charles was reminded again how much he missed her, and how badly he had been wanting her all afternoon to be at the ceremony. *How I miss Travis, too. I wish he were here.*

He resolved almost that minute to meet with Travis one more time. Charles was on shakier legal ground to make such a request, now that Travis was being adopted, but he wrote Travis anyway and asked him to come up to Raiford for one more visit. He told his son that he didn't have to come if he didn't want to. But if he wanted to sever contact and family ties with Charles, he would like it if he came and told his father so in person, face to face.

A few weeks later Charles came to the contact visit area early to wait for his visitors. He was very anxious, just as he had been for Travis's first visit with him at FSP.

It was Danielle's new husband, Gary, who drove Travis to FSP. Charles stood up to welcome Gary by shaking his hand. He looked at Gary and felt a shock of envy at the man who would soon, if he hadn't already, be designated by the state as Travis's father.

Charles hesitated at first but then took Travis into his arms and greeted him with a hug with as little self-consciousness as he could muster. *Why shouldn't I embrace my own flesh and blood? I don't have any idea of how Gary feels about it, and frankly, I don't care.*

Travis went along with Charles' hug but kept his arms limp at his side.

Charles showed them to seats opposite him at the picnic table. Travis sat beside Gary, who was trying his best to look relaxed and self-confident. Travis had his head down, a nervous adolescent boy. He was very withdrawn and visibly unhappy and uncomfortable.

Join the club, kid. What's he feeling right now? Embarrassment because of the hug? Nervousness at this initial meeting with the man who was about to become "Dad" and the man he had been accustomed to calling "Dad?" Sadness at having to say goodbye? I know I'm a tangled mess of every emotion in the dictionary.

They exchanged pleasantries. Charles asked Gary if he had trouble finding FSP.

"I always double-check the road map before heading somewhere where I've never been."

Looking directly at Travis's face, Charles asked him if this was going to be their last visit.

"Yes," Travis uttered in a whisper, not looking at Charles but the floor beneath them.

"I see," Charles said sadly. "If you ever change your mind, Travis, I won't be hard to find. Gary knows the way now."

Travis's face registered no emotion. Just stiffness at having to repeat the news to Charles face to face.

Charles had trouble putting words together into a sentence. The sting of sadness in his throat was unbearable.

"Travis, I want you to know that no matter what others around you say, no matter even what the court says, I did *not* kill your mother."

Charles barely got the whole sentence out before he could say no more. He couldn't hide his unspeakable hurt any longer. He was deeply, deeply wounded. After wiping the tears from his eyes, he reacted the way men often do when their feelings are overwhelming—he got angry. In prison it was usually safest to be angry. Charles stood up and said bitterly to Gary, "Take care of my son." He hoped that Gary was hurt by that.

Charles walked out. The final visit lasted only a few minutes. Charles' hot anger didn't last much longer either. But the wound still festered, and the hurt went on for a long time.

In the years ahead Charles sent Travis birthday cards and small gifts on other special occasions in his life until Danielle asked him to stop doing so and confusing the boy. Travis never wrote back, not that Charles really expected him to. Travis became for him just someone Dana's family knew, someone out there somewhere growing up, growing older year by year, someone growing farther and farther out of reach.

But Charles knew that he would always love him, and that Travis would always be the living embodiment of a loving marriage that ended far too soon. Charles still hoped that someday, by some miracle, he would get another chance to be his father again.

CHAPTER 41

SEPTEMBER 11, 2001

CHARLES HAD BEGUN TO FEEL that he had finally recovered from the trauma of Travis's cutting in two his relationship with him. The world beyond the prison, however, had jumped its tracks.

That morning in September, it was a typical start to the day at work in the library. Charles had stepped out of the library to retrieve whatever mail might have arrived for the Interlibrary Loan Program. He was anxious to see what had arrived since he had put in a request for a book not available, as many are not in the FSP library.

The inmate who handled the mail on some days casually asked Charles if he knew any more about the Twin Towers.

"What towers?" Charles asked.

"The Twin Towers in New York—what are they called? The World Trade Center. You haven't heard? They were knocked down by an airplane."

"No, I hadn't heard. By a drunken pilot?"

"No, worse than that. They're speculating that it's an act of terrorism."

Charles took the mail and left the mailroom. *Yeah, right! The huge World Trade Center towers knocked over by a plane. Like I'll hit the lottery tomorrow. Just as likely.*

But Charles heard a couple of guards talking together in the corridor, not about hunting this time but about the retribution they hoped President George W. Bush would unleash on whoever it was that attacked buildings on U.S. soil. Even in the locked-down world that they inhabited, news began to bleed out about what had happened in the Big Apple.

September 11 happened to be one of Charles' short workdays in the library. He skipped lunch after work, went directly to his house, and turned on the television. (He had his own in his cell now and didn't have to sit through WWE fights and interminable basketball games in the dayroom.) Charles was utterly transfixed. He couldn't believe the amount of destruction and devastation in the streets of New York. People were evacuating the financial district on foot, covered in white dust and looking like characters out of a zombie movie. The TV stations kept repeating the slow-motion replay of the collapse of the superstructure of the first tower. Then they showed a second plane hitting the other tower. Charles couldn't believe what he was seeing. It felt like the day in November 1963 when President Kennedy had been assassinated outside the Texas School Book Depository in Dallas. The same tears in the eyes of the onlookers. The same huddles of mourners. The same forbidding sense among all that now *anything* was possible.

As more and more facts and suspicions about the who, what, and where of the attacks were revealed in the TV news programs, Charles heard the growing drumbeats of war. Later at chow time he saw fear and confusion on the faces of many of the inmates for the first time. Charles felt a part of a terribly naked and vulnerable nation the way he and his middle school classmates did when it was verified that the Russians had placed ballistic missiles on Cuba in 1962.

The world outside had gone crazy. Everyone Charles loved was out there. Ironically, he felt safer in prison. Eighteen-year-old Travis returned to the forefront of his thoughts. Could this terrorist attack lead to the reinstatement of the draft?

Then, in relatively short order, life inside FSP went back to what passed as normal.

ONE MORNING A YEAR LATER, Charles was summoned to the superintendent's office to take a phone call. On the rare occasions when an inmate is summoned to the Head Honcho's lair, the guards are particularly on the q.t. As a couple walk the inmate down the corridors to the administrative area, they don't let on what's up or what's on the line, making the long walk an exercise in terror—a panicked brainstorm in the mind of who might be deadly sick or dead or what he might have done wrong to deserve a private audience with the Boss Man himself.

Damn! Just when I was finally getting accustomed—feeling rather at home, in fact. I don't need another setback.

Once at the office Charles discovered that he actually had good news. Ilona Lawrence was on the telephone wanting to talk with him. She was on Innocence Project business in Miami and wanted to get Charles' permission to come to FSP to discuss a few potentially good developments in his case.

"My *permission?"* Charles buzzed playfully. "Are you kidding me? You've got it. How soon can you get here?"

Charles had heard of Ms. Lawrence from Shillington, of course, but had never met her face to face. When was the last time a courteous, competent professional woman in her thirties asked to come visit him in prison? Not *ever*!

She had a couple of days of meetings scheduled with the prosecutors and defense attorneys for another client in Miami. She'd come up as soon as she completed her business with them.

Ilona Lawrence turned out not to be the beauty off the pages of *Vogue* that her low, sultry voice on the telephone had led Charles to imagine. She was dressed that day in blue jeans and a checked, green, oversized flannel shirt. Charles doubted that she would be dressed in that fashion when she met with prosecutors and defense attorneys. But she obviously knew prisons and had no reason for the moment to impress the prison administration. Nor, Charles figured, allow herself to be the object of the secret lascivious catcalls of Union County guards or the carnal fantasies of sexually repressed inmates who would encounter her in the corridor and wouldn't resist the urge to whistle at her.

Ms. Lawrence did not come to FSP alone, however. Sitting beside her in the anteroom to the superintendent's office was a tall, rail-thin man, also dressed down much like Lawrence. She introduced him to Charles as Sven Pressley, a professor at the law school at the University of Florida in Gainesville. Pressley was the lawyer identified by Shillington and Nelson as the capital case attorney who was local and who would do the appropriate groundwork on behalf of IP lawyers Lawrence and Scheck. Pressley was now on the defense team, replacing Shillington and Nelson. He was relatively well known in Florida legal circles for his popular law school course, "Wrongful Convictions: The Ultimate Failure of the Justice System." Pressley assigned members of the class, many of them journalism majors, to research at least one case in Florida that resulted in the wrongful conviction of a defendant.

After the customary preliminary pleasantries among people who had never met before, Lawrence segued to outlining some information for Charles about his case and Innocence Project strategy regarding it.

"We've devised a plan of attack," she began. "Sven has made application to the office of the new Palm Beach County District Attorney's for his access to the judicial records and proceedings in your case. Sven will base his request on the Florida Open

Government Statute—better known as the Sunshine Law—which defends the right of attorneys to demand to inspect the state's evidence in a case against a defendant, the right for which your attorneys Shillington and Nelson demanded unsuccessfully from the prosecutor at your trial."

"Ms. Lawrence," Charles interrupted, "did I hear you say, 'the *new* Palm Beach County District Attorney?' What became of Buck Davidson who was the county Sheriff who arrested me? Didn't he get elected as District Attorney after my trial?"

Pressley, being the local, answered for her. "He sure was, by a landslide. He got what he wanted out of you by your wrongful arrest and conviction. He became a law and order god. But alas, even some gods are mortal. Davidson died in 1998."

Charles hadn't heard that. For a fleeting moment Charles felt a sense of loss, as he would at the death of any person in his life. He and Davidson were forever linked. But, for God's sake, this was Davidson, the one who had engineered his legal "lynching" and handed him over to the State to try and sentence him to life in prison. *A solitary minute of routine acknowledgement is all I owe him. That's all. Palm Beach County is rid of him.*

"A guy named John Gorlick from Jacksonville was appointed as Davidson's successor," Pressley added. "The governor wanted someone from out of the county as the new District Attorney."

"Anyway, Charles, Sven has yet to hear back about the release of documents and the contents of files that he's asked for. He'll follow up on that."

"But what if the Clerk of Palm Beach County refuses to hand them over?" Charles asked with a doubtful tone in his voice. "They haven't exactly been examples of cooperation before."

"Then we'll sue them," Pressley inserted emphatically. "Remember the Florida Sunshine Law. It's on our side."

"We'll need your permission to do DNA tests on all the autopsy swabs taken from Dana's body by the medical examiner—everything from scrapings underneath her fingernails to the tiny hairs they found clutched in her hand. They might have been from the killer. The testing might provide evidence that would tell us with certainty whether Dana had been sexually assaulted in any way."

Something that I dread learning.

"The trial was fifteen years ago. Are all those swabs somehow still in good enough condition for DNA tests?" Charles wondered.

"In many cases the evidence has been carelessly stored while in a sheriff's or prosecutor's custody," Pressley explained like the professor that he was.

"Carelessly stored, accidentally on purpose?" Charles asked.

"Yes, too often. By the time they get to doing DNA tests much of the biological evidence has deteriorated. But DNA is pretty resilient stuff. Usually the forensic technicians can find at least one area on a piece of evidence, even a tiny area, where the DNA has persisted."

"Related to that, Barry, Sven, and I will apply for DNA testing on the sheet that was on your bed when Dana's body was discovered. Your prior attorneys told us that an investigator had discovered semen stains on it. Maybe yours, as the prosecutor said, or maybe someone else's—"

"Like the actual murderer's?" Charles cut in.

"The DNA test will be able to tell us."

The meeting with Lawrence and Pressley was over. Charles floated back to his cell—high on life for the first time he could remember in fifteen years. Maybe he was just intoxicated by the potential for good news and progress in his case. But there was something else about the meeting that made Charles a little giddy. For the first time since his meetings months ago with Shillington and Nelson, he had actually had the chance to speak with two intelligent, educated, polite, and compassionate people who were committed to his well-being and future. He couldn't remember any conversation recently with FSP staff like that. Even the most gentle-looking female guards had a sharp edge. Beneath their shallow, outward smiles, they were no more respectful or less hostile than the men.

Jacobson and Henderson had been interested only in punishing Charles for what they accused him of doing.

But with Lawrence and Pressley, he chatted and laughed. They were friendly and asked questions—even asked for his *permission*, for heaven's sake. They didn't yell at him derisively or issue orders or speak to him coarsely like guards but treated him as though he had equal worth. Just normal conversation, human being to human being.

CHAPTER 42

OCTOBER 2002

WHEN HE WAS A YOUNGSTER AT HOME in Buffalo, New York, Charles got up early every Sunday morning because he had some place he needed to be.

He would put on his nicest clothes—a gleaming white short-sleeved shirt, his good pants pressed, and his shined dress shoes that he and his mother had bought downtown. He'd brush his teeth, look in his mirror, and adjust his stiff kinky black hair as much as it allowed. Before he went downstairs to wait for his parents, Richard and Eileen, to be ready, he would add the last sartorial touch that just about every twelve-year-old boy in the early 1960s needed, be they black or white: a clip-on bow tie.

The family of three went to their church almost every week. Eileen would also have on her Sunday best—hose, heels, perhaps a string of pearls, and always a pretty dress. They would step out of their Cape Cod home, shiny and polished, and head for the First Baptist Church on Bingham Avenue.

In Sunday school Charles learned Bible stories about Adam and Eve, Noah's Ark, David and Goliath, and his favorite at that juncture in his life: David and Bathsheba.

In the church service after Sunday school, the preacher would apply the traditional lessons to their lives. Mostly, the preacher helped the congregation know the difference between right and wrong, heaven and hell, walking with God or walking off a cliff. The choice was easy, the preacher promised. All you had to do was know which was the right path.

But a few years later, Charles didn't find things so clear-cut and easy.

A teenage friend had teased Charles when they were talking about something that was clearly not on the Godlike path. It was something naughty, which meant it must have been about one of two things—beer or sex—the two primary temptations faced by teenage boys in those days. His friend told Charles that he couldn't possibly know what he was talking about since Charles was such a good, churchgoing type.

At that moment in the tight stranglehold of peer pressure, Charles decided that he would take that summer to live "off the leash" and dabble in some things that his mother dreaded, and in acts that his church frowned upon. He reasoned that he'd come back to the church where he had left off wiser, more experienced, as a man who had tasted freedom.

Now Charles realized, almost forty years later, he hadn't come back. There was a brief exception just before he and Dana got married when he took private instructions in Roman Catholicism from Dana's priest but that had been to reassure her family, and her, too, that he wasn't an atheistic nonbeliever.

He hadn't given God much thought since he was a seventeen-year-old until one night in FSP when he began to wonder what difference it would make for his life in prison if he reassessed the role of God in his life. He was simply too stunned, too rocked back on his heels at the low blow life had dealt to Travis and himself, trying so desperately to keep his head above the dark, swirling water that was washing him away.

When Dana was killed, people with good intentions told him that they would pray for him but he didn't know what that really meant. When he was wrongfully convicted, he was too enraged to find any comfort in the possibility that there were people bringing him into the presence of God so he discounted it. He was infuriated that fate had compounded the cruelty of Dana's murder by taking away Travis, and his own freedom, too. In prison that rage protected him from his hostile environment, and in a strange way comforted him. It kept Charles cynical about whatever happened to the man—or the boy—he used to be.

It dawned on him, however, that the anger had also kept him from looking deeper into himself.

Charles was familiar with the professed conversion experiences of some fellow inmates, their newfound satisfying relationship with Christ their Lord, at least as they gloried in it. But it seemed to Charles that these born-again conversions always occurred conveniently just before their parole hearings. Charles saw them as attempts by inmates to bargain with God, to find and try faith only *because* they wanted something.

Charles had never done that. He had never prayed for God's help when Dana was killed, or when Travis had his dangerous but life-saving surgery as a toddler. He never prayed to be found innocent by the jury. He had never promised to be a better person if God would intervene and transform some of the bigger obstacles in his journey into a more comfortable existence.

When Travis decided he didn't want to see Charles anymore, the blow had been so profound that Charles felt it physically, emotionally, psychologically, and ultimately *spiritually*.

Suddenly, the only anchor mooring him in the world was gone. Travis had been the only sanctuary he had left. Travis had been the receptacle of all his hopes and dreams, the light at the end of his long tunnel. Travis was Charles' idol and his religion—his reason for living, his everything.

The loss of that relationship colored all his thoughts. It was a cloud that prevented his eyes from seeing anything positive or good. The conversation with Ilona and Sven had provided a respite from the gloom but only a brief, transitory one. In his darkest moments alone in his cell, Charles couldn't believe that the news he heard from them were "really real." He didn't like feeling this way. The prospect of DNA tests certainly was a welcome reprieve from his dark mood but he suspected the journey was still long and stony. *A lot of things can sabotage this thing, and probably will.*

Now Charles was dangerously close to feeling hopeless, defeated, broken. He knew himself well enough to know he couldn't stand so close to those feelings for very long and survive what he still had to endure. So he did something that was so uncharacteristic for him: He cried out to God.

"I beg you, if you hear me, for some sign, for some reason to go on living. For a way out of the abyss and out of the pain, for some deliverance, some reassurance. Something."

But all Charles received was nothing. Only total silence and emptiness. Further proof that he had been right all along that there was really no one there. That he was truly alone. *I knew there wouldn't be one.*

Charles plodded along day after day without a sign. Each successive day was just another day in prison. There had been thousands like it for him in the past, and it appeared there could be thousands more in the future.

At the end of yet another tiresome, tedious day, a typical one, Charles pulled himself onto his bunk. It was late, and he was worn out. He put on his stereo headphones, switched off the small reading light beside his bed, closed his eyes, found a station that came in clearly, and began listening, prepared to be carried off to another night of dark and dreamless sleep.

With no warning whatsoever, a bright, blinding golden light burst into the cell like lightning. The light swallowed up everything and enveloped Charles totally. He felt wrapped in light, a warm, wonderful, comforting light, a sensation entirely unlike any he had previously experienced.

He felt he was floating fearlessly, effortlessly, blissfully above his bunk. The classical music from his stereo slowly receded and was replaced by an incomprehensible roar like the thunderous roll of a massive wind or the crash and rumble of great rushing waters. He felt he was being lifted up and supported by some monumental power, mighty but very gentle, formidable but forgiving somehow, more so than anything he had ever imagined before.

Is this happening to me? God visiting me? This must be a dream. I don't deserve this bliss. But I am the recipient of it, nonetheless.

Most of all, more than the exquisite light and the inspiriting roar of unseen winds or the pure rhapsody this unique experience gave him, what he remembered most acutely was the seemingly infinite peace and joy, the limitless compassion and intense love he felt aimed right at him. The power was not meant at that moment for all of humanity but intended specifically and particularly and exclusively for Charles.

He knew intuitively without being told by anyone that this experience was nothing less than God's unmediated, perfect, boundless love. After so many years in prison, after being rejected by so many, after being bounced in and out of courts and kept behind steel bars, after losing his wife, his son, his life, and after all those years of a bad conscience on the verge of self-loathing for no logical reason at all, he was assured that none of that could separate him from the immense love for him of this brilliant light.

He couldn't claim that in his spiritual experience he had seen Jesus or heard a disembodied voice telling him to build a huge ark and load in the animals two by two because a hard rain was gonna fall. What he had seen and heard and felt was a divine light, a holy presence, a power that in one way or another he had been seeking all his life.

That light was to stay with him through all the years of

challenges and disappointments yet to come, through fresh heartaches and the settling of old scores. On the morning after Charles had no way of knowing how much he would need the presence of that light to survive all that was to come.

He continued to lie on his bunk and revel in the peace. The next thing he knew his alarm was going off and the lights in the cell were on. He had no recollection of having switched them back on. His stereo headphones were hanging from the nail he had hammered into the edge of his bunk as a convenient place to put them. But Charles was convinced he had fallen asleep with the headphones still on his ears and hadn't woken to hang them on the nail. He didn't understand what had happened during the night or why. He fell back on Occam's Razor: Of all the possible explanations he could conjure up for the phenomenon, the simplest one was probably the best. He had cried out to God for a sign, and he received exactly what he was asking for.

Charles realized that he was still a work in progress. He wanted to be the kind of person who *deserved* to be in the presence of God.

Soon enough Charles was back in his same old cell, in the same wing, the same prison that had been his home for over a decade and a half.

But it was a new morning, a new day. He was a new Charles.

CHAPTER 43
SEPTEMBER 2005

THE INNOCENCE PROJECT TEAM put in requests for items of suppressed evidence from the Palm Beach County District Attorney's Office. They were savvy enough not to call the evidence they wanted "*suppressed* evidence" since it had never been designated as such in a court of law, which was in spite of the fact that Shillington and Nelson knew intuitively that there was almost certainly such evidence and had no trouble convincing the IP lawyers of it.

Prosecutorial suppression of evidence, usually favorable to the defendant, was one of the primary reasons for wrongful convictions of innocent defendants. It's where the IP begins its "sniffing" in most cases. If not prosecutorial suppression of evidence, other prominent sources of malfeasance are wrongful identification of the defendant by a witness, and false confessions of guilt by the defendant often under distress or pressure exerted by the arresting law enforcement entity. Often with IP applying pressure on the identifying witness or the law enforcement personnel, the truth usually leaks out and the IP is able to apply to the courts for a new trial for their client.

The process of requesting missing evidence or arrangements for DNA testing on the evidence once it is uncovered and made available frequently launches a game of "hurry up and wait"—"hurry up" to meet deadlines for making a request, then "wait" often for a year or more for the particular government agency to respond to the request.

Since he had heard from his legal team that they had submitted their requests, Charles had been waiting for over a year for more word. Despite the delays, Charles knew that his file was flying across time zones; the pounds of paperwork and peculiar details of his case were being evaluated by very smart lawyers looking at it all with fresh eyes and open minds. Charles' amazement at, and gratitude for, their generosity hadn't waned in the least. *They're doing all this without any reason to believe in me. I want to be worthy of their trust in me.*

Waiting during the seemingly interminable delays was buffered by the possibility of an exoneration, an up-and-down belief that the impossible might just happen, that his legal team might just pull it off.

His legal team had reached out to the relatively new District Attorney of Palm Beach County, John Gorlick, who assumed the office in 1998 after Buck Davidson died of stomach cancer. The attorneys hoped that cooperation would have improved in the D.A.'s office with Davidson gone and a new man behind the desk. They were disappointed. It seemed that Gorlick and Davidson were cut from the same cloth. Gorlick treated his office as a passport to unchallenged power in his realm. Initially, he refused the attorneys' request on Charles behalf for the transcripts of Charles' trial and any items of documents that the prosecution referred to in the trial. Gorlick seemed to regard such a request as an invasion of the D.A. office's privacy.

"That case was closed years ago, and it's *our* business," he said.

It wasn't until Pressley pointed out that the Florida Sunshine Laws gave Charles' lawyers the right to request the files and reason to expect to get a prompt affirmative response to such a request that Gorlick took a very tentative, reluctant step to back down.

"Thank you for your cooperation, Mr. Gorlick," Pressley said in his most courteous voice.

"It will probably be some time while I rummage through the storage area and locate what you're asking for," Gorlick warned them, still hanging on to his "right of possession." Then, under his breath he added, "We work at our own pace here, even if it's a bunch of high-priced New York lawyers and their local lackey who are telling me how to run this office."

"We'll be on the lookout in the mail soon, Mr. Gorlick, for the material we've requested," Lawrence said in a mildly threatening tone as she was going out the door from his office.

A FEW WEEKS AFTER LAWRENCE AND PRESSLEY paid their courtesy call at Gorlick's office, Pressley called Charles to say that the only piece of evidence sent to them by Gorlick was a bluish piece of cloth that looked like a bandana. He asked Charles about it.

"You have any idea what it is and why it's among the evidence? The transcripts of the trial make no mention of it."

"Yeah, my brother-in-law, a retired sheriff's deputy, found it as he was doing his own investigation of our property and the yard of the house that was being constructed next door."

"You never brought it to the attention of your attorneys?"

"I'm trying to remember; it's been so many years. I do remember that my brother-in-law reported it to Sheriff Davidson and asked that he send someone over to retrieve it and include it with the other evidence. Doug had gone to great lengths to pack it in a plastic baggie to prevent it being compromised in any way. But because Davidson and Henderson had possession of the bandana and the other evidence, that was the last we heard of the bandana."

"Well, we finally have it now. The preliminary testing indicates that there was some blood on it."

"Whose blood?"

"That's what we're wondering."

Suddenly, Charles felt fear shoot through him. *Is there any way that it could be* my *blood?* He knew that it was an irrational thought. He had no reason to fear that it was his blood. But he hadn't been thinking very logically in the past few weeks.

Later that evening Charles prayed as hard as he could for acceptance of what might come next. *The bandana might tell all secrets. I could be destined to live out my life behind these bars. Davidson and Henderson had access to the bandana for years. They could even have smeared a sample of my blood on the bandana. It wouldn't be beneath them.*

Charles braced himself for bad news from the DNA testing lab.

But late in May 2011, Charles was handed a letter from Ilona Lawrence. She wrote to say that she would be elsewhere in Florida later in the week and planned on popping in at FSP to visit him.

But the end of Ilona's letter left Charles unsettled. Ilona casually mentioned that Sven Pressley would be with her again. Charles' mind reeled with possibilities. Were both Ilona and Sven coming to share the good news from the forensics lab—or did they both want to be together to deliver the bad news Charles was fearing? Both scenarios made sense.

Charles barely slept a wink that night thinking over and over all the possibilities that might be played out in the visitation room the next morning. He flipped and flopped around on his bunk like a fish tossed onto the floor of a boat. He alternated between praying and nodding off, hitting the pillow and cradling his head in his hands, fantasizing and planning his reaction to good or bad news.

Or am I overthinking things?

It was now at such a late stage of his incarceration that he couldn't help allowing his imagination to get carried away. Finally, dawn arrived and put him out of his misery.

The prison was on "lockdown," which happened whenever the count of inmates present by the guard didn't match the number on the official roster. Moving through the prison, especially to receive visitors, was difficult. Charles had to jump through all kinds of official hoops and get permission from various and sundry officers to proceed. It took him an hour just to get out of the wing and reach the visitation area. Once he got there, he had to stand in the corridor and wait another hour or so. He worried that Ilona and Sven had had similar problems getting in, or they might have turned around, gone back to their rental car, and then driven Sven back to Gainesville.

Finally, through the small square window in the door, he saw his attorneys walk through the door into the visitation room.

Sven was at least a head taller than anyone else in the room, perhaps the whole prison. He was moving the way he always did—like he was racing the clock to make it to court on time. His customary "full-speed-ahead" stance reflected his approach to legal battles—every case was the invasion of Normandy all over again.

Ilona marched beside Sven and matched him step for step. She had a singular way of appearing to be ferociously and meticulously on top of everything but endearing at the same time.

But Charles was unprepared to see her smile so broadly. The smile was so big and beautiful and startlingly bright that Charles believed she could have been used to signal ships in distress on a foggy sea.

The three of them moved into their more private visiting cubicle reserved for lawyers' visits with clients. Charles' heart was beating so hard he was sure they could hear it. His whole body was trembling. He pressed his legs to his chair as hard as he could to hold them steady. Sven held the palm of his hand flat against the plate of plexiglass that separated the inmate from his attorneys. Charles took the cue and put his palm against Sven's. He was smiling at Charles, then at Ilona, and then looked back beaming at Charles.

"We have some good news for you."

Sven and Ilona excitedly passed the phone handset back and forth as they explained how the testing on the bandana confirmed that some of the blood on the bandana was Dana's. That was big. Doug had speculated at the outset that the bandana had been dropped in the neighbor's yard as the killer made his getaway.

Doug had been right.

Then the bombshell: The other DNA on the bandana—skin cells

intermingled with traces of dried sweat and of Dana's blood. The DNA wasn't Charles', apparently, but belonged to an unknown male.

"The man who killed my wife," Charles said with relief.

"Yes, the culprit who has gotten away with the murder—until now," Sven added.

"There's a chance we can run this man's DNA through a national database and get a hit. We could find him and arrest him," Ilona said.

In odd ways, this possibility awakened the suppressed hurt and despair he felt about losing Dana. Nearly twenty years after her death, Charles at long last faced the likely possibility of finding out who had done what he was still in prison for. Charles was totally unprepared for the new wave of almost palpable grief that washed over him. He was struggling just to swallow and breathe. One moment he felt he had the strength of ten men and could jump so high he could touch the ceiling, the next he thought he might sink to the floor.

It was not unlike the moment long ago when the jury foreman stood up and, without looking at Charles, declared, "We find the defendant guilty!" Only this time he was stunned in reverse.

"Take a few minutes, Charles," Sven said, "to simply breathe and process the information."

Sven was right. While Charles stood near the glass wall of the cubicle and then leaned against it to steady himself, Sven and Ilona stayed on the other side of the plexiglass and spoke some encouraging words to him. Charles' eyes were brimming with tears. Ilona kept talking while Charles regained his composure.

Ilona brought the conversation back to earth. Soberly, she reminded Charles that nothing was official yet. The forensic lab report hadn't been posted yet. Gorlick and his staff at the Palm Beach County D.A.'s office had fought them at every turn. "But we're going to keep on fighting if we have to. There's a marathon of legal wrangling still to come. It'll take a while, Charles."

Pressley continued. "Treat this interval time as you did the months between Dana's murder and the trial. *All* of your mail, *every* telephone call, and *every* conversation, you'll have to guard with your life. A single word from a jailhouse snitch that he heard you discussing the murder or the trial would set us back years. Many of the men behind these bars would do anything to get out faster. You know some of them would stop at nothing to snitch on another—or make up a lie."

Charles sensed that the meeting was coming to an end when Sven brought up something that just about put Charles over the edge.

"Charles, do you want me to find Travis and tell him the news?"

Charles realized again just how raw his feelings regarding Travis were. Huge, shameless tears welled up in his eyes and slid down his face. To Charles, Travis was still a little boy, even though he knew in his mind that he was now a fully grown man. His mother had written to Charles to inform him that she had heard that Travis was now married. He and Charles hadn't had any meaningful contact for years.

"No thanks, Sven. That's kind of you to offer. But I think I'll have to find some way to share the news with him myself."

His lawyers and he said their goodbyes. Ilona beamed as she walked away. Sven stepped out of the cubicle on his side of the glass, and then stepped back in, picked up the phone receiver, and said, "Prayer works."

Charles still wasn't totally comfortable talking about it, but he responded, "Yes, it does. It really does."

CHAPTER 44

IT WAS AS THOUGH THE PAST FEW DAYS in Charles' life had all been a dream. As he walked back from the visitation area where he had met with Ilona and Sven, he felt like a changed man with a new future. Yet, back in his cell, every aspect of his limited life remained unchanged: the buzzers, the undecipherable squawks from the P.A. system, the grinding of the metal doors and their slamming shut behind him, the endless jangling of the guards' keys and cuffs. He was still inside a prison.

As fervently as a few nights ago when he had prayed for acceptance, now he asked for the power of restraint. He had to keep himself from getting ahead of events. He recalled Ilona's words: "There's a marathon of legal wrangling still to do," she had warned him. He had to guard against letting his hurt and rage at the cruelty and incompetence of law enforcement and the legal system explode. He had to behave now as though he had heard nothing, and that he found to be the hardest of all.

To get through it all, Charles focused on the fact that somewhere out there a computer was searching through a massive database of convicted criminals looking for a match for the DNA found on the blue bandana. Thinking about that kept him sane. He might be so very close now to the conclusion but he must not allow himself to celebrate it too early. A lot could still go wrong.

It had been Charles' fifty-seventh birthday a few weeks after the initial good news about the DNA—another birthday in jail. But this one was different.

His work went well that day. When the guards began one of their numerous counts for the day, Charles heard the words of "Happy Birthday" being sung. The men on his wing formed an impromptu choir. After a few minutes one of the inmates, Chuck Woodley, nicknamed James Beard, produced a masterpiece of a prison cake he'd made for the occasion. It was a wild concoction of crushed Oreo cookies, peanut butter, and God knew what else. Then the whole thing was slathered with melted chocolate.

On the P.A. system a voice made an announcement, which

Charles deciphered to say, "Prisoner Wilkerson, report immediately to the law library." Charles hated to duck out of the illicit but innocent party put on for him. But this time he had a good feeling about the call.

Ilona and Sven were waiting for him on the telephone. On the line with them was Barry Scheck, one of the founders and now head of the Innocence Project.

"Charles, happy birthday," Sven said. "We have a birthday gift for you."

Scheck added, "The DNA database found a match, a man presently in California. We don't know his name yet, but it won't take more than a day or two."

Charles grew quiet. Later Sven told him he thought he had fainted. It wasn't far from the truth. He remembered Sven asking, "Charles, all you all right? You still there?"

"Yes, Sven," Charles answered after a pause. "Don't worry. I'm just trying to let all this wash over me."

"Congratulations, Charles," Barry said. "This must be huge for you."

"Tomorrow is the twenty-fifth anniversary of Dana's death. After all this time, I'm finally getting some of the answers I've been searching for."

"We're not quite at the finish line yet, of course," Barry added. "Charles, I've got another question for you. What do you know, if anything, about what Travis said to the therapist way back twenty-five years ago?"

"As I remember it, the therapist said she doubted that Travis had actually seen the 'monster with the red hands' in our house. He was simply experiencing very understandable ill effects of suddenly being separated from his mother."

Barry then read aloud from a transcript of a telephone conversation between Dana's mother and Sergeant Ramsden at the county sheriff's office. The legal team had gotten ahold of the transcript along with other files and documents in Henderson and Davidson's possession.

Shortly after Dana's funeral, her mother had called Ramsden about a conversation initiated by her grandson. "He told me he had seen a 'monster with red hands' who had hit his mother in the house. When I asked him if his Daddy was in the room or house, he said, 'No, just Mom and this monster. Not Daddy.'"

Charles recalled telling Shillington about what Travis had told him, pretty much the same as what he had told his grandmother, and that Shillington said that Travis's testimony would probably not be admitted in the trial because of Travis's age. It was pretty late in the game, but at least now his legal team had the transcript.

The trio of lawyers on the phone were understandably focused on the legal significance of the transcript.

"This is as clean and as irrefutable a case as we've seen of the state's suppressing exculpatory evidence," Scheck pronounced. "This is a textbook case. It was a bald violation of the Brady rule and blatantly illegal. Someone in Palm Beach County is in deep doo-doo."

Charles walked back to his cell, not knowing how he felt. He knew he should be feeling exultant about the increasing likelihood that his days at FSP were numbered. He'd be getting out soon—he hoped he wasn't jinxing his chances. It wouldn't be tomorrow or the next day but in the not-too-distant days ahead. It was finally happening!

But Charles was deeply troubled at the same time. Talking about Travis's eyewitness testimony to his grandmother and to him made him feel desperately sorry for Travis, that he had had to see his dead mother laid out on the bed and encounter the murderer face to face. *How long does a traumatic experience like that remain lodged in a boy's memory?*

Charles was also disgusted by the utter travesty of the sheriff department's investigation of Dana's death and his being put on trial and sitting a quarter of a century in jail. The files and documents that his legal team had managed to pry loose from the Palm Beach D.A.'s office proved how the investigation and prosecution had been even more incompetent, more corrupt, and more mean-spirited than even he imagined.

Davidson, with the full knowledge and cooperation of Henderson, had hidden Charles' neighbors' reports of an old green van lurking for days outside the wooded area behind the house. They had buried witness accounts of people living nearby who saw the van's driver hanging about in the woods. What a difference testimony like that might have made in the final verdict reached by the jury.

There would be a new trial now, seeking to vacate Charles' sentence. The judge in Palm Beach County who was assigned to hear Charles' case recused himself. Apparently, the prospect of rooting out the current D.A. and the former one, now deceased, as well as the prosecutor, now a fellow judge, did not appeal to him. Judge Erskine was deceased, and so a new judge who held court in Orlando would be brought in to oversee what happened next in Charles' case.

After the announcement that another man's DNA was discovered on the blue bandana, Palm Beach County D.A. John Gorlick spent the week trying to convince others that none of that mattered. It didn't compromise in any way the case against Charles Wilkerson.

What is it about this fraternity of district attorneys and prosecutors that they will defend and protect their colleagues, right or wrong, to the bitter end?

Gorlick was proving every day that he had no business being on the job, making life or death decisions about Charles' guilt or innocence. It was like watching an ancient tapestry unravel thread by thread. The case against Charles Wilkerson was coming apart lie by lie before their eyes. Anyone watching could see how it was going to end—everyone but the people in charge of the Palm Beach County system of justice.

In late September when Gorlick was still telling anyone who would listen that Charles was guilty and should be kept in prison, the other shoe dropped. Charles received another call from Ilona and Sven. They now had the identity of the man whose DNA was on the bandana. He was someone named Ernest Wilcox, a drifter who was employed from time to time as a carpet layer. He had a criminal record a mile long, mostly for burglary and assault. Now the FBI had matched Wilcox's DNA to yet *another* murder, one that was heartbreakingly similar to Dana's.

Delores Adams Whitehead was found killed on January 11, 1988. The house in which she had been living was several blocks away from the Wilkersons' home. She had been about Dana's age with similar long, black hair. She had been home alone that morning with her three-year-old son. Her body was stretched out on the bed in the bedroom underneath some baskets and a suitcase. She had died as the result of crushing blows to her head and face by a blunt object.

Charles realized that this was good news for him legally. But as a human being who had also lost a beautiful wife in the same manner, it was heartbreaking. Worse, if the Palm Beach County Sheriff's Office had done their job faithfully and correctly, if they had listened to his claims that an intruder had murdered Dana, Delores Adams Whitehead would still be with her child today.

The unsolved Whitehead case had been discovered by two student interns in Sven Pressley's office. They had started looking in the database for murders similar to Dana's. They hit the jackpot very quickly. Even before the DNA connection had been made, they were certain that the same murderer in Dana's case had been involved in Whitehead's. Wilcox had been renting a room in a house on the same block.

On October 1, 2011, Charles was told that he had another call in the law library. The Innocence Project and Sven had been involved in heated hearings over the next steps in his case so Charles figured they were calling to update him.

Instead, Scheck told Charles that John Gorlick—a man who had fought his attorneys tooth and nail and put up every obstacle he could devise—now wanted to cut a deal. Gorlick offered to release Charles from jail on Tuesday, October 4, if Charles agreed to some "reasonable conditions." Most of the conditions were designed to spare Palm Beach law enforcement personnel any fallout. Charles would sign an affidavit guaranteeing his promise not to file a lawsuit against the county or seek any kind of financial compensation for the wrongful conviction or his twenty-five years in prison. Charles was not to make contact with Dana's family and relatives without Gorlick's written permission. He needed to promise that upon release he would leave Palm Beach County and the State of Florida.

"Barry," Charles said categorically, "play hard ball with Gorlick. Tell him no deal."

Three hours later Scheck called Charles back to tell him that Gorlick had caved completely. "He agreed to all our conditions and didn't make any more of his own." Charles would be bench-warranted to Palm Beach County for a quick retrial and promptly released on Tuesday, October 4.

October 4 was only three days away. Charles was too overcome for words. He simply wept tears of inexpressible joy.

Chapter 45

ALL THREE OF CHARLES' ATTORNEYS were sincerely interested if he wanted to make contact with Travis now that he was on the verge of becoming a free man. Charles was also interested, to be sure, but not at all certain that after the months and years of their separation whether Travis would welcome renewed contact, or if indeed it was a wise thing to do for Travis psychologically.

Since Travis had been a toddler, Charles had been the "bad guy." He was the man who everyone, including the courts, agreed was the one who had killed his mother, the creep who broke the hearts of Dana's family, the jerk who was so dangerous that he had to be kept away from decent people, especially his son. But now, in the blink of an eye, a round of obscure, difficult to decipher DNA testing had proven that it had been a man named Ernest Wilcox who had killed his mother. Travis's life would be turned completely upside down. The truths he had been raised by Dana's family to believe turned out not to be true at all. A dirty bandana found on the ground years ago turned out to speak with more authority than the people who had raised him and whom he loved. Charles figured it was going to take a while, a very long while, for Travis to make sense of this new information.

Charles was unsure if the timing was right to reconnect with Travis.

Katie Pressley, Sven's wife and a social worker, in effect made the decision for him. Incredibly, Katie had formerly played tennis with Dana's mother and several other women. Through one of these women, Katie came to know a daughter of one of the women, Christine, who was now Travis's wife.

Katie and Christine became very instrumental in moving Charles' relationship with Travis a few important steps forward. Sven told Katie that Christine believed firmly in the healing power of the truth.

"We shouldn't shield Travis from the truth," Christine had told him, "even if it might be rather sudden and confusing for him to absorb."

For some reason unknown to her, Christine hadn't heard from

Dana's family that Charles was being exonerated until Katie told her.

"Although Travis doesn't mention his father very often," Christine responded to the news, "I do know he is confused and conflicted about his father and his feelings for him. Travis, the once child, still loves his father, but all his life he has heard nothing but bad things about him. As his wife, I know Travis's heart, and I think once he hears the news, he will be open to the idea of a meeting with Charles—and maybe good things will follow."

"That would be a blessing," Katie replied.

"I'm not sure if I should say anything to Charles about the exoneration or the possibility of a meeting until I hear from you if Charles would welcome a meeting with Travis."

"I'll try to find out as soon as possible."

"As you probably know, I've never met Charles but I'd like to meet him before he talks to Travis, if he is willing."

Christine also said to Katie, "I've never met Charles either, but if Travis is anything like his father, I'd like to meet him. If you think it's wise, please tell Charles so and that I would welcome a chance to speak with him before he talks with Travis if he's interested."

Charles was interested, *very* interested. Charles had an intuition that his son would choose a good and wise woman as a spouse, just as he had himself. There'd be nothing to lose by meeting with her privately.

He could see, however, that the better the news was for him from the legal authorities, the more painful and confusing it would become for Travis. Charles felt he was hurting Travis again without intending to, by being transformed suddenly from a wife-killer into an innocent man. *Rebuilding my relationship with Travis means embarking on another very long, very complicated journey. In any case, first I've got a few things to do.*

STANDING BY HIS BUNK IN HIS CELL, Charles began to sort through his property to decide what to take with him when he stepped out the front door for the last time. He actually possessed very little and wanted even less. He'd watched as other inmates prepared to leave the prison after performing this ritual, and he wanted to perform it, too. Like all liturgies, it marked the moment as a sacred one.

He figured that he still had two days to sort through his belongings and give away the things that he wanted other inmates to have. But the bench warrant calling Charles back to Palm Beach County had arrived at the prison. A guard came into the wing and shouted, "Wilkerson, get ready to leave for Palm Beach County. Pack up your stuff. Pronto!" Then he added, "But first you have to move to seg."

That was "segregated housing" where inmates were kept for punishment or protection, or a place to put you on your way out, a kind of prison "no-man's-land." *Figures I don't belong anywhere anymore, at least not in the joint. They had been in such a hurry to push me to get into this place, now I'm being rushed out.*

He asked the guard to wait another few minutes while he picked up some articles he had put on his bunk. He gathered his few family photos, toothpaste, toothbrush, deodorant, a comb, and the Bible his family had sent to him, and put them into one commissary bag. He put everything else—snacks he had bought for himself, some novels, writing supplies, his radio and headphones, his thermal underwear for the winter in the unheated wing, a pair of almost new sneakers, and extra hygiene items—into a larger commissary bag. This bag he wanted to give away to the two men on his wing who he trusted the most, Martin and Rojas. "Keep what you can use with my compliments, and distribute the rest as you see fit. I've got to vamoose."

It felt so satisfying to Charles to share what he had with those who might not have even that much. Doing so, he felt, was part of the sacred unspoken covenant between "brothers" who had lived through life in the "trenches" together and survived.

Charles sensed the guard hurrying him along impatiently. Before he crossed the threshold out into the corridor, he heard a commotion in the dayroom—whoops of delight, full-throated, old-fashioned hollering of good wishes and good-natured mayhem. Some saluted him with raised fists or drummed their hands on the metal tables and stomped their feet on the floor. Claps and cheers came down from the upper tier, a few men in quiet tears.

It was a heartfelt goodbye from the men he had lived with and sometimes loathed, guys who drove him crazy and made him angry or made him laugh. Charles got chills and began to choke up. He waved and kept on walking with the guard.

FSP had given him such a big send-off. He almost wanted to stay. Almost.

CHAPTER 46

TWO PALM BEACH COUNTY SHERIFF'S officers came to FSP to take Charles back to the place where he had been wrongfully convicted twenty-four years earlier. He had spent 8,980 days and nights of his life in prison for a crime he hadn't committed. It wasn't a lot of consolation for him that since the death penalty had been resumed by the order of the Supreme Court in 1976, there were 172 others like him in the United States originally sentenced to death row who were exonerated after wrongful conviction, many of them because of prosecutorial misconduct at the trial, the majority of them black. *There are a lot of Skip Hendersons and Buck Davidsons out there.*

Some time that afternoon, Charles' legal record would be set right—at least as right as it could be set after so many years and so much loss.

The deputies brought him a set of dark blue scrubs from the county jail, making Charles look more like a disheveled male nurse after two or three consecutive shifts in the emergency ward than a man about to be freed by the court. Charles' parents, now in their late seventies, were bringing a new set of street clothes for him to change into after the hearing.

As he dressed to leave the courthouse, he got one more reminder of just how incompetent the Palm Beach County system of justice could be. One of the deputies handed him a plastic bag containing new shoes—Crocs, of all things.

"Really? Are they serious?" Charles asked him when he got out of the vacant room he was using as a changing room. "Both shoes for the *left* foot?" The deputy just shrugged as Charles slipped the shoes on his feet.

When Charles was ready, the deputy placed the standard big house hardware on him, handcuffs and a short chain between his ankles. Before he finished, however, the deputy intimated to Charles that he had been only a boy of twelve years at the time of Charles' trial.

"I had nothing to do, believe me, with the injustice imposed on you. Many of us came to hate our boss Davidson so much that later you became a sort of a prison legend and hero."

The deputy helped Charles get into the back of the cruiser. *Here I am for one more ride in a Palm Beach County sheriff's cruiser. I feel different today from how I did the first time in 1987. Today I want to dangle my head out an open window and feel the wind against my face like a dog who finally got to ride in a car.*

The cruiser pulled into a gas station to fill up. *I'm still not used to an Exxon station instead of the old Esso.* "Do you want to do the honors?" the deputy asked.

"Sure, let me take a shot at it. I haven't done this since Ronald Reagan was president."

The gas pumps he had been accustomed to using had been replaced by a contraption that looked like a cross between a computer and an electronic billboard: flashing digital numbers, glaring ads, and even a television screen the consumer could watch while filling up the gas tank.

The deputies chuckled. "There have been a few changes in those years."

"No kidding," Charles agreed.

A few other customers at the gas station were staring at Charles in his blue scrubs and handcuffs. Charles thought he could read their minds: just another black creep getting what he deserves. They couldn't know that he was actually on his way to a very long-awaited public exoneration and sweet freedom.

When they arrived at the Palm Beach Detention Center, which had replaced the antiquated Palm Beach County Jail, things were different from his previous visits. They had cleared out the whole reception area for Charles. The drunks, the hookers, and other unfortunate souls waiting for their jailhouse check-in had been herded into enclosed glass tanks from where they watched Charles enviously being processed into—and then right back *out* of jail.

The entire occasion was videotaped by a sheriff's deputy, probably as proof that the powers-that-be in the county were treating an inmate—or now one to be *released*—with all due fairness and respect.

A young woman in a glass booth had Charles' paperwork. She needed more information to complete it. "What is your occupation, Mr. Wilkerson?"

What am I supposed to say? Professional prisoner?

Charles looked over at the deputy who was accompanying him. He shrugged.

"OK, Mr. Wilkerson. How about an address?"

"I don't have one. I've been at FSP for almost twenty-five years." *I'm being set free to rejoin society. But I possess none of the grounding elements that are part of normal life. No job, no home, no phone number, no plans for the future. Just bobbing between prison and the free world. Not truly belonging in either place.*

Charles was led by the deputy to a small windowless room between the detention center and the courtrooms. The clothes his parents had brought for him were handed to him in a small, neat stack, pressed and lovingly folded. He yanked off his crummy jailhouse blues and began putting on the new, free world garb. By the time he had pulled on new underwear and slacks, Charles knew he was in emotional trouble.

He didn't want to be so overwhelmed by putting on new clothes that he wept openly or collapsed in a pathetic heap and embarrassed himself before the deputies. He hadn't expected a new set of clothes to trigger his first fight to control his feelings.

He was completely unprepared for the fresh smell of clean clothes, the softness, the comfort, and the perfect fit of duds that had been designed to make him look and feel good. He had spent the last quarter of a century wearing prison-issued clothes designed to underline and further his punishment. The prison wardrobe was meant to strip the inmate of any sense of individual identity and dignity, to take away small comforts and crush any sense of pride that might still have remained after a trial or a conviction.

Charles had a catch in his throat as he tried to remember the last time he had pulled on a pair of clean khaki pants or a button-down shirt. The last time he had been decked out like this he and Dana had been to a Paul Simon concert. He didn't have any gray hair or laugh lines then. Culturally, Charles had missed so much that he didn't even know what he had missed.

Charles thought of himself as a contemporary Rip van Winkle, a man who had fallen off the face of the earth in 1987 and groggily reappeared nearly twenty-five years later.

Once finally dressed, he was ushered into a small hallway somewhere behind the judge's bench. Soon the area was filled with people who had fought selflessly every step of the way to get him to this point. Sven Pressley wrapped him in a massive bear hug. Ilona Lawrence and her unforgettable smile enveloped him, too. Barry Scheck had made the trip from New York to be there.

Charles looked up and saw the tall, lean figure of Steve Shillington walking toward him. If Shillington had not handed Charles' case to the Innocence Project, if Shillington had not cared, Charles might still be in FSP. Charles opened his arms to embrace Steve.

Charles looked at them all. He owed them all big-time. He owed them his life.

When the group entered the courtroom, Charles was stunned at how crowded it was. Standing room only. Charles' family was sitting in the front row. They were beaming in a way Charles hadn't seen since his wedding to Dana. There were his long-suffering parents who had been through so much—so many ups and downs in Charles' legal journey—there for him. Charles walked over and embraced them all, trying not to shed tears.

Charles took his seat at the defense table in the front with Barry, Sven, and Ilona. The bailiff called the court to order, and Judge Earle from Orlando began to speak. Charles assumed that Earle's words were moving and meaningful. But the truth is that he didn't really hear a thing, not a word, not a single syllable. Charles was in the courtroom but was still in shock that they were there for this purpose.

Barry Scheck, however, was in his element. He guided the attendees through the performance like a thorough and experienced ringmaster.

The hearing ended when Judge Earle issued an order that Charles be released from the state's custody on his own personal recognizance. *Bang* went the judge's gavel announcing that Charles' prison life had come to an end. *Can it be, Lord? Released? Prison life at an end? Can it really be?*

The crowd in the courtroom broke out into spontaneous, enthusiastic applause and joyful laughter. Charles was struggling not to cry.

Sven Pressley led Charles by the arm through the crowd. Just before they stepped through the open glass courthouse doors, Sven said, "When you get outside, Charles, breathe in the freedom. It's yours now."

Once he stepped through the doors, Charles closed his eyes and lifted his face into the bright October sunshine and let it bathe in. In

South Florida October is among the most pleasant months of the year. October 4, 2011, was a picture-perfect fall day: brilliant sunshine, not a cloud in the azure sky, a slight hint of the good Florida weather to come. *How I've taken these kinds of days for granted before now. From now on, I will treasure them as the precious, priceless gifts they are.*

Charles got into the car with his parents; they were about to pull out of the parking lot when he saw Barry Scheck walking toward them, holding a middle-aged woman gently by the arm. She was weeping.

She had been on Charles' jury, a retired high school teacher. Charles remembered her vaguely. For twenty-five years she had told her students that she had done her civic duty and voted to send a wife-killer to prison, originally to death row. But now she knew that what she had believed for so many years to be right had been revealed to be wrong. She stood outside the truck, tear-stained and aching with remorse. Charles' legal team was eager to get him out of the parking lot and Charles, too, was ready to get on with his life. *I can't just leave the poor woman. I know too well what it's like to hurt while alone.*

Charles reached out through the window and did the only thing he could at the moment. He cupped her cheek in his hand and tried to reassure the poor soul. "That was a long time ago, Ma'am. You had to make a difficult decision to the best of your reason and ability. I forgive you, Ma'am. Believe me, I do."

As the car pulled out into the street Charles looked back at the courthouse. There, lining the railing of a balcony on the second floor, was a row of uniformed deputies from the Palm Beach County sheriff's department, all waving to Charles and applauding him.

Later at the luncheon Ilona had planned for Charles, an attorney friend of Barry Scheck's commented that he had never seen anything like it in his life—law enforcement applauding a defendant they had apprehended unjustly. "Unbelievable."

How quickly life can turn. In one day, I've gone from being the villain to everybody's hero. From pauper to prince. From the object of prison guards' disdain to their admiration and applause. From having no future to anticipating a yet unknown but surely adventuresome one.

CHAPTER 47

IT WAS A GRAND "FREEDOM PARTY" that the Innocence Project team put on for Charles at the only hotel in nearby Starke that could provide the kind of hospitality that Ilona and Sven had in mind for Charles and the other guests.

Then, afterward, Charles settled into the back seat of his parents' car for the almost six-hour drive down to Palm Beach County. Eileen and Richard were quite restrained and reserved. Charles sensed that his father was exhausted by the party and Charles' long-anticipated release from FSP. Eileen offered to drive so that he could relax and adjust the passenger seat to a prone position to sleep if he needed to. Charles felt that he should offer to drive, but then remembered that his driver's license was one of the first pieces of personal I.D. that he had had to surrender when he entered the prison system. The Department of Transportation mug shot, along with his license, would be twenty-five years out of date.

Charles' mother repeated the heartfelt gratitude she had voiced publicly earlier at the party to Ilona and Barry for their invaluable assistance in making this momentous day a reality. "The Innocence Project is an amazing organization. God bless you, Barry and your colleague Peter Neufeld, for having the vision and the compassion for inmates wrongfully sentenced to start an organization like this."

Her voice broke as she spoke, even though neither Barry nor Peter nor Ilona were present in the car. Charles' eyes welled with tears.

"I owe them so much," he added. "I owe them my life."

"What will you do now?" his mother inquired.

Before he could answer, she continued, "You'll come and live with us in our spare bedroom, of course. I know it's not much, not very big. We hope it will do for a while until you get a sense of direction."

"Of course, I'll be there for a while. When I was checking out at FSP, they asked me for my address. I couldn't for the life of me remember yours."

"456 McLean Road," his father chimed in to prove he was awake and able to keep up with their conversation. "Boynton Beach, FL 32426."

"I can't wait to see 456 McLean Road again," Charles said and laughed. "After the places where I've been sleeping, the spare bedroom will feel like a suite at The Breakers. I've been dreaming of this ride home—for decades."

Truly for Charles, walking into his parents' home again was staggering. The house had the familiar aroma that brought him back instantaneously to his youth. At long last Charles felt safe. He hadn't realized how habitual it had become for him at FSP to always be on his guard—from other inmates who might have the crazed notion of harming him in some way, or a guard or several of them who might be hatching a plan to hijack him surreptitiously to introduce him again to the execution area. Charles also hoped that in the shelter of his dear parents' home he could reflect on the past few decades of his life and measure how far he had grown as a man.

"Are you sure you won't feel awkward with a fifty-seven-year-old man sleeping in your house?"

"Not if it's *you*, Charles. We've got so much to get caught up on," Eileen replied.

Charles settled in to enjoy the scenery. He felt his empty wallet in his back pocket. He thought of his old friend Billy DeLisle at FSP, who told him how the government of Texas provided wrongfully convicted inmates at their release $25,000 of compensation for every year served. The compensation covered only the ten first years of incarceration. But still, for the almost twenty-five years of Charles' confinement, he'd be leaving the prison with $250,000 in his bank account. But, alas, not in Florida. All Charles received was what they call a "prepaid credit card" with $50 on it, and an indifferent "good luck" greeting. Charles knew that the Innocence Project was working on getting changes in the resistance of fifteen states, including Florida, to do more to ease the transition of wrongly convicted inmates to life in society again.

A few weeks after Charles' release from FSP, his father suffered a mild stroke. Richard had been lying in his La-Z-Boy recliner in the living room when it happened. It wasn't a bad one. He regained his ability to speak clearly and began to recover within days. But for Charles it was sobering.

I'm here. I'm actually here in my family's home. I'm finally here to help my mom, to do what I can for my dad, at long last to step in and be an active, accountable, participating part of my family. I have unimaginable peace.

Charles got up from his seat on the couch to move the morning's newspaper to the small table closer beside Richard's recliner so that he could reach it himself if he wanted to read it.

God's universe really goes by its own clock and calendar. I moved into my parents' home at just the right time, just when Mom and Dad need me the most. My long journey to exoneration and release wasn't what it seemed like so many times—simply a series of arbitrary coincidences, good and bad. accidents, setbacks, and eventual unplanned victories. All this was meant to happen just the way they did.

WITHIN ANOTHER FEW WEEKS Charles was invited to Sven and Katie Pressleys' beautiful lakeside home in Bradford County. His parents were invited to come, too, even though Eileen didn't feel up to taking Richard along as well.

Not just to visit the Pressleys, however. The day before Charles and his mother were expected at their home, Sven had called to say that he and Katie had taken the liberty to invite Travis and Christine as well; he asked if Charles would be okay with that. Charles had actually been privately brainstorming ways he might be able himself to initiate and pull off a reunion with his son and his new wife.

"I'll be nervous, of course, Sven. But I look forward to seeing Travis again for the first time as a free and innocent man. I'm grateful, very grateful, to you and Katie for arranging it."

As his mother drove north, Charles navigated the route to rural Bradford County. He tried also to control his nervousness about the meeting with Travis and Christine. He so much wanted everything to go well. He knew that they probably had a long way to go before Travis could accept him again as his father. They had to overcome decades of misinformation and possible lies about who Charles really was and what his relationship with Dana had been like. Charles also felt the gaps in information about Travis's life as he grew into young adulthood. Travis had no idea about what had transpired miraculously to make it possible for Charles to be there now in person, a released prisoner whose false conviction of murdering Travis's mother had been overturned. The two of them had a great deal to get past. Charles was beyond eager to get started.

Travis and Christine had not arrived at the Pressleys' yet. Charles sat a little uneasily with Eileen, Sven, and Katie in the living room. *I feel like a teenager with the first date jitters.* Katie did her best to try to help Charles relax.

Finally, the doorbell rang. Charles' heart jumped. *Is this how the firefighters feel when the alarm at the station goes off?* The whole group got up out of their seats and gathered in the foyer. Sven opened the door and welcomed the new guests.

While still in FSP, Charles had seen a few photos of Travis taken and sent to him by Eileen. In the law library Charles had surreptitiously snuck a glance on the internet of the webpage of the Catholic school where Travis was working as an educator and looked up his photo with the rest of the staff. His mother had sent him pictures taken at Travis's college graduation. Since arriving at his parents' home, he had seen a display of photos taken by a professional photographer at his and Christine's wedding.

In his mind, however, Charles hadn't gone past the mental picture of the toddler before his heart surgery who relied on his parents to help him with virtually everything—the little tow-headed kid who held Charles' hand and talked to him when he was doing projects around the house, and who later sweetly fell asleep in Charles' arms.

To Charles, the boy who walked in the door at the Pressleys' had changed immeasurably. He had become a man. Of course, Charles had changed a lot, too, since the last meeting years ago at FSP. Changed, not just on the outside, but on the inside as well. Seeing Travis now felt a lot like attending a high school reunion and vaguely recognizing a face, and *knowing* for certain that you have a history with that person but being so separated by life experience and years apart that it takes you all evening and a lot of mental work to reconnect.

Charles recognized that over the years at FSP he had projected so much onto this moment. He understood that, undoubtedly, Travis had fears, too. Now and here the father was standing, an overly excited man deep into his middle age with more gray hair than brown, a villain turned victim, but still very much the man he had learned to hate. They shared a handshake that almost immediately morphed into a hug.

Sitting down again in the living room, they chatted stiffly.

Charles looked at Travis more closely and began to see small signs that he recognized as being part of their lost connection. He noticed that they were wearing virtually identical shoes and their khaki slacks looked like carbon copies. They had chosen almost matching shirts for the big day. When Charles looked into Travis's face, he was both gladdened and saddened that he saw Dana looking back at him. Charles had to struggle to keep his emotions in check. He didn't want to embarrass his son.

Charles talked with Christine.

"Charles, maybe this question is too personal so soon. But you were put away for twenty-five years for a crime you didn't commit. Can I ask you this: Aren't you angry or bitter at those who are responsible for the terrible injustice? I know I would be."

Charles chuckled. He thought Dana would have asked a similar question just as boldly.

"Bitter? Yes, I've had my moments. But I didn't allow those moments of vindictive feelings to last too long. I noticed that my fantasies of revenge against the prosecutor and the judge didn't seem to cause *them* any harm. The prosecutor was promoted to a judge, and Judge Erskine retired comfortably before dying. But *I* was being eaten up inside. My anger and bitterness were not hurting anyone but myself. That might be the most painful yet important lesson that I learned in the whole experience."

He saw that Travis had chosen a wife with the same stunning blue eyes and long ebony hair as his mother's. Charles found her to be warm and kind, encouraging and easy to talk with. Charles was profoundly grateful for her presence in his son's life. He didn't venture to say anything yet to her in case he was wrong, but she appeared to Charles to be pregnant.

Charles could feel himself talking faster and faster as if sheer speed of speech was a way to make up for lost time.

Sven came over to Charles and Travis and told them about the wooden glider he had suspended from the large live oak tree in the backyard. "It's perfect for two people."

It was getting dark already that fall evening, but still light enough for Charles and Travis to find the glider and take a seat. The others understood what was going on and remained inside. The glider creaked as Charles and Travis talked. Eventually, they found their rhythm and their common ground. They couldn't see each others' faces but Charles could sense Travis smiling, and Charles smiled, too.

For Charles, being with Travis felt like a homecoming.

"Travis, I feel as though I've won the lottery, having this surprise chance to be with you."

"I have to admit I was more than a little nervous about seeing you again," Travis said very quietly. "After all, I must have really hurt you when I was fourteen years old and asked not to see you again."

Charles was silent. He didn't know how honest he should be about feelings he had had in the past.

"I'm very sorry, Travis, that I missed you growing up and becoming a husband, father, and teacher. I'm so proud of you, son. I mean it."

Travis was visibly uncomfortable with the compliment. "I had my reasons for not wanting to come back up to the prison to see you. I didn't understand the reasons then. While growing up I had to live with the knowledge that my father was a bad man who had killed my mother. I had to close my mind and heart to you because that was what I believed—or was led to believe."

"I know you probably heard a lot of bad things about me. I hope that now you know those things are not true."

"Honestly, all that is still so new to me that I'm not used to feeling that way. But Dad, I will try to learn. I really *want* to try."

At that point Travis broke down and laid his head on Charles' shoulder and wept. Charles said nothing, just tried to be a sympathetic father and accept his son's feelings of regret.

Charles understood that Travis's whole understanding of his life was crumbling. He hadn't been told a lot about his mother. Charles' conviction in the case became such a terribly painful part of the family story that no one wanted, or even felt strong enough, to talk about it with Travis. Much of what Travis had learned about that chapter was from private, independent study of stories in back issues of *The Palm Beach Post* at the library. He had been immensely disappointed in Charles and shocked at the murder. He never brought up the subject with Dana's family, not even with Danielle who had adopted him, because he suspected they were afraid of the subject.

Charles dared to hope that if he and Travis might have the opportunity and the time to grow closer, he could fill in some of the blanks in Travis's knowledge of Dana. He so badly longed to tell Travis what he had been too young to remember: how Charles and Dana had lived together very happily as husband and wife for a decade and how full of hope they had been for the future.

That night in the foyer, as Travis and Christine said goodbye and hugged Charles tenderly, Charles hoped that they had made a good beginning. He knew they had only begun to scratch the surface of all that lay beneath the bare outlines of each other's lives.

They had a long road ahead, but now the journey had been launched.

Epilogue
June 2013

THE MEETING BETWEEN CHARLES and Travis at the Pressleys' in 2011 was, Charles hoped, the first in what would be a long, possibly lifelong, relationship. In the two years since that evening, Charles and Travis had gotten together as often as they could. Sometimes it was just the two of them attending a St. Louis Cardinals or Miami Marlins spring training game at the stadium the two teams shared in Jupiter, Florida. If they felt like a little longer drive, they'd go up to Port St. Lucie to catch a Mets game.

Occasionally, they made it a family get-together at Travis's home with all five of them—the two men plus Christine, almost two-year-old Grace, and the newest addition, Liam, born earlier in 2013. Even on the whole family occasions, at one point or another Christine would gather the kids and take a drive to go buy ice cream to give Charles and Travis space and time to talk without interruptions.

Part of the wisdom that washed over Charles in the past two years of freedom was the realization that Travis had had to make a more difficult journey in the past quarter of a century than he did. Through all those years Charles knew some significant things that Travis had not: Charles knew all along that he was innocent of the crime. He knew all along that he didn't stop loving his son. Charles had an intuitive certainty all along that someday the mess of errors and injustices would all be set right.

Travis had had to adjust repeatedly to different realities and versions of the truth. Charles was so grateful for the way that he welcomed him back into his life. He was hoping that in the years ahead he could compensate for the years of Travis's childhood and youth that he had missed by watching Grace and Liam grow up. He wanted to be a good grandpa.

Charles was also grateful that he could try to be a good husband. He and Cindy were married in 2012, about fifteen months after his release from FSP.

Charles and Cindy met the old-fashioned way—in church. She was a member of All Saints' Lutheran Church in Fort Lauderdale. She participated in an informal group within the church of persons who wanted to explore current social issues.

Charles felt he had a unique story to tell so added his name to a list compiled by the Innocence Project of volunteers willing to go out and talk about their experiences with the legal system, especially death row.

Not long after Charles had volunteered, he received a telephone call from the woman who served as the chair of All Saints' Lutheran's social issues group. They talked over the phone for over a half hour. Charles gave a synopsis of his long experience contending with the Florida legal system over his wrongful conviction and incarceration. The woman was utterly flabbergasted at what he related.

"Mr. Wilkerson, your story is an incredible one. I was not fully aware that such things can happen in Florida, and I doubt that many of our group's members are either. We definitely want you to come and share your story with our intimate little group."

Three or so weeks later, he was in Fort Lauderdale. Indeed, the group was small, about ten or so people, mostly women, sitting in a circle on metal folding chairs.

They gave Charles their rapt attention as he related his harrowing experience, uttering signs of disbelief at the injustice and looks of sympathy on their faces. While he tried not to focus too obviously on one face at the risk of seeming to disregard the others, there was the face of one particular woman in the group who kept looking at him while he spoke—not with sympathy exactly on her face but rather a look of *empathy,* not pity for this poor soul victimized by injustice but a look that bordered on *admiration* for his perseverance and determination to rise above his environment.

Following a time of questions and Charles' answers, the group was dismissed to enjoy coffee or juice or a plate of cookies and pastries. Several members of the group continued to address new questions to him until they seemed to come to an unspoken consensus that it was time to let the speaker enjoy the goodies as well.

"Thanks, ladies and gentlemen, for this evening. I have enjoyed being with you very much," Charles announced to the group. "If you still want to hear things I may have neglected or forgotten to say in my talk, you'll need to call me up and buy me a cup of coffee sometime."

The group chuckled at his joke. He sat alone on his folding chair and nibbled on a piece of pound cake. He could sense, however, that not everyone had finished with their comments or questions that they wanted Charles to hear.

The woman he had noticed as he was speaking approached him very respectfully and a little timidly. She was probably in her early fifties, a little younger than himself, he figured. She introduced herself as Cindy. "Well, actually it's Lucinda, but I've been Cindy since I was a child."

As they chatted together, Charles was struck by her gentleness and kindness that appeared to be genuine. But what impressed him the most was the real spark of intelligence in her eyes.

On the drive back up to Boynton Beach, Charles thought about the brief chat with Cindy. He was attracted to her, he recognized. But he filed the possibility of following up as "maybe someday." He certainly knew that he was not ready to jump into the dating pool. He still thought of Dana every day. Ironically, when he and Cindy were chatting, he thought of Dana again because that spark of intelligence in her eyes reminded him of her.

A few days later the phone at Charles' parents rang, which he answered. It was Cindy.

"I want to buy you that cup of coffee. I can drive up to West Palm if you like."

Charles was stricken. He didn't know how to answer. Needless to say, he had never been asked out by a woman. *Things have changed while I was in prison. I don't even know if this counts as being "asked out."* He realized anew how out of social practice he was. He'd just been handed a lit social firecracker.

He swallowed hard and said, "Yes, I mean no. Yes, let's have a cup of Joe. But no, I'll drive down to meet you in Fort Lauderdale. You name the place and time."

That cup of coffee was their beginning. They met at a gourmet coffee house and talked for four hours, but not about prison. The next week they did it again—the same coffee shop, the same engaging conversation, the same powerful electric connection between them.

He felt drawn to her sexually. But now it was not the feverish rush to roll in the hay and make love, as in the early days with Dana. Rather, what he imagined was a more relaxed, controlled, measured experience of the union of two mature, grown-up souls.

Cindy was widowed and had two delightful teenage daughters who took to Charles almost immediately.

Charles and Cindy shared a worldview and system of beliefs and dreams. Charles felt as though he had known her for a long time. He felt safe with her. They talked about books and laughed that they both adored *To Kill a Mockingbird* and wished just as ardently that F. Scott Fitzgerald could have duplicated in his later novels the beauty of the unparalleled prose and the compelling power of the plot of *The Great Gatsby*.

They started going out together to plays, restaurants, and her church, which became his church. She accompanied him when he gave talks about wrongful convictions at other churches and service clubs.

She was with him in Tallahassee when he lobbied for a new piece of legislation that would keep Charles' nightmare from being visited upon anyone else. Charles was initially embarrassed when the new proposed law was named *The Charles Wilkerson Act*. It codified exactly how and when prosecutors need to s*hare* information with accused defendants and their attorneys.

The proposal passed the Florida legislature on May 18, 2013. Cindy was there to keep Charles' head from getting too big when the governor and other prominent politicians shook his hand, patted him on the back, and led the assembly in a standing ovation. He loved Cindy for that.

She was there with him at Skip Henderson's Court of Inquiry mandated by the Attorney-General to be investigated for all of the cases he had prosecuted before and after Charles' trial. Cindy was there to hold his hand as they heard a judge rule that Henderson would have to face a criminal proceeding for his actions in Charles' trial. Later, Henderson resigned his position on the bench and surrendered his law license.

Charles hadn't particularly thirsted for revenge. But he did feel satisfaction that the Palm Beach legal establishment was rid of a dangerous cancer that had been infecting the system for so many years.

Charles and Cindy became husband and wife shortly before Ernest Wilcox was tried for Dana's murder. After conviction for that murder, Wilcox was tried and convicted for the murder of Delores Adams Whitehead. Charles was curious about Wilcox's motivation for the murders but declined to attend the trial as an observer. He had new and promising adventures to explore.

Shortly thereafter, they sold Cindy's home in Fort Lauderdale and bought a comfortable ranch house not far from the beach in

Delray Beach, still within a short drive from Travis and his family.

Cindy and Charles had a huge wooden backyard deck overlooking a small inland lake along with a majestic blue heron as a regular visitor in the evenings. For the first time since 1986, Charles could look out from his deck with his arm around Cindy and take grateful inventory: a devoted wife, a renewed relationship with his son and his wife, two adorable grandchildren, his prison days behind him, his cleared name, and his restored future.

"Life is good," he said many evenings to the blue heron. "Life is *very* good."

WORKS CONSULTED IN WRITING

John Grisham. *The Innocent Man: Murder and Injustice in a Small Town*. Doubleday, 2006.

Michael Morton. *Getting Life*. Simon and Schuster, 2014.

Sister Helen Prejean. *The Death of Innocents: An Eyewitness Account of Wrongful Convictions*. Vintage Books, 2006.

Steffen Hou. *The Deprived: Innocent on Death Row*. Nook Book, 2019.

Karl Johnson, Jr. *Depraved Prosecution Redux*. Mondale Publishing, 2012.

Scott Turow. *Irreversible Errors*. Grand Central Publishing, 2002.

Television Series: *The Innocence Files* on Netflix.

About the Author

Jack is currently living in his third country. He was born in Finland; in 1955, he and his family emigrated to Toronto, Canada. From 1971 to 1974, he studied at Yale Divinity School in New Haven, CT, and in 1981 he took up residence in Florida. He currently lives in Wyncote, PA.

He has been married since Richard M. Nixon occupied the Oval Office and two years before he relinquished the office in disgrace. His wife, Diane, is a native Pennsylvanian. They are the grateful parents of two adult sons: Luke of Wyncote, PA, and Jesse of Gainesville, FL.

Jack remains a Canadian citizen.

In June 2015, he retired after over 40 years as a Lutheran clergyman in Canada, Florida, Connecticut, and Pennsylvania. Since retirement, his viewpoint has changed from scanning the environment for sermon material to seeing the world as a novelist. He'd always wanted to write one since reading *The Great Gatsby* in high school and then studying English literature at the University of Toronto. So he did write one. Four, actually! In October 2016, his immigration novel, *Beginning Again at Zero,* was self-published at Lulu Press. His next books have been published on the "Can't Put It Down Books" imprint of Open Door Publications. He is currently working on his fourth book, *The Long and Stony Road*, on the Civil Rights era.

OTHER NOVELS
BY JACK A. SAARELA

I hope you have enjoyed *A Perfect Storm of Injustice*. I invite you to explore my other novels.

Beginning Again at Zero – Onni is still only a teenager when he gets restless and, like many others, decides to emigrate from his home in Finland to Canada in 1938. A whole new world of opportunity and possibility awaits him there. Follow Onni as he encounters unexpected challenges in adjusting to a new land. His thoughts shift back to his native land when in November 1939 the Russians attack his native land from the east and the Winter War begins. Onni has a difficult decision to make.

Accidental Saviors – Felix and Algot are two Finnish expatriates who happen to be in Berlin in 1938 to witness the horrors of *Kristallnacht* and hear reports of further Nazi atrocities against the Jews across Europe. They have never met or even know of the existence of one another. But each in his own way is moved to use his expertise to help transport endangered Jews out of the reach of the Nazi persecutors into safety. Together but separately, they rescue thousands of Jewish lives. This novel is based on actual historical events.

Love Out of Reach – World War II is raging all around them as thirty-six-year-old pastor/theologian Dietrich Bonhoeffer meets and develops a romantic connection with Maria von Wedemeyers, sixteen years his junior. Dietrich is arrested and imprisoned by the Nazis for various anti-Nazi activities in 1942. He and Maria become engaged to be married when the war is over. However, while in prison, Dietrich joins other resistors in an ambitious conspiracy to assassinate Hitler. Dietrich remains in a Nazi prison until he is executed a mere few weeks before the end of the war in Europe. This novel is a partially fictionalized retelling of Dietrich and Maria's actual relationship.

All of Jack A. Saarela's books are available on www.amazon.com.

ACKNOWLEDGMENTS

Before an historical novelist proceeds to put any words of a story into a manuscript that will eventually become a novel, he or she must initially discover a passion within for a particular historical era. Then in the process of imagining a plot and inhabiting it with engaging characters, the novelist must have a fierce love for them, or else the reader will remain indifferent about what happens to them in the story.

When the novelist begins writing, he or she discovers, if he or she didn't know already, that it takes a team of persons with diverse talents and a strong desire to help the author produce the best possible result for all the often painstaking work. If he or she were being honest, he/she would recognize and publicly acknowledge that no one produces good literature alone—no matter the number of hours spent by the author in solitude at a keyboard.

The seeds for this novel began to germinate at the Florida State Prison and later at its neighbor, the Union Correctional Institution, when I served as a volunteer spiritual advisor to death row inmates in the 1980s and 1990s. I met so many memorable people and heard so many compelling stories from them that I began to envision writing a novel based on their experiences—and in that way share their stories and that of other inmates that I discovered in books. So I express my gratitude to Susan for recommending me to several death row inmates as their spiritual adviser and soul friend, as well as to Dennis, the late Ray, Roy, Kenny, and Francis. I continue to maintain a friendship with four of them to this day by exchanging letters or via email.

"Beta-Readers" Marty Weiss and Cindy Raff read each chapter as I completed the first draft and offered helpful suggestions from their perspective, as did members of my weekly "virtual writers'" group Wendy and Sherri. Federal Prosecutor Albert Glenn provided invaluable feedback and suggestions for creating an accurate portrayal of the courtroom scenes, as well as contributing the flattering headshot of me as the author. Colleague Larry Reimer, a fellow spiritual advisor, offered a spirited "pre-review" of the novel and kind words of encouragement.

Before *A Perfect Storm of Injustice* was submitted to a printer and prepared for release, publisher/editor Karen Hodges Miller oversaw the writing and "midwifed" the novel into life. Karen, this is now the third novel in which we have collaborated for Can't Put It Down Books, and I am truly grateful once again for your pushing and pulling me when necessary, raking me over the coals, or uplifting me with welcome words of encouragement when appropriate.

Eric Labacz designed the one-of-a-kind cover, and Vivian Fransen (author of *The Straight Spouse: A Memoir*) proofread the manuscript to ensure it was easier for you to read and enjoy.

www.ingramcontent.com/pod-product-compliance
Lightning Source LLC
Chambersburg PA
CBHW051942220626
47052CB00004B/766